reprint series, 2006

ROSE CLARK.

BY

FANNY FERN.

NEW YORK:
PUBLISHED BY MASON BROTHERS.
1856.

STEREOTYPED BY
THOMAS B. SMITH,
82 & 84 Beekman Street.

PRINTED BY
JOHN A. GRAY,
97 Cliff St.

Reader !

When the frost curtains the windows, when the wind whistles fiercely at the key-hole, when the bright fire glows, and the tea-tray is removed, and father ·in his slippered feet lolls in his arm-chair ; and mother with her nimble needle " makes auld claes look amaist as weel as new," and grandmamma draws closer to the chimney-corner, and Tommy with his plate of chestnuts nestles contentedly at her feet ; then let my unpretending story be read. For such an hour, for such an audience, was it written.

Should any *dictionary on legs* rap inopportunely at the door for admittance, send him away to the groaning shelves of some musty library, where "literature" lies embalmed, with its stony eyes, fleshless joints, and ossified heart, in faultless preservation.

Then, should the smile, and the tear, have passed round, while the candle flickers in the socket, if but one kindly voice murmur low,

"MAY GOD BLESS HER!"

it will brighten the dreams of

FANNY FERN.

CONTENTS.

CHAPTER I.

PAGE

THE ORPHAN ASYLUM—ROSE'S INTRODUCTION TO IT—MRS. MARKHAM—ROSE'S INITIATION—TIMMINS 15

CHAPTER II.

MR. BALCH.. 27

CHAPTER III.

ROSE'S COMPANIONS—THE DINING-TABLE AND THE SCHOOLROOM. 30

CHAPTER IV.

AUNT DOLLY—HOW IT CAME TO PASS—TWO OLD MAIDS' OPINIONS ON LITERATURE, MEN AND MARRIAGE GENERALLY, AND ON THE BACHELORS OF DIFFTOWN PARTICULARLY.......... 34

CHAPTER V.

LITTLE TIBBS—AN INSTANCE OF MRS. MARKHAM'S "MOTHERLY CARE" OF THE ORPHANS............................... 39

CHAPTER VI.

THE FASHIONABLE UNDERTAKER...................... 45

CHAPTER VII.

THE INVESTIGATING COMMITTEE "INSPECT" THE ASYLUM—MR.
BALCH PRIVATELY RECORDS THE VERDICT ON THE HAND OF
THE MATRON...................................... 48

CHAPTER VIII.

TIBBS' GHOST..................................... 54

CHAPTER IX.

AUNT DOLLY REMOVES ROSE FROM THE ASYLUM—THE RIDE
"HOME"—DOLLY'S IDEAS OF NATURE, SENTIMENT, AND DUTY. 57

CHAPTER X.

AUNT DOLLY REFUSES ROSE'S REQUEST TO BE SENT TO SCHOOL,
AND ATTEMPTS TO CONVINCE HER THAT LYING IS THE BEST
POLICY.. 68

CHAPTER XI.

MR. CLIFTON, THE VILLAGE MINISTER—THE PARSONAGE..... 71

CHAPTER XII.

MR. CLIFTON'S PASTORAL CALL ON DOLLY—THE CONVERSATION
ABOUT ROSE.... 76

CHAPTER XIII.

PAGE

DEATH AT THE PARSONAGE............................... 82

CHAPTER XIV.

ROSE REQUESTS OF AUNT DOLLY A MEMENTO OF HER MOTHER. 86

CHAPTER XV.

ROSE IN THE MILLINER SHOP............................. 90

CHAPTER XVI.

MRS. CLIFTON VISITS "THE BABY'S" GRAVE—A PLEASANT SUR-
PRISE—DOLLY'S SICKNESS—DAFFY'S SOLILOQUY........... 94

CHAPTER XVII.

DOLLY CONVALESCES AND EFFERVESCES—BAKING-DAY, AND
ROSE'S FIRST ATTEMPT AT COOKING—HEART'S-EASE........ 101

CHAPTER XVIII.

VILLAGE GOSSIP—THE DESOLATE PARSONAGE............... 109

CHAPTER XIX.

THE CHILD-MOTHER—AUNT DOLLY'S LETTER................ 112

CHAPTER XX.

PAGE

A GLIMPSE AT BACHELOR QUARTERS...................... 119

CHAPTER XXI.

ROSE'S SICK BABE—AUNT DOLLY, AS THE FASHIONABLE MRS.
JOHN HOWE...................................... 122

CHAPTER XXII.

OLD MRS. BOND'S VISIT TO THE CITY—SILENT REPROOF....... 128

CHAPTER XXIII.

MR. FINELS, MRS. HOWE'S INTIMATE FRIEND—MRS. BOND'S IN-
TERVIEW WITH ROSE............................... 133

CHAPTER XXIV.

A PASSAGE-AT-ARMS BETWEEN MRS. HOWE AND HER FASHION-
ABLE FEMALE FRIEND............................... 147

CHAPTER XXV.

MR. HOWE ATTEMPTS AN INDEPENDENT COURSE OF ACTION—
HE REMOVES ROSE AND LITTLE CHARLEY FROM THE ATTIC
TO THE BEST SPARE ROOM—MRS. HOWE "LETS HIM HEAR
FROM IT."....................................... 152

CHAPTER XXVI.

ROSE MAKES AN ASTOUNDING DISCOVERY—MR. HOWE VEN-
TURES ON A CONNUBIAL JOKE—THE RESULT OF MR. HOWE'S
JOKE—ROSE AND HER SICK BABE IN THE STAGE-COACH..... 158

CHAPTER XXVII.

PAGE

MRS. BOND'S RECEPTION OF ROSE—THE OLD LADY'S CHRISTIAN FAITH AND PHILOSOPHY......................... 170

CHAPTER XXVIII.

THE WASH-ROOM—THE BRUTAL REMARK.................. 172

CHAPTER XXIX.

MISS BODKIN'S ACCOUNT OF THE RISE AND PROGRESS OF MRS. JOHN HOWE....................................... 176

CHAPTER XXX.

THE FLIGHT OF ROSE, WITH LITTLE CHARLEY.............. 181

CHAPTER XXXI.

THE CHRISTENING, AT MRS. HOWE'S—THE SECRET WHISPER —THE DENOUEMENT................................ 184

CHAPTER XXXII.

ROSE AT SEA—CAPTAIN LUCAS—FRITZ—DOCTOR PERRY—THE MARRIAGE PROPOSAL 189

CHAPTER XXXIII.

THE CAPTAIN AND DR. PERRY—ARRIVAL IN NEW ORLEANS. 198

CHAPTER XXXIV.

PAGE

Rose's New Home—The Maniac's Story—News of Vin-

cent... 202

CHAPTER XXXV.

Mrs. Howe thinks it time to go to the Springs—Mr. Howe

attempts to cherish an Opinion of his own—The Magic

Whisper.. 209

CHAPTER XXXVI.

The Mystery Explained.............................. 212

CHAPTER XXXVII.

Rose's Illness 215

CHAPTER XXXVIII.

The Lady Artist.................................... 218

CHAPTER XXXIX.

Gertrude's Story 226

CHAPTER XL.

Mr. and Mrs Howe on the road to the Springs—A Rail-

road Accident—The Tables Turned.................. 256

CHAPTER XLI.

PAGE

CHARLEY'S INTRODUCTION TO THE VINCENT MANSION—DOCTOR PERRY AGAIN SEEKS TO MAKE ROSE HIS WIFE—GERTRUDE'S LOCKET—THE RECOGNITION................. 264

CHAPTER XLII.

MADAME VINCENT'S PRESENT TO CHARLEY................. 278

CHAPTER XLIII.

JOHN AND GERTRUDE—A BIT OF WOMAN'S PHILOSOPHY...... 280

CHAPTER XLIV.

ROSE PROPOSES TO TURN AUTHORESS—GERTRUDE GIVES HER SOME CHOICE SPECIMENS OF CRITICISM.................... 286

CHAPTER XLV.

MISS ANNE COOPER—MADAME VINCENT'S SEXAGENARIAN LOVE REMINISCENCES...................................... 291

CHAPTER XLVI.

MADAME VINCENT'S VISIT TO ROSE........................ 300

CHAPTER XLVII.

MISS ANNE COOPER'S DIPLOMACY......................... 304

CHAPTER XLVIII.

MADAME MACQUE TURNS ROSE OUT OF DOORS............... 369

CHAPTER XLIX.

CUPID IN THE KITCHEN—HIGH LIFE BELOW STAIRS.......... 312

CHAPTER L.

A LETTER FROM MR. FINELS........................... 320

CHAPTER LI.

ROSE, GERTRUDE, AND JOHN, AT NIAGARA—THE AGED COUPLE
—THE HUSBAND CARRIED OVER THE FALLS, AND THE MOURN-
ER'S STORY.. 323

CHAPTER LII.

A CHAPTER ON MAN'S VANITY.......................... 335

CHAPTER LIII.

MARKHAM FOUND OUT—BALCH REPENTENT................ 340

CHAPTER LIV.

THE UNEXPECTED APPEARANCE OF MR. STAHLE, AND ITS CON-
SEQUENCES 344

CHAPTER LV.

ROSE'S DREAM...................................... 349

CHAPTER LVI.

A SCENE IN MRS. HOWE'S PARLOR...................... 353

CHAPTER LVII.

MRS. BOND'S STRANGE VISITOR........................... 359

CHAPTER LVIII.

ANOTHER LETTER FROM MR. FINELS....................... 366

CHAPTER LIX.

A CHAPTER ON BOSTON, ITS INHABITANTS AND ENVIRONS...... 368

CHAPTER LX.

JOHN'S DREAM... 376

CHAPTER LXI.

SCENE ON BOARD CAPTAIN LUCAS'S SHIP................... 379

CHAPTER LXII.

GERTRUDE'S SORROWFUL DAY............................ 383

CHAPTER LXIII.

A THIRD LETTER FROM MR. FINELS....................... 385

CHAPTER LXIV.

CHARLEY'S CHILD-SORROW............................... 389

CHAPTER LXV.

MRS. BOND'S FUNERAL.................................. 394

CHAPTER LXVI.

THE MEETING OF JOHN AND THE STRANGER.................... 379

CHAPTER LXVII.

THE STRANGER IN GERTRUDE'S STUDIO—ROSE'S PICTURE REC-
OGNIZED—THE MEETING.............................. 402

CHAPTER LXVIII.

VINCENT'S STORY.. 405

CHAPTER LXIX.

JOHN'S TRIUMPH.. 410

CHAPTER LXX.

JOHN AND VINCENT...................................... 412

CHAPTER LXXI.

PEACE—RETRIBUTION.................................... 414

ROSE CLARK.

CHAPTER I.

"HERE is number fifty-four, Timmins," said the matron of a charity-school to her factotum, as she led in a little girl about six years of age; "number fifty-four; you must put another cot in the long hall, and another plate in the eating-room. What is your name, child?"

"Rose," replied the little one, vailing her soft, dark eyes under their curtaining lashes, and twisting the corner of a cotton shawl.

"Rose!" repeated the matron, in a contemptuous aside, to Timmins; "I knew it would be sure to be something fanciful; beggars always go on stilts."

"I am not a beggar," said the child, "I am mother's little Rose."

"Mother's little Rose?" repeated the matron, again, in the same sneering tone; "well—who was mother?"

"Mother is dead," said the child, with a quivering lip.

"No loss, either," said Mrs. Markham to Timmins, "since she did not know better than to let the child run in the streets."

"Mother was sick, and I had to go of errands," said the child, defensively.

"Ah, yes—always an excuse; but do you know that I am the matron of this establishment? and that you must never answer me back, in that way? Do you know that you must do exactly as I and the committee say? Timmins, bring me the scissors and let us lop off this mop of a wig," and she lifted up the clustering curls, behind which Rose seemed trying to hide.

"There—now you look proper and more befitting your condition," said Mrs. Markham, as the sheared lamb rose from its kneeling posture and stood before her. "Timmins, Timmins!" Mrs. Markham whispered, "don't throw away those curls; the hairdresser always allows me something handsome for them. It is curious what thick hair beggar children always have."

"But I am not a beggar," said Rose again, standing up very straight before Mrs. Markham.

"Look at it," said Mrs. Markham, with a sneer; "look at it, Timmins, it is 'not a beggar.' Look at its ragged frock, and soiled shawl, and torn pinafore; it 'is not a beggar.' We shall have some work to do here, Timmins. Come here, Rose."

"Did you hear me, child?" she repeated, as Rose remained stationary.

The child moved slowly toward Mrs. Markham.

" Look me in the eye."

Rose cast a furtive glance at the stern, hard face before her.

"Do you know that naughty girls, in this house, stay in dark closets."

Rose shuddered, but made no reply.

" Ah, I thought so ; you had better remember that. Now, go away with Timmins, and have the school uniform put on ; 'not a beggar!' was there ever the like of that?" and Mrs. Markham settled herself in her rocking-chair, put her feet upon the sofa, and composed herself for her after-dinner nap.

As she reclines there, we will venture to take a look at her : not a phrenological glance, for she has a cap on her head ; under its frilled borders peep some wiry artificial curls ; her lips are thin and vixenish ; her nose sharp and long, with a bridge which seems to defy the beholder to cross her will ; her dress clings very tightly to her bean-pole figure ; and on her long arm hangs a black velvet bag, containing her spectacles, snuff-box, and some checkerberry lozenges, which she has a pleasant way of chewing before the children in school hours. You may know that she expects a call to-day, because she has on her festal gilt breast-pin with a green stone in the center.

"Beg your pardon, ma'am; sorry to wake you," said Timmins, with a very flushed face; "but I can't do nothing with that young one, though I have tried my best. I went up stairs to wash her all over, according to rule, before I put on the school uniform; and when I began to strip her, she pulled her clothes all about her, and held them tight, and cried, and took on, saying that nobody ever saw her all undressed but her mother, and all that sort of thing."

"The affected little prude! and to break up my nap, too!" said Mrs. Markham. "I'll teach her—come along, Timmins."

True enough; there stood Rose in the corner, as Timmins had said; her dress half torn off in the scuffle, leaving exposed her beautifully-molded shoulders and back, while with her little hands she clutched the remaining rags closely about her person. With her dilated nostrils, flushed cheeks, and flashing eyes, she made a tableau worth looking at.

"Come here," hissed Mrs. Markham, in a tone that made Rose's flesh creep.

Rose moved slowly toward her.

"Take off those rags—every one of them."

"I can not," said Rose; "oh, don't make me; I can not."

"Take them off, I say. What! do you mean to resist me?" (as Rose held them more tenaciously about her;) and grasping her tightly by the wrist, she drew her through a long passage-way, down a steep pair of stairs, and pushing her into a dark closet, turned the key on her and strode away.

"Obstinate little minx," she said, as she passed Timmins, on her return to her rocking-chair and to her nap.

"Hark! Mrs. Markham! Mrs. Markham!—what's that groan? Had n't I better open the door and peep in?"

"That is always the way with you, Timmins: no, of course not. She can affect groaning as well as she can affect delicacy; let her stay there till her spirit is well broke; when I get ready I will let her out myself;" and Mrs. Markham walked away.

But Timmins was superstitious, and that groan haunted her, and so she went back to the closet to listen. It was all very still; perhaps it was not Rose, after all; and Timmins breathed easier, and walked a few steps away; and then again, perhaps it was, and Timmins walked back again. It would do no harm to peep, at any rate; the key was in the lock, and Mrs. Markham never would know it. Timmins softly turned it;—she called,

"Rose!"

No answer. She threw open the blind in the entry, that the light might stream into the closet. There lay the child in strong convulsions. Timmins knew she risked nothing in calling Mrs. Markham now.

"Come quick—quick—she is dying!"

"Pshaw! only a trick," said Mrs. Markham, more nervous than she chose to acknowledge, as she consulted her watch and thought of the visitor she was expecting.

"Take her up, Timmins," said she, after satisfying herself the child was senseless, "take her into my room, and put her on the bed."

"Gracious! how can I?" asked Timmins, looking with dismay at the blood flowing profusely from a wound in the temple, occasioned by her fall; "she looks so dreadful, Mrs. Markham."

"Fool!" exclaimed that lady, as she snatched up the little sufferer in her arms, and walked rapidly through the entry. "That's the door bell, Timmins; that is Mr. Balch; tell him I will be there directly—mind—not a word about the child, as you value your place. I have not forgotten that brown soap business."

The cowed Timmins retired as she was bid; and Mrs. Markham, laying the insensible child on the bed, closed the door of her room and applied the proper restoratives; for her position involved some little knowledge of the healing art. After a while, Rose opened her eyes, but as suddenly closed them again, as they revealed the form of her persecutor.

"*You* can attend to her now," said Mrs. Markham to Timmins, about half an hour after, as she went down to receive Mr. Balch.

Timmins walked about the room uneasily, for Rose's ghastly face distressed her.

"If she would only speak, or open her eyes!" but the child did neither. Timmins coughed and hemmed, but Rose did not seem to notice it; at last, going up to the bed-side, she passed her hand over her forehead.

"Don't," whispered Rose, glancing round the room as if afraid of seeing Mrs. Markham; "don't try to make me well, I want to die."

"Oh, no, you don't," exclaimed Timmins, more frightened than ever; "that's awful—you won't go to Heaven, if you talk that way."

"Won't I?" asked the child; "won't I go to Heaven and be with my mother?"

"No," said Timmins, oracularly; "no—in course you won't; all of us has to wait till we are sent for; we can't, none of us, hurry the time, or put it off, nuther, when it comes."

"When will my time come?" asked Rose, sadly.

"Lor'! how you talk—don't go on that way; you've got a while to live yet; you are nothing but a baby."

"Shall I always live here?" asked Rose, looking round again, as if in fear of Mrs. Markham.

"You'll live here till you are bound out, I reckon."

"What's that?" asked Rose, innocently.

"Wall, I never!" exclaimed Timmins; "have n't you never heern about being bound out?"

"No," answered Rose, a little ashamed of her ignorance.

"Wall, the upshot of it is, that you are sent away to live with any body that Mrs. Markham and the committee say, and work for them just as long as they tell you, for your meat, and drink, and clothing."

"What is a committee?" asked Rose.

"Why, it's Mr. Balch, and Mr. Skinner, and Mr. Flint, and Mr. Stone, and Mr. Grant, and them."

"Can't you ever get away from the place where they send you?" asked Rose.

"What a thing you are to ask questions. Yes, I spose you kin, if you die or get married—it amounts to about the same thing," said Timmins, with a shrug of her divorced shoulders.

"To whom shall I be bound out?" asked the child.

"Land's sake, as if I could tell; perhaps to one person, perhaps to another."

This answer not being very satisfactory to Rose, she turned her face to the pillow and heaved a deep sigh.

"Have n't you got no folks?" asked Timmins.

"What?"

"No folks? no relations, like?"

"None but Aunt Dolly."

"Who is Aunt Dolly?"

"I don't know; I never saw her till she brought me here."

"Where did she bring you from ?"

"My mother's grave."

"Yes—but what house did you live in when she took you ?"

"I did n't live in any house ; all day long I sat on my mother's grave, and, at night, I crept behind some boards, by the grave-yard, and slept.

"Land's sake, did n't you have nothing to eat ?"

"Sometimes—I was not much hungry, my heart ached so bad ; sometimes the children gave me pieces of bread and cake, as they went to school."

"What did you do all day at your mother's grave ?"

"Talked to mamma."

"Land's sake, child, dead folks can't hear."

"Can't they ?" asked Rose, with a quivering lip. "Did n't my mamma hear what I said to her ?"

"In course not," answered Timmins. "Why, what a chick you are. If you were n't so bright, I should think you was an idiot."

"What are you crying for ?"

Rose kept on sobbing.

"Come now, don't take on so," said the uneasy Timmins, "you are not the only person who has had a hard time of it. I was a little girl once."

"Were you ?" asked Rose, wiping her eyes, and surveying Timmins's Meg Merrilees proportions.

"Yes, of course," said Timmins, laughing ; "just as

if you did n't know that every grown-up woman must have been a little girl once. Do you say those things a purpose, or do they come by accident, like ?"

" Did *your* mother die ?" asked Rose, not appearing to hear Timmins's last question.

" Yes—and father, and brother, and sister, and the hull on 'em."

" Did you cry ?"

" I 'spose so ; I know I was awful hungry."

" But did you cry because your mother was dead ?"

" Partly, I suppose."

" When you went to bed, did you think you saw her face with a cloud all around it, and did you call ' Mother?' and did the eyes look sad at you, but stay still where they were? and when you went up toward the cloud and the face, did it all go away ?"

" Lor', no ; how you talk," said Timmins, as Rose's face grew still paler. " Don't—you make my flesh creep."

" You would n't be afraid of your own dear mamma, would you ?" asked Rose.

" Lor', yes, if she came to me that way," answered Timmins. " It is n't natur', child ; you saw a—a—," and Timmins hesitated to pronounce the word ghost.

" I know you would n't run away from it, if it looked so sweet and loving at you," said Rose ; " but why did it not come nearer to me ? and why did it all fade away when I put out my arms to clasp it ? That made me think it could n't be my mamma, after all; and yet it was mamma, too, but so pale and sad."

" Wall—I don't know," said the perplexed Timmins; "you are beyond me; I don't know nothing about sperrits, and I don't want to; but come here; you 've been asking me all sorts of questions, now I should like to ask you one."

" Well," said Rose, abstractedly.

" What on airth made you carry on so like sixty about my washing you? Don't you like me?"

" Y—e—s," replied Rose, blushing deeply.

" Wall, then, what was the matter with you? any scars on your body, or any thing?"

" No," said Rose.

" What *did* ail you, then? for I 'm curous to know; why did n't you want me to wash you?"

" It made me feel ashamed," said Rose; "nobody ever washed me but mamma; I did n't mind my mamma."

" Wall, I 'm beat if I can understand that," said Timmins, looking meditatively down upon the carpet; " and one of your own sect, as they call it, too. It seems ridikilis; but let me tell you, you 'd better make no fuss here; none of the other childern does."

" Other children?" asked Rose, " are there more children here? I did not hear any noise or playing."

" No, I reckon you did n't," said Timmins, laughing. (" I wish to the land Mrs. Markham had heard you say

2

that;") and Timmins laughed again, as if it was too good a joke to be thrown away on one listener.

"Are *their* mothers dead, too, Timmins?"

"I dare say—I reckon some on 'em don't know much who their fathers and mothers was," said Timmins.

"They had some, did n't they?"

"In course," said Timmins; "why, you are enough to kill old folks; sometimes you are away beyond me, and sometimes not quite up to me, as one may say, but you'd better shut up now, for Mrs. Markham will be along presently."

"Do you think Mrs. Markham is a good woman?" asked Rose.

"About as good as you've seen," said the diplomatic Timmins, touching the cut on Rose's temple; "the quicker you mind her when she speaks, the better—that's all."

"Do *you* like her?" asked Rose.

"No—sh—yes—why, what a thing you are to make people say what they don't mean to. I like you, any how. But don't you never act as if I did, before folks, because my hands is tied, you see."

"I don't know what you mean," said Rose.

"Sh—sh—did n't I tell you to shut up? Somebody is as stealthy as a cat;" and Timmins looked uneasily at the key-hole of the door.

CHAPTER II.

MR. BALCH was a bachelor of forty-five, with a small fortune, and a large bump of credulity. Like all ancient and modern bachelors, he liked "to be made of," and Mrs. Markham's hawk eye discovered this little weakness, and turned it to her own advantage. A moneyed man's vote on a committee is of some importance, and Markham had an eye to the perpetuity of her salary; further than that, we have no right to probe the secrets of her unappropriated heart.

On the visit in question, she received Mr. Balch very graciously, inquired with great solicitude concerning his rheumatism, which she averred was quite prevalent that year among *young* people; gave him the most eligible seat on the sofa, and apologized for having kept him waiting so long.

"Not a word, my dear lady, not a word," said the pleased Balch. "We all know how onerous are your duties, and how indefatigably conscientious you are in the performance of them. It was spoken of at the last meeting of the Board; I wish you to know that your services are fully appreciated by us."

"Oh! thank you—thank you, Mr. Balch. You are too kind. None of us can say that we are insensible to appreciation, or independent of our fellow-creatures. It is particularly grateful to me in my lonely condition" (and here Markham heaved a sigh as long as her corsets would allow her,) "for these dear little orphans are all I have to love, and I think I may say I have won their little hearts."

"We know it, we all know it, my dear lady; but you must not allow your duties to press *too* heavily. I thought you looked over-weary this evening."

"Do I?" asked Markham, snapping her eyes to make them look brighter. "Ah, well—it is very likely—the poor little darling who came here to-day, was taken in a fit. I find she is subject to them, and I had just brought her safely out of it, when I came to you. One can't help feeling at such a time, you know, unless indeed, one is a stock, or a stone, and my sensibilities are almost too acute for my situation."

"Very true, my dear lady; but for *our* sakes, for *my* sake," and Mr. Balch lowered his tone, "do try to control them, though to me, a female without sensibility is a—a—monster, Mrs. Markham."

"I can't conceive of it," said that lady, in extreme disgust.

"No, of course you can not; how should you?" asked Balch. "I wish that I—we—I—dared say how much we think of you."

"Oh!" said Markham, with a little deprecatory waive of her hand, "I only do my duty, Mr. Balch."

"Yes, you do—a great deal more—much more than any one with less heart would think of doing; you are too modest, Mrs. Markham; you underrate yourself, Mrs. Markham; I shall move at the next meeting of the Board to have your salary raised," said Balch, with enthusiasm.

"Oh, I beg—I beg"—said Markham, covering her face with her hands—"pray don't, Mr. Balch—I am not at all mercenary."

"My *dear* lady," seizing her hands—"as if we—I—we—could think so—and of *you?* I shall certainly propose it at our next meeting, and if the Board have n't the means to do it, I know who has;" and Balch squeezed Markham's hand.

CHAPTER III.

In a large, uncarpeted, barren-looking room, round narrow strips of table, were seated Mrs. Markham's collected charge, at dinner. Each little head was as closely shaven as if the doctor had ordered it done for blistering purposes; and each little form was closely swathed in indigo-blue factory cotton, drawn bag-fashion round the neck; their lack-luster eyes, stooping forms, and pale faces, telling to the observant eye their own eloquent tale of suffering

The stereotyped blessing was duly mumbled over by Mrs. Markham, and the bread and molasses distributed among the wooden plates. There was little havoc made, for appetizing fresh air and exercise had been sparingly dealt out by Mrs. Markham, who had her reward in being spoken of, in the Reports of the Committee, as "a most economical, trustworthy person, every way qualified for her important position." For all that, it was sad to see the hopeless, weary look on those subdued faces, and to listen to the languid, monotonous tone in which they replied to any question addressed them.

Rose sat over the untasted morsel, looking vainly from one face to another, for some glance of sympathy for the new comer.

They were once new comers—some long since, some more newly; their hearts, too, like Rose's, had yearned for sympathy; their ears ached, as did hers, for one kind tone; but that was all past. Many suns had risen and set on that hopeless search; risen and set, but never on their sports or plays.

The moon sometimes looked in upon them asleep in their little narrow cots. She saw the bitter waking from some mocking dream of home. She saw them spring suddenly from their couches, as they dreamed that the inexorable bell summoned them to rise. She saw them murmuring in their restless slumbers, the tasks which their overworked brains had failed to commit, and for which their much abused physiques were held responsible.

Morning came; no eye brightened at their waking; no little tongue bade a silver-toned 'good-morrow;' no little foot tripped deftly out of bed: for Markham stood at the door—Markham with her bell, and her bunch of keys, and her ferule—Markham, stern and immovable as if she never were a little child, or as if God had forgotten, when he made her, to give her a heart.

And so, as I said before, Rose sat looking round the table, over her untasted food, and wondering why it was the children looked so old, so different from any

children she ever saw before; and then she thought
that, perhaps, when they were all alone together (as if
the hawk-eyed Markham would ever leave them alone
together), some little child might come up, and put its
arm around her neck, and pity and love her. But day
after day went monotonously by; they all went speechless to dinner, speechless to the school-room, speechless
to bed.

Twice a day they were walked in file round the
paved yard, through which not a blade of grass dared
struggle; walled in from the little children outside,
whose merry laughs and shouts startled the little pris-
oners as if *those* tones were unnatural, and only *their*
listless life real. As evening came on, they sat drow-
sily stooping over their tasks, or clicking the monotonous knitting-needle, till weary lids *would* droop, and
tired fingers resumed their task only at the rap from
Markham's ferule.

Rose saw it all now—she felt it—the torpor—gradually creeping over her, and numbing her senses; she
ceased to talk about her mother. She did mechanically
what she was bid; and, in the approving words of
Markham, was

"Quite a subdued child."

At stated times, the committee came in to look at
them, and remarked how inevitably children of the
lower classes inherited poor constitutions from their
depraved parents, and went away as satisfied as if,

granting this to be the case, they were humanely endeavoring to remedy the inherited curse; as if they were not keeping those growing limbs in overstrained positions for hours, and depriving them of the blessed air and sunshine, which God intended childhood to revel in as freely as the birds and flowers.

2*

CHAPTER IV.

"WELL, what did you see in the city, Dolly?" asked a village gossip of the village milliner.

"What are the summer fashions? Any thing new? Flounces worn, I suppose? Always will be, for tall people, they are so becoming. Mantillas worn, or shawls? Do they trim bonnets with flowers or ribbons? Do they wear heels on the shoes or tread spat down on the pavement? What is there new for sleeves? I am going to have a ninepenny calico made up, and I want to know all about every thing."

"I had n't as much time to look round as I wanted, not by half," answered Dolly, "for the stores are full of splendid goods. I had to put that child of Maria's into the orphan asylum. People began to talk because I did n't look after it. I am sure I can't support it, at least not till it is big enough to pay, by helping me in the shop here. People always die just at the wrong time. If Maria had only waited a year or two, now, till that young one had grown bigger; and if she had brought her up to be good for any thing (she is a little shy kind of a whimpering thing, no more life in her then a stick) ; but I don't intend her living shall come out of me. I have worked hard for what money I have, and I know how to keep it. She shall stay at that asylum till she is big enough to help me, as I said before, and then she must work enough here to pay for her bread and butter."

"That's it," said Miss Kip. "People who can't live to take care of children have no business to have them, that is my creed. Was your sister like you, Dolly?"

"No; I guess she wasn't. She was after every book she could find, before she could speak plain, and when she got hold of one, you might fire off a pistol in the room, and she wouldn't hear it. She crammed her head inside, and I crammed mine outside," said Dolly, laughing; "for I had a real milliner's knack before I left off pantalettes. Why, you never saw any thing like our Maria. She went and sold the only silk gown she had to buy a grammar and dictionary, to learn what she acknowledged was a dead language."

"What a fool!" exclaimed Miss Kip.

"Of course," said Dolly; "letting alone the gown, which was bran new, what was the use of her learning a language that was dead and out of fashion? Well, there was a Professor Clark, who used to come to see her, and you ought to have heard the heathenish noises they made with that 'dead language,' as they called it; it was perfectly ridikilis.

He said Maria was an extraordinary girl! as if that
was any news, when every body knew she never did
any thing like other folks. Why, she 'd pretend she
saw bears, and dippers, and ple—pleasure-rides, I believe she called them, up among the stars."

"What a fool!" exclaimed Kip, again.

"Yes; and she said the earth was round and hollow, just as if any of us could live in safety, hanging
on the outside of an egg-shell, and *it* turning round all
the time, too—it was ridikilis!

"Well, Professor Clark married her, and their house
was fixed up with books, and pictures, and every thing
of that sort which Maria liked. I never went to see
them, for they never talked about any thing that interested me. Maria did n't care a penny whether her
bonnet was an old or a new one, so long as it was
clean and whole. She had no eyes nor ears for any
thing but her books and her husband, till that child
was born, and then she acted just so about that.
When it was five years old, its father died, and then
nothing would do but Maria must go after him, as
if there was nobody in the world worth looking at but
Professor Clark. She might have got married again,
and then I should not have had that child to look
after. I know she will turn out just like her mother.
She looks just like her, and has all her superfine, good-
for-nothing lady ways already.

—"No, I did not have any time at all to look after

the fashions in the city. The things there are enough to drive you distracted. Such beautiful big plaid and striped silks; such gay trimmings, and bright shawls. I declare every thing looks so homely here in this village, when I come back, that I am perfectly disgusted. Those old poke bonnets of the Cramm girls, trimmed with that pink ribbon they have worn two seasons, and Mrs. Munroe's rusty-looking black mantilla—it is perfectly disgusting."

"So it is," said the sympathizing Kip, "I am tired to death of them, myself. I really wonder, Dolly, you can make up your mind to stay here in this dull place. Why don't you move into the city?"

"Perhaps, I shall, one of these days," said Dolly, with a toss of her head. "I feel as though I was born to better things. It is dull work for a woman to live all her life alone."

"I know it," said Kip, disconsolately.

"There are men enough in the world, no doubt of that," said Dolly, "and when I go about with them, in the city, I quite enjoy it; but one sees nothing here, except frogs and crickets; it is perfectly disgusting."

"So it is," chimed Kip; "and such splendid moonlight-nights as we have, too, and such nice places to walk."

"Yes, but to walk with a *woman!*" said Dolly. "I like you very well, Kip; but when one *has* had gentlemen's society, it is like swallowing the parings, after having eaten the peach."

"So it is," said Kip (quite willing in such a cause to be tossed unceremoniously among the parings).

"Well, it is just here," said Dolly, "I will own it to *you*, Kip, I mean to get married!"

"You don't!" screamed Kip; "to whom?"

"Lord knows, I don't, but I feel sure I shall do it."

"How?" asked Kip, with great interest.

"Never you mind," said Dolly; "see if I don't live in the city before long. Such times as they have there! Theaters, concerts, shows, balls, and every body so pleased with every body; such a delightful noise and bustle and racket. And just look round this village! you might hear the town clock tick; it is perfectly digusting. There is not a man in it, of any account, but Sprigg's the blacksmith, and he has but one foot; sometimes I want to scream."

"So do I," said Kip.

CHAPTER V.

MRS. MARKHAM sat in her private parlor, comfortably sipping her tea. Whatever might be said of the children's bill of fare, there was nothing meager about hers. No Chinaman's tongue was ever a safer tea detector than Markham's. No spurious mixture found a place in her tea-caddy; no water-pot was allowed to wash away its strength when made. The warm biscuit were as fragrant as the tea, and the butter might have won the prize at any agricultural fair. The room too, in which the tea-table was spread, had every appliance for the consolation of a single woman. Comfortably plump sofas and chairs, a looking-glass, selected for its peculiar faculty of adding breadth to an unnecessarily elongated face; a handsome, well-filled bottle of Cologne, another of Bay Water, and a work-box, with all sorts of industrial appendages, the gift of Mr. Balch. Then, for the look of the thing, a few books, newspapers, pamphlets, etc., for Mrs. Markham never read; partly because she had a surfeit in the book line in the school-room, but principally, because publishers and editors had a sad way

of making their types so indistinct now-a-days; or in
other words, Markham had a strong aversion to spectacles.

There were no pictures or flowers in the room, because the former "marked the walls," and the latter
"kept dropping their leaves on the carpet;" but there
were two smart, gilt candelabras on the mantle, and a
small clock between them, and an hour glass, and a
stuffed owl. There was also a light kid glove, which
always lay there, because it served for a text for Mr.
Balch's little complimentary speeches about hands and
hearts, and pairs, etc. Mrs. Markham was always
going to put it away, but somehow she never did so.

"Ah, Timmins, is that you? come in. Is Tibbs any better," asked Mrs. Markham, comfortably sipping her tea.

"No ma'm, she 's awful; her wrists look as if they
would snap in two; and her neck looks so slender;
and her head so big. Oh, she 's a sight, ma'am."

"Pooh, you are always sight-seeing, Timmins; the
child always had a miserable constitution. As the
committee say, it is not much use to try to rear these
children; the seeds of disease are in them."

"Well, Tibbs is going fast enough, that 's certain.
She 's mostly stupid-like, but now and then she smiles
and reaches out her arms, for all the world as if she
saw the angels, and wanted them to come and take her."

"What nonsense, Timmins. Hand me that toast.
Just as if a pauper-child would have such notions."

"Well, ma'am, if you only would stay long enough by the child, you'd see it; it is awful to watch with her all alone."

"Afraid of a sick child," said Mrs. Markham, pouring out another cup of hyson.

"No, not the child exactly—Tibbs is a good little thing; but the sperrets, about the room. I do believe," said Timmins, solemnly, "that sperrets are all round these childern. You don't see things as I do, Mrs. Markham."

"I hope I don't," answered that lady, laughing, as she pushed back her empty cup. "A pretty matron I should make, filled with such fanciful whims; and a great while the committee would keep me."

"Perhaps so," answered Timmins. "Sometimes I think—"

"What?" asked Markham.

"And then again I don't know," said the perplexed Timmins; "but I must run back to Tibbs—if you only *would* look in on her, Mrs. Markham," said Timmins beseechingly, as she closed the door.

While the above conversation was passing, the film gathered slowly over little Tibbs's eyes; the feet and hands grew colder—colder; drops of moisture gathered on the marble temples; the lips moved, but no sound came; a convulsive spasm shook the slight form,

and little Tibbs was dead!   None stood by to hold the
feeble hand, or wipe the gathering death-damp from
the pale lips and brow.   No warm breath was proof
to the dimmed eye and dulled ear of Love's dear
presence.

Tibbs died *alone.*

And yet not alone, for He who loveth little children, folded her to His bosom.

"It is quite time she took her drops," said Timmins,
re-entering the room ; and holding the phial up to the
light, and placing a spoon under its mouth, she commenced counting, " One — two — three — four— here
Tibbie.

" What !"

The horror-struck Timmins darted through the door,
and back to Mrs. Markham.

" Oh, ma'am — oh, ma'am—she 's gone—all alone,
too—oh, Mrs. Markham—"

" Who 's gone ? what are you talking about, Tim-
mons ?"

" Tibbs, ma'am—Tibbs—while I was down here talking to you—and all alone, too—oh dear—oh dear—"

" Hold your tongue, Timmins ; as if *your* being
there would have done any good ?"

" Don't you think so, ma'am ?" asked the relieved
Timmins.

" No, of course not ; the child's time had come—it

is all well enough; you couldn't have helped it. Call Watkins, and tell her to go lay her out. I will be up when I have taken my nap. You stay there till Watkins has done, and then lock the door and take the key. What o'clock is it?"

"Oh, I don't know," said Timmins. "Are you *sure* it was just as well for Tibbs to die alone? I hope *I* shan't die alone." Should *you* like to die alone, Mrs. Markham?"

"That has nothing to do with it," answered Mrs. Markham, angrily; "go along, Timmins, and don't make a fool of yourself."

"Poor thing! poor thing!" exclaimed Watkins, as she untied little Tibbs's night-dress to wash her thin limbs, "*her* sufferings are over. I tell you, Timmins, there'll be a long reckoning for this some day. I had rather be Tibbs here than Mrs. Markham. She isn't a sparrow's weight," said Watkins, lifting the child. "Was she sensible when she died, Timmins?"

"Don't ask me—don't ask me. Oh, Watkins, *could* I help it? I ran down to speak to Mrs. Markham, and—and—"

"She didn't die alone?" asked the horror-struck Watkins, laying the corpse back upon the pillow.

Timmins nodded her head, and sat rocking her figure to and fro.

"Now, don't say a word—don't say a word," said

Timmins, "I know I shall be punished for it; but in deed I did n't mean no harm. I can't stay much longer in this house, Watkins."

Watkins made no reply, except by slow shakes of the head, as she drew on the little charity night-dress which was to answer for a shroud, smoothed the soft silken hair, and folded the small hands over the weary little heart.

"Do you know a prayer, Watkins?" asked Timmins, looking at the dead child.

"I know 'Our Father,'" replied Watkins, smoothing a fold in the shroud.

"Say it," said Timmins, reverently; "it won't do *her* no good, but it will *me*."

"Our Father——"

"Got all through?" asked Mrs. Markham, throwing open the door; "that's all right. Now spread the sheet over her face—open the window—lock the door, and give me the key."

"Won't you come in, ma'am, and look at the child?" asked Watkins, stepping one side.

"No, it don't signify; you washed her and all that, I suppose. Come out, Timmins; and you, Watkins, run for the undertaker—the sooner the child is taken away the better; it is not healthy to have a corpse in the house," and Mrs. Markham applied her smelling-salts to her nose.

Watkins tied on her bonnet, and went sorrowfully down street for the undertaker.

CHAPTER VI.

Mr. Pall prided himself on the reverent manner in which he performed his necessary funereal duties. He always dressed in black, and sat, handkerchief in hand, in the middle of his coffin ware-room, in a prepared state of mind to receive customers.

He had every variety of coffin—from plain pine-wood up to the most polished mahogany and rosewood. His latest invention was "the casket," daintly lined throughout with white satin, and the lid so constructed as to expose the whole person instead of the face only, as in more common coffins. This was what Mr. Pall called "a dress coffin," and was perfectly consistent with any variety of adornment in the shroud that the fancy of grief-stricken affection might suggest.

When Watkins entered, Mr. Pall sat complacently in his chair amid his piles of coffins, with his hands solemnly folded over his handkerchief. He would have scorned to disgrace his profession, like many others of the craft, by reading the newspapers in his sanctum, smoking a cigar, or in any other way convey-ing the idea that he had lost sight of his mournful calling. We are not bound, therefore, to believe, on the authority of a prying policeman's limited vision through the key-hole, that when the shop was closed, Mr. Pall nightly drew from an old-fashioned coffin a bottle of whisky and a box of cigars, wherewith to console him-self for the day's solemn and self-inflicted penance.

"Good morning, m–a–a–m," drawled the dolorous Pall.

> "'Hark! from the tombs a doleful sound,
> Mine ears attend the cry.'

"Want my mournful services, ma'am? I shall take a melancholy pleasure in showing you my coffins. Age of the corpse, ma'am?" and Pall used his white handkerchief.

"Six years."

> "'Death strikes down all,
> Both great and small—'

"Place of residence, ma'am?

"Orphan Asylum, eh?" repeated the disappointed Pall, as his vision of the costly casket pattern faded away; "pine coffin, of course—no satin lining or silver nails—no carriages—night burial, Potters' Field, etc.

> "'Lie in the dust,
> We all must.'

"Tell the afflicted matron of the Orphan Asylum

that I will send up directly and take the deceased child's measure."

And Pall flourished his white handkerchief as long as was consistent with the demise of a charity orphan, and the small sum invested in the pine coffin.

CHAPTER VII.

It was the day for the committee to make their stated visit of examination at the Asylum. Timmins had swept the school-room floor very carefully, scoured off the black-board, dusted the benches, and placed a bunch of flowers on Mrs. Markham's desk, just as that lady entered on her tour of inspection.

"How on earth came that green trash on my desk?" asked the offended matron.

"I did it, ma'am, to make it look kind o' cheerful like;" said Timmins, a little abashed at exhibiting such a weakness in such an august presence. "It looks so dry and hard here, and children, poor things, is fond of flowers," and Timmins sighed as she thought of poor Tibbie.

"Are you in your dotage, Timmins, to bring such a frivolous thing as a bouquet into a school-room? who ever heard of such a folly?" and Mrs. Markham sent it spinning through the nearest window.

Timmins sighed again, and rubbed off one of the benches with a corner of her apron; then, looking up as if a bright thought had struck her, she said:

"They say, ma'am, that this world is nothing but a school for us, and yet God has strewn flowers all over it. He must have done it for something."

"Pshaw!" exclaimed Mrs. Markham, in extreme disgust; "go, bring in the chairs for the committee, and then ring the bell for the children."

Clang—clang—clang went the bell, and in wound the mournful procession; all habited alike, all with the same listless air, flabby-looking limbs, and leaden complexions.

"Seems to me you look uncommonly stupid," remarked the matron, by way of encouragement to the children; "see if you can't throw a little animation into your faces."

The poor little victims stared open their eyes, and made an ineffectual attempt at a smile, more painful to witness than their former listlessness.

"Stand up straighter, can't you?"

The little crooked spines made a feeble and ineffectual attempt to remedy the irreparable injury Mrs. Markham had inflicted upon them.

"Now, let every toe touch that crack on the floor.

"Now, cross your arms behind, every one of you.

"There—don't you stir a hair till the committee come in; it is now eleven; they will be here at quarter before twelve; now mind what I tell you about throwing a little animation into your faces;" and Mrs

3

Markham having laid the ferule in sight, seated herself in an easy position in a very comfortable chair, put a checkerberry lozenge in her mouth, and prepared herself to punish the first child whose overstrained limbs relaxed from weariness.

Every one knows how much more easily one can walk a mile than stand perfectly still, in the same position, for fifteen minutes; and no one who has ever seen the martyrdom which restless childhood is compelled to undergo, in this respect (even in our best schools), sometimes in the scorching vicinity of a redhot stove, sometimes in a shivering draught, for an hour or more, while the teacher, comfortably seated, leisurely experiments upon their intellects, can help wishing that he might have it in his power to subject thoughtless teachers, and as thoughtlessly criminal parents, to the same daily and intolerable torture; can help wishing that, having placed them in such positions, he could have liberty to punish *them* for the non-committal of tasks which their aching heads and limbs have rendered impossible.

Let every parent satisfy himself or herself, by *personal inspection*, with regard to these things; not on farce exhibition days, but by unexpected calls, at such times as he or she may see fit; and let any teacher who would debar a parent from such an inalienable right, be deposed from his station.

Many a grave now filled with moldering dust would

have been tenantless, had parents, not trusting to show-circulars, satisfied themselves on these points, instead of merely paying the term-bills when due.

" Rose !"

The little drooping head righted itself; the child had fallen asleep; a thump on the head with the ever-ready ferule brought on a head-ache, which rendered a repetition of the offense improbable.

" Quarter before twelve."

Markham slides her little gold watch back under her basque. The committee have arrived. Now she smiles all over. Her hypocritical voice is pitched to the company key. She glides round the benches, and calls to " Rose, dear," and "Mabel, dear," and "Anna, dear," patting them on their shrinking shoulders with her serpent touch.

Now one of the committee makes a prayer, and thanks God that these dear children, rescued from sinks of pollution and crime, and from depraved parents, have here found a Christian home, under the guardianship of a mother in Israel; he prays that God will reward her abundantly for her self-sacrificing devotion to them, and that the children may feel unfeignedly grateful for all their blessings.

The committee then seat themselves, and Markham asks a list of questions, cut and dried beforehand, to which parrot tongues respond. The children then wail out a hymn, composed by a friend of Mrs. Mark-

ham's in which they are made to express to that lady
their affectionate gratitude, as well as to the philan-
thropic and discriminating committee present, who
blow their noses sympathetically, and wipe their spectacles.   The children are then dismissed to their bread
and molasses, and so the farce ends.

(Pity, that the munificent bequests of great and
good men to such institutions as these, should, for
want of a little investigation, sometimes be so sadly
misappropriated.)

The next day the readers of *The Morning Budget*
are informed, with a pretty show of statistics, of the
flourishing condition of that humane institution the
CHARITY ORPHAN ASYLUM, and of the spiritual and
temporal well-to-do-a-tiveness of its inmates, under the
judicious supervision of its energetic, self-denying, and
Christian matron, Mrs. Clara Markham; who forth-
with orders a dozen copies of *The Morning Budget*,
which she distributes among her friends, reserving one
for a fixture on her parlor table, to edify chance visitors.

Meanwhile little Tibbie sleeps peacefully in her pine
coffin in the Potters Field, and Rose sits up in her little
cot, while all around her sleep, and stretches out her
imploring arms to the peaceful stars that shimmer
through the window.

On the evening of examination-day, Mr. Balch, as
usual, takes his leave with the rest of the committee,
but after seeing them safely round the corner, returns

as usual, to tea with Markham in the cosy little parlor;
and Markham smiles on him as only an unappropriated
elderly female knows how; and Mr. Balch, what with
the smile and the Hyson, considers Webster and Worcester united too meager to express his feelings, and
falls back upon Markham's hand, upon which he makes
an unmistakable record of his bachelor emotions.

CHAPTER VIII.

"MERCY on us! you don't expect me to sleep in that room, do you?" asked Timmins of Mrs. Markham, as they stopped before the door of the room where little Tibbie died.

"I wouldn't do it for a purse of gold. I know I should see her ghost; oh, it would be awful;" and Timmins put her hands before her face, as if the ghost were looming up in the depths of the dimly-lighted entry.

"Nonsense!" said Mrs. Markham; "how superstitious you are! I am going to sleep there with you."

"Are you? Well, that alters the case," and Mrs. Markham led the way, while Timmins followed her with distended eyes.

"I really can't help thinking she *will* come back," said Timmins, as Mrs. Markham extinguished the light and crept into bed. "I can't seem to get over it, about her dying all alone. How very thin she was. Did you ever think she was unhappy, Mrs. Markham?"

"I don't think any thing about it, Timmins. I go to bed for the purpose of sleeping;" and turning her back upon Timmins, she buried her frilled night-cap in the pillow.

"Don't cuddle up so close, Timmins," said Mrs. Markham, about ten minutes after; "you make me insufferably hot."

"Lor', ma'am, I can't help it; I can't see nothing, and you won't speak to me, and how am I going to know that you are there?"

"Guess at it," said Markham, giving another hitch away toward the wall, and soon her sonorous breathing announced her departure to the land of dreams.

"Goodness alive! if she ain't asleep," said Timmins; "what if Tibbie *should* come back? Oh dear! I am sure I am sorry enough I left her so. I'll put my head under the bed-clothes. No I won't—because if it *is* coming, Mrs. Markham must wake up, for I shan't be good for nothing; I never spoke to a ghost in my life."

"What's—that?" she whispered hoarsely, as, by the dim light of the street-lamp on the window-glass, she saw the door open slowly, and a little figure dressed in white, glide in. "Oh Lor'—oh Mrs. Markham—(griping that lady by the arm)—it's come! Hist—there—there—oh—oh, it's coming *here*," whispered Timmins, as Mrs. Markham, now thoroughly roused, trembled as violently as Timmins, and both made a shuddering plunge under the bed-clothes.

" *You* look out, Timmins?"

" No—*you*, Mrs. Markham!" and both night-caps were thrust carefully from under the sides of the raised sheets.

There was the little figure—it was no illusion—fluttering, gliding about the room; now here, now more distant, and now, with its pale, wan face and outstretched arms, it approaches the bed. Timmins and Markham both jump shrieking from it through the door, and fall senseless upon the entry floor.

The wicked flee when none pursueth.

Poor innocent little Rose! Waked suddenly from her somnambulistic sleep, she stands gazing about her, the unconscious avenger of little Tibbie's sufferings, and her own.

CHAPTER IX.

Years pass on. Some of the children have been bound out, others Death has more mercifully indentured into his own service. Rose has grown tall. Her step is slow and feeble, and her form has lost its roundness; but her eyes are beautiful from the light within, and her wee mouth has a grieved look which makes the beholder long to clasp her to his heart. Even the ugly charity-school bonnet which Markham has just tied under her chin, can not make her look ugly.

Dolly stands waiting to take her to Difftown; she has no bundle to pack up, she has no regrets at leaving the Asylum, she has no hope for the future, for she has looked into Dolly's face with her clear calm eyes, and read her doom.

"Rose, come and kiss me, darling, before you go," said Markham. "I always feel *so* melancholy," she added, in an aside, to Dolly, "at parting with these dear children. It is quite impossible not to feel a motherly interest and solicitude after being with them so long. Good-by, dear Rose—don't *quite* forget me."

3*

Rose thought there was little fear of that, as she followed Dolly out of the house.

"A very nice woman, that Mrs. Markham," said Dolly, as they walked to the stable where she had left her horse and chaise, "a very nice woman."

Rose made no reply.

"I dare say though, you don't like her at all, do you?"

"No," said Rose.

"Why not, I should like to know?" asked Dolly, tartly.

"I had rather not tell, if you please," answered Rose.

The civil manner in which the refusal was couched irritated Dolly.

"You are as like your mother as two peas," said she, angrily; "you look just like her, and speak just like her."

"Do you think so?" asked the child, her whole face brightening.

"I don't know why you should look so pleased about it. Maria was a thriftless creature. No learning but book learning."

"Please don't speak so of my mamma," and the tears stood in Rose's eyes.

"I shall speak just as I please of her," said Dolly; "she was my sister before she was your mother, by a long spell, and I don't know why I am bound to love her for that reason, when there was nothing to love in her."

"But there was," said Rose. "She was sweet, and gentle, and loving, and oh, Aunt Dolly, she was every thing to *me*," and the hot tears trickled through Rose's slender fingers.

"Fiddle-faddle! Now ain't you ashamed, you great baby, to be bawling here in the street, as if I was some terrible dragon making off with you? That's all the thanks I get for taking you out of the church-yard and putting you in that nice Orphan Asylum."

"If you had only left me in the church-yard," sobbed Rose.

Dolly was quite too angry to reply. The very bows on her bonnet trembled with rage.

After a pause, she turned round, and laying her hands on Rose's trembling shoulders, said,

"Now, look here, Rose Clark, now just take a fair and square look at me. I don't look much like your *gentle* mother, as you call her, do I?"

"No, no," sobbed Rose, with a fresh burst of tears.

"Well, I ain't like her in any thing. I ain't a-going to pet you, nor make of you, nor spoil you, as she did. You are bound out to me, and you have got your bread and butter to earn. I have no taste for cry-babies nor idlers, and if you don't work and mind too, the committee of the Orphan Asylum shall know the reason why; you may find worse quarters than my

milliner's shop," and Dolly stopped, not that the subject, but her breath, was exhausted.

The morning was calm and serene, and the road
through which Dolly's old horse plodded, very lovely.
There had been heavy rains for days before, and now,
as they left the city behind them, the sun shone out,
and bright drops hung glistening on the trees, shrubs,
and grass blades, and the spicy pines and way-side
flowers sent forth their sweetest odors. The little
birds, too, came out, pluming their wings for a sunny
flight far—far into the clear blue ether, whither Rose
longed to follow them.

Such a burst of song as they went !

It thrilled through every fibre of the child's frame.

Rose glanced at the frowning face beside her. There
was no appreciation there. No, Dolly was thinking
how much work she could get out of the feeble child
by her side, the helpless orphan in whose veins her
own blood flowed.

On they went—the old horse, and Dolly, and Rose.

Wreaths of mist rolled up from the valleys, crept
along the hill-sides, and were eagerly drunk up by the
sun's warm breath, leaving the earth fresh and fair as
when it first came from the forming hand of God.

Cottages they passed, nestled among the trees, on
whose happy thresholds children clambered on a
mother's knee.

Churches too, whose glistening spires pointed to

that Heaven where Rose longed to be at rest; and far, far away, the silver lake gleamed in the bright sunlight; oh, how gladly, on its peaceful bosom, would the child have floated away!

"For mercy's sake, what are you thinking about," asked Dolly, "with that curious look in your eyes, and the color coming and going in your face that way?"

"I was thinking," said the child, her eyes still fixed on the silver lake, "how beautiful God made the earth, and how sad it was there should be—"

"*What* now?" asked Dolly tartly.

"Any sorrow in it," said Rose.

"The earth is well enough, I s'pose," said Dolly. "I never looked at it much, and as to the rest of your remark, I hope you will remember it when you get home, and not plague my life out, when I want you to work. Let 's see; you will have the shop to sweep out, the window shutters to take down and put up, night and morning, errands to run, sewing, washing, ironing, and scrubbing to do, dishes to wash, beside a few other little things.

"Of course you will have your own clothes to make and to mend, the sheets and towels to hem, and be learning meanwhile to wait on customers in the shop; I shan't trust you with the money-drawer till I know whether you are honest."

Rose's face became crimson, and she involuntarily moved further away from Dolly.

"None of that now," said that lady, "such airs won't go down with me. It is a pity if I can't speak to my own sister's child."

Rose thought this was the only light in which she was likely to view the relationship, but she was too wise to reply.

"There's no knowing," said Dolly, "what you may have learned among those children at the Asylum."

"You put me there, Aunt Dolly," said Rose.

"Of course I put you there, but did I tell you to learn all the bad things you saw?"

"You didn't tell me not; but I never would take what belonged to another."

"Shut up now—you are just like your mother ex—actly;" and Dolly stopped here, considering that she could go no further in the way of invective.

And now they were nearing the village. Rose thought it looked much prettier at a distance than near.

There was an ugly, dirty tavern in the main street, on whose gaudy sign-board was painted "The Rising Sun;" and on whose piazza were congregated knots of men, smoking, chewing, swearing, and bargaining, by turns; for it was cattle-fair Monday, and the whole population was astir.

Herds of cattle; sheep, cows, calves, oxen, and pigs, divided off into little crowded pens, stood bleating and lowing in the blazing sun, half dead with thirst, while their owners were chaffering about prices.

On the opposite side of the street were temporary booths, whose owners were making the most of the day by opening oysters, and uncorking bottles for the ravenous farmers; little boys stood by, greedily devouring the dregs of the glasses whenever they could dodge a boxed ear. A few sickly trees were planted here and there, at the sides of the road, which seemed to have dwindled away in disgust at their location. On a small patch of green, dignified by the name of the Park, an ill-assorted, heterogeneous company were drilling for 'lection, presenting arms, etc., in a manner that would have struck Napoleon dumb.

Dolly's house was on the further side of "the Park," a two story wooden tenement, of a bright red color, planted on a sand bank close to the road side, unornamented with a single green thing, if we may except some gawky boys who were eyeing the tin soldiers and peppermint candy in the milliner's window, and who had been attentively listening to the swearing cattle-dealers and picking up stray lobster-claws which good fortune had thrown in their way.

"That *her?*" whispered Daffodil (Dolly's factotum), pointing to Rose, as she assisted Dolly to alight. Dolly nodded.

"Why—she'd be a real beauty if she was only a

little fatter, and did n't stoop, and her eyes were n't so big, and she was n't so pale."

"I don't see any beauty," mumbled Dolly, "she looks exactly like her mother."

"O no—of course she is n't a beauty," said Daffy, retracting her involuntary mistake, "she don't favor you in the least Dolly; I said she would be pretty if—"

"Never mind your ifs now, I'm as hungry as a catamount, give me something to eat, and then I'll talk; some of that cold ham, and warm over some tea; goodness, how faint I am, that young one has tired me all out argufying—she's just like her mother—exactly."

"Shall I set a plate for her too?" asked Daffy.

"Of course not, till I get through; children always cram all before them, there would n't be a mortal thing left for me—let her wait till I have done. Rose —here! take off your bonnet, sit down and unpack those boxes, don't break the strings now, untie the knots carefully, the strings may do to use again, and don't litter up the shop floor, and don't —— Lord-a-mercy, Daffy, if she ain't undone the wrong boxes, I knew she would."

"T-h-o-s-e," she thundered in Rose's ear, pulling her along to the right pile, and bending her over till her nose touched the boxes; "now see if you can see them, and don't make another mistake *short* of ten minutes," and Dolly threw off her bonnet and sat down to her tea.

Rose stooped down as she was bid, and commenced her task, but the excitement she had undergone, so different from the monotonous life she had led, the heat of the day, and her insufficient breakfast before starting, brought on a sudden vertigo, and as she stooped to execute her task, she fell forward upon the floor.

"Sick now, the very first day," exclaimed Dolly, turning to Daffy, "now ain't that enough to provoke any body? Her mother used to be just so, always fainting away at every thing; she's got to get cured of that trick; get up Rose!" and Dolly shook her roughly by the arm.

"I really think she can't," said Daffy, looking at her white lips and relaxed limbs.

Dolly seized a pitcher of water near, and dashed it with rather more force than was necessary in the child's face.

"That's warm water," said Daffy.

"How did I know that?" muttered Dolly, "bring some cold then;" and Dolly repeated the application, at a different temperature.

Rose shivered slightly, but did not open her eyes.

"She intends taking her own time to come to," said Dolly, "and I have something else to do, beside stand by to wait for it."

"But it won't do for her to lie here," said Daffy. "Suppose Mrs. John Meigs should come in after that new bonnet of hern? It don't look well."

Dolly appreciated that argument, and Daffy had permission to carry her out of sight, into a back sitting-room, on the same floor.

"She *does it* remarkable, if she *is* making believe," soliloquized Daffy, as she laid Rose on the bed; "and she *is* pretty, too, I can say it now Dolly is n't round, pretty as a waxen doll, and not much heavier; she is not fit for hard work anyhow, with those bit-fingers. I should n't wonder if Dolly is too hard on the child, but I dare n't say so. What can that little scar be on her left temple?" and Daffy lifted the curls to look at that indelible proof of Mrs. Markham's affection on Rose's initiation day.

"Well, she 's a pretty cretur!" said Daffodil again, as she took one more glance at her from the half open door. "I could n't find it in my heart to speak cross to the poor motherless thing; but it won't do for me to stay up here."

"Shall I make a cup of tea for Rose, agin she wakes up?" asked Daffy.

"Sick folks ought not to eat and drink," said Dolly, sarcastically; "no, of course not; clear away the table, and put things to rights here. Our Maria was always acting just so; if she did n't have her breakfast ready to put in her mouth the minute she got out of bed, she 'd up and faint away; she 'd faint if it was hot, and she 'd faint if it was cold. She 'd faint if she was glad, and faint if she was sorry. She was always a-fainting; I never fainted in my life."

"Sisters are different, you know;" said Daffy, polishing a tea-cup with a towel.

"I believe you," said Dolly. "It is lucky they are; I am glad I ain't such a miserable stick; but Rose has got to get out of that," added she.

"You don't really believe she, nor Maria, as you call her, could help it, do you?" asked Daffy.

"Help a fiddlestick," said Dolly, jerking down her pea-green paper window-curtain; "ridikilis!"

Daffy knew that word was Dolly's ultimatum, and pursued the subject no further.

CHAPTER X.

"AUNT DOLLY," said Rose, timidly, about a month after the events above related, "Aunt Dolly"—and here Rose stopped short.

"Out with it," said Dolly, "if you 've got any thing to say. You make me as nervous as an eel, twisting that apron-string, and Aunt Dolly-ing such an eternity; if you have got any thing to say, out with it."

"May I go to the evening school?" asked Rose, "it is a free school."

"Well—you are not free to go, if it is; you know how to read and write, and I have taught you how to make change pretty well, that is all you need for *my* purposes."

"But I should like to learn other things, Aunt Dolly."

"What other things, I 'd like to know? that 's your mother all over. She never was content without a book at the end of her nose. She could n't have earned her living to have saved her life, if she had n't got married."

"It was partly to earn my living I wanted to learn, Aunt Dolly; perhaps I could be a teacher."

"Too grand to trim caps and bonnets like your Aunt Dolly, I suppose," added she, sneeringly; "it is quite beneath a charity orphan, I suppose."

"No," said Rose; "but I should like to teach, better."

"Well, you won't do it; never—no time. So there's all there is to that: now take that ribbon and make the bows to old Mrs. Griffin's cap—the idea of wanting to be a school-teacher when you have it at your fingers' ends to twist up a ribbon so easy—it is ridikilis. Did Miss Snow come here last night, after I went out, for her bonnet?"

"Yes," answered Rose.

"Did you tell her that it was all finished but the cap frill?" asked Dolly,

"No; because I knew that it was not yet begun, and I could not tell a—a—"

"Lie! I suppose," screamed Dolly, putting her face very close to Rose's, as if to defy her to say the obnoxious word; "is that it."

"Yes," said Rose, courageously.

"Good girl—good girl" said Dolly; "shall have a medal, so it shall;" and cutting a large oval out of a bit of pasteboard, and passing a twine string through it, she hung it round her neck—"Good little Rosy-Posy—just like its conscientious mamma."

"I wish I were half as good as my mamma," said Rose, with a trembling voice.

"I suppose you think that Aunt Dolly is a great sinner!" said that lady.

"We are all great sinners, are we not?" answered Rose.

"All but little Rosy Posy;" sneered Dolly, "*she* is perfect, only needs a pair of wings to take her straight up to heaven."

"Many a true word is spoken in jest," muttered Daffy, as she waxed the end of a bit of sewing silk, behind the counter.

CHAPTER XI.

MR. CLIFTON, the minister of Difftown village was one of those few clergymen who possessed of decided talent was yet content to labor in an humble sphere. Many of his brother clergymen had left their country parishes to become stars in cities. Some, unspoiled by the breath of applause, had laid their honors meekly at the Saviour's feet; others, inflated with pride and self-conceit, preached soft things to those who built them palaces of ease, and healed the hurt of the daughter of God's people slightly.

Mr. Clifton feared the test. Appreciation is as dear to the sanctified as the unsanctified heart. It *were* pleasant to see the heart's dear ones, fitted by nature to enjoy the refinements of life, in full possession of them; it were pleasant to have daily intercourse with the large circle of the gifted who congregate in cities—but what shall it profit a man if he gain the whole world and lose his own soul? Mr. Clifton felt that with his ardent social and impulsive temperament, his quiet village parish, with its home endearments, was most favorable to his growth in grace; and so, turning a deaf ear to the Syren voices which would have called him away, he cheerfully broke the bread of life, year after year, to his humble flock.

It was Sabbath evening—Mr. Clifton lay upon the sofa, suffering under one of those torturing head-aches which excessive mental excitement was sure to bring on. He loved his calling—it was not mere lip service for him to expound the word of God, and teach its sacred truths—the humblest among his people knew this; the tremor in his voice, the moisture in his eye, told their own eloquent tale. There must have been something to enchain those whose active limbs, never still during the other days of the week from dawn till dark, could sit on those narrow seats and never droop with uneasiness or sleep.

But the physical reaction was too apt to come to the delicately strung frame; and with closed eyelids, Mr. Clifton lay upon the sofa in the parlor of the little parsonage, while his wife bent over him, bathing his aching temples.

The parsonage parlor! how difficult to furnish it to suit every carping eye, for there were those, even in Mr. Clifton's parish, as in all others, whom his blameless life and welling sympathies could neither appease nor conciliate.

The parsonage parlor! The father of Mary Clifton would gladly have filled it with luxuries for his only daughter; but Mary shook her little head, and planted

her little foot firmly on the plain Kidderminster carpet, and sat down contentedly in the bamboo rocking-
chair, and hung the pretty pictures her girlhood had
cherished in a spare room up-stairs, and looked round
upon the bare walls of the parlor without a murmur of
dissatisfaction.

Flowers she still clung to. The parsonage parlor
was never without them. They were on the breakfast
and tea-table—sometimes but a single blossom, for
Mary had little time to cull them—sometimes only a
green branch or sprig, whose wondrously beautiful
leaves, shaded with the nicest skill, had given her a
thrill of pleasure—sometimes a bunch of simple clover
—sometimes a tuft of moss, or a waving corn tassel,
mixed with spears of oats and grass-blades.

Mr. Clifton loved Mary all the better that she loved
these things; and when she came to him with her blue
eye beaming, and her cheek flushed with pleasure, and
held up to him some tiny floral treasure, whose beauty
no eye less spiritual than her's could have discerned,
and pointed out its delicate tinting, he thanked God
her heart could be made happy by such pure, innocent,
and simple pleasures.

But it was at such times as I have alluded to, when
Mr. Clifton sank under his pastoral duties, that Mary's
love shone forth the brightest. On the Sabbath eve
of which we speak, his eyes were closed, but he heard
the rustle of her dress and her light foot-fall on the

4

carpet. He felt her fragrant breath upon his cheek, and the touch of her soft fingers charming the fever from his temples. Gradually it crept away, yielding to her magnetic touch, and the smile came back to her husband's lip, and the beam to his languid eye. And now the healing cup of tea was prepared, and the little stand with its tray set before him, and Mary herself sweetened it, more with the smile on her lip and the love-beam in her eye than with the big lump of sugar she dropped into it; and as her husband drained the cup and laid his head back again upon the cushions, he thanked God, as many a convalescent has done, for the untold wealth of love which sickness may draw forth.

"Did you see that sweet child, George, in Dolly Smith's pew to-day?" asked Mary. "Her little face quite fascinated me. It was as sad as it was sweet. I fancied the child must have known sorrow; perhaps be motherless," and Mary kissed her own little blue-eyed baby. "You know, George, things sometimes come to me like a revelation. I am sure that child's heart is sore. When you read the hymn I saw the tears standing in her eyes, but then your voice is so musical, George, it might have been from excess of pleasure."

"Foolish little wife," said her husband; "as if every body saw me through your eyes, and heard me with your partial ears."

"Well, be that as it may," said Mary, "I want you to call at Dolly's and see that child; get her into my Sabbath-school class if you can, and if she has a sorrow, we will try to lighten it."

CHAPTER XII.

NOT the least difficult part of a clergyman's duty is his round of parochial calls. They must be rightly timed with regard to the domestic arrangements of each family. This he is supposed to know by a sort of intuition. They must not be too infrequent. He must remember the number of the inmates, and be sure to inquire after the new baby. He must stay no longer at Mrs. Wheeler's than he did at Mrs. Brown's. He must swallow, at any physical cost, whatever is set before him in the way of eating or drinking.

Mr. Clifton was fully aware of all these parochial shoals, and, as far as mortal man could do it, steered clear of shipwreck; but "offenses will come," and Dolly was at the wash-tub, up to her elbows in soap-suds, when "the minister" was announced by the breathless Daffy, who was unaware that Monday is generally the day when all clergymen turn their backs upon the study and recruit their exhausted energies by locomotion.

"Why, in the name of common sense, could n't he have called Saturday?" asked Dolly, hastily, wiping the suds from her parboiled fingers; "then I had on my green silk, and should as lief have seen him as not ; but ministers never have any consideration. Daffy—Daffy, here—where's my scalloped petticoat and under-sleeves? I dare say now that the sitting-room center-table is all awry. Daffy, is the Bible on the light stand? and the hymn-book too? Hand me my silk apron trimmed with the pink bows, and get my breast-pin quick, for goodness' sake; men prink forever themselves, but they never can wait a minute for a woman to dress; how do I look, Daffy? I do wish people had sense enough to stay away of a Monday morning. Don't let these calicos lay soaking in the tub, now, till I come back; give 'em a wring and hang 'em out ."

"Good morning, Mr. Clifton," said Dolly, dropping a bobbing courtesy; "it is quite a pleasure to see you."

"Thank you, Miss Dolly," replied the minister, with a gravity truly commendable, when the fact is taken into consideration that he had heard every syllable of the foregoing conversation, through the thin partition ; "thank you, Miss Dolly."

"Yes, I was just saying to Daffy," resumed Dolly, "how long it was since you called here, and how welcome you were at any time, when you felt *inclined* to come. I don't think it at all strange that you should prefer calling oftener at Lawyer Briggs's and Squire

Beadle's, than at my poor place. I know it is hardly fit to ask a clergyman into."

"Lawyer Briggs and Squire Beadle are my wife's relatives, you know, Miss Dolly."

"Oh, I was n't complaining, at all," said Dolly; "they are eddicated people, it is n't at all strange; how's your folks?"

"Very well, I thank you; the baby is getting through his teeth bravely."

"I saw Mrs. Clifton go into Mrs. Messenger's the other day," said Dolly. "I see she has her *favorites* in the parish."

"Mrs. Messenger's little boy was taken in a fit," said Mr. Clifton, "and they sent over in great haste for my wife."

"Ah," said Dolly, "well, I did n't blame her, of course not; I would n't have you think so. Mrs. Messenger is considered very genteel here in the village; Mrs. Messenger and I are two very different persons."

"I see you brought me a new parishioner last Sunday," said Mr. Clifton, glad to change the conversation.

"Yes; she is a poor child whom I took out of pity to bring up; her mother is dead, and so I offered her a home."

"That's right," said Mr. Clifton, who had his own views about Dolly's motives. "I hope she will attend the Sabbath-school; Mrs. Clifton, I know, would like her to be in her class."

Dolly's countenance fell. "Well, I don't know about that, though I 'm obleeged to Mrs. Clifton. I don't think Rose would be willing to go."

"She might be shy at first," said the minister, "but my wife has quite a gift at drawing out children's hearts. I think little Rose would soon love her."

"I don't think she will be able to go," said Dolly, coldly; "but I 'll think of it."

"Do," replied Mr. Clifton, "and perhaps you would allow her sometimes to run over and see the baby and the garden. Children are sociable little creatures, you know. Is she fond of flowers?"

"I guess not," said Dolly. "I am sure I never could see any use in them, except to make artificial ones by, to trim bonnets."

Mr. Clifton smiled, in spite of himself, at this professional view of the subject. "Well, the baby then," he added; "it is just beginning to be interesting. I think she would like the baby."

"She don't seem to have much inclination to go about," answered Dolly, "and it is not best to put her up to it; home is the best place for children."

Ay, *home*, thought Mr. Clifton, as Rose's sweet sad eyes and pale face passed before him.

"Well, good morning, Miss Dolly; perhaps, after all, you will change your mind about the little girl."

"Good morning, Mr. Clifton," and Dolly bobbed a succession of little courtesys, and avoided answering his last remark. " Good morning, Mr. Clifton ; thank you even for a *short* visit, but I don't complain. It is a poor place, after all, to invite a clergyman into."

"I think I see Rose going to Sabbath-school," said Dolly, as she folded up her finery, put it away, rolled up her sleeves and went back to the wash-tub; "I think I see *her* going off to Sunday-school and me doing up the work; visiting at the minister's house too; 'baby and flowers,' and all that: she'd be so set up in a fortnight that there would be no getting along with her: all sorts of notions put in her head, instead of thinking herself well off here as she is, with her head under shelter, ten to one she would imagine she was terribly abused. No—Rose don't make any acquaintances if I can help it, and as to Sunday-school, there's the Bible, she might as well study it in one place as another; there's something behind all this ; I verily believe that child is going to bewitch folks, just as her mother did before her; the amount of it is, they took a fancy to her, Sunday, in meetin'; Rose is just like her mother exactly; *she* always looked just so innocent, as if she didn't know that she was— (Dolly couldn't say *pretty* even to herself, so she added—artful). No, that child shan't go any where, nor see any body, nor do any thing, but work for me ;"

and Dolly gave the towel she was wringing out, as vigorous a twist as if it had been Rose's neck.

The kind-hearted clergyman and his wife made many after attempts to show Rose some little kindness, but Dolly was always sure to out-general them, and fearing at last that the situation of the child might be made still more irksome by their persistence, they reluctantly confined themselves to sympathetic glances, and nods, when they met her; and this was much to poor Rose, for Dolly's voice grew each day harsher and colder, and Rose's future, hour by hour, looked more dark and rayless.

4*

CHAPTER XIII.

AND now the minister and his gentle wife had their own sorrow to bear.

The baby was dead.

There are those to whom that phrase conveys but little meaning; there are others whose every heart-string thrills to it. "The baby" may not be pretty to any, save those who gave it being. Its first smile, its first word, its first tottering step, are trifles all to the busy world without; but ah, not in the little home circle: not to *him* who contending all day long with the jostling world of trade, sickened and disgusted with its trickeries and overreaching, selfishness, and duplicity, weary with the clamorous din of traffic, crosses at length his own peaceful threshhold, and sitting down by that little cradle, bends a brow seamed with care, over the little sleeper, with heaven's own smile upon its lip, heaven's own purity on its baby brow.

Not to *her ;* to whom its faintest smile were reward enough for mortal pangs and throes; its faintest wail of pain loud enough to drown the united call of hunger, thirst, and weariness.

Not to *those* who, folding it to their *united* hearts, say— *Our baby.*

Is *their* love the less when disease lays its withering finger on the roses of its cheek and lip? Can they spare "the baby" even though other children cluster round the hearth? And when death's shadow falls, can they forget the night-watch nestling of that little velvet cheek? the imploring look of that fading, upturned eye? Can such chords be rudely snapped without a jarring discord? No, *let* them weep; Jesus wept.

Inexpressibly dreadful is the touch of careless fingers upon the loved dead; the careless robing and unrobing of limbs in life so dearly cherished, so delicately draped.

Inexpressibly beautiful are the services weeping love jealously renders to the departed; bearing on its own shoulders to its last resting-place the coffin and the pall, lowering it carefully, reverently, as if the pulseless heart within would be pained by a stranger touch.

It was Mary Clifton's own fingers which shrouded the baby; it was the father's own hands which placed it in the coffin, it was in their own arms by the light of the quiet stars, it was borne to its garden grave.

"Ridikilis!" exclaimed Dolly, "as if nobody was

good enough to touch that child; minister's folks, too, having sich stuck-up notions; as if the child knew who carried it, as if the sexton did n't understand his business, as if the whole village ought n't to have seen 'em bury it, if they wanted to. Polly Smith was up in a tree, and saw the whole of it. She said she was determined to. She said they cried like every thing; now that just shows how much they believe what they preach about 'heaven's being the best place;' if that is so, they 'd naterally be glad the young one had gone there; pooh, it is all stuff—they don't believe it no more nor I do; any how, I shall make the most of this world, and then, if there 's nothing better in t' other, I shall have at least gained something.

"It was perfectly ridikilis, there not being a funeral time; I should have sold yards and yards of black ribbon, for the parish to wear; but minister's folks never think of any body but themselves. I 've found that out."

Mary Clifton sits at her nursery-window; the empty cradle is by her side, with its snowy pillow and coverlid, the baby's rattle lies on the mantle, and its little cloak and silken hood hang just in sight within the closet.

That window was her favorite seat; there she used to toss the baby up and down, to catch the woodbine branches that clambered over the open window; *they* still stirred with life—but oh, where was the little dimpled hand, so late outstretched in glee to reach them?

Just one short week ago that day (before "the baby" was taken sick), oh, how well she remembered it, how bright it looked that morning, with its snowy frock and blue ribbons, she stood just in that spot with it; a pane of glass had lately been broken, and the cement in the new one was yet fresh; the baby pressed its tiny little finger on it, and left its impress. No wonder Mary sits there passing her own finger slowly over the indentation, while the tears chase each other down her face; oh, to how many maternal hearts have such memories been at once a sorrow and a solace?

CHAPTER XIV.

"OH, Aunt Dolly!" said Rose, coming in with her face all a-glow, "will you please tell me is this my mother's thimble? I found it in the drawer, and *may* I have it?" she asked, pressing it to her lips.

"It don't take me long to answer questions," said Dolly; "it *is* your mother's, and you may *not* have it. You had no business to go ferreting round among my things."

"You told me to go to the drawer, and get the thread," answered Rose, "and it lay right there, and I could not help seeing it. Won't you please let me have it? I shall be *so* happy if you will."

Poor child! This was the worst argument she could have used.

"I will do any thing, Aunt Dolly, if you will," said she, pressing the coveted treasure on her tiny finger. "I'll—I'll—"

"Won't you ever say another word to me again about going to school, as long as you live?"

Rose hesitated, and looked at the thimble. "I don't like to promise that, Aunt Dolly."

"Then I don't like to give you the thimble," answered Dolly, snatching it from Rose's finger, and stuffing it into her own pocket. "Now go back to your work, miss."

"I would have given it to her, had I been you," said the good-natured Daffy (adding the only argument which she knew would tell on Dolly); "I really believe the child would do twice the work with that thimble on her finger."

"I did n't think of that," replied Dolly, "perhaps she would—Rose?"

Rose came back with traces of tears upon her face.

"Will you be a very, very good girl, and do every thing I tell you, always?"

Rose could not answer for sobbing.

"Give it to her," whispered the tortured Daffy, "you 'll see how it will work."

"Well, there 's the thimble," said Dolly, throwing it at her.

"Oh, Aunt Dolly," said Rose, "I thank you. I 'll try; indeed I 'll try."

"Well, go along, and see that you keep your word. I have n't much faith in it, though."

"I declare," said Dolly, leaning back in her chair, "our Maria was the beater for one thing; every body who ever saw her used to carry on about her just like that child; even the cats and dogs liked a kick from her, better than a petting from any body else, and as to her husband, he thought the model was broke (as that image man said) after his wife was made. I don't suppose fire could burn out the love of that young one for her mother, for all she was so little when Maria died. I am sure I have done my best, but the fact was, Maria had a way with her."

Ah, selfish Dolly! Thy sister had a heart. It shone in her eyes, lingered in her smile, sweetened her voice. *Love* was the open sesame by which she unlocked all hearts, and without which thy grasping fingers shall try in vain.

"Aunt Dolly," said Rose, returning, "there is a boy in the shop who wants to know if you can make three mourning bonnets right away. Mrs. Sharp died this morning."

"Oh! that's very nice. To be sure I can. Go tell him I will begin them this minute. Those hats, Daffy, must not cost less than eight dollars a-piece. It don't do for people in affliction to chaffer about prices and make bargains beforehand, that's one comfort; they must be made of the most expensive English crape, Daffy."

"I thought the Sharps were not very well off," suggested Daffy.

"That's nothing. They ought to pay a proper respect to the dead, if they ain't; beside, they have rich relations. I shall be sure to get it out of some of 'em, never fear. Hand the black crape, Daffy. I wonder

what ailed Mrs. Sharp? She was out to meetin' last
Sunday. I hope her husband will call to settle the bill.
Daffy, don't it make you laugh to see what a fuss
widowers make *trying* to grieve for their wives? It is
ridikilis! Mr. Sharp is n't a bad man to look at. How
many children has he, Daffy?"

"Ten," said Daffy.

"Could n't stand it," said Dolly. "Rose is enough
of a pill for me. I shall certainly refuse him."

CHAPTER XV.

"GOOD afternoon, Dolly," said one of her neighbors, coming into the back room, and tossing off her shawl, which served the double purpose of cloak and bonnet. "Who *is* that pretty girl you have there in the shop?"

"Who can she mean?" asked Dolly of Daffy, in affected surprise.

"Why," said Miss Tufts, anticipating Daffy, "that pretty creature with the curly hair and large eyes, who is rolling up your ribbons; she is a real beauty."

"She can't mean Rose?" asked Dolly of Daffy, looking innocent again.

(Simple Daffy, puzzled to know how Dolly wished her to answer, contented herself with a little doubtful shake of the head.)

"Call *her* pretty?" said Dolly, returning from a tour of observation into the shop, as if she had not the slightest idea who was there; "call Rose pretty. Well, I'm beat now."

"Why—don't you?" asked Miss Tufts. "I don't see how you can help it; her hair curls so beautiful, and she has such a way with her, it took right hold of me; her voice sounds as if a little bird was singing in her mouth."

"Ridikilis!" said Dolly; "how you talk. Has your pa got over his pleurisy? That's right. How do you like this ribbon? It is new style, you see; one side is green, and the other red."

The visitor's eyes being fixed on the ribbon which she had taken to the window to examine, Dolly took the opportunity to whisper to Daffy, "Go tell Rose to go out of the shop into the back part of the house."

"It is a first-rate ribbon," said Miss Tufts, refolding it; "but look, there's Mrs. Clifton going down street. She has n't held her head up since her baby died. How she does take it to heart, Dolly."

"Yes," said Dolly, snipping off the end of her thread, "that's the way with those people who are always talking about 'another and a better world.' I don't see but they hold on to this one with just as tight a grip as other folks."

"It is n't nature not to feel bad, when a friend dies," remarked Miss Tufts.

"Well, there's no need of making such a blubbering about it," said Dolly. "I did n't, when our Maria died, I restrained my feelings; it is perfectly disgusting."

"Here Daffy," said Dolly, as Miss Tufts tossed her shawl over her head, and bade them good-by, "here's

the trimmings Nancy Dawes brought for her bonnet;
it is not much matter how you put them on, she has no
taste you know; it will be all one to her, if you only
tell her it is the fashion; that is the right kind of customer for me, your knowing people are a sight of
bother, with their fussing. Daffy, mind you save me
enough of Nancy Dawes's ribbon for a bow for my neck,
three quarters will make a very decent one, but I had
rather have a yard; and Daffy, when Lawyer Grant's
wife comes in to ask how much ribbon it will take to
trim her bonnet, mind that you tell her a yard extra.
She has all her ribbons from the city, and they are just
the thing for neck-ribbons. She never will know but
it is all put on her bonnet, when the bows are cut up
and twisted together; she never asks no questions,
there's nothing mean about Lawyer Grant's wife; she
don't mind milliners and mantua-makers taking their
little perquisites."

"Sometimes I think it isn't right," said Daffy.

"You do? that's a good one, I'd like to see your
year's profits on any other system. Why, Mrs. Bond
gets all hers and her children's aprons out of the silk,
and de-laine, and thibet-cloth that ladies bring her for
dresses; it is all right enough. We must take it out
some way, when ladies beat us down to the lowest possible price for work; talk to me about its not being
right—'self-preservation is the first law of natur,' as
the Bible says."

Daffy did not dispute the questionable authority of the quotation, but rolling the responsibility of the anticipated sin she had assumed, off on Dolly's broad shoulders, proceeded to do her bidding.

CHAPTER XVI.

MRS. CLIFTON *was* going down street, as Miss Tufts
had said; going to "the baby's" grave, for she could
bear the deserted nursery and empty cradle no longer.
It was something to be near the little form, though the
spirit which shone through the sweet eyes had winged
its way to Him who gave it; and so she passes the little
wicket-gate, and winds her way among other graves,
over which other mothers, like her, have wept. Some
of them, carefully kept, others overrun with briars and
nettles; seas perhaps, rolling between some babe and
her under whose heart it once stirred with embryo
life; or, far away, perhaps, the mother too, may be
sleeping, waiting, as does her solitary babe, for that day
when the dead who are in their graves, shall hear *His*
voice, and come forth!

Mrs. Clifton nears her baby's grave. A little form
is bending over it, a slender, delicate child, whose clustering curls, as she stoops, quite hide her sweet face.
Somebody else loves "the baby," for the little grave is
dotted over with flowers, simple enough, indeed, but
love's own offering. The mother draws nearer, smiling

through her tears the while—the child looks up; it is Rose.

"Bless you! bless you, my darling," Mrs. Clifton murmurs, and draws her to her bosom.

"Why did you strew flowers on my baby, dear?" asked Mrs. Clifton, wiping her eyes.

"Because I was so sorry for you," said Rose, timidly, "I thought perhaps it would make you happy, when you came here, to see them."

"Did any one ever die whom you loved?" asked Mary.

Rose's lip quivered, the tears gathered slowly in her eyes, and hung trembling on her lashes, as she nodded her little head.

"Who, my darling?" asked Mary, drawing the child nearer to her.

"My mother, my own dear mother!" said the weeping child, drawn to her kind questioner by the mutual sympathy of sorrow.

"Rose—Rose—Rose!" screamed the shrill voice of Dolly from over the wall.

"Oh, I must go! indeed I must; please don't tell, please don't say any thing," and Rose, hastily wiping away her tears, ran breathlessly toward the little wicket-gate.

"Now I'd just like to know, miss, where you have been without leave?" asked Dolly.

"Daffy told me you wanted me to go out of sight

till after the company was gone," said Rose, "and I thought I would just step over into the church-yard, and put some daisies on the baby's grave."

"Ridikilis!" exclaimed Dolly; "just as if that baby knew what was top of it; it is perfectly disgusting—you are just like your mother exactly. Now go along into the house."

Rose entered the back parlor and sat down at the little window to her work.

"Rose," said Dolly, about half an hour after, "don't your hair trouble you when you are sewing?"

Rose looked up in astonishment at this demonstration of interest on the part of her tormentor.

"I don't know," she answered; "I never thought any thing about it."

("Now don't go to cutting it," whispered Daffy; "it looks so pretty.")

"I think it is spoiling her eyes," said Dolly; "bring me the scissors, Rose," and Dolly notched her locks in and out, in as jagged a manner as she knew how. As for the offending eyes which Miss Tufts had complimented, they were too useful to be extinguished, and as there was no helping the "bird in her mouth," or the "pretty way she had with her," Dolly resolved to keep Rose out of sight as much as possible, with her sewing in the attic, which she designated as Rose's bed-room; and, in pursuance of this determination, she was ordered up there.

Every body knows what a country attic is, with its hot, sloping, pitch-oozing roof, with its indescribable paraphernalia of dried mullen, elder-blow, thorough-wort, and tansy ; with its refuse garden-tools, boxes, baskets, and chests of odds and ends ; its spider-webs and its rat-holes.

A salamander could scarcely have endured Dolly's attic that hot August noon. Rose sat down on the rickety old bed, under the heated eaves, to ply her needle. There was an opening in the roof, but the breeze seemed to blow over it, not into it. Rose made little progress with her sewing, for her temples began to throb painfully, and her fingers almost refused their office. Now she rubs her forehead and eyes, for a mist seems to be gathering over them ; now she pulls her needle slowly out again, and now dizziness over-powers her, and she falls forward upon the floor.

"Now just hear that noise," exclaimed Dolly; "hear that young one capering round that attic in-stead of doing her work. I'll soon settle that :" and taking her little riding-whip from behind the old-fashioned claw-footed clock in the corner, she mounted up stairs into the attic.

Phew ! how hot it was—the perspiration started at every step, and this fact did not tend to the diminu-tion of Dolly's rage.

"You need n't play asleep now, because it won't do," said she, laying the whip vigorously round the prostra;e child. "I shall whip you till you get up and ask my pardon, d' ye hear?"

There is not much satisfaction in whipping a person who does not appear to feel it, and Dolly turned Rose over to see what was the cause of her obtuseness; the face was so ghastly white that even she was for a moment daunted.

But it is *only* for a moment. Going to the head of the stairs, she calls, "Daffy?"

"Look here, now," said Dolly, "see what comes of that young one's going into grave-yards, where all those horrid dead people lie moldering; take her up, Daffy, and carry her down into your bed-room; there's a whole day's work lost now for that nonsense; she won't be able to do another stitch today."

Days, weeks, and months passed on, no lightening of the heavy load; but now the active spirit which seemed always devising fresh means of torture for the child, was itself prostrated by sickness. A fever had settled upon Dolly's strong frame and iron nerves, and reduced her to almost childish helplessness. Ah—who glides so gently, so tirelessly up stairs and down, bearing burdens under which her feeble frame totters? Who runs to the doctor's, and the apothecary's, who spreads the napkin over the little light-stand, that no rattle of spoons, glasses, and phials, may disturb the chance naps or jar the nerves of the invalid? And who, when she has done her best to please, bears the querulous fretfulness of disease and ill temper, with lamb-like patience?

Who but Rose?

"Why are you crying?" asked Daffy, as Rose stood by the kitchen table upon which she had just set down some glasses. "What is the matter with you?"

"I am so sorry that I can not please Aunt Dolly; she says I have not done a single thing right for her since she was sick; and indeed, Daffy, I have tried *very* hard," and Rose sobbed again: "I thought perhaps—that—Aunt—Dolly—might love me a little when she got well."

"Never you mind, Rose," said the distressed Daffy, twitching at her thread, "never you mind, she's a—a —there's a six-pence for you Rose."

"No, I thank you," said Rose, returning it, "I don't want money—I want—I want—somebody to love me," said the poor tired child, hiding her face in her apron.

"Never you mind," said Daffy, again, rubbing her sleeve into her own eyes, "you shall—you shall—

"Lor', I don't know what to say to you—Dolly's a— a—well she's sick and childish," said Daffy, ending her sentence in a very different manner from what she had intended.

"Perhaps it *is* that," said the good little creature, brightening up, "I did not think of that. How cruel it was for me to think her unkind, when she was only sick; I am glad you said that, Daffy," and Rose wiped her eyes and went back into the sick chamber.

"It's awful to hold in when a body's so rampageous mad," said Daffy, jumping up and oversetting her basket of spools, cotton, needles, pins, etc. "I shouldn't wonder if I burst right out some day, to think of that poor, patient little creature being snubbed so, after being on her tired little legs these six weeks, traveling up and down, here and there, and lying on the floor side of Dolly's bed, night after night, and all after the way she has been treated too (for I have eyes if I don't say nothing), and as long as nobody hears me, I'll just out with it; Dolly has no more heart than that pine table," and Daffy gave it a vindictive thump.

"There—now I feel better—I wish I dared tell her so to her face—but it isn't in me; she makes me shrivel all up, when she puts on one of her horrid looks, and I can't be looking out for a new place with this rheumatism fastening on me every time the wind blows; I don't know what is to become of the poor child, bless her sweet face."

CHAPTER XVII.

It is a long lane that has no turning, and Dolly now began to get about once more.

"Dear me"—she exclaimed one morning, as she crawled round the shop, enveloped in a woolen shawl—"how every thing *has* gone to rack and ruin since I have been sick; one month more sickness and I should have had to fail. See that yellow ribbon, all faded out, a lying in that window; when I was about, I moved it from the show-case to the window, and from the window to the show-case, according to the sun; three shillings a yard too, bought of Bixby & Co., the last time I went to the city; and there's the dress-caps put into the bonnet-boxes, and the bonnets put into the dress-cap boxes. Whose work is that I'd like to know? And as I live, if there isn't a hole in the cushion of my rocking chair, and the tassel torn off the window shade. O—d-e-a-r—m-e!" and Dolly sank into a chair, and looked pins and needles at the helpless Daffy.

"You forget how much we have had to do, don't you, Dolly? I have hardly sat down half an hour at

a time.   What with waiting on customers, and looking
after housekeeping matters, I am as tired as an old
horse.   I tried to do the best I could, Dolly."

"That's what people always say when they have
left every thing at sixes and sevens; but that don't
put the color back into Bixby & Co.'s yellow ribbon,
nor mend the shade tassel, nor the hole in my chair
cushion.   For mercy's sake, did n't you have Rose to
help you?   You make such a fuss about being tired."

"It took about all Rose's time to wait on you," answered Daffy.

"That's a good one!" exclaimed Dolly; "all on
earth I wanted was to be kept quiet, take my medicines, and have a little gruel now and then.   You
can't make me believe that."

"It takes a great many steps to do even that," said
Daffy, meekly; "but you are weak yet, Dolly, and a
little thing troubles you."

"Do you mean to tell me that sickness has injured
my mind?" said the incensed milliner; "that's a pretty
story to get about among my customers.   I could trim
twenty bonnets if I chose.   I am not so far gone as you
think for; perhaps you was looking forward to the
time when Dolly Smith would be taken off the sign-
board, and Daffodil put up instead; perhaps Rose was
to be your head apprentice; perhaps so."

"Oh, Dolly," said Daffy, shrinking away from her
cutting tone, "how can you?"

"Well, I'm good for a *little* while longer," said Dolly, "any how; now see that child," said she, pointing to Rose, who had just entered the door, "I bought those shoes just before I was sick, and now her toes are all out of 'em. See there, now. Do you suppose I can afford to find you in shoes at that rate?" and she seized Rose by the shoulders, pressing her thumb into her arm-pit, in a way to make her wince.

"I'm very sorry, Aunt Dolly, but I had so much running to do. Had I thought of it, I would have taken off my shoes."

"And worn your stockings all out," said Dolly, "that would have been a great saving, indeed."

"I would have taken them off, too, had I thought you would have liked it, Aunt Dolly."

"And gone barefoot here, in my house, so that the neighbors might say I did n't half clothe you. You never will pay for what you cost," said Dolly, pushing her roughly away. "You are just like your mother—ex-actly. Now begin to cry—that's mother, too, all over."

"If I were only with her," thought Rose, as she seated herself at her work.

Daffy stooped near to Rose, ostensibly to pick up a spool of thread, but in fact to whisper, "Never you mind, Rose; it is always the darkest just before day."

A few weeks of returning health and successful bonnet-making made the amiable Dolly a little more en-

durable to every body but our heroine; for she had
settled it in her mind that scant fare and harsh treat-
ment were the only means to keep Maria's child where
she should be.

It was Saturday morning, or, in other words, Dolly's
baking-day. You might have known it by the way the
tables and chairs spun round, the window-sashes flew
up and down, and by the pop-gun curtness of Dolly's
questions and answers. Every body gave Dolly a wide
berth on Saturday; even the cat kept out of doors till
the last smoking loaf was taken from the oven, and
Dolly had reseated herself at her usual post behind the
counter. Poor Daffy dodged round in the most diplomatic manner, and never ventured a disclaimer for any
sin, how heinous soever, with which Dolly might wrong-
fully charge her. With Rose it was *always* 'Saturday,'
and so she experienced no unusual flutter when Dolly
bade her follow her into the kitchen, "as it was high
time she learned to do the baking."

"Here, now," said Dolly, "down with you in that
chair, and see if you can stone those raisins decently.
Mind that you whistle all the while you are doing it, I
don't want them all eat up; raisins cost something,
they are very much like you in that respect."

Rose took the wooden bowl in her lap, and commenced her task, though she could not exactly understand how she was to learn to bake with her eyes fixed
on the raisins.

"What is that?" asked Rose, as Dolly measured out some lard, and put it on the table.

"What do you suppose it is, for mercy's sake? I dare say you thought it was cheese. It would be just like you; its lard, of course."

"How much did you put in, Aunt Dolly?"

"The usual quantity; how do you suppose my pies would taste, if I made them helter-skelter?"

"That's why I asked you," answered Rose, meekly.

"Well, how much did I put in? Why, there's that bowl full," said Dolly, "have n't you got eyes?"

"But if that bowl should get broke, Aunt Dolly, I could n't tell, unless I had another exactly that size, how much to take."

"I suppose it must needs be a yellow bowl, too," sneered Dolly, "just like this, with a black rim round the edge; how ridikilis!

"Is n't there any rule?" asked Rose, despondingly; "how shall I know when I get it right?"

"Why, go by your common sense, of course; how ridikilis; there, now, just see how you have cut those apples, all sorts of ways; wasted half of 'em in the parings."

"I am sorry," said Rose, "I was trying to learn how you made that crust—how much butter is there there, Aunt Dolly?"

"Why, those two pieces, don't you see? what silly questions you ask."

"I am afraid I shall never learn," said the bewildered Rose, " I don't believe I could do it."

" I dare say you couldn't; you are just as stupid about that as you are about every thing else. You are just like your mother, ex-actly."

" What did you do that for?" asked Rose, as Dolly, having made her paste, put a small dab of dough in the mouth of the oven.

" 'Cause I felt like it," said Dolly, " it don't look like a pudding, does it, and it is n't a pie; I dare say you'd stare at it till the millennium, without ever guessing what it was for; come, stone your raisins; you won't get done till next Christmas; of course, if you had any sense, you'd know that it was a piece of dough put there to try the heat of the oven—you are the tiresomest little young one I ever saw; you always talk at me, till I 'm all gone at the stomach."

" Why did you stand some of the pies up on bricks in the oven, and set others on the oven floor?" asked Rose, a short time after.

" Well," exclaimed Dolly, " that goes ahead of any thing you have said yet; if it was n't for letting my oven cool, I could hold my sides and laugh an hour; a smart cook you'd make; don't you see that there's either too many pies or too small an oven, and that by standing bricks endways between the plates, and putting pies on top of 'em, I can get lots more room, you born fool! Did you ever see such a stupid thing?" asked Dolly, turning to Daffy.

"But it's all new to her, you know," said Daffy, apologetically.

"Well, new or old, that child never will be good for any thing, with all my trying; she's just like her mother, ex-actly."

"There, now," said Dolly, "I am going into the bed-room to lie down; now see if you have sense enough to clear up here; get the dough off that pan and rolling-pin, put away the dredging-box, and salt, and lard, and butter, and things; throw away those apple chunks and raisin stuns, wash off the table, scrub up the floor, rinse out the dish-towels, and don't be all day about it."

As Dolly slammed the door to behind her, Rose sat down on one of the kitchen chairs, leaned her head on the table, and wept; she was growing older, and more capable of judging of the gross injustice done her.

Bitter, despairing thoughts came into her gentle heart, for it seemed as if the more patiently she bore her cross, the heavier it grew. She wondered if she could be worse off if she ran away, with the earth for her pillow, the skies for her shelter? Surely, strangers would not be more unfeeling than Dolly.

Oh, how could Dolly be sister to the gentle mother, whom she had seen drooping away day by day, and whose sweet, tender eyes had never yet faded from her sight. Rose remembered the murmured prayer with which she drew her little head upon her bosom the day she died, and now—she looked hopelessly about her. Hark—she thought she heard her name murmured in those same sweet, loving, maternal accents.

"*Rose!*"

Was it fancy? No! A bunch of flowers glanced through the open window and fell at her feet; a paper was twisted round the stem, and on it was written,

"FOR THE BABY'S FRIEND, LITTLE ROSE.

"When thy father and thy mother forsake thee, then the Lord will take thee up."

A bright smile came to Rose's lip, and with a hurried glance around the kitchen, she hid the bouquet in her bosom, and stepped lightly to her tasks.

The baby's mother loved her; the flowers were rightly named—Heart's-ease.

CHAPTER XVIII.

"Don't you think you are l-i-t-t-le hard on Rose?" asked Daffy, as Dolly reseated herself behind the counter, after her nap.

"Hard on her? to feed her, and clothe her, and keep her out of the alms-house," said Dolly. "Dreadful hard, that is."

"But you know you speak pretty sharp to her, and she does try to do right, Dolly."

"So she ought," said Dolly, tartly.

"Yes—but you know some children would get clean discouraged, if they were never praised."

"Let her get discouraged, then, I don't care, so long as she does what I tell her."

"I am afraid it will spoil her temper, by and by, and make it hard for you to get along with her."

"No fear of that," answered Dolly, glancing up at her small riding-whip.

"I have finished in the kitchen, Aunt Dolly," said Rose. "Shall I go take my sewing."

"Of course," said Dolly. "You might know that, without asking."

"Looking pale, is she?" said Dolly, turning to Daffy, "did you see what a bright color she had when she came in, and how her eyes sparkled?"

"I never saw her look so before," replied Daffy; "I wonder what has come over her."

"Nothing has come over her, except that it has done her good to work;" said Dolly "talk about my being 'hard on her,' indeed."

"Good morning, Dolly! A paper of No. nine needles, sharps, if you please—have you heard the news?"

"No," exclaimed Dolly and Daffy in a breath.

"Well—Miss Pettingill was down to Miss Gill's to tea last night, and Miss Gill was to work the day before at Deacon Grant's; and she said Deacon Grant and Deacon Tufts were closeted in the back parlor all the afternoon, and Miss Gill listened at the key-hole, and she heard them say, that the minister ought to go off on a little journey with his wife, because they were so low sperrited about the baby, and they are going to raise the funds to send him to the springs or somewhere, I don't know where. Miss Gill couldn't hear the whole of it, because she was afraid of being caught listening."

"I can tell them they won't raise any funds out of me," said Dolly—"Do I ever go to the springs? Do I ever get low-spirited? When minister's folks want to go on a frolic they always get up some such nonsense, and the parish has to pay the fiddler. It won't do," said Dolly. "I shan't give the first red cent toward it. His wife is going too, I 'spose."

"Yes—both on 'em—they are both all down at the heel. I 'm sorry for 'em."

"Well, I ain't," said Dolly—"babies is as plenty as blackberries, for the matter of that; they may have a dozen more yet, and if they don't, why then they will have more time to call on the parish, and make sermons and things—it is ridikilis!

Years rolled slowly away. Difftown, doomed to stereotyped dullness, remained in *statu quo*. It had still its "trainings" on the green, its cattle-fair Mondays, and its preceding Sabbaths in which herds of cattle, driven into the village on that day to 'save time' (as if time was ever saved or gained by breaking the fourth commandment), ran bleating round the little church, and with the whoas of their drivers, drowned the feeble Mr. Clifton's voice; feeble, though he still labored on, for consumption lent its unnatural brightness to his eye, and burned upon his hollow cheek;—the parsonage was doubly drear now, for the gentle form which flitted around it, had lain down long since with "the baby," and the broken band was destined soon to be complete.

CHAPTER XIX.

"''Most there, driver?" thundered out a red-faced man, as he thrust his frowsy head out of the stage-coach window.

"''Most there? Sahara is nothing to this sand-hill; phew! touch up yer hosses, can't you? I'm perspiring like an eel in a frying-pan."

"So are my horses," answered the driver, sulkily, "I can't run them up hill, this weather, to please you."

It was hot. The dust-begrimed leaves by the road-side hung limp and motionless: the cattle lay with protruding tongues under the broad tree shadows; not a single friendly cloud obscured the fierce bright-ness of the sun-rays, while the locust shrilly piped his simoom song in triumph.

"In-fern-al!" growled the fat man on the back seat, as he wiped his rubicund face with a soiled cotton handkerchief.

"Swearing will not make thee any cooler, friend," quietly remarked a drab bonnet by his side.

"Did thee ever try it, ma'am?" asked the irritated

Falstaff, mimicking her tone, "'cause if thee has n't, thee is not qualified to judge on that point."

"Did thee ever roll down that precipice?" asked the drab bonnet, "yet thee knows if thee should it would certainly harm thee."

"Keen," muttered the fat man to a young lady who sat near him, as a suppressed titter ran round the coach. "These women always trip up a man in an argument, not by any fair play either, but by some such metaphorical twist as that now. Well—nature gives strength to us, cunning to them; I suppose she knows what she is about. Women are necessary evils; if we can not get along with them, we certainly can not without them; I suppose it is all right;" and he looked for a reply in the face of the young lady whom he had addressed.

She seemed not to have heard any thing which had passed; her large, dark eyes were bent upon an infant who lay asleep on her lap, a very cupid for grace and beauty. The child could scarcely have been her own, for she could not have numbered more than sixteen summers; and yet there was the same full red lip, the same straight nose, and the same long curved lashes. The intense heat which had coarsened the features of her companions served only to have heightened the beauty of the young girl; deepening the rose on her lip and cheek, and moistening her tresses till they curled round her open brow like vine tendrils.

"This is the house miss," said the driver, throwing open the door, and looking in. "This is old Ma'am Bond's, miss."

The young girl colored slightly, and roused the little sleeper on her lap, who opened his large brown eyes, and yawned just enough to show off two little snowy teeth, and a very bewitching dimple, and then cuddled his little head into the girl's neck as the driver held out his arms to take him.

The driver deposited his charge and their scanty baggage, on the front stoop of the old wooden house, and remounting his box, gave his horses' ears a professional touch with his long whiplash. Turning to give his ex-passengers a parting glance, he said:

"Wonder if that girl *is* the child's mother? Can't be, though," said he, still gazing at her slight figure; "she's nothing but a child herself. That boy is a beauty, any how, should n't mind owning him myself. I'm beat if any parson could call *him* totally depraved. That girl can't be his mother, though—she's too young."

Yes, young in years; but what is the dial's finger to those who live years in a lightning moment, or to whom an hour may be the tortoise creep of a century?

Yes, young in years; the face may be smooth and fair, while the heart is wrinkled; the eye may be bright, though the fire which feeds it is drying up the life-blood.

Yes, young in years; but old in sorrow—a child, and yet a woman!—a mother, but the world said, not a wife.

Rat—tat—the dilapidated brass knocker is as old as its mistress. The young girl draws a glove from her small hand, and applies her knuckles to the sun-blistered door. Old Mrs. Bond toddles to the threshhold. With what a stony look the stranger meets her curious gaze! With what a firm step she crosses the threshhold; as if, child-mother as she was, she had rights that must not be trampled on. But see, her eye moistens, and her lip quivers. Harshness she was prepared for—kindness she knows not how to bear.

"You must be very weary," said good Mrs. Bond to Rose, as she held out her matronly arms for little Charley. "Poor little fellow!" and she held a glass of cold spring water to his parched lips; "how pleasant he is; and the weather so warm too."

"Charley is a good boy," said the young mother, pushing back the moist curls from his temples, with a sad pride.

"It is a very pleasant country through which you passed to-day," said Mrs. Bond, "though mayhap you were too weary to look at it."

"Is it?" answered Rose, languidly.

"Perhaps you would like to lie down," suggested the old lady, kindly; "and your little room is quite

ready.   Your aunt, Mrs. Howe, sent us word you
would be here to-day."

The old stony look came back to Rose's face, and
she stepped like a young queen, as she tossed the boy
carelessly over her shoulder, and followed the old lady
up the narrow stairs to her own room.

"Mrs. Howe was here yesterday in her carriage,"
said Mrs. Bond. "She left this letter for you," handing it to Rose as she spoke. "Here are water and
towels, if you would like to bathe the little fellow.
We have no closets, but I have driven up some nails
for your clothes. I hope you will be comfortable.
Shall I close the blinds for you ?"

"No, thank you," said Rose; "I am obliged to you;
it is very comfor—" but the word died upon her lips,
and she stooped over Charley to conceal the rebellious
tears, as Mrs. Bond left the room.

Yes, every thing was neat and clean—but so bare
and desolate. The old-fashioned windows were mere
port-holes, and so high that as Rose sat she could only
see the blue sky, and the tops of the waving trees.
There was a yellow wash-stand, a bed, a table, and
two chairs. Colored engravings of Joan of Arc and
Mary Queen of Scots habited alike, hung in wooden
frames on the wall. The floor was uncarpeted, and
huge beams crossed the ceiling.

As Rose looked about her, she drew a long weary
breath, and stretched out her arms, as if imploring

some invisible aid. The babe crowed and smiled; the trail of the serpent was not in his Eden.

Untying her bonnet, Rose broke the seal of the letter in her hand, and read as follows:

"You must be aware that you have built up a wall between yourself and the virtuous of your own sex; you must know that you have no claim upon the love or sympathy of any such. I presume, like others of your class, you excuse your sin to yourself, and are quite ready to meet me, your only relative, whom you have disgraced, with a plausible story of your marriage. It is quite useless. I shall never associate with you. Still I am willing to provide you a shelter with Mrs. Bond for two months, till your child (it is a great pity it lived) is that much older. I shall pay but a small sum for your board, as I expect you to do your own washing and the child's, and assist Mrs. Bond in the house work. You are a sad disgrace to us. My husband is just nominated for mayor. I have given orders to Mrs. Bond and some of the neighbors to watch you closely. If you walk out alone, or receive visitors, my allowance is at once withdrawn. One would think, however, you would have little desire to show yourself. I hope you will repent of the disgrace you have brought upon us.   DOLLY HOWE."

Rose sprung up and paced the chamber floor. The veins in her temples swelled almost to bursting. Her large dark eyes flashed, and her teeth closed over her full red lip till the blood almost started, and tearing the letter into pieces, she trampled it under foot. The babe crept smiling after picking up the bits as they fell from her hand. With a quick grasp she wrenched them from his tiny hand, trampling them again under foot. Then, as the boy uttered a low, grieved cry, she snatched him to her breast, covered him with kisses, and throwing herself upon the bed, burst into a long and passionate fit of weeping.

And thus they sobbed themselves to sleep, the child and the child mother, pure alike in His eyes who judgeth not by outward appearance, and to whom the secrets of all hearts are known.

CHAPTER XX.

In a private parlor of one of our great Southern cities sat two young men, in dressing-gowns, smoking-caps, and slippers. On a table between them stood a silver cigar-stand, a bottle of wine covered with cob-webs, and two empty glasses. The room was exqui-sitely furnished, with the exception of some questionable drawings upon the walls, and the young men them-selves were what boarding-school misses would have called "perfect loves." Their hands were very white, their whiskers in a high state of cultivation, their cravats were quite miraculous, and their diamond rings of the purest water.

"Is this your last trophy?" asked Grey, poising a slipper of Cinderella dimensions on the palm of his hand.

"That? not by a score," carelessly answered Vin-cent, changing his diamond ring to the other hand; "that belongs to the pretty boarding-school girl. I really had quite forgotten her. I wonder what ever became of her? She was a perfect little Hebe, effer-vescent as Champagne, quite worth a three months' siege."

"And believed herself married to you, I suppose?" asked Grey.

"Of course," said Vincent, laughing; "she was the most trusting little thing you ever saw, primevally innocent in fact; it was quite refreshing. How's the wine, Grey?"

"Capital," answered his friend, refilling his glass and holding it up to the light with the gusto of a connoisseur. "Capital; but, Vincent, you are a wicked dog."

"Think so?" drawled Vincent quite proudly, surveying his handsome face in an opposite mirror.

"Yes," said Grey, "I am bad enough; but shoot me if I could be the first to lead a woman astray."

"You sneaking poltroon," laughed Vincent; "if you did not, somebody else would."

"That does not follow," answered Grey; "don't you believe that there are virtuous women?"

"Ha! ha! you ought to have your picture taken now," laughed Vincent. "Propound that question, most innocent Joseph, at our next club-meeting, will you? The explosion of a basket of Champagne corks would be nothing to the fizz it would make. A virtuous woman! no woman, my dear boy, was ever virtuous but for lack of temptation and opportunity."

"I will never subscribe to that," said Grey, with a flushed cheek; "no—not as I honor my mother and my sister."

Vincent's only answer was a slight elevation of the eyebrow, as he pushed the bottle again toward Grey.

"No, thank you; no more for me," answered Grey, in disgust, as he left the room.

"Green yet," said Vincent, lighting a cigar. "I can remember when I was just such a simpleton. 'Virtuous women!' If women are virtuous, why do they give the cold shoulder to steady moral fellows, to smile on a reckless dog like me? I have always found women much more anxious to ascertain the state of a man's purse than the state of his morals. If I am an infidel on the subject of female virtue, women have only themselves to thank for it. I believed in it once."

6

CHAPTER XXI.

"She's down stairs, she's back again, the young woman and her baby. I knew you would n't like to hear it, ma'am."

"Go down stairs, and tell her I am not at home, Patty."

"I did tell her so, knowing your mind, ma'am; but she said I was mistaken, for that she saw you at the window."

"Say that I am sick, then, and can not be disturbed; and, Patty, tell the cook to see that her custards are ready for dessert; Mr. Finels dines here to-day."

Patty retired with her instructions, but presently returned in great haste.

"Bless us all, ma'am, the baby is taken in a fit in the entry, and is rolling up its eyes horrid! Shall I tell her to go away with it?"

"Yes!" said Mrs. Howe—"yes—no—how provoking! I don't believe it—I 'll go down myself, Patty."

Throwing a large cashmere shawl over her robe-de-chambre, Mrs. Howe went reluctantly down stairs.

The baby did look "horrid," as Patty had said, and Rose stood over it wringing her hands.

"I don't see what you have come back for," grumbled Mrs. Howe, turning her back upon the convulsed baby.

"What shall I do? oh, tell me what to do for him!" said the young mother—"he will die! Charley will die!"

"All the better for him, if he should," said Mrs. Howe.

"Oh," said Rose, kneeling at her feet, "you have lost a little one, can not you pity me."

Even this touching appeal would have been powerless to move Mrs. Howe, had not the twitch of the bell-wire announced a visitor at the front door. Hastily running to Patty, she said, "Take that child up stairs and lay it on your bed. I am sure I don't know what to do with him; my nerves are all unstrung; take him away; I suppose he will come out of his fit before long."

Patty stooped to take Charley in her arms, but Rose anticipated her, and carried the poor tortured child up into the attic. He came out of that fit only to go into another, and Rose, agonized beyond endurance, fell senseless across the bed.

"They are dying, both of 'em!" screamed Patty, bursting into Mrs. Howe's room again; "you will *have* to attend to it now, ma'am, sure. I know *I* can't stay by them."

"Go for the doctor, then," said Mrs. Howe, thinking this might be preferable to a coroner's inquest; "not *our* doctor, but the one in the next street."

"Your doctor is the nearest, ma'am," suggested Patty.

"Do as I tell you!" said the frowning Mrs. Howe, going leisurely up stairs.

"Just see what a spot of work, ma'am," said the cook, who had run up to see what was the matter; "that child must be undressed, ma'am, and put into a warm bath."

"Let it alone," said Mrs. Howe; "the doctor will be here presently. How do you know it is the right thing to do with the child?"

"I am sure of it, ma'am, begging your pardon; my sister's child had just the like of those fits, and that was what we always did for him, but just as you please, ma'am—had n't you better hold some smelling-salts to its mother's face? she 's in a faint, like."

Patty arrived at length with the doctor, who puffed considerably at climbing so many stairs, and disconcerted Mrs. Howe still more by his keen survey of the barren attic, Mrs. Howe's expensive apparel, and the two patients before him.

Charley he pronounced in a critical state, owing to the length of time he had lain in the fit; he then wrote a prescription, applied some remedies, and recommended perfect quiet, and attentive nursing.

"He can not be moved, then?" asked Rose, who had recovered sufficiently to know what was passing.

"By no means," said the doctor, "is it your child?" he asked, looking with surprise at the girlish form before him.

Rose bowed her head.

"In fact," said the doctor, "I should n't think you were fit to go yourself, if that were your intention."

Mrs. Howe's face flushed, and she walked up and down the floor uneasily.

"How long before he will be able to be moved?" asked Rose.

"It is impossible to tell. I think he may have a run of fever. I can tell better to-morrow. Perhaps it would be better, on account of this window," suggested the doctor, as he pointed to the broken panes of glass, "to remove the child into another room. Don't you think so, madam?" he asked, turning to Mrs. Howe.

"Oh, of course, certainly," replied Mrs. Howe, "he ought to have every comfort the house affords."

Had the doctor known Mrs. Howe better, he would not have been deceived at the seeming Samaritanism of this sarcastic reply. Rose could only groan in anguish.

"It would be well to have those recipes attended to as soon as possible, madam," said the doctor, handing them to Mrs. Howe, "shall you take charge of my patient, madam?"

"Certainly," said Mrs. Howe, with another withering aside glance at Rose.

"Well, then, madam, if you will have the goodness to watch the child closely, until after he has taken his second powder—you see there are two of them, one to be taken as soon as it arrives, and the other three hours after. Should any thing unforeseen occur, you know my address," and the doctor, resuming his hat and cane, left the room, followed by Mrs. Howe.

"Oh! Charley, Charley!" murmured Rose, pressing her lips to the little hot hand which lay upon the bed, "do not leave me."

But the desolate mother had little time for reflection, for Mrs. Howe returned immediately after having seen the doctor down stairs, and coming up to the bed-side, demanded of Rose "what she meant by bringing that sick child into town to burden her?"

"He was quite well when I started; I am very sorry, very, that I can not go back. I lost a letter here, the only one I ever had from—"

"Your *husband*, I suppose you would say," said Mrs. Howe. "It is astonishing that you will persist in keeping up that humbug; I should think you might have learned by this time that your husband, as you call him, could never have had much love for a woman whom he has neglected so long; and so all this bother has come of a search for a precious piece of his writing? 'Tis all a pretense, and you need n't believe that I don't see through it."

Rose knew it was quite useless to attempt any justification of herself, and made no reply.

"I am glad you have sense enough not to deny it," said Mrs. Howe, bent upon irritating her; "I am quite a match for your cunning in every respect, Rose. I suppose you will have to stay here now, till the child gets a little better, but I want you distinctly to understand that you must wait upon yourself; my servants have something else to do, and when you have occasion to go below, see that you go down the back stairs, and do not allow yourself to be seen. You can move into the next room, Bridget's room, if the Doctor cares for that broken window; that is some of Patty's carelessness, I suppose. I shall insist upon your leaving the house at the earliest possible opportunity; when the medicine comes you must attend to it yourself;" and gathering up her flowing skirts, Mrs. Howe left the room.

CHAPTER XXII.

"It is very curious that Rose does not come back; it is only five miles into the city. I begin to think that something has happened to the poor child," said old Mrs. Bond. "I feel quite uneasy. Mrs. Howe certainly would not keep her any longer than she could help. Something *must* have happened;" and she walked from one window to the other, put up her spectacles, and took them out, then took a book down from the shelf, and after reading it upside down a few minutes, returned it to its place again.

"I must certainly go into town and see what is the matter," said she. "I never shall rest easy till I know;" and going out to the barn, she called the cowboy, and by his help, harnessed the old gray horse into the chaise, for a drive into the city.

It was slow work, that ride; for the old, stiff-jointed creature, knowing well the all-enduring patience of his mistress, crawled leisurely up and down the long hills, stopped to pay his respects to every water-trough he came across, and nosed round the sides of the road after the grass-patches, in the most zig-zag fashion;

now and then stopping short, and insisting upon an entire reprieve from locomotion, to be lengthened or shortened, at his own discretion. As to the whip, old Gray stood in no fear of that, because his mistress never used it for any thing but to drive off the flies. It is not astonishing, therefore, that it was well on toward noon before he and Mrs. Bond reached the city. It was as much of an event for old Gray, as for his mistress, to see it. It was many years since either had been there. Its kaleidoscope frivolities had little charm for Mrs. Bond; her necessary wants were easily supplied from the village, and she was so fortunate as to have no artificial ones.

Old Gray stopped short, as the city's din fell upon his unsophisticated ear; and as he moved on and listened to the lashings less favored nags were receiving from merciless drivers, as he saw the enormous loads under which they staggered—stumbled—and oftentimes fell upon the plentifully watered, and slippery pavement, rising (if they rose at all) with strained and excoriated limbs, he probably thought, if horses ever think, that "God made the country, and man made the town."

"Whip up your old skeleton. Get out of the way there, can't ye?" muttered one of the progressives. "Drive to the left there, ma'am; drive to the right; halt there, ma'am," and similar other expostulations, coupled with invectives, were thundered in the ears of

Mrs. Bond; who, in her benevolence of heart, jerked this way and that, backed, sidled, and went forward, and in the vain attempt to oblige all, displeased every body; still she maintained her placidity, and smiled as sweetly as if every person in the blockaded thorough-fare were not wishing her in the torrid zone.

The old lady's greatest trouble, was her fear of running over some one of the many pedestrians, of all sizes and ages, who traversed so fearlessly that Babel of horses and carriages.

"Dear heart!" she would ejaculate, as some little child made his unprotected way through the vehicles. "Dear heart! it will certainly get killed!"

Good old soul! she did not know how miraculously city children live on, in spite of crowded streets, school-teachers, milk-men, and foolish mammas.

But at length, a stable is reached near Mrs. Howe's; and the jolly hostlers nudge each other in the ribs, as the old ark rattles into the paved yard; and Mrs. Bond climbs carefully out, and resigns old Gray into their hands, with many charges as to his plentiful supply of water and oats. As the nice old lady turns her back, they go into convulsions of merriment over the whole establishment, from harness to hub; interrogating old Gray about his pedigree in a way which they think immensely funny.

Mrs. Bond threads her way along on foot, now good-naturedly picking up a parcel for some person who had unconsciously dropped one, now fumbling out from her pocket a penny for the little vagrants who are tossing mud back and forth over the crossings, with very questionable stubs of brooms, to the imminent risk of pedestrians; and now she slides a newspaper, which the truant wind has displaced, under the door crack for which it was destined.

Now she sees a group of ragged, dirty little children, nestled upon a door-step, upon which they have spread out a dingy cloth, containing old bones, bits of meat, cold potatoes, and crusts of bread, upon which their hungry eyes are gloating. It is too much for the old lady. She points to the gutter, where she wishes their unwholesome meal thrown, and beckoning them toward a baker's window, plentifully supplies the whole party with fresh bread and crackers.

And now she stops short, for she hears a name uttered dear as her hopes of heaven.

" Jesus Christ !"

The speaker's hands are not clasped, his head is not bowed, no prayer followed that dear name ; it was not reverently spoken. She turns on the gentleman who uttered it a look, not of reproof but pity—such a look as might have lingered on the Saviour's face when he said, " Father forgive them ; they know not what they do."

A crimson blush overspread his face, and his " Pardon me, madam" was answered only by a gathering tear in the old lady's eye as she bowed her head and turned slowly away, her lips moving as if in prayer. *He* felt it—and the jest died upon his lip as his eyes involuntarily followed her feeble footsteps, and thoughts of a sainted mother's long-forgotten prayers came rushing through his mind with childhood's freshness.

Ah, who shall say into what pits of selfish and unhallowed pleasure that look shall haunt the recipient? What night shall be dark enough to hide it, what day bright enough to absorb its intensity? Who shall say that hallelujahs shall not yet tremble on the lips where erst were curses?

CHAPTER XXIII.

Mrs. Howe was lying on a sofa in her boudoir, in a showy *robe-de-chambre* of green, with cherry facings, over an elaborately embroidered white petticoat. She had on also toilet slippers, with green and cherry trimmings, and a very fanciful breakfast cap.

"Fall fashions open to-day, eh?" said she, laying a nicely printed envelope, scented with "millefleurs," with which Madame Du Pont had announced that important fact to her customers.

"Madame will have loves of things, just as she always does. I shall be so happy in looking them over. I think I must have a lilac hat; madame thinks lilac best suited to my complexion. Mr. Finels likes me in lilac; as to John, he don't appear to know one color from another. I don't think, however, a man ever knows what his wife has on. Madame Du Pont would make very little if we had only our husbands to dress for; yes, I will have a lilac hat, and I will go there before any other woman has a chance to make a selection of the best. I must go in a carriage: Madame Du Pont never pays any attention to a lady who comes on

foot ; a hackney-coach is terribly vulgar. I must per-
suade John to set up a carriage. I will contrive the
livery myself. I wonder what is our family coat-of-
arms ? I must go to the heraldry office, I think, and
buy one ; a bear would be most emblematical of John
—how cross he is getting! I never should get along
at all without Finels." And Mrs. Howe drew out her
gold watch, and then rising, surveyed herself in the
long glass.

"Well, Mary, what is wanted ?"

"If you please, ma'am, Mr. —— Mr. ——, I forget
his name, is below, and wants to speak with you a
few minutes."

" You stupid creature, you should have brought up
his card. How am I to know who it is ? or whether it
is worth while to make any change in my dress or not?"

"I guess it is, ma'am," said Polly, with a sly look.
"It is—Mr. ——, Mr. —— Fin— Tin—"

" Finels ?" asked Mrs. Howe, innocently.

" That 's just the name, ma'am. I never can remember it. It is the gentleman who always says to me if
Mr. Howe is busy not to call him ; that *Mrs.* Howe
will do just as well," and Polly grinned behind her
apron corner.

" How tiresome to call so early !" exclaimed Mrs.
Howe, with ill-concealed delight. " Well, I suppose
you must tell him that I will be down directly. Is the
parlor all right, Mary ?"

"Yes, ma'am, and Mr. Howe has just gone out."

This last remark, of course, was not heeded by Mrs. Howe, who was playing in a very indifferent manner with her cap strings.

"You must really excuse my *robe-de-chambre*, Mr. Finels," said Mrs. Howe, making use of the only French phrase she knew, to draw attention to her new *negligée* which a poor dress-maker had set up all night to finish for the present occasion.

"I could not have excused you had you not worn it," said Finels, quite accustomed to the little transparent trickeries of the sex, "it is in perfect taste, as is every thing you wear; and I feel more particularly flattered by your wearing it on the present occasion, because I consider that when a lady dispenses with etiquette in this way toward a gentleman friend, she pays a silent compliment to the good sense of her visitor," and Finels made one of his Chesterfieldian bows, and placed his right hand on his velvet vest. "Beside, my dear madam, one who is so superior as yourself to all the adornments of dress, should at any rate be exempt from the tyranny of custom."

"Oh, thank you," minced Mrs. Howe, playing with her robe tassels, and trying to improvise a blush.

"Here is a volume of poems which I had the luck to stumble upon yesterday. I have brought them to you, because I like to share such a pleasure with an *appreciative* spirit," said the wily Finels, who always complimented a woman for some mental, or physical perfection, of which she knew herself to be entirely destitute. "It is a book I could speak of to but *few* persons, for I hoard such a treasure as a miser does his gold."

Mrs. Howe *really*—blushed with pleasure. The diplomatic Finels was not astonished, he was accustomed to such results.

"You will find some marked passages here," said Finels, turning over the leaves. "They are perfect gems; I thought of you when I read them. I risk nothing in hoping that you will admire them equally with myself," and he handed her the book. "Is Mr. Howe not yet in?" he asked in a loud tone of voice as he heard that gentleman's footsteps approaching. "Ah— how d' ye do, Howe? I was beginning to despair of seeing you."

"Thank you, thank you," muttered John, gruffly, throwing up the window in extreme disgust at the strong odor of patchouli on Finel's handkerchief, "thank you, you are *too* good."

"I came," said Finels, "this morning to consult you on important business matters. We literary people are sadly deficient in practical affairs, and I know of no one in whose judgment I could so safely rely as your own. Can you give me your arm down street?"

"Any time to-morrow I will be happy to oblige you," said the mollified John; "to-day I have an unpostponable business engagement with the stock-holders of the —— Railroad."

"Any time—any time, my dear fellow," said Finnels, who was not at all sorry for the reprieve; "I shall not think of deciding, at any rate, until I see you again," and with as faultless a bow to Mrs. Howe as Finels alone could make in a husband's presence, he backed gracefully out.

"Finels is a *pretty* good fellow, after all," said Mr. Howe, "*rather* too much of a fop. What's this?" he asked, taking up the book which that gentleman had left.

"Good gracious, Mr. Howe! see the paint on your new coat," said his wife, remembering the marked passages and marginal notes, in the poems, intended for her eye alone; "good gracious, Mr. Howe! do come up into my dressing-room, and let me take it off while it is fresh."

A little sponge wet with spirits of turpentine, if it did not obliterate the paint that never was there, at least obliterated all recollection of the book from John's innocent mind; and Mrs. Howe, seeing her lord safely out of the house with his spotless coat, prepared for her call at Du Pont's.

"Please, ma'am," said Patty, "there is an old woman below, as wants to see you bad."

"Did n't I tell you to send away all beggars, Patty?"

"She is not a beggar, and yet she is not a lady ex-

actly, and yet she *is*," said the puzzled Patty. "She
is very respectable, ma'am; she said her name was—
was—I declare ma'am, I am shocking at names."

"Well—send her off, any way," said Mrs. Howe;
"tell her I am out."

"But I have told her you was *in*, ma'am, not knowing as you might want to see her."

"You never should do that, Patty, you should
always say that you will see if I am in; that gives me
a chance, you see. Go tell her then, that I am engaged."

"Please ma'am," said Patty, returning after a few
minutes, "she says her name is 'Mrs. Bond,' and wants
to know if she can see the young woman, and the sick
baby; shall I show her up there?"

"Yes—yes—don't bother—I never shall get off to
Madame Du Pont's."

One—two—three—four—five pair of back stairs, dark
as only city back stairs can be. Poor old Mrs. Bond
stumbled and panted, panted and stumbled breathlessly up toward the attic.

Patty threw open the door of the cook's room
which Mrs. Howe, out of her abundance, had ben-
evolently appropriated to the use of the sick child.
The floor was uncarpeted, the window was without a
blind, and the fat cook's ample petticoat had been
nned up by Mrs. Howe, not out of kindness to

the sick child, but to keep out the eyes of prying neighbors.

Rose sat on the only seat in the room, a low cricket, swaying to and fro with Charley in her lap, vainly trying to hush his moanings; her eyes were swollen with weeping, and her face was even whiter than Charley's, for through the long weary hours, she had paced the floor with him, or sat on the cricket, lulling him as best she could, watching every change of expression in his little wan face.

At sight of Mrs. Bond, her pent up heart found vent, and laying her head upon her shoulder she sobbed aloud.

"Don't, darling, don't," said Mrs. Bond, with difficulty restraining her own emotions at Rose's distress, and the comfortless look of every thing about her. "Dear heart, don't cry;" and taking Charley in her matronly arms, she pushed Rose gently toward the bed, and sat down beside her.

"I see—I see"—she whispered, looking round the room, "you needn't say a word, dear, it is hard to bear; but turn over, and try to catch a nap while I hold the baby; and cuddling him up into her comfortably fat neck, the good hearted old lady commenced her weary walk up and down the attic floor. Her gentle lulling and gentler touch, for babies know well how to appreciate an experienced and skillful hand, soon soothed the little sufferer. Rose, too, relieved

from the pressure of responsibility which had weighed
so heavily on her inexperience, yielded to the exhaustion which overpowered her, and sank into a fitful
slumber.

Mrs. Bond laid Charley down on the foot of the
bed, enveloped in her own warm shawl, and with
velvet tread and noiseless touch, rinsed the glasses and
spoons which stood on the window-seat near her, re-
arranged the cook's petticoat over the window, and
sat down to watch her charge.

How even those few hours' sickness had blanched
Charley's cheek, and paled Rose's lip!—" How *could*
Mrs. Howe?"—but no, she would not think about it, if
she could help it; and yet it *was* cruel; no, no, she
would not think of it, and laying her head forward
upon the bed, she prayed God to make the stony heart
a heart of flesh.

Rose started up—she was not dreaming, for there
sat good Mrs. Bond, with her snowy cap and heart-
warming smile.

"Dear heart! what a nice little nap you have had,"
she says, kissing Rose's forehead; "try and sleep
again, dear."

"No," replied Rose, rising slowly; "lie down yourself—how very tired you must be, and how kind you
are! I don't know how to bear such wretched hours
as I have had here; oh, mother—mother!" and Rose
sobbed again.

"There—there!" said Mrs. Bond, wiping Rose's eyes with her handkerchief; "don't now, there's a dear. *I don't know why this is, but I know God loves us all, though we may not sometimes think so. Bear it, and trust Him, dear; we shall know all by and by. There, don't cry, now;" and Mrs. Bond wiped away her own tears.

A little stifled moan from the shawl announced Charley's waking. Rose took him up, and sat down with him upon her lap; how hot was his little head and hand, and how heavy his eye!

"Give him a sup of cold water, dear; see how parched his lips are."

"There is none up here," said Rose. "Mrs. Howe said I must not call upon the servants, and I could not leave Charley alone to get it; now that you are here, I will go down for some, if you will take Charley."

Mrs. Bond shook her head, and motioning Rose to sit still, took a mug in her hand, and slowly felt her way down the dark back stairway.

On the third landing she had a little more light on more than one subject, as Mrs. Howe's "boudoir" door was then open for the purpose of cleaning it. What soft, downy sofas and cushions!—what a mossy carpet!—what luxurious curtains and chairs! The old lady shook her head mournfully; and, supporting herself by the balustrade, descended another pair. There was light there, too, for the drawing-room door

was open; no niggard hand had furnished its gilded
mirrors and pictures, its lounges, tête-à-têtes, and candelabras; there was no parsimony in that ample China
closet, with its groaning shelves of porcelain, silver,
gold, and cut glass. Down still another pair to the
kitchen, whose savory odors already greeted her nostrils; no parsimony there, with its turkeys and chickens roasting, its pies and puddings making, its custards
and jellies quivering in costly cut glasses—no parsimony there.

"Will you have the goodness to show me to the
pump in the yard?" asked the unsophisticated Mrs.
Bond.

"Pump in the yard! won't this pump do as well?"
asked the "professed cook," with a grin at one of her
underlings.

"Yes, thank you," said the dignified old lady, dis-
covering her mistake, and moving toward the pump.

"Civil," whispered the cook to her assistant, "I am
sorry I laughed at her. Let me pump it for you,"
she said, taking the pitcher from the old lady's hand.

"I will be obliged to you if you will," she said, "I
don't understand the handle of the pump. Thank you,"
said Mrs. Bond, with one of her disarming smiles, as
she held out her hand for the pitcher.

"Let me carry it up for you," said the cook, "it is
such a way up."

"Oh, no!" said Mrs. Bond, quickly, remembering

what Rose had told about Mrs. Howe's order not to call on the servants.

But the cook was already out the door with the pitcher, and Mrs. Bond followed her.

"What has come over you, now, I'd like to know," said Patty, as the breathless cook returned to her turkeys, "it is the first time I ever saw you put yourself out to oblige any body."

"Well, it won't be the last time, if that old lady stays here; there's good enough in me, if people only knew how to draw it out; she does, that's the amount of it. I wish my tongue had been torn out before I made fun of her; I felt worse when she said 'thank you,' so civil, than as if she had struck me with that rolling-pin; she's one of the Bible sort; there ain't many of 'em; she'll go to heaven, she will."

"Well, let her go, I'm willing," said Patty, "now sing us the rest of 'Rosy-cheeked Molly.'"

"Oh, I can't," said the cook, breaking down at the end of the first verse, "I wish you would just stir that custard while I run up with this rocking-chair to that old lady; there's nothing on earth but a cricket in that room for her to sit on."

"You'd better not," said Patty, "Mrs. Howe said we were n't one of us to do nothing for them folks up stairs, no how."

"For all that, I shall," said the cook, shouldering the chair; "I am not afraid of Mrs. Howe; I know my value. She would n't part with me for her eyes, first because she likes my cooking, and second, because Mrs. Flynn, whom she hates, wants to get me away from her; so now;" and up stairs she trudged, with the rocking-chair.

"P-h-e-w! there 's some difference between that garret and this kitchen," said Nancy, when she returned, "both as to distance, and as to accommodations in 'em," said she, looking round upon the plentiful supply of viands. "I begin to think that young girl up there, and her baby, are awful misused; I don't believe Mrs. Howe's story about her; she don't look as if she was n't clever."

"Well, you 'd better not say so," said Patty; "it is always my rule never to burn my fingers pulling other folks' pies out of the oven."

"I should think so," said Nancy, "just smell that pastry burning now; that rule won't work in this kitchen, any how; if Mrs. Howe comes home, she 'll be sure to scent it on the front door step, she has *such* a nose."

"So you think the little boy will get along?" asked Mrs. Bond, following the doctor out into the entry.

"Oh, yes, madam, with time, and careful nursing; though he would stand a better chance if he had a larger apartment; these attics are bad for sick people. His mother appears to be quite worn out."

"She 's young yet," said the old lady, desirous of attributing Rose's distress mainly to her anxiety for Charley; "she has had little experience."

The doctor would have liked to know more about his patients, but he had too much delicacy to ask questions; and placing a new recipe in Mrs. Bond's hand, he withdrew, musing, as he went down the stairs, on the many painful phases of life to which his profession introduced him, and which his skill was powerless to remedy.

Mrs. Bond kissed Rose and Charley, tenderly, as she bade them good-by, for she could not leave her own household over night; and with a promise to come again, and an entreaty to the tearful Rose to bear up, she took a reluctant leave.

She would like to have seen Mrs. Howe before leaving the house, but Patty told her she had not yet returned. As she went through the front entry, she met Mr. Howe returning to dinner.

"Good-day, sir; I am glad to see you before I go; I have only a word; you will take it from an old lady who means well: The baby and its mother, sir—'As ye would that others should do unto you, do ye even so to them;'" and with a gentle pressure of his hand, she smiled, bowed, and went out.

"'As—ye—would—do—unto—them!' What does she mean?" said Mr. Howe. "I supposed they were comfortable enough. Mrs. Howe told me so. She said they had a room and every thing they needed.

7

Mrs. Howe likes to manage things her own way, and I let her," said the easy man, hanging his coat on the peg; "but if they are not comfortable, that's another thing. That old lady meant something. I must look into it—after dinner; I am too hungry now."

CHAPTER XXIV.

Mrs. Howe returned with the lilac hat in her possession, and her purse lighter by some scores of dollars. She had also a new Honiton pelerine, a thirty-dollar *mouchoir*, and a gold bracelet, all of which she spread out upon the silken coverlet of her bed, walking round and round it, with very unequivocal glances of admiration.

"Has that old woman gone?" she asked, as Patty answered the bell.

"Yes, ma'am; just gone, and desired her respects to you."

"Well, her room is better than her company. Hand me my wine-colored brocade, Patty, from the wardrobe, a pair of silk stockings, and my black satin slippers. Now give me my frilled under-sleeves. Dinner going on, Patty? I thought I smelt something burning as I came in; perhaps it was only my fancy."

"I am sure it was, ma'am—the pies has had a lovely bake, and so has the custards and puddings."

"I hope Nancy put vanilla in her custards," said Mrs. Howe. "Tell her I want wine in the pudding-sauce; and tell her to strew grapes over the dishes of oranges."

" Yes, ma'am."

" And, Patty?"

" Yes, ma'am."

" Tell Betty—where's my other slipper? Oh! here it is—tell Betty—did you take down my wine-colored brocade, Patty?—tell Betty—it's no matter, Patty; I don't know what I was going to tell you."

Patty had nearly closed the door, when she again heard her name called.

" I've just thought what I wanted to say, Patty: did you clean the silver, this morning?"

" Yes, ma'am."

" And wash the parlor looking-glass?"

" You told me not to do that, ma'am."

" Oh! so I did. Where's my other under-sleeve? Gracious! you burned a hole in it, ironing it. Oh, no; it is a fuzz of black silk sticking to it. There, do go along, Patty; I want to dress;" and the fussy Mrs. Howe locked the door, and gave herself up to the undisturbed contemplation of her new Honiton pelerine and gold bracelet.

Dinner had been satisfactorily discussed, and Mrs. Howe sat back in her cushioned chair to the work of digestion, and self-appreciation, while John retired to smoke.

A visitor is announced. (*Enter Mrs. Flynn.*)

The usual very sincere compliments, were tossed shuttle-cock fashion from one lady to the other, Mrs. Howe, meanwhile, losing no opportunity to display her new bracelet and settle the folds of her new pelerine, which Mrs. Flynn persistently declined observing.

"I am *so* tired," groaned Mrs. Howe, at length; "if I am stupid, my dear creature, you really must pardon me, for I have been at Du Pont's all the morning. I bought a few trifles of her, this pelerine, only forty dollars, and this cheap bracelet for fifty. Du Pont never is easy till I give her my opinion of her new millinery."

"She prefers the opinion of one qualified, by experience, to be a judge," said the vexed Flynn, alluding to Dolly's former chrysalis state.

Mrs. Howe bit her lip, and pulling the *mouchoir* from her pocket, said, "I forgot to show you this seventy-five dollar handkerchief. I did not need any *common* handkerchiefs, but I bought this to please Du Pont."

"I fancied I had seen that, as well as your pelerine and bracelet at Mrs. Gardiner's party last winter," said the fibbing, irritating Flynn.

"Last winter!"—screamed Mrs. Howe—"my dear creature, I wouldn't wear the same garter two winters."

"O, I must have been thinking of somebody else; pardon me, dear, my memory is *so* bad. What kind of servants have you, dear? I am so plagued with servants."

"I have no trouble," replied Mrs. Howe, folding her hands complacently over her pelerine, "for I always pay the highest prices." The rising flush on Flynn's face announced this to be a dead shot.

Taking breath again, however, she came gallantly to the rescue.

"Yes my dear creature, but they are all alike about gossiping; now our Margy, came to me with a long story about a baby which she declares she saw up in your attic, and a young girl, beautiful as an angel, tending it, and an old woman, and a young doctor, and goodness knows what. I told her it was all nonsense, sheer nonsense, for of course you would have spoken of it had there been a baby in your house; did you ever hear such stuff?" asked Flynn, with a triumphant air.

"Never," replied the exasperated Mrs. Howe, stooping to settle her bracelet to conceal her vexation; "I never heed what they say."

"Of course not," said Flynn, who having accomplished her mission, was now ready to depart, before the enemy rallied sufficiently to charge back. "Call and see me, my dear creature; intimate friends like us should not stand upon ceremony. O, I forgot to tell you Finels called on me yesterday. Bon jour;" and Flynn made good her retreat with flying colors.

"Spiteful creature!" said Mrs. Howe, "she knows she never saw that pelerine, or bracelet, or *mouchoir*, before this morning. I shall go mad. And that baby business, too; if she had not floored me so unexpectedly on that, I could have said a few things that would have shut her mouth. I know that an own cousin of her husband is servant-man at Mr. Jenks's; but my bright thoughts never come till afterward. Yes, I will go and see her, as she requested. She shall hear of it yet, and then we will see. Finels call on *her!* Finels requires *mind* in a female friend," and Dolly turned to the "marked passages" for consolation.

CHAPTER XXV.

"Bless my soul! you don't mean to say you have been up *here* all this time, Rose?" asked John, throwing open the door of the attic. "Why, bless my soul! Mrs. Howe told me that you were fixed very comfortable, and all that. I did not know any thing about it," said the penitent John, gazing at Charley's pale face. "This won't do; you must go down stairs. Why, bless my soul! you *shall* go down stairs," and before Rose could reply, John had called Patty.

"Look here," said John, "take all those medicines and traps down into the best spare chamber, and bring up a blanket to wrap the baby in; for these folks are going down stairs."

"But, Mrs. Howe, sir, said that none of us was to wait on 'em on no account, sir, and I—"

"Do what I tell you," said John, "down with these medicines, quick. Why, bless me," he muttered, looking around, "no carpet on the floor, no—why—bless me—" and the good-natured John looked from Rose to the baby, and from the baby to Rose, and at last stooped and gave Charley an atoning kiss.

"Had you not better let us stay where we are?" asked Rose, wishing to avert from the head of her *pro tem.* protector the storm she knew would be sure to burst upon it. "I am very sorry that Charley was taken sick here, and that we have been so much trouble to you; very sorry that I"—and Rose's voice began to tremble.

"You need not be sorry for any thing at all, any thing," said the distressed John, "so, don't cry, it is a burning sha—well—never mind; give me that little fellow, and follow me down stairs. Why, bless my soul! no carpet on the floor—no—I had no idea of it."

"There now, Patty," said he, facing that astonished damsel, "go fill that ewer with fresh water, and don't wait for these folks to ring to find out whether they want any thing or not."

Patty stared at him as if she thought he were drunk or dreaming.

"D'ye hear?" said John.

"Y—e—s, s—i—r," said Patty, leaving her mouth wide open after this reply, as though there were several little remarks she might make, if she only dared.

Ah, well might little Charley open his wondering eyes at the crimson silk bed-curtains, looped away over his cherub head. He had never lain on so dainty a bed of roses as was embroidered on that gorgeous coverlet; and as Rose sank down beside him into one

7*

of those luxuriously-cushioned chairs, and laid her
beautiful head back, with her finely-chiseled profile relieved against its crimson damask, John thought how
well both mother and child became their new sur-
roundings.

Yes, Rose's picture should have been taken at that
moment, with her unbound tresses, and her little
hands crossed in her lap in such dreary hopelessness.
But when was she not a picture? and what has beauty
ever brought its possessor, but a broken heart?

"You will see the end of this," said Patty, to the
cook, laying her forefinger mysteriously on the bridge
of her nose. "You will see what's what, when Mrs.
Howe comes home; those folks will be tramped back
into the attic in double quick time."

"What will you bet on that?" said Nancy; "men
get tired after awhile of being led by the nose. I will
bet you that pair of gold ear-rings you have been
hankering after, that they will stay where they are."

"Done!" exclaimed Patty, "and I will bet you my
new silk apron, with the satin pockets, that they go
back in the attic in less than twenty-four hours from
now. Hark! there comes Mrs. Howe home this minute; now we shall see;" and Patty set the kitchen
door wide open, that no sound might escape her.

John was pacing up and down the library, whither
he had retired, after moving Rose into the best spare

chamber. He was naturally a good-hearted fellow, but his constitutional indolence had made him a willing slave of his crafty, designing wife. John hated nothing so much as trouble. Inch after inch of ground he had yielded to the enemy, rather than contend for its possession. Now that the excitement of his late involuntary declaration of independence was over, he began to reflect upon the probable consequences, to listen nervously for the door-bell, and in fact, he felt very much more like running away than "facing the music."

He had done penance before now, by drinking muddy coffee, eating half-boiled potatoes, raw meat, and smoky puddings. He had groaned under three weeks of sulks, with which Mrs. Howe had been afflicted, on account of what she considered his conjugal misdemeanors. He had missed his business memorandum-book for days together; been obliged to go out the back door, instead of the front; had stood on one leg three quarters of an hour at a friend's house, whither he had escorted Mrs. Howe to a party, waiting for that lady to rejoin him to enter the drawing-room; she, meanwhile, reclining composedly in an arm-chair in the ladies' dressing-room, leisurely enjoying the penance she was inflicting. He had been called *out* of the party at an early hour, to wait upon her ladyship home, merely because he seemed to be enjoying it; he had slept with the window open when it was cold, and slept with it shut when it was hot. No wonder John felt a little nervous.

"There it is—there it is," said Patty, rubbing her hands, "there 's the bell for me," and up she ran, confident of winning the coveted gold ear-rings.

"Patty?"

"Yes, ma'am."

Mrs. Howe's face was pale with rage as, beckoning Patty to follow her, she pointed through the open door of the best chamber at Rose and the baby, to whom she had not deigned to speak.

"It was Mr. Howe's doings, ma'am. I told him you would be angry, and so I did n't want to have no hand in it, but Lor', ma'am, he made me ; it was n't no fault of mine, because I know'd it was agin' your wishes, and so I made bold to tell him, ma'am."

"Hold your tongue. Take those messes (pointing to the medicines) up into the attic, and then come back and get that baby."

Rose clasped Charley closer to her bosom, for Mrs. Howe's face was demoniac in its rage.

"Out with you," said Mrs. Howe, taking Rose by the shoulder and pointing to the door.

"Patty."

"Yes, ma'am."

"You see now," said that amiable lady, locking the door of the spare room, and putting the key into her pocket, "whom you are to mind—who is master in this house—do you? Go down into the kitchen."

"There—did n't I tell you so?" asked the triumphant Patty of the crest-fallen cook; "now for my gold ear-rings."

"Not that you know of," said Nancy.

"What do you mean? Did n't you say that if—"

"I said," said Nancy, crossing her two stubby forefingers, "that I would bet you that pair of gold ear-rings you wanted, that *they would stay where they were;* meaning that the ear-rings would stay where they were—in the jeweler's shop."

"It is right down mean," said the pouting Patty; "see if I am not even with you before the week is out."

CHAPTER XXVI.

Poor Rose sat down in her old quarters, with Charley in her lap, trying to read in his pale face the probable duration of his sickness. Poor little fellow! he did not like the change. He missed the sheen of the pretty satin curtains, and the glitter of their gilded cornices. They were something for baby eyes to wonder and look at. He had quite exhausted those ugly attic walls, hung with the cook's dingy wardrobe. Even the pretty sunbeams in which babies love to see the little motes glitter and float, had been jealously excluded by the tyrannical Aunt Dolly; so poor Charley had nothing to do but roll his little restless head from side to side, and whimper.

Ah, there is something now to look at! The door creaks on its hinges, and an old crone, bent almost double, her nose and chin meeting, totters in, leaning on a stick. A striped cotton handkerchief thrown over her spare gray locks, and tied under her chin, and an old shawl over her cotton gown, complete her wardrobe.

At any other time this little weird figure, appearing

so suddenly, would have terrified Rose; now her despairing thoughts had crowded out every other feeling, so she sat quite still as the old woman hobbled, mumbling, toward her.

"Why, Maria! there now. I *knew* you were not dead. I told them so, but they would not believe a word I said. You look as sweet as a lily. Where is your husband, dear? and little Rose? and all of 'em, and every body? I can't find any body I want to see. I am so tired and lonely. Don't *you* go away now, Maria. Did you buy that little doll for me to play with?" she asked, catching sight of Charley. "It opens and shuts its eyes, don't it dear, just like the waxen dolls? I like it—chut—chut—chut," and the old lady touched Charley under the chin with her wrinkled fingers. "Pull the wire and make the doll laugh again, dear," she said, looking up in Rose's face. "I would like it to play with. I get *so* tired, *so* tired. I stole away to-day; Dolly did n't know it. Do you know Dolly? does Dolly strike *you?* What made you stay away such a long time, Maria? Let us go to your house. I don't like to be locked up in Dolly's house. I get *so* tired, *so* tired—dearie me—dearie me—where's little Rose, Maria?"

Rose did not answer, for a light was struggling dimly through her brain. She remembered long years ago, when she first came to Dolly's, that an old woman came there, not so bent as this old crone was

now, but yet gray haired and wrinkled, and that
Dolly spoke harshly to her, and tried to make her go
away, and that the old lady cried, and said it was cold
at the poor house, and that she was hungry, and then
Dolly said she would give her a small piece of money,
and something to eat, if she would promise never to
come there again; and that Dolly sent her (Rose) into
the kitchen till the old lady was gone, but that she
had heard all they said through the thin green baize
door.

"Maria? why don't you speak? where is little
Rose?"

"Is not this little Rose?" asked Rose, compassion-
ately, as she pointed to Charley.

"Sure enough," said the pleased old lady; "I
thought it was a doll—sure enough—why—I shall
find 'em all by and by, who knows?—But—Maria,
why don't it grow any? it is just as little as it was
when I saw it last—where did I see it last, Maria?—
chut—chut—chut—" she said, tickling Charley's chin
again. "Maria? you won't go away again, will you?
—*you* won't strike me, will you? I'll be very good.
Can't I stay here, dear, with you, and the little doll,
little Rose? Why don't it grow bigger, Maria?
Are you hungry? I am hungry—oh, dearie me—
dearie me—"

"Dear, dear grandmother," sobbed Rose, "I love
you."

"Love me! do you! what for? did Dolly make you cry too? Maria, where's Rose? Maria, what makes you call your mother grandmother? Do you know Dolly? Dolly is down stairs; I don't go down stairs. See here," and she touched her old faded gown and shawl, "I can't, you see, Dolly would n't like it. Oh! dearie me—dearie me! I am *so* tired," and the old lady laid her wrinkled face against her granddaughter's.

" Voices! and in Rose's room! what new treason now?" and Mrs. Howe applied her ear to the keyhole. The thin gray locks rested lovingly on Rose's glossy auburn tresses. Rose's arm was about her withered neck, and tears fell trickling from her eyes. It was a sweet picture; but the artist might have found a foil to it, in the demoniac face outside the door.

Ah! Rose, the hated Rose, in possession of her secret! Her face grew darker—deadlier. But perhaps she was not *yet* in possession of it; not a moment was to be lost.

Opening the door, she said, coaxingly, "Why, Betty, are you in here? This won't do. What will the doctor say? You must go back to bed, Betty," and Dolly fixed her basilisk eyes on her cowering victim, who nestled more closely to Rose.

" Poor crazed thing," said Mrs. Howe, " she imagines every body is going to hurt her; by and by she will think so of you. She may kill Charley. I ought to send her to the Lunatic Asylum; but she is an old servant who used to live in Mr. Howe's family, and so I keep her, though she is so troublesome. Come, Betty!"

"Maria!" whispered the old lady, hoarsely, clutching at Rose's dress—"Maria, tell her *you* love me, Maria."

"I do—I do!" sobbed Rose, unable to restrain herself, as she threw her arms around her.

"Love that lunatic? What should you love her for, I'd like to know?" asked the startled Dolly.

"Because she is my grandmother—my own dear grandmother. Oh Aunt Dolly! hate me, if you will, but love her; she will not live long to trouble anybody," and Rose kissed the furrowed temples and stroked back the thin gray locks.

"Well, if I ever!" said Dolly, looking innocent; "I believe the whole world is going mad! Come along, Betty."

"Maria! Maria!" whispered the old lady, again nestling up to Rose.

"There, you see, she is quite out; she fancies you are somebody she has seen before."

"No—she takes me for Maria, my mother," said Rose; "you say that I look like her exactly."

"Come along, Betty!" said the infuriated Mrs. Howe. "Mother and grandmother! you are both as mad as March hares," and seizing "Betty" by the arm, she drew her across the entry into her own den, and turning the key on her, put it in her pocket, and went down into the dining-room.

We have no desire to record her reflections as she sat down to "Moses in the Bulrushes," upon which she had already expended pounds and pounds of German worsted, and who, if ever found by his mother "Miriam," would scarcely have been recognized.

John was in his arm-chair reading the *Daily Bulletin*. He was perfectly aware of the late overthrow of his domestic authority by Dolly; not that it was by any means the first instance of the kind, but the others had been known to no third party. He trusted for the perpetuity of the declaration of domestic independence which he had lately set up, to its being made publicly before the servants. Mistaken man! Dolly's pride lay in a different direction. Well, it was all over now; he only wondered in his cool moments how he had ever been so mad as to attempt to make Rose more comfortable; but let no man ever say what he will or will not do till he has seen a pretty woman in tears.

Still, John had a rod in pickle for Dolly; his publicly-wounded pride must have some satisfaction. He saw by the gleam of her eye, as she sat down to Moses, that she was that morning particularly deficient in his "meekness." It was a good chance. John cleared his throat, preparatory to improving it.

"Oh, I forgot to tell you, Mrs. Howe," said he, laying down his newspaper, as if a sudden thought had struck him, "Finels asked me the other day who Rose was?"

"Finels! Finels!" screamed Mrs. Howe, sticking her needle vigorously into Moses, "how came Finels to see Rose?"

John's eyes gleamed. "When I waited upon him to the door the other day, Rose was just passing through the entry, with a pitcher of water."

"Just like her, and I told her expressly to go down the back stairs."

"But the carpenter was fixing the back stairs, that day," said John, "she could n't pass, I suppose."

"I don't suppose any such thing," said Mrs. Howe, "she did it on purpose; I know she did. Well, what did Finels say of her?"

"He said she had the loveliest eyes he ever saw, and that her face was without a flaw."

"What o'clock is it?" asked Mrs. Howe, in a husky voice.

"Just one," said John, "Why?"

"What time does the stage go to Exeter?"

"Three, I believe."

"Believe! don't you know?"

"Yes, I know it goes at three."

"Well, go and order it here at our door by that time. Rose shall go back to old Bond this very day; I won't stand it."

"Is the baby well enough?" asked John, not looking for this painful termination to his little bit of connubial fun.

"I don't care whether it is or not; if you don't get that stage, I will."

"I'll get it," said John, "but—"

"There's no but about it, I tell you she shall go, if that child dies on the road; that's all there is to that," and Mrs. Howe went up stairs to inform Rose of her determination.

Rose had just succeeded in lulling the restless baby to sleep upon her bosom. Upon Mrs. Howe's violent bang of the door after entering the room, he uttered a loud, frightened cry.

"Stop that child, will you?" said Mrs. Howe, "I have something to say to you."

The quick blood rushed to Rose's face, as she nestled Charley to her bosom.

"It is now one o'clock," said Mrs. Howe, drawing out her gold watch, with its glittering chain and trinkets; "the stage will be at the door to take you to Exeter, at three o'clock precisely. Do you understand?" said she, as Rose bent an anxious glance at the sick baby's face.

"I will be ready," said Rose, in a trembling voice.

This mild, acquiescent reply was not what Mrs. Howe desired; she would have preferred something upon which to hinge her pent-up wrath.

"How came that rocking-chair up here, I should like to know?"

"Betty brought it up for old Mrs. Bond."

"Likely story; and Betty told you, I suppose, to parade yourself through the front entry, when Mr. Howe was talking with a gentleman; I know your tricks. I should think you had had enough of *gentlemen* to last you one while.

"The carpenter was—"

"Don't talk to me about 'carpenters;' where there is a will there is a way; you might have waited for the water."

"It was to mix Charley's medicine," said Rose, with brimming eyes.

"I dare say—such things don't go down with me; pick up your things quick and get ready."

Rose attempted to lay Charley down on the bed, but he began to cry most piteously.

"There is no need of your stopping for him now; he might as well cry for one thing as another; he is always crying, I am sick to death of hearing him; he is perfectly spoiled."

"He is sick," said Rose, stooping to kiss Charley as if he could be pained by Mrs. Howe's heartlessness.

"Well—any how, I am sick of both of you; so hurry, and don't think you are going to stay, because it is beginning to sprinkle," said she, drawing carefully aside one corner of the cook's petticoat as she peered out the window—"come, make haste now," and Aunt Dolly swept down stairs.

Poor afflicted Mrs. Howe! Flynn had robbed the pelerine and bracelet of their power to charm, and the "marked passages" no longer gave her consolation, for Finels had admired Rose's eyes. Consuielo, too, lies wheezing in his embroidered blanket; dear little Consuielo! it could not be that *he* was going to be sick! And Mrs. Howe takes him up gently, strokes his long silken ears, looks into his eyes, and offers him some food, which the pampered little cur refuses.

A scrambling in the blanket!

Consuielo is in a fit!

So is his mistress.

"O, John, for heaven's sake, run for Thomas, he knows all about dogs. Supposing he should die? O dear—make haste ; my darling, my darling !" and Mrs. Howe ran up stairs, and ran down stairs, ran for water, and ran for physic, opened the windows, and shut them, pulled round Betty, and Sally, and Bridget, and threatened the whole crew, unless they helped Consuielo, to turn them all out of doors. And then Thomas came, and manipulated Consuielo as only his humbug-ship knew how, and restored the convalescent jewel to its mistress, who wept with delight, and crossed his palm with a five-dollar gold piece, and then Thomas retired, calling down blessings on all over-fed puppies in particular, and credulous women in general.

And Rose!

She crept down stairs as well as her tears would let her, stopping to kneel before the door through which the wailing "dearie me—dearie me," was issuing.

Wrapping Charley in the only shawl she owned, to defend him from the falling rain, she clambered unassisted, up into the stage. The passengers growled when they saw the baby; the rain spattered on the roof, and windows, and the coachman slamming to the door with an oath, cracked his whip, and the stage rolled away.

What pen can do justice to the atmosphere of a stage, omnibus, or railroad car, of a rainy day?

The fumes of alternate whisky and onions, the steaming, cigar-odored coats, the dirty straw soaking under foot, a deluge if you open the window, poison by inhalation if you do not. Charley became more and more restless, while Rose grew still paler, and the drops stood on her forehead, in dread of his prolonged cry.

"I think he will be good with me; let me take him, please," pleaded a sweet voice at her side.

Rose turned, and saw a lady dressed in black, whom she had not before noticed, extending her arms for Charley. Her face was sufficient to win confidence, and Rose accepted her offer. Handling him as only an experienced hand can handle a babe, she changed him with perfect ease from side to side, laid him now up on her shoulder, now down on her lap, without the slightest appearance of discomfort to herself.

Rose looked the thanks she could not speak; then, stupified with exhaustion and sorrow, she leaned back in the dark corner where she sat, and closed her eyes.

The lady made no attempt to draw her into conversation, but gazed lovingly upon Charley's face. Living sorrows, she had none; but on a little tombstone in a church yard far away, the stranger's foot paused as he read:

"OUR FRANK!"

Oh, how many visions of home joys and home sorrows, did those two little words call up!

Our Frank! More than one heart had bled when that little tombstone was reared, and though the hands which placed it there were far away, yet the little grave had ever its garland, or its wreath, for even stranger eyes involuntarily dropped tears, when they read,

"OUR FRANK."

And so Frank's mother sat gazing on Charley's little cherub face, and wondering what grief a *mother* could know, with her *breathing* babe beside her.

Pity us, oh God! for every heart knoweth its own bitterness, and a stranger intermeddleth not therewith.

8

CHAPTER XXVII.

"WHAT is that?" exclaimed old Mrs. Bond, as she saw the stage, dimly, through the pelting rain, plowing through the clayey mud, up the steep hill toward her door. Somebody must be coming here, else the driver would have taken the easier cut to the village," and she pressed her face closer against the moist window-pane to get a clearer view.

"It is going to stop here, sure as the world," she exclaimed. "Who can be coming a visiting in such a rain as this? It is not time for old Cousin Patty, these three months yet."

"Dear heart," she said, as the driver jumped off his box, and opened the stage-door, "if it is n't Rose, and that sick baby! Dear heart—dear heart, it is as much as its life is worth. I hope I shall have grace to forgive that woman, but I don't know, I don't know; who could have believed it?" and by this time, the baby was handed into her outstretched arms, and Rose stepped dripping across the threshold.

"Cry, dear—do cry. I am going to cry myself. It is dreadful hard." And she drew the chairs up to the fire, and gazed by its light into Rose's brimming eyes and Charley's pale face.

"May God forgive her," she said, at last; "can't you say it, dear? Try."

Rose answered by pointing to Charley.

"I know it, dear heart; I know it; but you remember the 'crown of thorns,' and the mocking 'sponge,' and the cruel 'spear,'" said the old lady, struggling down her own incensed feelings.

"Take Charley now, dear, he is quite warm, while I run and make you a cup of hot tea," and the old lady piled fresh wood upon the huge andirons, and drew out her little tea-table, stopping now to wipe her eyes, now to kiss Rose and the baby, and whispering, "Try, dear, do; it will make you feel happier; try."

The cheerful warmth of the fire, and Mrs. Bond's motherly kindness, brought a little color into Rose's pale face, and Charley kicked his little cold toes out of his frock, and winked his eyes at the crackling blaze, as if to say,

"Now, this is something like."

After tea, Rose narrated to Mrs. Bond the visit of the old crone to her attic, and expressed her firm belief that she was Dolly's mother.

This was even worse in Mrs. Bond's eyes than Mrs. Howe's cruelty to Rose, and not trusting herself to speak, she gave vent to her feelings by alternately raising her hands and eyes to heaven.

"There will be a sad reckoning-day—a sad reckoning-day, dear," said the old lady solemnly. "He that keepeth Israel shall neither slumber nor sleep."

CHAPTER XXVIII.

It was Monday morning. Mrs. Bond's little kitchen was full of the steam of boiling clothes. Little Charley, with one of Mrs. Bond's long calico aprons pinned over his frock, was pursuing on all fours his infantile investigations.

On the bench before the door stood two wash-tubs, at one of which stood a strapping Irish girl with red arms and petticoats, scrubbing the plowman's clothes with superhuman energy. At the other stood Rose, her curls knotted up on the back of her head, her sleeves rolled up above her round, white elbows, and her calico skirt pinned away from one of the prettiest ankles in the world; even this homespun attire could not disguise her beauty.

Three hours, by the old-fashioned clock in the corner, she had stood there; and yet, though she had rubbed the skin from her little hands, the pile of clothes before her seemed scarcely to have diminished, owing partly to her unskillfulness, and partly that she was obliged to leave off every few minutes to extricate Charley from some scrape with the shovel, tongs, or poker, or to barricade some door through which he seemed quite determined to go; added to this, her heart was very heavy, and one's fingers are apt to keep time with the heart pulses.

Oh, where was Vincent? Would he never return, as he had promised? Was he still "at his father's dying bed?" How strange she did not hear from him. How strange he had not told her where he was. He loved her? Oh, yes—"more than all the world beside." Had he not told her so? He could not have deserted her? Oh—no—no—and yet, poor Rose, there was such a weary pain at her heart; but see, there is Charley again, little mischief, between the andirons. Rose wipes the suds from her hands, and runs to extricate him for the twentieth time. She pats him petulantly; the boy does not cry, but he looks up at her with his father's eyes. Rose kisses those eyes; she dashes away her tears, and goes back again to her work. She tries to believe it will be all right. Mrs. Bond comes in to make the pudding for dinner. She sees how little progress Rose is making, and though Rose does her best to hide them, she sees the tell-tale tears, trembling on her long eyelashes.

Mrs. Bond has the best heart in the world; she never treads on the little ant-houses in the gravel walks, she says the robins have earned a right to the cherries by keeping the insects from the trees, she has turned veterinary surgeon to keep the breath of life in an old skeleton of a horse which Zedekiah "vowed oughter been shot long ago," she puts crumbs on the piazza for the ground birds, and is very careful to provide for the motherly yellow cat a soft bed. The peddler always is sure of a warm cup of tea, and the wooden-ware man of a bit of cheese or pie. Rose's tears make her quite miserable, so she says to Bridget, in her soft kind way, "I should think *you* might help wash the baby's clothes, Bridget."

"Not for the likes of her," retorted the vixen, with her red arms a-kimbo. "Thank the Virgin, *I* am an honest woman."

Rose snatched Charley from the floor and darted through the open door, with the fleetness of a deer; not weary now; strong to bear any thing, every thing but that coarse, cruel taunt. Away!—away from it! but where? Oh, Vincent, will it always follow! Strong, is she? Poor Rose! She falls earthward with her tender burden. Charley utters a cry of pain as his temples strike a sharp stone. Rose heeds not his cry, for she is insensible.

When her consciousness returns, some two hours after, she finds herself in her own little bed, with Mrs. Bond beside her. There are phials upon the table, and a strong smell of camphor; a bandage is around her forehead, and the blinds are closed, and Charley is

not there, but she hears him crowing below stairs.
Mrs. Bond puts her finger on her lip, and says, "Try
to sleep, dear," and Rose gladly closes her eyes; she
only wishes it were forever.

CHAPTER XXIX.

"Six rows of the ruffling, edged with lace, and two tucks between each ruffle. Mind you don't make a mistake, now; had you not better write it down? You will remember to make the upper tuck about a fifth of an inch narrower than the others. Do it very nicely, you know I am particular about my work. Remember—let me have it, without fail, by next Thursday evening," and the speaker gathered her voluminous skirts in her hand and tripped through the door and into her carriage.

"For good gracious' sake, who's that?" asked Miss Snecker.

"Yes—who's that? Every body who sees her fine airs and gay dresses, asks me that question. I suppose you wouldn't believe if I should tell you what caterpillar that butterfly came from;" and Miss Bodkin put her feet upon the cricket, and took up the interminable yards of ruffling and commenced her work and her history.

"Well—that's Mrs. Howe, and *how* she ever became Howe, is more of a mystery to other people than it is

to me.—'Mrs. John Howe'—a very well sounding
name you see, but for all that it never can make a lady
of her. 'Mrs. John Howe.' It used to be 'Dolly
Smith;' it was 'Dolly Smith' much longer than its
owner liked. It was painted in large, green letters
over a little milliner's shop in Difftown. Such a fidget
as it was in to get its name changed; but nobody
seemed to want it. It tried the minister, it tried the
deacon, it tried the poor, bony old sexton (mercy
knows it never would have taken so much pains, had it
known as much about men as I do), however, that's
neither here nor there. It was a way it had. Well—
by and by a shoe-maker from the city came up to our
village for three weeks' fishing, and while he was bait-
ing for fish, Dolly baited for him. She used to stand
at the door of an evening, when he came up the village street, with his fishing tackle and basket; by and
by he got to stopping a bit, to rest, and to buy a
watch-ribbon and one thing and another, as a man naturally would, where he was sure of a welcome. Well,
one evening when he came, Dolly was seized with a
horrid cramp—I never had no faith in that cramp—
such a fuss as she made. Well, John said he might be
in the way, and so he would leave, till she was better.
Simpleton! That was just what she did n't want him
to do. Well, every body else round was sent flying
for 'doctors and medicines,' and John staid through
that cramp; and the next thing I heard, the bonnets

8*

was took down out of the shop, it was shut up, and that's the way Dolly Smith became Mrs. John Howe. Of course it don't set very well on me to have her come in here with her patronizing airs, to bring me her work to do; but a body must pocket their pride such hard times as these. I shall nurse my wrath, any way, till I get a little richer."

"Well, I never!" exclaimed Miss Snecker, "how artful some women is! I suppose now she has every thing she wants, and has a beautiful time—the hateful creature."

"Yes, she is rich enough," said Miss Bodkin, "her husband gave up the shoe business long ago. She is as stingy as she is rich; she beats me down to the lowest possible price for every stitch I do for her.

"She was dreadful mortified about her niece Rose; suppose you know all about that? No! Well, Dolly took her when she was a little thing to bring up, as she said (the child was an orphan), and a poor sorry little drudge she made of her. She didn't have no childhood at all. She had a great faculty for reading, and wanted to devour every book she could get, which wasn't many, you may be sure, where Dolly was round. The child had no peace of her life, day nor night; was worried and hunted round like a wild beast.

"After Dolly married, she sent Rose away to school, making a great talk about her 'generosity in

giving her an eddication,' but the fact was, that Mr.
Howe was younger than Dolly, and Rose was hand-
some : you see where the shoe pinched," said Miss
Bodkin, giving Miss Snecker a nudge in the ribs.

" Certain," said Miss Snecker ; " well, what became
of the girl ?"

" Well, Rose was handsome, as I told you, though
she did n't know it, and good as she was handsome ;
but sad-like, for she never had any body to love her.
I don't think she was sorry to leave her aunt, but still
you know the world is a great wide cold place to
push a young thing like that out into. However, she
started off with her little trunk to Mrs. Graw's
school.

"Mrs. Graw used to be chambermaid to a real Count's
wife, and as soon as she found out that Rose was a
poor relation, she kinder trod her down, and the
school-girls disliked her, because she was handsomer
than they, and so she was miserable enough, till she
made the acquaintance of Captain Vincent, who took
her away from school, to be married, as he said, and
then ran off and left her. Of course, her aunt was
dreadful hard on her, and drove her almost crazy with
her reproaches. She would n't believe any thing she
said about her being really married ; and was just as
bitter as if she herself had n't been man-hunting all
her life.

" *She* held Rose off at arm's length, as if the poor

betrayed child's touch were poison; shut her doors in her face, and all that; and why the poor thing did n't take to bad ways nobody knows. She went to a Lying-in Hospital, and staid there till the babe was born, and then there was a great noise, when it was found out how rich her aunt was; and when Mrs. Howe found out that people's tongues were wagging about it, she came forward and offered to pay her board in the country awhile.

"Mrs. Howe herself lives up in St. John's Square. She is trying to ride into fashionable society with her carriage and liveried servants; and that poor girl so heart-broken.

"Well, the Lord only knows what is going to become of poor Rose! Beauty and misery—beauty and misery—I 've seen what came of that partnership before now."

CHAPTER XXX.

Mrs. Bond had drank her cup of tea and eaten her one slice of toast. Rose had not yet come down to breakfast, and she hesitated to disturb her slumbers. So she put the tea-pot down by the fire, covered over the toast, and sat back in her great leathern chair.

How beautiful they looked, Rose and the boy, the night before, when she crept in, shading her lamp with her hand, to see if they were comfortable. The boy's rosy cheek lay close to his mother's blue-veined breast, and one of his little dimpled arms was thrown carelessly about her neck. Rose with her long hair unbound vailing her neck and shoulders, the tears still glistening on her long lashes, heaving now and then a sigh that it was pitiful to hear.

"Ah!" thought Mrs. Bond, "the father of the child should have looked in upon that scene! Those sighs, those tears, went they not up to heaven as swift witnesses against him?"

And so Mrs. Bond, the previous night, extinguished her small lamp, and knelt by the bed-side; she prayed for those wronged sleepers from the gushing fullness of

her Christian motherly heart. Poor children!—for
what was Rose but a child ?

And now Mrs. Bond sat there over her breakfast-
table thinking it all over. Her own life had been as
placid as the little lake you could see from the cottage
door ; it was pitiful to her the storm of sorrow beating
down upon that fair young head. She tried to see
something bright in her future. She knew that though
she herself had no wish beyond those humble walls,
save to lie in the pleasant church-yard when her work
was done, yet that life must be monotonous and dull
there for one like Rose. She knew that the heart,
when wretched and inactive, must prey upon itself.
She wished she knew how to interest Rose in something. There was Charley, to be sure, dear little fellow, but he was at once a pain and a pleasure—a comfort and a reproach. Poor little lamb ! he did not know
why the caress he proffered was at one time so joy-
fully welcomed, then again repulsed with coldness ; he
did not know how cruelly the poor heart against which
he nestled was rent with alternate hopes and fears ; he
did not know why he involuntarily hid his head from
the strange, cold look, in those sometime—loving eyes.

Mrs. Bond sat a long time thinking of all this ; yes,
very long, for an hour and a half was a great while for
her to sit still of a morning. She thought she might as
well creep up softly, and see if Rose were waking.
She knocks gently—no answer ; they still sleep, she

must waken them. She opens the door—there is no one there but herself; the clothes have all gone from their pegs, and a note lies upon the table.

Mrs. Bond takes her spectacles from their leathern case, and her hand trembles as she breaks the seal. It is in a delicate, beautiful hand. Her dim eyes can scarce see the small letters; her hand trembles too, for an indefinable fear has taken possession of her.

The letter ran thus:—

" MOTHER,—

"For so I will call you always, even though I am going to leave you. You thought I was sleeping when you knelt by my bed-side last night, and prayed for Charley and me. Every word I heard distinctly—every word was balm to my heart, and *yet* I leave you.

Oh! do not ask me why—I love *him*, the father of my child—it is life where he is, it is death where he is not. I go to seek him, the wide earth over. What else is left me, when my heart wearies even of *your* kindness, wearies of poor Charley? Mother! pray for

" Your ROSE."

Mrs. Bond did " pray," long and earnestly ; she shed reproachful tears, too—good, motherly Mrs. Bond, that she had not done impossibilities. Would that none of us more needed forgiveness.

CHAPTER XXXI.

THE setting sun streamed in upon a parlor on St. John's Square. One might have mistaken it for an upholsterer's ware-room, so loaded was it with chairs, sofas, and *tête-à-têtes*, of every conceivable size and pattern. The same taste had hung the walls with pictures, whose coloring, perspectives, and foreshortening would have driven a true artist mad; the gaudy frames, with their elaborate gildings, being the magnet which had drawn the money from the pocket of the lady hostess.

Distorted mythology, in various forms, looked down from little gilt roosts in the corners, peeped at you from under tables, stared at you from out niches. Books there were, whose principal merit was their "pretty binding," the exception to this being in the shape of a large Family Bible, splendidly bound, and on the present occasion ostentatiously placed on the center-table, for Mrs. Howe had at last a baby, and this was christening-day.

Mrs. Howe had an idea that it was more exclusive and genteel to have this little ceremony performed in the house. There was to be a splendid christening—

cake and wine, after the baptism, and only the appreciative select were to be present.

Mrs. Howe had expended a small fortune on the baby's christening-cap and robe, not to speak of her own dress, which she considered, coiffure and tournure, to be unsurpassable; and now she was flying in and out, with that vulgar fussiness so common to your would-be-fine-lady; giving orders, and countermanding them in the same breath, screaming up stairs and down to the servants; at one moment foolishly familiar with them, and at the next reprehensibly severe; pulling the furniture this way and that, and making her servants as much trouble, and herself as red in the face as possible. "Dolly Smith," was too much for "Mrs. John Howe." St. John's Square had an odor of the milliner's shop.

The baby slept as quietly as if it were not the heroine of the day; as if all the novels, and poems, and newspaper stories had not been ransacked for fitting appellations; as if its mother had not nudged its father in the ribs for fourteen consecutive nights, to know if "he had thought of any thing."

Mr. John Howe! who had married on purpose to get *rid* of thinking; who had no more sentiment than a stove funnel; who would not have cared had his baby been named Zerubbabel or Kerenhappuch; who was contented to let the world wag on in its own fashion, provided it did not meddle with his "pipe."

Yes, Mr. Howe smoked " a pipe." Mrs. Howe got up several hysteric fits about it, but on that point only he was immovable, spite of smelling-salts and burned feathers. Finally, Mrs. Howe made up her mind to remove the odium by artistifying it, and with the sweetest conjugal smile presented him with an expensive chibouk, to take the place of that leveling clay pipe. She also added a crimson velvet smoking-cap, in which she declared he looked " as Oriental as a dervish."

" Thunder !" exclaimed Mr. Howe, as he caught sight of himself in a glass, " you have made me look like that foreign fool of a conjuror we went to see the other evening, who turned eggs into watches. You don't expect me to wear this gimcrack ?"

Mrs. Howe whispered something in Mr. Howe's ear. Whatever it was, the effect was electrifying. Husband's have their weak points like other mortals. The smoking-cap was received into favor—so was the chibouk.

In default of any preference of Mr. Howe's for the baby's name, Mrs. Howe had selected " Fenella Fatima Cecilia." It was written on a card, all ready for the Reverend Doctor Knott, who had the misfortune to be a little deaf, laid by the side of the gilt Bible, and held down to the table by an alabaster hand, with a *real* diamond ring on the third finger.

The baptismal basin was of silver, with two doves perched on the edges. The water to be used on the occasion, said to have come from the river Jordan, was in a state of preparedness in a corked bottle in the china closet.

All the preparations were completed, but still the baby slept on. Mrs. Howe was rather glad than otherwise, partly because it gave her plenty of time to survey her new apparel in a full-length mirror, partly because the baby always had " such a pretty color in its cheeks when it first 'woke," and she wanted to carry it in when the flush was on.

The last pin was adjusted in the maternal headdress; the Reverend Dr. Knott had arrived, so had the appreciative select; Mr. Howe's cravat and waistcoat had been duly jerked into place by his wife, and now the baby "really must be woke." Mrs. Howe sprinkles a little jockey-club on Mr. Howe's handkerchief, takes one last lingering look in the mirror, readjusts a stray ribbon, changes the latitude of a gold head pin, then steps up to the rose-wood cradle, and draws aside the lace curtains.

What a pity! There is no flush on the babe's face! and how very pale she looks! Mrs. Howe takes hold of the plump little waxen hand that lies out upon the coverlid. What is there in the touch of her own flesh and blood to blanch her lip and palsy her tongue?

Ah! she can not face death, who could gaze with stony eyes on misery worse than death?

"Vengeance is mine—I will repay, saith the Lord."

CHAPTER XXXII.

"A STIFF breeze, captain; we shall soon be in New Orleans at this rate. Talk about yellow fever; it can not be worse than sea-sickness. If a good appetite does not come to my rescue, on reaching land I shall pass for a live skeleton.

"But, captain, who is this pretty stewardess you have on board? and you a family-man, too; eh, captain? And what child is that she has the care of? And what the deuce ails her?—so young and so sedate, so pretty and so uncome-atable! I don't understand it."

"I don't know that it is necessary you should," said the old captain, dryly.

"That's true enough; and if she were homely, she might sigh her soul out before my curiosity would be piqued; but a pretty woman in trouble is another thing, you know. I feel an immense desire to raise a smile on that pretty face, though it could hardly look more enchanting under any circumstances."

"Look here, Fritz," said the captain; "while that young creature is aboard my ship, she is under my

protection. Understand? Not that any of your cox-
combical nonsense could make any impression on her,
for her heart is heavy with sorrow of some kind, but I
won't have her annoyed or insulted. I don't know her
history myself, nor shall I ask to know; her post as
stewardess is a mere sinecure, though she does not
know it.

"She came to me with that child in her arms, in
great distress to get to New Orleans, and proposed
herself as stewardess. I saw she was in trouble, somehow—young, beautiful, and unprotected; I have daughters just her age; I imagined them in a similar position.
Her dignified modesty was a sufficient recommendation
and guaranty. I knew she would be hurt at the offer
of a *free* passage, so I told her that I needed a second
stewardess. That is all I know about her; and, as I
said before, while she is aboard my ship, I will protect
her as if she were my own child;" and the old man
stowed away a tobacco-quid, and walked fore and aft
the cabin, with a determined step.

"Certainly," said the foiled Fritz; "your sentiments
do you honor, captain. But I have not seen her for
two or three days; is she sick?"

"No; but the boy is, and I told her to let every
thing go by the board, and attend to him till he was
better. Beautiful child he is too; I have never seen a
finer one. Doctor Perry thinks he will soon right
him."

"Doctor Perry!" exclaimed Fritz, with a spasm of jealousy; "it is my opinion he will make a long job curing that boy."

"The doctor is not one of *your* sort," said the captain; "her very defenselessness would be to him her surest shield. The doctor is a fine man, Mr. Fritz."

"Yes, and young and unmarried," answered Fritz, with a prolonged whistle. "We shall see," said he, taking the captain's spy-glass to look at a vessel that was looming up in the distance.

"Charley appears brighter to-day," said Rose to Doctor Perry. "Captain Lucas is very kind to me; but I am very anxious to get about to fulfill my engagements. Don't you think my boy will be well soon?"

"There is every prospect of it," said Doctor Perry. "He is improving fast. I will stay by him, if you will allow me," said he, more anxious to give Rose a reprieve from the confined air of the cabin than solicitous for the "fulfillment of her engagements."

"Thank you," replied Rose, in her usual grave tone, without raising her eyes; "but I would not like to trouble you."

"Nothing *you* could ask would trouble me," replied the doctor, "unless you asked me to leave your presence."

Rose drew her girlish form up to its full height as

she answered: "I did not think you would take advantage of my position to insult me, sir."

"Nor have I, nor do I," replied the doctor, with a flushed brow. "I love you—I love you honorably; I would make you my wife; I am incapable of insulting any woman."

Tears sprang to Rose's eyes as she answered, "Forgive me; I can not explain to you *why* I am so sensitive to a fancied insult."

"Nor need you," replied the doctor, as an expression of acute pain passed over his fine features; "Rose, let me stand between you and harm; be my wife—my own, dear, honored wife."

"Oh no, no, no!" gasped Rose, retreating as he approached her; "you do not know—or you would not. Sir!" and the color receded from her lip and cheek—"that boy!—God knows I believed myself an honored wife."

"Rose," again repeated the doctor, without heeding her confession, "will you be my wife?"

"I can not," said Rose, moved to tears by his generous confidence, "*that* would be sin—I have no heart to give you. Though all is mystery, though I never more may see him, I love the father of my boy."

The doctor rose, and walked the little cabin.

"Is this your final answer?" asked he, returning to the side of Rose.

"I can give no other, much as I thank you for this proof of your—" and here her voice again failed her.

"Rose," exclaimed the doctor, passionately seizing her hand, "I will not ask you to love *me*. I will be satisfied if you will allow me to love *you*."

Poor Rose, none knew better than herself how eloquently the heart may plead; and *because* she knew this, because only to the voice of the loved one would the chords of *her* heart vibrate, did she turn away from that pleading voice and those brimming eyes.

For a long time Rose sat with her face buried in her hands after the doctor left her. It was hard so to repay such trust. Could he only be her brother—her counselor—but no—her path in life must be solitary.

Would the cloud never roll away?

Must it always be so?

Would Vincent never come to claim her?

Would a life of purest rectitude *never* meet its reward?

Would the world's scornful "Magdalena" be her earth-baptism?

Would the sweet fount of her boy's life be turned to bitterness?

Would he grow up to blush at his mother's name?

Would his hand be raised in deadly fray to avenge the undeserved taunt which yet he knew not how to repel?

O, Vincent!

9

Rose's refusal of Doctor Perry but added fuel to the flame; it is the unattainable we seek, the unattainable only that we fancy can satisfy; the unattainable that at any cost we must have.

How could he give her up? How think of her in the great, busy, wicked city, to which she was going, unfriended and penniless? Was there no way he could be of service to her? No way in which, without offending her sensitiveness, he could shield her from suffering and insult. Who was the father of her child? She "still loved him," believed him true to her—looked forward to the time when his honor should be vindicated on her behalf.

The doctor knew more of the world. The film would fall from her eyes by and by; he would wait patiently for that moment: then, perhaps, she would not turn away from him. She was too noble to cherish the memory of one she believed to be base. What alliance could purity have with pollution? Poor, trusting, wronged Rose! How immeasurably superior was she even now, and scorned thus, to the pharisaical of her own sex who, intrenched outwardly in purity, and pointing the finger of scorn at the suspected of their own sex, yet hold out the ready hand of welcome to him who comes into their presence, foul from the pollution of promiscuous harlotry.

Beautiful consistency! Pure Christianity! From

the decision of such an incompetent tribunal, thank God! Rose could appeal to a Higher Court.

Rose was a daily marvel to the conceited Fritz. Accustomed in his grosser moments to those debasing *liasons* which so infallibly unfit a man for the society of the pure in heart, he could not comprehend the reserve—even *hauteur*—with which the pretty Rose repelled every advance to an acquaintance.

At first, his surprised vanity whispered that it was only a cunning little *ruse*, to enhance the value of surrender, but this astute conclusion was doomed to be quenched by Rose's determinate and continued persisttency. Then Fritz had fallen into the common error of fancying that to know *one* woman was to know the whole sex; not dreaming that it is necessary to begin with a different alphabet, in order to read understandingly *each* new female acquaintance ;—a little fact which most men blunder through life without finding out.

In vain he displayed his white hands. In vain he donned successively his black suit, his gray suit, and his drab suit (which last he never resorted to except in very obstinate cases) ; in vain he tied his cravats in all sorts of fanciful forms ; in vain he played "sick" in his crimson silk dressing-gown, or languished on deck in his Jersey overcoat. In vain he, who detested children, made advances through Charley, who was now convalescent ; in vain he remarked in Rose's hearing that "his gloves needed mending," and that "the but-

tons were off his linen." Rose might as well have been
deaf, dumb, and blind, for all the notice she took of
him.

It was unaccountable. Fritz was piqued—in fact he
did not like it, and consulted his never-failing solace,
the looking-glass, to see what was the matter. There
was still Fritz enough left (such was the verdict of the
looking-glass), spite of sea-sickness, to satisfy any reasonable woman.

" Pooh! Rose was a stupid little thing; that was
the amount of it; there was no use wasting his time on
her ;" and this last, by the way, was the only sensible
reflection he had yet arrived at. He could fancy very
well why she had not liked Doctor Perry (the doctor's
distrait manner of late had attracted his notice). "Perry
was well enough, but"—and Fritz finished the sentence
by affectionately caressing his adolescent mustache."

" Yes, Rose was a stupid little automaton—she had
no soul." Fritz had so much soul himself, that he considered that article a *sine quâ non* in any woman he
honored with his notice.

Meanwhile the gallant vessel plowed her plashing
way through the pathless waters. Over the mermaids,
if there were any, over the coral reefs, over the wondrously beautiful sea-weeds, over the sheeted dead in
their monumentless sepulchers; dashing—plunging—
creaking—soaring and sinking—defying winds and

storms—scattering the dolphins—startling the sea-birds
—hailing cheerily the homeward and outward bound—
careering as gayly over the treacherous waves, as if the
shivering of a mast, a little water in the hold, or the
leaden lids of the pilot, might not land the passengers
with their joys, sorrows, and embryo plans on that
measureless shore whence there is no return boat.

CHAPTER XXXIII.

"I am sorry for you, my dear Perry," replied the captain. "Rose is a glorious, little creature, and you are a whole-souled fellow, and I wish I could pilot your boat into the port of matrimony; but women are queer things, you can no more tell which way they 'd be likely to jump, than I can tell what wind will next blow my vessel. Now, I should have thought she is all alone so, and unprovided—but it is no use talking, cheer up, Perry. I will do all you ask; I 'll disburse the funds for you, and she shall never know where it comes from; you are a good fellow, Perry; there are not many rejected suitors that would act as magnanimously as you have; but do you suppose when you get to New Orleans you can watch over her, without her finding it out?"

"Yes," said the doctor. "I think so, with the aid of a little disguise, false whiskers, etc. At any rate, it is no use for me to try to fix my mind on any thing. I never was in love before, never saw a woman whom I did not shudder to think of, in the light of a life-companion. Perhaps you marvel that I can overlook, what to most men would be an insuperable obstacle to marriage with Rose; and yet, viewing it through the world's spectacles, why should you? Do not priests and parents every day legalize the prostitution of youth to toothless Mammon; beside Rose has been deceived. She is at heart pure. In God's sight, she is innocent. I would stand between her and the scorn of the world. She has been more sinned against than sinning,"

"True," said the captain, "and loves the rascal in spite of it."

"Because, with a woman's generous devotion, she does not believe him false; she looks yet to have the mystery cleared up, and to find his honor untarnished."

"God grant it, for her sake," replied the captain.

"Amen!" exclaimed Perry; for in truth his love for Rose, surpassing the love of men, was capable even of this magnanimity.

"Shipwreck me!" exclaimed the captain, consoling himself with a bit of tobacco, "if I can make out how it is, that the finest women invariable throw themselves away on these good-for-nothing fellows. It is always so, Perry."

"Not always," said the doctor. "Not in your case, at least," and he grasped the captain's hand.

"Thank you—thank you," replied Captain Lucas, with emotion. "I believe my Mary is a happy wife."

And this was New Orleans! its hot breath swept across Rose's cheek, as she stood upon the deck of the Neptune, gazing upon its nearing spires, roofs, and chimneys. The city's distant hum even now falls upon her watchful ear. Amid its motley population should she find him whom she had come to seek? Would he take the pain from out her young heart? claim her, and his boy? or should she walk the crowded streets day by day, reading faces, measuring forms, listening to voices, and return at nightfall with eye, ear, and heart, dissatisfied.

"Rose?"

She turned her head. "A few words with you," said Captain Lucas.

Ah—that was what she had been dreading, payment for her services, and they had been so slight, so inter-rupted by Charley's sickness, and so she told the cap-tain with her usual ingenuousness, for she had begun to fear latterly that Captain Lucas had not needed them at all, and that his engagement with her was a delicate cover for his charity. But it was useless talk-ing; the captain was as peremptory as if he were on quarter-deck among his sailors, instead of talking there in the cabin to a little woman four feet high; he said "he was in a hurry," he said (presenting her with Doctor Perry's roll of bills after he had himself paid her) that "that was a present from himself for Charley," and he said that as she was all alone, she must let an old man like him direct her where to find proper lodgings; so he penciled on a card the address of an old lady, whose quiet house he thought would just suit her; and then he said, kissing Charley, "God bless you both," and drew his hand across his eyes.

Good Captain Lucas! when was ever a sailor's heart callous to the touch of sorrow? May there not be something in the strong brave element on which he rides to quicken what is grand and noble in his nature?

CHAPTER XXXIV.

ROSE found the new quarters to which Captain Lucas had directed her, very comfortable. Her French landlady seemed altogether too busy, attending to her domestic matters, and nursing her poodle, to trouble herself about Rose's private affairs. This of itself was an infinite relief, for she had learned to shrink from the scrutiny of strangers. Her apartment was furnished neatly, and Charley's delight was unbounded to be able to pursue his educational baby instincts, untrameled by the pitching of the vessel. But Rose counted every moment lost, in which she was not pursuing her search for Vincent; a night of broken slumber, a hurried breakfast, a hasty toilet, and she started with Charley in her arms on her almost hopeless errand, she scarce knew whither.

Past the large hotel, on whose broad piazza strangers and citizens congregated, past the busy stores, past the quays and wharves, turning hastily the street corners, gazing into shops, now startled by the tone of a voice, now quickening her pace at the deceptive outline of a distant form. Fear found no place in her throbbing heart, and if it had, was there not an angel in her arms? It is a sweet thought, that the presence of a little child is often to an unattended woman the surest protection. The abandoned idler recognizes and respects this holy tie. He, too, was once a pure and stainless child—the lisping little voice seems to whisper in his sin-dulled ear, "Go and sin no more."

Rose could not have told why, of all the Southern cities, she had selected New Orleans for her search for Vincent. Had you asked, she could have given no reason for the magnetism which had drawn her thither.

Still she pursued her search day after day, spite of discouragement; still the great busy human tide ebbed and flowed past her, bearing on its surface barks without ballast—barks without rudder or compass—drifting hither and thither, careless how surely Time's rapids were hurrying them on to the shoreless ocean of eternity.

It was evening. Rose had put Charley in his little bed to sleep, and sat at the open window, as she had done many an evening before, watching and listening. It was now a fortnight since she came to New Orleans, and still no clew of Vincent. She could not always live in this way; she had not the purse of Fortunatus; she must soon again seek employment. Rose's heart grew sick and faint with hope deferred.

A low moan of pain fell upon her ear. She started to her feet and ran up to the little bed. It was not

Charley; he was quietly sleeping. She looked out of the window; a woman had fallen upon the pavement beneath it. Rose ran down the steps to her assistance. She had only turned her ankle, but the pain was so acute that she was unable to rise unaided.

"Lean on me," said Rose, as she gently placed her arm at her disposal, and guided her up the steps and into her little parlor; then kneeling before her, she gently drew off the stocking, and laved the pained foot with cold water. It was a pretty foot, small, white, and if a high instep, as some would have us believe, is proof of "blood," an aristocratic foot. The stranger might have been twenty-five years of age, and had the remains of great beauty.

"You are very kind," said she, at length, opening her large eyes; "very kind—and beautiful too; more's the pity. I was once beautiful; look at me now. You don't believe it, perhaps. *He* thought so; he said, 'my eyes were stars, my teeth pearls.' Did you ever love? It is very sweet to be loved. My mother died; my father had a new wife. In their happiness they forgot me, and in my loneliness I prayed for death. Then *he* came. Oh, *now* I prayed to live! he made earth so fair to me. I was glad that I was beautiful for his sake. He asked me to be his wife. So one night, when the stars came out, I put my hand in his, and looked on my home for the last time. I knew my father and his new wife would not miss me. Oh, I was so happy! I did not see the face of the priest who married us; it was down by the old church, and the stars were the only witnesses. That night I slept on my husband's breast, and I wished my mother were living to know how blest was her child. You are glad I was so happy; you think some day *you* will be happy too; you think you will madden some fiery heart with love. So you may; and then you will be the blighted thing I am; for our marriage was a mockery; the priest was his servant. One night, as I sat at the window watching for him, I heard voices; I heard him, my husband, speak my name lightly to this servant. I, who believed myself his wife; I, who had thought to turn my back on misery forever, and hug happiness to my bosom; I, who had trusted all, given all, and asked for no surety! I heard him plan with his servant to decoy a young school-girl to his arms, and blight her as he had me. The roof over my head stifled me; I did not stay to upbraid him; I could not have taken a drop of water from his hand had I been dying. I fled from the house;—but oh! not as I left my childhood's home! I sought labor; for I loathed sin. None would employ me; I hungered for bread; all turned coldly away. Then one saw me, who knew my story, and wherever I turned, scorn pointed her finger. The 'good' closed their doors, and said, 'Stand aside, I am holier than thou;' the bad opened theirs, and said, 'Eat, drink, and be merry.' Then

Despair took me by the hand, and led me in. Sin fed me, clothed me ; sin baptized my child.

" One night, with other revelers, *he* came to that unholy place ; *he*, my ' husband !'—oh, it was gay ! He smiled the old smile ; he said, ' Right, my girl, a short life and a merry one ; there is no future—we die and there 's an end !' My tortured soul gave these false words the lie ; but I smiled back—he was to be *my* victim now ! Peace was lost, heaven was lost ; what should hold me back ? The wine cup went round. ' Pledge me,' I said, ' here 's to your happy future !' He drained it, poison and all, to the dregs— why not ? Men make the laws to suit themselves, so they make no law for the seducer. I had to be judge and jury ; oh it was gay ! He writhed—why not ? What was it to the writhings of my spirit every hour in that accursed gilded prison-house ! He died, my seducer ; then I fled hither.

" Down—down—down I am going ; beauty buys me no bread now ; down—down !" and the fire died out from her eyes, and her head drooped upon her breast.

" Dreadful," said the horror-struck Rose, " don't talk so, I am a stranger here ; but surely," and the crimson flush overspread her cheeks, " there must be Magdalen Asylums here."

" Oh, that 's gay," said the half-crazed woman, laugh- ing hysterically, " gay ; they write ' Magdalen' over the door where you go in and out, they tell visitors you are a 'Magdalen,' when you want to hide your shame, and be good. They drag you *away* from heaven, and then tell you to go there. Listen," and she lowered her voice, and laid her thin hand on that of Rose. "Listen, and I will tell you a story. Once, at the Magdalen Asylum, a young girl, half starved, and out of employment, came and asked for a shelter. They asked her 'if she was virtuous,' she said 'yes,' then they shut the door in her face, saying 'that their house was for Magdalens;' she wept, and wrung her hands, as she turned away into the dark night. Next day she came back, and said, 'take me in, now, I'm a Magdalen, now I shall have a shelter.' Oh it was gay; children of this world are wiser in their generation than the children of light. Satan is too busy; down, down. If Vincent sees your pretty face you'll go down, down, too, but Vincent's dead. Good-by, you are beautiful, more's the pity."

The poor, half-crazed creature pressed Rose's robe to her lips, and limped away, and like one under the influence of night-mare, Rose sat gazing spell-bound, after her retreating form without the power of speech or motion.

Shine on, as ye have shone, gentle stars!

Look down upon crushed innocence and triumphant guilt, upon ragged virtue, and ermined vice—upon the wretched who pray to die, and the loved and loving whose uplifted hands, and tears of agony, fail to stay death's dart.

Roll on, gentle stars!

Shall not He, who feedeth your never-consuming fires, yet make every crooked path straight, every rough place plain ? What though the tares grow amid the wheat until the harvest, shall not the great Husband-man surely winnow them out, and gather the wheat into the heavenly granary ?

Roll on, gentle stars !

CHAPTER XXXV.

Mr. John Howe sat comfortably in his easy-chair, smoking his chibouk. Mrs. Howe sat opposite to him, dressed in a fashionable suit of black, with her gaiter-boots on a bronze hound.

"John?"

John smoked away as imperturbably as if he were a bachelor.

"Mr. Howe?"

"Well," replied John, complacently regarding the curling smoke.

"Do you know this is the last day of June?"

"Well," repeated John.

"'Well—well!' Mr. Howe, I do wish you'd stop thinking of that contemptible political paper you are reading, and attend to me. But before I begin, I wish to say that I *should* like a paper in the house that has something in it. There is not an account of the fashions in that newspaper from one year's end to the other; in fact, there is nothing in it but politics—politics; it is the stupidest paper I ever read. Why don't you take the 'Lady's Garland,' now, or 'The Parlor

Weekly,' or some such interesting periodical, with those lovely fashion-prints, and cuff and collar patterns, and crochet guides? One would think you imagined a woman's mind needed no nutriment at all. What are you laughing at, Mr. Howe?"

"Your thirst for knowledge," replied John.

"Laugh away—it is a great point gained to get one's husband good-humored. Now, listen: Mrs. St. Pierre has gone into the country, so has Mrs. Ralph Denys, and Mrs. George Cook goes to-morrow."

"What the deuce has that to do with us?" asked John.

"It is so vulgar to stay in the city in summer," replied Mrs. Howe. "Nobody does it but tradespeople, and those who can not afford to migrate. I tell you it is indispensable for people in our station not to be seen here in the summer months."

"I don't want to be seen," said John, still puffing. "Shut the front window-shutters; let the silver door-plate grow rusty, and the cobwebs gather on the blinds and front-door; live in the back part of the house; never go out except in the evening. That's the way half the fashionables 'go into the country;' confounded cheap way, too," and John laughed merrily.

"Now, John," said his wife, "where did you pick that up? I took good care not to tell you that, because I knew I should never hear the last of it; but even that is better than to be thought unfashionable. Still, it is not like having a country seat."

"A country-seat!" ejaculated John, wheeling square round, so as to face his wife; "catch me at it! Eat up by musquitos, kept awake by bull-frogs, serenaded by tree-toads, bored to death by riding-parties from the city, who devour your fruit, break off your flowers, and bark your trees; horses and carriages to keep, two or three extra servants, conservatory, hot-house, stables, barns, garden-tools, ice-house—shan't do it, Mrs. Howe;" and John turned his back, put his heels deliberately up on the window-seat, and resumed his chibouk.

Mrs. Howe smiled a little quiet smile, snapped her finger, as if at some invisible enemy, and tiptoeing up behind her husband's chair, whispered something in his conjugal ear.

The *second* time that magic whisper had conquered Mr. Howe!

CHAPTER XXXVI.

SLOWLY Rose regained her consciousness. Had she been dreaming about Vincent's death? The dim light of morning was struggling in through the vines that latticed the window. She raised herself from the floor. Ah, now she remembered. It was only the incoherent ravings of the poor crazed being who had been in the evening before; how foolish to let it make her so miserable! As if there were not more than one person of the name of Vincent in the world. She tried to shake off her miserable thoughts; she knelt by the side of little Charley's bed, and kissed his blue eyes awake, although it was scarcely daylight; for she felt so lonely, just as if *her* Vincent were *really* dead, and the wide earth held but one. She took Charley up and held him in her arms, and laid her cheek to his. Strange she could not shake off that leaden feeling. It must be that she were ill, she was so excitable. She would be better after breakfast. Sad work those trembling fingers made with Charley's toilet that morning. Still she kept tying, and buttoning, and pinning, and rolling his curls over her fingers—for the restless, unquiet heart finds relief in motion; ay, motion—when the brain reels and despair tugs at the heart-strings. Oh, Time be merciful! bear swiftly on the restless spirit to meet its fate ; torture it no longer, suspended by a hair over the dread abyss!

It had commenced raining. Rose believed it was that which made her linger on that morning, forgetting through how many drenching rains she had patiently traversed those streets.

She walks back and forth from the window irresolutely. She thinks she will wait till the skies clear. Poor Rose! will thy sky *ever* be clear ? Now she listlessly takes up a newspaper, with which Charley has been playing. She smooths out its crumpled folds, and reads mechanically through advertisements of runaway negroes, sales of slaves at the auction block, ship-news, casualties, marriages, deaths. Ah! what is that ?

"THE MYSTERY EXPLAINED.

"It is at length ascertained that the young man who was poisoned in Natchez, in a house of questionable reputation, by an abandoned female, was Vincent L'Estrange Vincent. The deceased was about twenty-five, of splendid personal appearance, and will doubtless be much regretted by the large and fashionable circle in which he moved. The murderess has not yet been apprehended."

The arrow has reached its mark—the bolt has sped —the weary search is ended—Vincent is found. Rose's Vincent ?

No, not *hers*.

The idol is dethroned forever: the Vincent *her* innocent heart loved was good, and pure, and true. Rose suffers, but she no longer loves. There is a deep sense of wrong and injury, a hurried look back upon all that is lost, a shuddering look forward, from youth's blighted threshhold, at the long, dreary years yet to come—a helpless folding of the hands at Fate —a hopeless, tearless, measureless grief.

Blessed tears come quickly; lighten that heavy load; moisten those burning eyelids; unclasp those icy hands; give to those dumb lips speech; take from young life death's stony semblance!

Speak to her, Charley. Stir the deep fountains of a mother's love, poor fatherless one! Nestle close to her desolate heart. Bid her live for *thee*, Charley. Tell her that 'mid thorns roses are found. Tell her that to the *night* alone, many a dew-gemmed flower yields up its incense.

CHAPTER XXXVII.

"THAT will do, Mrs. Macque, thank you; now a small wine-glass and another tea-spoon, if you please, for the light stand. I think we can leave nurse Chloe with my patient now," said the speaker, turning to a tall negress. "You understand, Chloe, give her the drops at four in the morning, if she should waken; if the effect of the opiate lasts longer, do not disturb her. I shall be in by six in the morning," and Doctor Perry took his leave.

No, not his leave; he might not stay with Rose, but he could pace up and down beneath her window; he could see by the faint light of the shaded night-lamp, the shadow of the nurse's figure on the muslin window-curtains, and know that she was faithful at her post; yes, he could walk there, and the time would not seem long while he thought of Rose.

Did she think, poor child, that his love could be chilled by aught but unworthiness?

Did she think it could die out though no encouraging breath of her's fanned the flame?

Did she think he could leave her to traverse the

crowded streets of that great Sodom, with no defense but her helplessness?

Did she think that a rejected lover could not be a trustworthy, firm, and untiring friend?

Did she think that, like other men, he would mete out his attendance, only so far as it met with an equivalent?

Dear Rose!

How often he had longed, as he had followed her at a distance through the crowded streets, and seen her slight form bend under Charley's burden, to offer her his protecting arm. How he had longed, when the day's fruitless tramp was over, to go to her in the little parlor, and bid her lay her weary head, fearlessly, as if on a brother's breast, and now, when the heart's tonic— hope—had been suddenly withdrawn, would the drooping spirit sink? Medicine, he knew, could do little for the soul's malady, but what it could do, she should be benefited by.

The old colored nurse Chloe drew aside the bed-curtains to look at her charge. How still she lay—how white and wan. "Berry sick," she muttered, with a shake of her turbaned head, "missis berry sick," and she moved gently a long tress of hair which lay across Rose's forehead. "Missis berry young," she muttered, "no wrinkles dere; missis' heart is wrinkled, pr'aps; young face an' ole heart; some trouble been dere," and the old negress touched the little snow-flake of a hand which lay upon the coverlid. "Most see trough it," she muttered, following the tracery of the blue veins. "No ring on de wedding-finger; ah! pr'aps dat 's it," said the old negress, "den she'd better nebber wake up again. Black skins and white skins, de Lord sends 'em both trouble to make it all even. Some one ting, some anodder. My ole missis Vincent berry rich, but had berry bad son; handsome, but berry bad; lub nobody but himself; die like a dog wid all his money. De Lord he makes it all even, dis nigger knows dat; ole missis Vincent good to gib ole Chloe her freedom, but missis' son berry bad. De Lord sends some one ting, some anodder," and Chloe folded her arms philosophically, and leaned back in her chair.

10

CHAPTER XXXVIII.

THE door of Gertrude's studio was ajar, for the day was warm, and the lady had sat persistently at her easel, as was her wont (when the glow was on), since early day-light.

Pictures and picture frames, canvas and brushes, sketches in oils, engravings and crayons, were scattered round, with as little regard to housewife-ly order, as if the apartment had been tenanted by one of the disorderly sex; the light was fine, and that was the most Gertrude cared about.

She was a picture herself as she sat there, and though a woman, was not aware of it. The loose, white wrapper she wore had become unfastened at the throat, and fallen partially off one shoulder, revealing as perfect a bust as ever set a sculptor or lover dreaming. No prettier ornament could have been found to keep back her light brown tresses than her tiny white ears. And as the light fell upon the arm and hand which held her palette, one ceased marveling, with such a model before her, at her successful reproductions of it in the female pictures.

There are some kinds of hair which always look poetical, whether arranged or disarranged; their glossy waves changing in the sun's rays like the arched neck of the peerless golden pheasant; now brown, now golden, beautiful whether in light or shade. This was one of Gertrude's greatest charms. And yet Gertrude was no beauty; but somehow there was a witchery about her which made you think so. It might have been the play of expression on the flexible lips, the warming up of the complexion, the sudden kindling of the eye with smiles, to be as suddenly quenched by tears; the rapid transitions from pensive sadness to mischievous mirth. When she spoke, you thought the charm in her musical voice, when she moved, in the symmetry of her form; every dress she wore you wished she would always wear, every thing she did struck you as being most perfectly and gracefully done; every thing she said was pertinent and piquant; she had thought much, and read little, hence she was always fresh and original; she was an independent thinker, and though strong-minded and clearheaded, was strictly feminine. You looked your watch in the face incredulously when you left her, as if *it*, not *she*, were at fault.

"I really do not think I can do better than that," she soliloquized, laying down her brushes, and stepping back to look at her picture, "that is a success; I feel it."

"Saints and angels!" she exclaimed as the door creaked slightly on its hinges; "where did you come from, you delicious little cherub?"

Well might she exclaim. There was Charley, the little truant, just as he had crept out of bed, looking (as a babe always does when it first wakes) like a delicate morning-glory, whose dewy beauty the first sun's ray will exhale. His little white night-robe hung loosely about him; his large lustrous eyes were full of childish wonder, his dark hair curled in moist rings round his white temples, and his cheek was yet warm with the flush of sleep.

"Where did you come from, you beautiful creature?" said Gertrude, snatching him up, and kissing first his cherry lips, then his bare, dimpled foot, with its pink-tipped toes, then his ivory shoulders; "I never saw any thing half so beautiful—who *are* you, you little dumb angel?"

Charley only replied by cuddling his little curly head on Gertrude's shoulder, for even infancy's ear may be won by the musical sweetness of a voice, and Gertrude's tones were heart-tones.

"You trusting little innocent," said Gertrude, as her eye moistened, "you are sweet and holy enough for an Infant Saviour. There, sit there now, darling," said she, placing him on the middle of the floor, and scattering a bunch of flowers about him by way of bribe, "sit there now, while I sketch you for one," and she flew to her easel.

"Yah—yah," said a voice at the door, as another model presented itself, in the picturesque turbaned head of Chloe, "yah—yah—you cheat ole nurse dis time, Massa Charley—"

"Oh, don't take him away," said Gertrude; "lend him to me a little while—whose child is it? I almost hoped he belonged to nobody."

"Missis, down stairs," answered Chloe; "I don't know her name; she berry sick, I only came las' night to nurse her, and while I busy here and dere, Massa Charley take hisself off."

"Your mistress is sick?" said Gertrude; "then of course she does not want this little piece of quicksilver squirming round her; I want to make a picture of him like those that you see," said Gertrude, pointing to her sketches about the room;—"he is as handsome as an angel; leave him with me, never fear, I can charm babies like a rattlesnake, and bite them too," she added, touching her lips to Charley's tempting shoulders.

"But my missis—" remonstrated Chloe.

"Oh, never mind," said Gertrude, with her usual independence; "no mother ever was angry yet because her child was admired. I will bring him down to your door when he gets weary—there, do go away—he grows more lovely every minute, and I am losing time."

It was not strange that Gertrude should have been

unaware of the presence of the new lodger, rarely
leaving her studio and the little room adjoining, where
she had her meals served, except in the evening, when
Rose was shut up in her own apartment, a prey to
sorrowful thoughts.

Gertrude was as unlike other women in her dislike
of gossip as in various other items we might name.
Provided she were not interfered with, it mattered
nothing to her who occupied the rooms about her. It
is only the empty-minded who, having no resources
of their own, busy themselves with the affairs of their
neighbors. It was unaccountable to her how the number of another woman's dresses, or bonnets, the hours
and the places in which she promenaded, the visitors
she had, or refused to have, her hours for rising, eating,
and retiring, or the exact state of her finances, could
be matters of such momentous interest. Living contentedly in a world of her own, she had neither time
nor inclination for such petty researches.

A month had elapsed since Rose's sickness; she was
now convalescent, and able to part with the faithful
Chloe, who claimed the privilege of calling in occasionally to see Massa Charley. Rose was again alone—no,
not quite alone, for Gertrude had made her acquaintance, to explain her capture of Charley, and ask the
loan of him till the picture should be finished.

Gertrude was at a loss to comprehend Rose's manner: at one moment frank and sisterly, at the next

cold, silent, and repellant. Rose was struggling with two contending feelings; her straightforward ingenuousness made her shrink from the idea of concealing from one of her own sex, who thus sought her acquaintance, her real history. She shrank from a friendship based on deception.

Simple, straightforward Rose! as if half the friendships in the world would not snap in twain, placed on any other basis! If each heart, with its disingenuous trickeries, its selfish purposes and aims, were laid bare to its neighbor, if the real motives for seeming kindness, the inner life, whose pure outward seeming is often in direct inversion to the hidden corruption were as transparent to the human as to the Omniscient eye, who could stand the test?

A few interviews with Gertrude served to dispel, in a great measure, these feelings. Her ready tact, and quick, womanly sympathies, served to bridge over the chasm to Rose's naturally trusting heart.

Oh, that parting with the life-boat of faith—that unsettled, drifting, sinking, weary feeling—that turning away even from the substance, for fear of the mocking shadow—that heart-isolation which makes a desert of the green earth, with all its fragrance, and music, and sunshine—who that has known misfortune has not deplored it? Who has not striven in vain to get anchored back again where never a ripple of distrust might disturb his peace,

"Tell me how you like it," said Gertrude, placing Charley's finished picture in the most favorable light. "Now don't say you are no connoisseur, that is only a polite way of declining to give an unfavorable opinion. Find all the fault you can with it; you at least should know if it is true to life."

"It is perfect," said Rose, delightedly; "it is Charley's own self; he *is* a pretty boy," said the proud mother, looking alternately from him to the picture.

"You must remember," said Gertrude, "that of all the different expressions of a loved face, which the heart has daguerreotyped, the artist can catch but one, and that one may not always be to friends the favorite expression; hence you see, with all our good intentions, the craft sometimes labor to disadvantage. However, I seldom paint portraits; my forte is 'still life;' so, of course," she added, laughing; "your mercurial little *Charley* was quite out of my orbit, but thanks to flowers and lump-sugar, I think I may say there is his double."

"A mother's eye sees no flaw in it," said Rose.

"Thank you," said Gertrude, with a gratified smile. "It has already found a purchaser. A gentleman who was in my studio this morning thought it a fancy sketch, and would not believe me when I told him that there was a beautiful living type; he offered me a sum for it that would at one time have made my heart leap; I can afford to refuse it now."

"How early did your artistic talent develop itself?" asked Rose.

"I was always fond of pictures," replied Gertrude; "but the 'talent' which prosperity 'folded in a napkin,' the rough hand of adversity shook out."

"Adversity?" repeated the astonished Rose, looking at Gertrude's sunny face.

"You are skeptical," said Gertrude. "I forgive you, but I have learned not to wear my heart dangling like a lady's chatelaine at my girdle, to be plucked at by every idle, curious, or malicious hand.

"Listen!" And she drew her chair nearer to Rose.

10*

CHAPTER XXXIX.

"WHEN I was about fifteen, I lost both my parents with an epidemic, which raged in the neighborhood. Up to that time, I had known poverty and sorrow only through an occasional novel, which fell in my way. My dear father, whose silver head I never can think of without involuntarily and reverentially bowing my own, had made my child-life one dream of delight. I felt free to think aloud in his presence. I feared no monastic severity at my childish blunders, or indiscretions; he was my friend, my play-fellow, as well as my teacher and guardian.

"I had an only brother, who had imbibed an unconquerable passion for travel and adventure, and the only mistake my father ever made educationally, was shutting him off from any mention of the subject. He thought himself right in this, and meant it kindly; but it resulted in my brother's secretly leaving home in disguise for a foreign port; he has never since been heard from, and was probably lost at sea.

"Upon the death of my parents there was found nothing left for my support, and I was left to the care of a distant relative. It was an unexpected and unwelcome legacy, for Mrs. Bluff had five children of her own, and though in comfortable circumstances, desired no addition to her family. The knowledge of this added poignancy to the grief which already burdened my heart. Upon entering this new life, I made many awkward attempts, with my city-bred fingers, to propitiate Mrs. Bluff on such occasions as baking-days, cleaning-days, washing-days, and ironing-days. Mrs. Bluff's daughters were as round as pumpkins, and as flaunting as sun-flowers; could spin and weave, and quilt, and bake, and brew, and had the reputation of driving the best bargain at the village store, of any customer for miles round; they pushed me this way and that, laughed at my small, baby hands and pale face, wondered where I had been brought up that I never saw a churn; 'swapped off' my dear books, my only comforts, unknown to me, to a traveling peddler for some bright-red ribbon, and voted me on all occasions a most useless piece of furniture. As for Mr. Bluff, provided his horses, hens, cows, pigs, and chickens, fulfilled their barn-yard destiny, and Squire Tompkins's rabbits did not girdle his young trees, and his mug of cider was ready for his cobwebbed throat as soon as his oxen's horns were seen turning down the lane, the world might turn round or stand still.

"Every effort I made to conciliate the Bluffs, or to

render myself useful, met with a rude rebuff. I could not understand it then. I see now that it was the rough but involuntary tribute which uneducated minds involuntarily paid to a more refined one. Yet why should they feel thus? If I could have taught them many things I had learned from books, they, on the other hand, could have initiated me into the practical duties of every-day life, without a knowledge of which any woman is in a pitiable state of helplessness, for though she may be rich enough to have servants, she is yet at their mercy, for if she chooses to order a certain pudding for dinner, they may make a reply, which her ignorance can not controvert, as to the time necessary to prepare it, or the quantity of ingredients, not on hand, to make it.

"Deprived of my books, my mind preyed upon itself. I wandered off, in my leisure hours, in the woods and fields, and built such air-castles as architects of sixteen are apt to construct. So fond I became of my wood-rambles in all weathers, and talking to my-self for want of company, that an old lady in the village asked Mrs. Bluff, with the most commiserating concern, 'if it was n't a heap of trouble to look after that crazy critter?'

" I had been at Greytown about a year when a new pastor was settled over the village church. It was an event commensurate with the taking of Sebastopol. There was not an unwedded female in the parish, my

cousins included, who did not *give him a call* in the
most unmistakable manner. What with utter disgust
at these open advances,and renewed signs of hostility
on the part of my cousins since his advent, I resolved
to absent myself on the occasion of every parochial
call, and to confine my eyes to the pew crickets on
Sunday.

"The barriers which my obstinacy thus built up
chance threw down. City bred as I was, I had an
extraordinary gift at climbing trees and scaling fences.
In one of my rambles, trusting too much to my agile
ankles, when climbing over a stone wall, I lost my foot-
hold, and was precipitated to the ground, bringing
down a large stone upon my foot. The pain was so
great that I fainted.

"When I came to myself, the minister was bathing
my face with some water he had brought from a brook
near by. I roused myself, and after making several
ineffectual attempts to bear my own weight, was
obliged to accept his offered arm. I was vexed to
have been seen in so awkward a predicament, vexed
that the dread of the storm that was sure to burst on
my head on my appearance with him at my aunt's,
should render me incapable of even the most common-
place conversation. For some reason or other, he
seemed equally embarrassed with myself, and I shut
myself up on reaching home, to give full vent to my
mortification. From that moment I endured every

species of persecution from my aunt and cousins, who, with their scheming eyes, saw in it only a well-planned stratagem, and drove me nearly distracted by speaking of it in that light to those who would be sure to report it to the party most concerned. Whether this suggested thoughts in the young minister he would not otherwise have entertained, I can not say—certain it is, that he very soon invited me to become mistress of the parsonage, and from its flowered windows, a few weeks after, with my husband's arm about me, I could smile on my parishioners, both male and female.

"Never was a wife blessed with a truer heart to rest upon—never was a wife nearer forgetting that happiness is but the exception in this world of change. What is this modern clamor about ' obedience' in the marriage relation? How easy to ' obey' when the heart can not yield enough to the loved one? Ah, the chain can not fret when it hangs so lightly! I never heard the clanking of mine. Oh, the deep, unalloyed happiness of those five short years! I look back upon it from this distance as one remembers some lovely scene in a sunny, far-off land, where earth and heaven put on such dazzling glory as dimmed the eyes forever after, making night's leaden pall denser, gloomier, for the brightness which had gone before. These are murmuring words; but Rose, if you ever loved deeply; if, after drifting about alone in a stormy sea of trouble, you gained some gallant vessel, saw the port of peace in sight, and then were again shipwrecked and en-gulfed—but you are weak yet, dear Rose; I should not talk to you thus," said Gertrude, observing Rose's tears.

"It eases my heart sometimes to weep," was Rose's low reply. "Go on."

"I left the roof under which no sound of discord was ever heard, my child and I. The world is full of widows and orphans. One meets their sabled forms at every step. No one turns to look at them, unless perhaps some tearful one at whose hearthstone also death has been busy. And so we passed along, won-dering, as thousands have done before us, as thousands will in time to come, how the sun *could* shine, how the birds *could* sing, how the flowers *could* bloom, and we so grief-stricken! I found the world what all find it who need it. Why weary you with a repetition of its repulses—of my humiliations, and struggles, and vigils? Years of privation and suffering passed over my head.

"Amid my ceaseless searches for employment I met a Mr. Stahle. He was a widower, with two little boys who were at that time with his first wife's relatives. He proposed marriage to me. My heart recoiled at the thought, for my husband was ever before me. I told him so, but still he urged his suit. I then told him that I feared to undertake the responsibilities of a step-mother. He replied that was the strongest argu-

ment in favor of my fitness for the office. He told me
that *my* child should be to him dear and cherished as
his own. These were the first words that moved me.
For my child's sake should not I accept such a comfortable home ? Often he had been sick and suffered
for medicines not within my means to procure; was I
not selfish in declining? I vacillated. Stahle saw his
advantage, and pursued it. A promise of employment
which had been held out to me that morning failed.
I gave a reluctant consent. Mr. Stahle's delight
was unbounded; his buoyant spirits oppressed me;
his protestations of love and fidelity pained me; I
shrank away from his caresses, and when, after a few
days, he, fearful of a change in my resolution, urged a
speedy union, I told him that the marriage must not be
consummated—that my heart was in my husband's
grave—that I could not love him as I saw he desired,
and that our union under such circumstances could
never be a happy one.

"He would listen to no argument; said I had treated
him unkindly; that my promise was binding, and
that I could not in honor retract it; that he did not
expect me to love him as he loved me, and that if I
could yield him no warmer feeling than friendship, he
would rather have that than the love of any other
woman. Perplexed, wearied, and desponding, I ceased
to object rather than consented, while Stahle hurried
the preparations for our union. Worn out in mind

and body, I resigned myself as in a sort of stupor, like the wretch whom drowsiness overpowers in the midst of pathless snows. Oh, had I *but then* woke up to the consciousness of my own powers! But I will not anticipate.

"Mr. Stahle took a house much larger than I thought necessary, for he had only a limited salary. I begged him to expend nothing in show; that if his object were to gratify me, I cared for none of those things. He always had some reason, however, which he considered plausible, for every purchase he made; and skipped from room to room with the glee of a child in possession of a new toy, giving orders here and there for the arrangement of carpets, furniture, and curtains, occasionally referring to me. On such occasions I would answer at random, memory picturing *another* home, whose every nook and corner was cherished as he who had made it for me an earthly heaven!

"One morning early, Stahle came to my lodgings in great haste, saying, 'Gertrude, we must be married immediately; this very morning; see here,' and he drew from his pocket a paper, in which he read: 'Married, last night, by Rev. Dr. Briggs, Mrs. Gertrude Deane to John H. Stahle.'

"'Who could have done that?' asked I, no suspicion of the truth crossing my mind.

"'It is impossible to tell,' replied Mr. Stahle; 'at all

events, there is only one course for us to pursue; here is the marriage-license—the clergyman will wait upon us in fifteen minutes. Never mind your dress,' said he, as I cast my eye down upon my sable robes—(alas! they were all too fitting)—' you always look pretty, Gertrude,' and he took my hand in his own, which trembled with agitation.

"I was bewildered, paralyzed; for up to that moment I had hoped for some unexpected deliverance. I was hardly conscious during the ceremony. I remembered the face of my child, and of a friend who was witness. I remember Stahle's convulsive pressure of my arm against his side. I remember how like a knell fell these words upon my ear, 'I now pronounce you man and wife.' I remember my dread of the clergyman's taking leave of us; and I remember that the gleam of Stahle's eye, as he did so, made me shiver.

"Stahle was mentally infinitely my inferior; still I believed him a conscientious *Christian*. Now when I look back, I only wonder that I did not lose my faith in the very belief he so disgraced by his professorship. His external religious duties were most punctiliously performed. He never was absent, how inclement soever the weather, from church or vestry-meeting; he never, under any circumstances, omitted family devotions; the Bible was as familiar to him as A, B, C, and as often on his lips. I myself was religiously inclined; it was this alone which had buoyed me up when wave after wave of trouble dashed over me. I had thought sometimes that on this ground we could meet, if on no other. This alone inspired me with confidence that his promises to me and my child would be conscientiously kept.

"How can I describe to you my gradual waking up from this delusion? The conviction that came slowly —but surely—that he was a hypocrite, and a gross sensualist. That it was passion, not love, which he felt for me, and that marriage was only the stepping-stone to an else impossible gratification.

"Now I understood why that, which, to a delicate mind, would have been an insuperable obstacle to our union, was but a straw in his path. It was not the *soul* of which he desired possession, it was not that which he craved or could appreciate. I was wild with despair. O, the creeping horror with which I listened to his coming footsteps! I sprang from my seat when his footfall announced his approach—not to meet him, as a wife should meet her husband, as I in happier days had met Arthur—but to fly from him—to throw out my arms despairingly for help, and then to sink back into my chair, and nerve myself with a calm voice and shrouded eye to meet his unacceptable caresses.

"O, what a fate—and for me! I who had soared with the eagle, to burrow with the mole!

"How aggravated the misery that one must bear

alone! My perfect self-control could not be penetrated by Stahle's imperfect vision;—to him my disgust was only coyness, and served but as fuel to the flame. This was my penance, for a sin against God, of which every woman is guilty who goes from the altar with perjured lips. But alas! little by little, as a drop of water may wear away the stone, had poverty, and sorrow, and discouragement robbed me of my energy, and made me the helpless tool I was. Still it comforted me that I had not deceived Stahle;—he knew my heart was not his, and but for the trick to which I was now sure his fears and passion had alike urged him on that fatal morning, I might have roused myself ere too late, from the benumbing spell of despair.

" Still, before God I resolved conscientiously to perform the duties I had assumed. The more my heart recoiled, the more strict was my outward observance. I patiently repaired the dilapidations of Stahle's widower wardrobe; I attended to his minutest wishes with regard to the management of his household; I saw that his favorite dishes were set before him.

"*Duty* in place of *Love!* O, the difference in the two watchwords! The irresistible trumpet tones of the two combined!

"During the day, the labor of my hands served as an escape-valve for the restlessness of my heart; but the evenings—the long, long evenings!—for Stahle never left my side. I proposed his reading to me, as a reprieve from his caresses. I did not care what, so that his arms were not round my waist, or his lip near mine. The plan succeeded but very indifferently; the books which I had on hand were not suited to his understanding, or his taste. I then procured some novels, involved him in tracing the fates of distressed lovers and their adjuncts, and succeeded better; not but that even then there were occasional parantheses which recalled me from the dream-land into which I had wandered away from the book and its reader, while employed with my needle. This reading also served as a pretext for lengthening the evenings—which, paradoxical as it may appear, was very desirable to me.

"I have said Stahle had two absent children. I had urged him ever since our marriage to bring them home. His reply always was: 'I can not leave you yet, Gertrude, to go for them.' I urged their separation from him, and the necessity that probably existed for those who had passed through so many different hands, of some system, as to their government and education. He seemed quite insensible to these appeals, having only one thought, that of leaving me, although the journey required but one day.

"I am, as you have seen, Rose, very fond of children. I determined, God helping me, to fulfill my duty to the utmost in regard to his. I hoped to make this a pleasant duty.

"It was evening. I was alone; a cheerful fire blazed

upon the hearth; the tea-table was spread, the lamps
lighted, and my little Arthur was amusing himself
making rabbits with his fingers upon the walls. I sat in
my little rocking-chair thinking. It was so blessed to
be again alone with only my little Arthur. Lip, eye,
and brow to be out of school! True, my bill of sale
every where met my eye; the roof over my head was
his—I could not say *ours*.

"Hark!—away with such thoughts—that step was
Stahle's! He had returned from his day's journey.
He came in, leading by the hand two little boys. My
heart warmed toward the motherless; these little ones,
still clad in the badge of mourning for her whose loss,
with my best efforts, I could never hope to repair;—
these little ones, looking wonderingly about them,
in their meek helplessness, at the strange aspect of
every thing! It was to me an inexpressibly touching
sight. Before I could caress them, Stahle stepped between us, and threw his arms passionately about me.
It was so like him, that mistake. The children felt
supplanted, cast frightened glances at me, and nestled
closer to each other. I lost not a moment in disengag-
ing myself from Stahle, and took them both in my
lap.

"Fragile little things they were. They had out-
grown their scanty garments, the brush had not
brought out the gloss on their silky locks, their
little finger-nails were all untrimmed, their flesh out

of sight not scrupulously clean; in short, they looked as childhood ever looks when the watchful eye and busy hand of the mother is cold in death.

"We soon became friends. The searching glances they bent on me, in which I felt they were, to the best of their childish ability, taking my measure, I returned with looks of heartfelt pity and love.

"The next day, and many succeeding days, I busied myself in supplying their wardrobe. I had a natural skill in cutting and making children's garments, which, in my search for employment, I had sometimes hoped to turn to account, and which rendered it a matter of little expense to Stahle. This was a great gratification to me; it seemed to me to repay, in some sort, an irksome obligation. I worked diligently and assiduously, and had the satisfaction of hearing Stahle say that 'he had not thought his children were so pretty;' and yet I expended nothing in ornament, so unnecessary on childhood; but their limbs had free play in their clothes; the colors of which their dresses were composed were suited to their complexions; their feet were not compressed with tight shoes; their hair was nicely kept, and they gradually lost that shy, startled look which so distressed me when they first came.

"I taught Authur to yield his natural rights in his own property to them. It was a lesson I was desirous early to teach him, who was in danger of becoming selfish from always having played alone.

"Children have quick instincts. Little Edgar and Harry soon learned to love me, whom they knew to be their friend; they would put their arms about my neck, and call me 'dear mother.' This troubled me; it seemed as if it must pain *her*. I never taught them to call me so. I never taught my child to call Stahle father. It seemed to me this should not be forced, but should flow out spontaneously; even then I almost shrank from accepting the sacred appellation. I talked to them often of their own mother, lest years should efface the indistinct recollections of infancy. I learned from their childish prattle, that she was 'always sick.' I could readily believe it, for they had inherited her fragility; also that she 'taught them a little prayer,' which they 'could not remember,' though I repeated several which childhood oftenest lisps.

"They said mother's hair was not curly, like mine, and that she was 'ever so much little-er'; and that she coughed very bad, and could not play with them much. Consumption then was the enemy I was to ward off; so I protected their little lungs with flannel. I dressed them warmly, and then tried to inure them to all weathers, as I had always done my own child.

"I found a sort of quiet happiness in thus attempting to perform my duty, for I really loved the children, who were quite as good as they could be, after having passed through so many different hands. We had been some time married when all the little ones were seized with scarlatina, and after a painful prostration by it, and a partial convalescence, the doctor advised a change of air, and we accordingly commenced all needful preparations for the journey.

"Up to this time I had not been into public with Stahle; even in my first married life I had never done this, (why should I have done so when *home* was Paradise?) and now—what availed change of place, when, go where I might, the arrow was still quivering in my heart?

"Occasionally we had callers, business friends of Stahle's, to whom he requested me to be, and to whom I was, punctiliously civil.

"But we were now to move out of this orbit into a wider one; we were to meet more than one class of persons, for the facilities of travel have made north and south, east and west, mere nominal terms.

"One day, on our journey, I took my seat at a public dinner-table with Stahle. Some gentlemen were already seated, and engaged in conversation. As we entered, one of them glancing at us, said to his companion, 'Look there, Howard, how in the name of —— did such a fellow,' nodding at Stahle, 'get such a fine-looking woman as that for a wife?'

"Stahle overheard it; his lips were livid with suppressed rage, while in spite of all my efforts to keep

11

the tell-tale blood from my face, it was quite crimsoned. From that moment he became changed; for
the first time the disparity between us seemed to
dawn upon him. He thought every body else was
looking at us through the same pair of spectacles.
He grew moody, silent, and abstracted; was ever on
the alert when we were in company, overhearing every
word, watching every look, noticing every motion,
magnifying every thing into an affront to him, or an
overture to me.

"I have not described Stahle's physique to you. He
was under-sized, with a pale complexion, and light
brown beard. He wore his hair long, and parted on
the left temple, its sleek, shining look, giving him a
meek appearance; his lips were thin, and, in a woman,
would have been called shrewish; this tell-tale feature
he dexterously concealed with his beard. I have never
seen such a mouth since, that I have not shuddered;
his eyes were a pale gray, and were always averted in
talking, as if he feared his secret thoughts might shine
through them. He appeared to great disadvantage in
company, both from his inferior personal appearance
and his total inability to sustain a conversation on any
subject. Of this he seemed to be unaware until we
appeared in company together. I soon found that the
monosyllabic system to which he was necessarily confined, it would be necessary for me also to adopt,
when addressed. This, apart from the tyranny which

prompted it, was no trial to me, for I never liked going into company, and never was at a party which paid me for the bore of dressing.

"Of course I saw all these things as though I saw them not. I was perfectly aware of my position, and I resolved, under all circumstances, to control myself, and never descend, whatever might transpire, to a war of words. I appeared in public as seldom as possible, lest Stahle should find cause of offense. I was as scrupulously attentive to him and his interests as if I did not know that my best endeavors would now be misconstrued. I felt no faltering in my desire to make his innocent children happy and comfortable. I spoke to no one of my discomfort. I said to myself, I have made a great mistake, and must bear the consequences with what fortitude I may.

"I little knew the deadly malignity of Stahle's disposition. I little knew the penalty I was to pay for the difference which nature and education had made between us.

"One day Stahle came home looking unusually moody and sullen. He found his dinner nicely prepared, and the children neatly washed and dressed. The parlor was tidy, I was courteous; there was nothing to find fault with, nothing to irritate, not the most slender foundation for a quarrel.

"Stahle saw this—he could have wished it were otherwise. He was at a loss how to proceed. After

taking one or two turns across the room, he said, 'Gertrude, I want all the children's clothes packed in a
trunk, and ready by noon to-morrow.'

" ' The children,' asked I, in surprise, ' are you going
to send the children away ? Where are they going ?'

" ' That 's my affair,' he rudely answered.

" I asked no questions; I simply said ' The trunk shall
be ready,' and went on with my sewing. I did not know
then as I do now, that it was the first of a projected
and deliberate series of attempts to injure me, by creating the impression that the children were not well cared
for. He could not well have wounded me more deeply.
I—who had so conscientiously striven to perform my
duty to the motherless. I—who, when any little question between the children was to be decided, gave the
preference to *his* children, lest I might wrong them
even in a trifle—those ' trifles,' which, to childhood are
matters of as grave importance as our adult affairs.

" The cunning malignity of this act was worthy of
Stahle. I made no complaint, I asked the children no
question which I was too proud to ask the father. The
little trunk was packed, and Stahle remarking that he
should be gone two days, the carriage drove off. It
was some comfort that the children ran up to me, and
put up their lips spontaneously for a kiss, as they were
leaving; it was more still that my conscience acquitted
me before God of any intentional sin of omission toward them.

"I had just begun to see the good effect of systematic training on natures sweet and good, though neglected and misdirected. Their wardrobes were amply supplied, the books purchased to teach them—and now —well, I bore the cross uncomplainingly at least, and when Stahle returned, no trace of what had occurred was perceptible in my manner, or habits. He was evidently as much at a loss to understand my self-control, as to cope with it. He had expected a scene—an outburst of indignant feeling—an angry altercation in which his nature might vent itself in a brutal reply. He judged me by the women whom he had all his life known. He was at fault.

"His next step was to break up housekeeping and board out; for this also, he gave me no reason. Whole days he passed without speaking to me, and yet, at the same time, no inmate of a harem was ever more slavishly subject to the gross appetite of her master. It was now midwinter; I had a bad cough, and was suffering from want of flannels and thick under-clothes; he furnished me with no funds for the purpose. This was to compel me to do what would give him some advantage over me—run in debt. I foresaw this, and avoided it, confining myself to my insufficient clothing.

"Stahle always selected a boarding-house for our residence, the mistress of which was *her own mistress*—(*i. e.*, a widow or a single woman). Immediately upon going to such a house, a private understanding sprung up between Stahle and herself, and the servants taking their cue from their mistress, I found it quite impossible to get any thing I wanted. This was less of a trial to me than it might have been, had I not been accustomed to wait upon myself; but one is necessarily circumscribed in a boarding-house; the cellar may not be visited for coal, or the kitchen for water, if the landlady does not see fit to have the bells answered; neither, if she chooses to decree otherwise, and your husband is in the conspiracy, can you be waited on at the table till every one else has been served. Stahle often finished his dinner and rose from the table while my plate and Arthur's, had not been once filled. He studiously insulted me by this public neglect, and to make it still more marked, helped every one else, even the men, within reach. Of this, also, I took no outward notice.

"One day the landlady came to me with a manner so bland that I was instantly on my guard. She complimented my hair, my figure, my manners. She wondered I never came down out of my room into the public parlor. She intimated that the gentlemen were very desirous of making my acquaintance, particularly one, by the name of Voom—with whom, by the way, I had seen Stahle leave the house, arm in arm. I saw through the plot at once—but received it as if I did not, treated her just as civilly as if she were not a female Judas, and resolutely kept my own apartment.

To show you the pettiness of Stahle's revenge, I will mention one or two incidents:

"One evening, while walking my room, a needle penetrated the thin sole of my slipper, and was at once half buried in my foot. Three times, with all my strength, I tried to extricate it; the fourth, and I was still unsuccessful; both strength and courage now failed me. Stahle, from the other side of the room, looked coolly on, and, with a Satanic smile, said, 'Why don't you pull again?' With the courage inspired by this brutal question, I seized the protruding point of the needle with my trembling fingers, and finally succeeded in withdrawing it.

"That evening sharp pains commenced shooting through my foot, extending quite to my side. I began to grow uneasy as they increased, and requested Stahle to send for the doctor. This he peremptorily refused to do. I waited a while longer, my limb in the mean time growing more and more painful. Again I requested Stahle to go for the doctor, or I should be obliged to send some one. At this he put on his hat and coat, and went out. After a prolonged absence he returned, not with a doctor, but a bottle of leeches, which he said 'had been ordered,' and set down the bottle containing them on a table at the further end of the room.

"It had become by that time quite difficult for me to step, as the needle had penetrated the sole of my foot; but, by the help of chairs, I pushed myself along until I reached the bottle.

"I am not given to faintings or womanish fears, but from my childhood I have had a shuddering horror of any thing like a snake; so unconquerable was this aversion, that I was forced to date it back prior to my birth.

"Stahle was aware of this weakness, and as, with a strong effort at self-command, I took up the bottle and then set it down again in a paroxysm of terror at the squirming inmates, he laughed derisively. That laugh nerved me with new strength. I uncorked the bottle, holding its mouth close to my foot, that the leeches might fasten on it, without my touching them with my fingers.

"As the first one greedily struck at my foot, I fainted. The effort at self-control in my nervous, excited state, was too much for me.

"When I recovered, the broken bottle lay upon the floor, the leeches had disappeared, save the one which had fastened upon my foot, and Stahle had gone to bed.

"Not long after this, unable to go out myself, I sent my little Arthur of a necessary errand. He had attended to it successfully, and was returning, when a gig, furiously driven by two young men, turned rapidly a street-corner, ran against and prostrated him. Arthur was a very spirited little fellow, and, beside, had much of the Spartan in his temperament. A policeman who saw the transaction, stepped up and raised him upon his feet, the brave child stoutly maintaining that he was 'not much hurt.' With all this bravery, Arthur was also shy and sensitive, and the gathering crowd and the immediate proximity of the policeman annoyed and mortified him. The policeman, however, true to his duty, would not leave him, and Arthur, whose love to me no thought of self could ever obliterate, gave him the number of Stahle's place of business instead of our residence, lest I should be distressed or frightened in my invalid state by their sudden appearance.

"The policeman accordingly left him there, satisfied that he would be kindly cared for by a father. After he had gone, Stahle put his pen behind his ear, his hands in his pockets, and, surveying my boy a moment, said, 'Well, sir, go home to your mother.'

"Child as he was, he would have died rather than ask for the conveyance which he so much needed, or even for Stahle's helping hand on the way—for it was a long distance to our lodgings—and Stahle saw him limp out without offering either.

"The door opened, and with white lips my brave boy staggered into the room, and briefly narrated his misfortune, still persisting, though the pain was even then forcing tears from his eyes, that he was 'not hurt.' I took off his clothes, and found his side already quite black with the bruise he had received, and so sore that, though he still refrained from complaining, he winced at the lightest touch of my finger.

"I had not a cent in my possession. I had not had
11*

for a long time, for I never had asked Stahle for money. This Stahle knew, and that day and night, and half of the following day he purposely absented himself, leaving me to get along in these circumstances as best I could with the child. On his return he asked no questions and took no notice of the occurrence, although Arthur was still a prisoner to the sofa. Not a word passed my lips either on the subject, though this, to my maternal heart, had been the heaviest trial it had yet been called to bear.

"Time passed on, and Arthur had become convalescent. I was now so extremely nervous from mental suffering, that I found it impossible to sleep unless I first wearied myself with out-door exercise.

"Tying on my bonnet, I went out one afternoon for this purpose. The noise and whirl of the street was an untold relief to me.

"Motion—motion—when the brain reels, and despair tugs at the heart-strings!

"On my return I was not obliged to ring at the front door, as some persons were standing upon the steps talking; I passed them and my light footfall on the carpet, being noiseless, I entered the door of my room unheralded.

"Judge of my astonishment when I saw Stahle standing with his back to me, quite unaware of my presence, inspecting (by means of false keys) the contents of my private writing-desk! opening my husband's letters, sacred to me as the memory of his love; reading others from valued friends, received before my marriage with Stahle—not one of which, for any stain they cast on me, might not have been bared to the world's censorious eye.

"He then took up my husband's miniature—O, how unlike the craven face which bent over it! At last, I was choking with passion; this was the brimming drop in my cup; you might have known it by the low, calm tone with which I almost whispered as I laid my trembling hand on my treasures—'these are *mine* not yours—"

"They were the only words which escaped my lips, but there must have been something in the tone and in my face, before which his spirit cowered. He made no attempt to resist me as I took possession of them, but turning doggedly on his heel, muttered: 'the law says you can have nothing that is not mine.' O, how many crushed and bleeding hearts all over our land can endorse the truth of this brutal answer.

"Stahle began now to spend his nights away from home; I had never yet made a complaint or remonstrance except in the case just stated. I did not now. If it was his purpose with his usual want of insight into my character, to give me a long cord with which to hang myself, it failed, for my boy and I slumbered innocently and peacefully.

"You may ask why, with these feelings toward me,

he did not desert me; for two reasons. 1st. He had a
religious character to sustain; during all this time he
was more constant than ever, if that were possible, at
every church and vestry-meeting, often taking part in
the exercises, and always out-singing and out-praying
every other church-member. 2d. It was his expecta-
tion by these continuous private indignities, which
many a wife suffers in silence, to force *me* to leave
him, and thus preserve his pietistic reputation untarnished. All these plans, which I perfectly understood,
failed. He could find nothing upon which to sustain
a charge against me, either in my daily conduct, or in
my private correspondence, dated, long years before
he knew me, but which the *law allowed him to inspect.*

"I contracted no debts because he would not supply
my necessary wants. I took no advantage of his absence
from home to forfeit my own self-respect. What was to
be done? He must move cautiously, for the mainten-
ance of a religious character was his stock in trade.

"Returning from a walk one day with my little
Arthur, I found a note on my table from Stahle, saying 'that he had suddenly been called South on business, and should remain a few days.' I have never
seen him since. Not that I did not hear from him, for
the plan was legally concocted. Letters were written
to me by him, saying 'that he was searching for a
good business-situation, and would send for me when
he found it.' Sending for me to join him, but making

no mention of my boy. Sending for me to come hundreds of miles away under the escort of his brother, whom I had ascertained to have uttered the foulest slanders about me (and who was to be my protector and purser on the occasion). Every letter was legally worded; 'my dear Gertrude' was at the top of the letter, and ' your affectionate husband' at the bottom. They were always delivered to me by two witnesses, that I might not dodge having received them. And yet each one, though without a flaw in the eye of the law, was so managed as to render compliance with it impossible, had I desired to rejoin a man who had done, and was still covertly doing, all in his power to injure my good name. In the meanwhile, what he dared not do openly, he did by the underground railroad of slander; insinuations were made by those in his employ; eyebrows were raised, shoulders were shrugged, hints thrown out that my extravagance had rendered it necessary for him to leave me. (I, who had never asked for a cent since our marriage, whose nimble needle had replenished his own and his children's dilapidated wardrobes.)

"Men stared insolently at me in the street; women cast self-righteous scornful glances; 'friends' worse than foes, were emboldened by *his* villainy to subject themselves to a withering repulse from her who sought to earn her *honest* bread.

"Did I go out in search of employment—I was

'parading to show myself.' Did I stay within doors—
'there was no doubt a good reason why I *dared* not
go out.' Did I keep my own and my boy's small
stock of clothing whole, tidy, and neat—'they would
like to know who kept me in clothes now."

"Surely," said Rose, interrupting her, "surely, dear
Gertrude, there must have been those who knew, and
could bear witness, that you were good and innocent."

"True," answered Gertrude, "there were those who
could do so, but admitting this fact, what plausible excuse could they make for not being my helpers and defenders on all needful occasions? No, dear Rose, the
world is a selfish one, and degrading as it is to human
nature to assert it, it is nevertheless true, that there are
many, like those summer friends of mine, who would
stand by with dumb lips and see the slanderer distill,
drop by drop, his poison into the life-blood of his victim, rather than bring forward, at some probable cost
to themselves, the antidote of truth in their possession.
Even blood relations have been known to circulate
what they knew to be a slander to cover their parsimony. And those people, who are the most greedy
listeners to the slanderer's racy tale, are the people
who "never meddle in such things," when called upon
to refute it.

"Did these bitter taunts crush me? Was I to become, through despair, the vile thing Stahle and his
agents wished?

"No! The nights I walked my chamber-floor, with my finger-nails piercing my clinched palms till the blood came, were not without their use. I weighed every faculty God had given me, measured every power, with a view to its marketable use. I found one yet untried. I seized my pencil, and I triumphed even with the blood-hounds on my track, for God helped the innocent."

"Oh, teach me that, strong-hearted, noble Gertrude, teach me that! for I have no stay this side Heaven!" and, with sobbing utterance, Rose poured into Gertrude's sympathizing heart the checkered story of her life.

Did she whose courage had parted the stormy waters of trouble, and who had come out triumphant, turn a deaf ear to that wail of despair?

Is woman *always* the bitterest foe of her crushed sister? always the first to throw a stone at her?

No—God be thanked! For the first time Rose was folded to a loving sister's heart, and in the sweet words of Ruth to Naomi, Gertrude said, as she bade Rose good-night,

"Whither thou goest I will go; whither thou lodgest I will lodge; naught but death shall part thee and me."

Was the watchman's midnight cry, "All's well," beneath the window, a prophecy?

CHAPTER XL.

" SEEMS to me that you are nudging a fellow for his ticket every five minutes," said a lantern-jawed looking individual to the railroad conductor, as he roused himself from his nap, and pulled a bit of red pasteboard from his hat-band. " I feel as if my gastronomic region had been scooped out, and rubbed dry with a crash-towel; how long before we stop, hey?"

" Buy some books, sir?" said a young itinerant bookseller to our hungry traveler.

"Have you the 'True guide for travelers to preserve their temper?'" said our friend to the urchin.

The boy looked anxiously over the titles of his little library, and replied, with a shake of the head, " No, sir, I never heard of it."

" Nor I either," responded the hungry growler; " so get about your business; the best book that was ever written can neither be ate nor drank; I 'd give a whole library for a glass of brandy and water this minute," and the unhappy man folded his arms over his waistband, and doubled himself up like a hedge-hog in the corner.

" I am always sure to get a seat on the sunny side

of the cars, and next to an Irish woman," muttered a young lady. "I wonder do the Irish never feed on any thing but rum and onions?"

"Very uncomfortable, these seats," muttered a gentleman who had tried all sorts of positions to accommodate his vertebræ; "the corporation really should attend to it. I will write an article about it in my paper, as soon as I reach home. I will annihilate the whole concern; they ought to remember that editors occasionally travel, and remember which side their bread is buttered. Shade of Franklin! how my bones ache; they shall hear of this in 'The Weekly Scimeter.' It is a downright imposition."

In fact, every body was cross; every body was hungry and begrimed with dust; every body was ready to explode at the next feather's weight of annoyance.

Not every body; there was one dear little girl who found sunshine even there, and ran about extracting honey from what to others were only bitter herbs. Holding on by the seats, she passed up and down the narrow avenue between the benches, peeping with the brightest smile in the world into the faces of the cross passengers, drinking from the little tin-cup at the water-tank, clapping her hands at the sound of the whistle, and touching the sleeve even of the hedgehog gentleman rolled up in the corner. The child's mother sat on the back seat, looking after her as kindly as she was able; but, poor thing, traveling made her sick, and she held her camphor-bottle to her nostrils, and leaned gasping against the window-sill to catch every stray breath of air.

What's that?

Crash goes the window-glass; clouds of scalding steam pour into the cars, which seem to be vibrating in mid-air; benches, baskets, bags, and passengers are all jumbled pell-mell together; every face is blanched with terror.

"Oh, it's nothing, only the cars run off the track— only the engine smashed, and baggage-car a wreck— only the passengers' trunks disemboweled in a muddy brook—only the engineer scalded, and the passengers turned out into a wet meadow in a pelting shower of rain; that's all. Not a son of Adam was to blame for it—of course not," growls the exasperated editor. "Thank Heaven the Superintendent of the road and the Directors were in the forward car and got the first baptism in that muddy brook."

"Zounds!" he exclaimed, pinning up his torn coat-flap, and punching out the crown of his hat; "they shall hear of this in 'The Weekly Scimeter.' Railroad companies should remember that editors sometimes travel."

"May! my little May!" gasped the poor sick woman, recovering herself, and looking about for her child; "where's May?"

Ah, where's May? Folded in His arms who carries the little lambs so safely in his bosom—gone with the smile yet bright on her lip.

Blithe little May!

They take the little lifeless form and bear it across the fields to the nearest farm-house, and the mother falls senseless, with her face to the damp grass—the last tie of her widowed heart broken.

" Sad accident, ma'am—hope you are not hurt," said the bustling village doctor to a lady who held her handkerchief over her mouth. " Deplorable !" exclaimed the delighted doctor. " My engagements are very pressing in the village—five cases of typhoid fever, two of chicken-pox—hurried up here in the face of promise to a lady, wife of one of our richest men, not to be gone over half an hour, in *case* she should want me. Ladies can't always tell *exactly*, you know, ma'am.

" Jaw-bone fractured ? I'm somewhat in a hurry. Senator Scott's wife, too, was very unwilling I should leave my office—;" and the doctor drew out a Lepine watch, as if his moments were so much gold-dust—as if he had not sat in his leathern chair, week in and week out, watching the spiders catch flies, and wishing he were a spider, and the flies were his patients.

" Jaw-bone broke, ma'am ?" he asked, again.

" She is not hurt at all, I tell you," growled Mr. Howe, shaking the rain from his hat, as he stood knee-deep in the tall meadow-grass. "She lost her set of false teeth in the collision, and if you jabber at her till the last day you won't catch her to open her mouth till she gets another set."

"*Mr.* Howe," said that gentleman's wife, in a muffled voice from behind the handkerchief, "how *can* you?"

"How can I? I can do any thing, Mrs. Howe. Are not our trunks all emptied into that cursed brook? All that French trumpery spoiled for which you have been draining my pocket all the spring to go to Saratoga. Did I want to come on this journey? Don't I hate journeying? Have n't I been obliged to go a whole day at a time with next to nothing on my stomach? Have n't I been poked in the ribs every fifteen minutes for the conductor to amuse himself by snipping off the ends of my railroad tickets? Don't my head feel as if Dodworth's brass band were playing Yankee Doodle inside of it? Refreshments! Yes— what are the refreshments? A rush round a semi-circular counter by all sorts of barbarians—bowls of oysters, scalding hot, and ten minutes to swallow them —tea without milk—coffee without sugar—bread without butter, and unmitigated egg—no pepper—no salt —no nothing, and, seventy-five cents to pay; the whole thing is an outrageous humbug; and now here 's this collision, and your false teeth gone, not to mention other things."

Another muffled groan from behind the handkerchief.

"I'll have damages, heavy damages—let me see, there is the teeth, $200."

"Good heaven's, Mr. Howe," shrieked his wife— "you don't mean to mention *them* to the corporation?"

"But I do, though," said John, "you never will be easy till you get another set, and I mean they shall find 'em."

Another groan from behind the handkerchief.

"Passengers, please go through the meadow, and the cow-yard, yonder, and cross the stile to get into the cars beyond," shouted the brakeman.

Down jumped the ladies from their perches on the fences where they had been roosting, like draggled hens in the rain, for the last half hour, and all made a rush for the cow-yard.

"There now, Mrs. Howe—do you hear that? A pretty tramp through that high grass for your skirts and thin gaiter-boots. This is what tourists call the delights of traveling, I suppose—humph!"

"We shan't get to —— till the middle of the night, I suppose—*i. e.*, provided the conductor concludes not to have another smash-up. There will be no refreshments, of course, to be had, that are good for any thing, at that time o' night; waiters sleepy and surly, and I as hungry as a bear who has had nothing but his claws to eat all winter. Pleasant prospect that. You need n't hold up your skirts Mrs. Howe; there's no

dodging that tall grass. Trip to Saratoga! Mr.
John Howe and lady—ha—ha! Catch me in such a
trap again, Mrs. Howe."

Precisely at two o'clock in the morning, our hungry
and jaded travelers arrived at——. A warm cup of
tea and some cold chicken, somewhat mollified our
hero, and he was just subsiding into that Christian
frame of mind common to his sex when their hunger
is appeased, when happening to remark to the waiter
who stood beside him, that he was glad to find so good
a supper so late at night—that worthy unfortunately
replied:

"Oh—yes! massa! de cars keep running off de
track so often dat we have to keep de food ready all
de time, 'cause dere's no knowing, you see, when de
travelers will come; and dey is always powerful hungry."

"Do you hear that?" said Mr. Howe to his wife,
who was munching, as well as she was able, behind her
handkerchief; "and we have got to go back the same
road. You may not want that other set of teeth,
after all, my dear."

"Sh—sh—sh—" said that lady, treading not very
gently on his corns under the table—"are you mad,
Mr. Howe?"

"Yes," muttered her husband—"stark, staring mad,
I have been mad all day—mad ever since I started on
this journey; and I shall continue mad till I get back

to St. John's Square and my old arm-chair and slippers;" and long after the light was extinguished, Mr. Howe was muttering in his sleep, "I'll have damages —let me see, there's $200 for the teeth."

From that journey Mr. Howe dated his final and triumphant Declaration of Domestic Independence. The spell of Mrs. Howe's cabalistic whisper was broken. Mr. Howe had a counter-spell. Mrs. Howe's day was over. Mr. Howe could smoke up stairs and down stairs, and in my lady's chamber; he could brush his coat in the best parlor; put his booted feet on the sofa, and read his political newspaper as long as he pleased. The word "damages," arrested Mrs. Howe in her wildest flights, and brought her to his feet, like a shot pigeon.

CHAPTER XLI.

A KNOCK at the door—it was Chloe, with her gay bandanna, and shining teeth, and eyeballs. She had come to take Charley out, ostensibly "for an airing," but in fact to make a public exhibition of him, for, in her eyes, he was the very perfection of childish beauty.

"He's tired, missis, stayin' in de house," said Chloe, as Charley crept toward the door, "let me take him out a bit;" and Chloe raised him from the floor, and tied his cap down over his bright curls, stoutly resisting all Rose's attempts to cover his massive white shoulders, promising to protect them from the sun's rays, with her old-fashioned parasol.

Rose smiled, as Chloe sauntered off down the street with her pretty charge; Charley's dimpled hand making ineffectual attempts to gain possession of the floating ends of her gay-colored head-dress.

And well might Chloe be proud of him; she had been nurse to many a fair southern child in her day, but never a cherub like Charley. One and another stopped to look at him. Mothers who had lost their little ones, fathers in whose far-absent homes crowed some cherished baby-pet, and blessed little children, with more love than their little hearts could carry, stopped, and asked "to kiss the baby."

Chloe was in a halo of glory. It was such a pity that missis was not rich, that she might be Charley's nurse. She was sure she was not, because her clothes and Charley's, though nice, had been so carefully repaired, and then Chloe fell to romancing about it.

"Chloe?"

"Oh, missis, is that you? Berry glad to see you," said the negress, with a not ungraceful courtesy, as she tried to keep out of the way of the lady's prancing horses.

"Whose lovely baby is that?" asked the old lady, putting on her glasses, "hand him to me, Chloe."

The old lady seemed to be strangely moved as Chloe sat him on her knee, and tears chased each other down her face.

"He is so like, Chloe, so like my poor dear boy at his age; just such eyes, just such a forehead, just such beautiful shoulders—poor Vincent! Whose child is it, Chloe?" asked the old lady, as she untied the baby's cap, and pushed back the curls from his forehead.

"He belongs to a northern lady I have been nursing, missis. *She* is berry handsome, too."

"I can't spare him, yet," said the old lady, as Chloe held out her arms for him. "I can not let him go; see, he likes me," said she, delightedly, as Charley, with

12

one of his caressing little ways, laid his head down on her shoulder. He is my dear Vincent back again. Get in, Chloe, I'll drive you where you want to go. I can not give up the child yet."

The gay, prancing horses, with their flowing tails and manes, the silver-mounted harness, and the bright buttons of the liveried coachman, sent a brighter sparkle to the baby's eyes, and a richer glow to his cheeks. He crowed, and laughed, and clapped his little hands, till wearied with pleasure, and lulled by the rapid motion of the carriage, his little limbs relaxed, and he fell asleep.

What is so lovely as a sleeping babe?

The evening star gemming the edge of a sunset cloud? the bent lily too heavy with dew to chime its silver bells to the night wind? the closed rose-bud whose fragrant heart waits for the warm sun-ray to kiss open its loveliness?

Unable to account for the powerful magnetism by which she was drawn to the beautiful child, the old lady sat, without speaking, passing her fingers over his ivory arm, and gazing upon the rich glow of his cheek, the perfect outline of his limbs, and the shining curls of his clustering hair.

"Is this baby's mother a widow, Chloe?" she asked, at length.

"I think so, missis—I don't know—I ax no questions."

"Is she wealthy?"

"Lor', bless you, no, missis; her clothes all mended berry carful."

"I wish I had this baby," said the old lady, half musingly, as she again looked at Charley.

"Oh, Lor', missis, she lub him like her life—'t ain't no use, I tink."

The old lady seemed scarcely to hear Chloe's answer, but sat looking at Charley.

"It would be a great comfort to me," she continued. "Where does his mother live, Chloe?"

"In —— street," answered the negress.

"That is close by, I will drive you to the door, and you must ask leave to bring him to see me, Chloe;" and impressing a kiss on the face of the sleeping child, she resigned him to his nurse.

Rose sat rocking to and fro in her small parlor, in a loose muslin wrapper, and little lace cap, languid from the excitement of the previous day, thinking of Gertrude, and wishing she had but a tithe of that indomitable energy to which obstacles only served as stimulants; and then Gertrude was talented, what had *she* but her pretty face? and that, alas! had brought her only misery!

"Come in," said Rose, in answer to a slight tap on the door.

"Ah, sit down, Gertrude. Chloe has just carried Charley away, and I am quite alone."

"I must make a sketch of that ebony Venus, some day," said Gertrude.

"I confess," said she, as she seated herself in Rose's little rocking-chair, "to a strong penchant for the African. His welling sympathies, his rollicksome nature, and his punctilious observance of etiquette in his intercourse with his fellows, both amuse and interest me.

"Your genuine African has dancing in his heels, cooking at his fingers' ends, music on his lips, and a trust in Providence for the supply of his future wants equaled only by the birds of the air.

"He dances and prays with a will, nor thinks the two inconsistent, as they are not. You should have gone with me, Rose, to an African church not long since. I had grown weary of fine churches, and superfine ministers, and congregations so polished that they had the coldness as well as the smoothness of marble. I wearied of tasseled prayer-books, with gilt clasps, and all the mummeries which modern religionists seem to have substituted for true worship.

"So I wandered out into the by-streets and poor places to find *nature*, rough and uncultivated though it might be. A tumble-down looking church, set among some old tenement-houses, caught my eye. Bareheaded children were hanging round the door, scarcely kept in abeyance by a venerable-looking negro sexton in the porch, with grizzled locks and white neckerchief, whose admonitory shakes of the head habit had evidently made second nature, as he bestowed them promiscuously, right and left, till service was closed.

"I entered and took my seat among the audience. No surly pew occupant placed a forbidding hand on the pew door. Seats, hymn-books, crickets, and fans were at my disposal. The hymn was found for me. I found myself (minus 'a voice') joining in the hearty chorus. Who could help it? 'God save the King' and the Marseillaise were tame in comparison. Every body sang. It was infectious. The bent old negress, with her cracked voice, her broad shouldered, muscular son, her sweet-voiced mulatto daughter, and her chubby little grandchild, with swelling chest, to whom Sunday was neither a bugbear nor a bore. And such *hearty* singing!—sometimes too fast, sometimes too slow, but to my ear music, because it was soul, not cold science.

"It was communion-Sabbath, and so I went up to the chancel and knelt side by side with my dusky friends. The clergyman was a white man, and it was millennial to see his loving hand of blessing laid on those dusky brows. This is as it should be, said I—this is worship; and as we retired to make room for other communicants, the clergyman himself stepped forward to assist to the chancel a gray old negress, of fourscore years, whose tottering steps were even then at the grave's brink. I went home happy, for I had not fed on husks.

"Ah! visitors? Then I must run," said Gertrude, springing up at a rap on the door.

"It is Chloe, I fancy," said Rose.

"Well, good-by," said she, stooping to kiss Charley, whom she passed on the threshhold, "I must back to my easel. Ah! it is the locket you want, not me, you rogue," said she to Charley, as she disengaged a chain from her neck, and threw it over the child's, "mercenary, like the rest of your sex."

Chloe marched in with Charley, who, now wide awake, sat perched upon her shoulder, looking as imperial as young Napoleon.

"This yere boy has got to go, missis," said Chloe, still marching round the room, as if treading all objections under foot. "Whar's his frocks and pinafores? My ole missis. Vincent, see him, and take him to ride in her fine carriage, and cry over him, cause she say he so berry like her poor murdered boy."

"De Lor'! missis," exclaimed Chloe, "how white you look! Whar's your salts?"

"Open the window," said Rose, faintly, "the room is too close, Chloe."

"Thar—will you hab some water, missis? you ain't nowise strong yet," said Chloe. "Had n't you better lie down, missis?"

"No, thank you. What were you saying, Chloe, about Charley?"

"Well, you see, my ole missis. Vincent, she gib me

my freedom, you know; good missis, but hab berry
bad son; berry handsome, but berry bad; bad for
wine, and bad for women; gambled, and ebery ting;
broke his ole fadder's heart clean in two, and den got
killed hisself by some bad woman.

"Ole missis berry rich now, but her money ain't no
comfort, cause she hab to lib all alone. To-day she met
me wid Massa Charley here. De Lor', how she did
take on! She say he look jess like young Massa Vincent, when he was little piccaninny, and she kiss him,
and hold him, and hab such a time ober him, and not-
ing would do but he must go ride in de carriage, and
she bring us way home to de door.

"She wants you, missis, to let her hab Charley. I
told her you would n't, certain," said Chloe, with a
scrutinizing glance at Rose, for in truth, Chloe secretly
wished, in that African heart of hers, that the matter
might be brought about, and that she might be in-
stalled nurse for the handsome boy.

"No, of course, you would n't, missis; but would n't
it be a fine thing for *you*, Massa Charley?" said she,
perching him on the edge of her knee, "to ride all de
blessed time in dat fine carriage, and one day hab it all
yourself, and de house, and de silver, and de money,
for missis hab no relations now, no chick, nor child,
and you 're just handsome enough to do it," said Chloe,
with another sly glance at Rose's face. "You 're jess
born for dat same—dat 's a fac—so ole Chloe tinks,

yah, yah—jess as well to laff about it, missis," said the
cunning Chole, "no harm in dat, you know; but he
took to the ole lady jess as nat'ral, and set up in her
lap, just as if he belonged dere in dat carriage; it made
ole Chloe laff—yah, yah. Massa Charley, he make his
way in de world wid dat handsome face of his'n. Ole
Chloe is always stumbling on good luck," said the old
negress, laughing, "all for dis," said she, exhibiting an
old metal "charm" attached to a string inside her
dress. "Good-by—we shall see. I come for you agin,
Massa Charley, for my ole missis berry childish, when
she wants a ting she *will* hab it, and de debbel hisself
can't help it—yah, yah."

As the door closed on old Chloe's weird figure,
Rose almost felt as if her words were prophecies.
What if the law of nature should set aside all other
law and bring in a verdict for Charley? Should she,
regardless of her strong maternal feelings, yield him
up? Away from *her* he would escape the taunt of his
birth, and yet how could she school her heart to such
a parting. What was wealth and position compared
to high moral principle and a pure life? If Vincent's
mother knew not how to instill these into her own son,
might she not wreck Charley on the same fatal rock?
But what wild dream was her brain weaving? She
could not, would not deceive Madam Vincent, and
then would there not be a revulsion of feeling when
the proud old lady knew the truth? for how could

Rose mention the great wrong she had suffered, and not wound the doting mother's heart? or how could she yield up Charley to one who would ignore his mother? No, no. She would think no more of it; and yet that Vincent's mother should have petted and fondled, even unconsciously, Vincent's boy—there *was* comfort in that thought.

"Are you well enough to receive a visitor this morning," asked Doctor Perry, as he entered the room.

"Physicians do not consider it necessary to ask that question," said Rose, with some little embarrassment in her manner. "I have much to thank you for, doctor, and am none the less grateful for your kind attentions, that I was unconscious of them. But how happened it?" asked she, with surprise. "I thought you had left town with Captain Lucas. How did you find us?"

"No," said the doctor, "I was unexpectedly detained by business. The morning of the day you were taken ill, happening to pass, I saw you accidentally at the window, and resolved to call that very evening. It happened quite opportunely, you see."

"Yes—thank you; I think I had become overpowered with the heat and fatigue."

"I was apprehensive of brain fever," said the doctor; "you talked so incoherently."

12*

Rose's face instantly became suffused, and the doctor added kindly:

" Whatever I may have heard, is of course, safe with me, Rose."

" No one else heard ?" she asked.

" No one. Your landlady is too deaf, and Chloe seemed absorbed in taking care of Charley, and preparing your medicines."

" Rose," said the doctor, " if my possession of your secret distresses you, suppose I give you one in exchange : I had, and have, no business in New Orleans, save to watch over you and yours. Every weary footstep of yours, my eye has tracked ; nay, do not be angry with me, for how could love like mine abandon your helplessness in this great strange city ? I am not about to weary you by a repetition of what you have already heard, or distress you by alluding to what you unconsciously revealed. I know that your heart is cold and benumbed; but Rose, it is not dead. You say you are grateful to me for what, after all, was mere selfishness on my part, for my greatest happiness was, though unseen, to be near you. I will be satisfied with that gratitude. Will you not accept *for life*, my services on those terms?" and the doctor drew his chair nearer to Rose, and took her hand in his own.

" You know not what you ask," mournfully replied Rose. " You are deceiving yourself. You think that in time, gratitude will ripen into a warmer feeling. I feel that this can never be. My heart has lost its spring; it is capable only of a calm, sisterly feeling, and the intensity of your love for me would lead you after awhile to weary of, and reject this; you would be a prey to chagrin and disappointment. How can I bring such a misery on the heart to whose kindness I owe so much?"

"Rose, you do not know me." said the doctor, passionately. "Do not judge me by other men. As far as my own happiness is concerned, I fearlessly encounter the risk."

"Then," said Rose, thoughtfully, "there would be dark days when even *your* society would be irksome to me, when solitude alone could restore the tension of my mind."

"I should respect those days," replied her lover; "I would never intrude upon their sacredness; I would never love you the less for their recurrence."

"Then," said the ingenuous Rose, blushing as she spoke, "the sin which the world wrongly imputes to me will never be forgiven of earth. As your *wife* I must appear in society; how would you bear the whisper of malice? the sneer of envy?—no, no!" said Rose, while tears stole down her face; "I must meet this alone."

"Rose, you shall not choose!" said the doctor, passionately. "I must stand between you and all this; I declare to you that I will never leave you. If you refuse me the right to protect you legally, I will still watch over you at a distance;—but oh Rose, dear Rose, do *not* deny me. I have no relations whose averted faces you need fear; my parents are dead. I had a sister once; but whether living or dead I know not. There are none to interfere between us; let us be all the world to each other.

"Charley! plead for me," said the doctor, as he raised the beautiful child in his arms; "who shall pilot your little bark safely? *This* little hand is all too fragile," and he took that of Rose tenderly in his own —"Nay, do not answer me now; I am selfish so to distress you," said he, as Rose made an ineffectual attempt to speak;—"think of it, dear Rose, and let your answer be kindly; oh, trust me, Rose."

As he stooped to place Charley on the floor, the locket which the child had around his neck became separated from the chain to which it was attached, and, striking upon the floor, touched a spring which opened the lid; under it was a miniature. The doctor gazed at it as if spell-bound.

"Where did you get this, Rose? Surely it can not be yours," and a deadly paleness overspread his face.

"It belongs to a lady who boards here," said Rose, ' and who transferred it from her neck to Charley's this morning. Has it any interest for you?"

"What is her name? let me see her!" said the doctor, still looking at the picture.

"Her name? Gertrude Dean," said Rose.

"Dean?" repeated the doctor, looking disappointed, "Dean? Rose, that is a picture of my own father."

While they were speaking, Gertrude tapped on the door. "My locket, dear Rose; I hope 'tis not lost."

Turning suddenly, her eye fell upon the doctor With a wild cry of joy she flew into his arms, ex claiming, "My brother! my own long-lost Walter?

CHAPTER XLII.

"GOOD morning, missis," and Chloe's turbaned head followed the salutation. "Did n't I tell you dat Massa Charley be born wid a silver spoon in his mouf? His dish right side up when it rains, for certain.

"See here, missis," and she handed Rose a small package, containing a pair of coral and gold sleeve-ties for Charley's dimpled shoulders. "Did n't I tell you dat missis could n't lose sight of him? and she sent me here for him to come ride in de carriage wid her again to-day, and eat dinner at de big house, and all dat," and Chloe rubbed her hands together, and looked the very incarnation of delight.

"Well," said Rose, "Charley has nothing fine to wear; only a simple white frock, Chloe."

"All de same, missis; he handsome enuff widout any ting. Missis must take powerful liking to give him dese; dey are Massa Vincent's gold sleeve-ties *he* wore when *he* little piccaninny like Charley dare."

Rose took them in her hand, and was lost in thought.

"Jess as good, for all dat, misses," said Chloe, thinking Rose objected to them because they were second-

hand. " Missis would n't gib dem away to every
body, but she say Charley so like young Massa Vincent, dat she could n't talk of nuffing else de whole
bressed time. Hope you won't tink of sending them
back, missis," said Chloe, apologetically ; " she is old
and childish, you know."

" No," said Rose, sadly ; " Charley may wear
them ;" and she looped them up over his little white
shoulders, with a prayer that his manhood might better
fulfill the promise of *his* youth.

" Ki !" exclaimed Chloe, as she held him off at arm's
length. " Won't ole missis' servants—Betty, and
Nancy, and Dolly, and John, and de coachman, and
all dat white trash, tink dey nebber see de like of dis
before ? And won't Massa Charley make 'em all step
round, one of dese days, wid dem big black eyes of
his ?"

Chloe's soliloquies were very suggestive, and Rose
sat a long while after her departure analyzing Charley's disposition, and wondering if the seeds of *such* a
spirit lay dormant in her child, waiting only the sun
of prosperity to quicken them into life. How many
mothers, as they rocked their babes, have pondered
these things in their hearts ; and how many more,
alas ! have reaped the bitter harvest of those who
take no thought for the soul's morrow !

CHAPTER XLIII.

"AND so you will not give me the poor satisfaction of punishing and exposing the scoundrel who has treated you so basely?" said John to his sister, as they sat in her little studio.

"No," said Gertrude; "he has taken that trouble off your hands—he has punished himself. He has traveled all over the Union in search of employment, and succeeded in nothing he has undertaken. He has met with losses and disappointments in every shape, and occupies, at present, a most inferior business position, I am told. Now that I have become famous, and it is out of his power to injure me, he quails at the mention of my name in public, and dreads nothing so much as recognition by those who are acquainted with his baseness. He sneaks through life, with the consciousness that he has played the part of a scoundrel—what could even you add to this?"

"But the idea of such a miserable apology for a man getting a divorce from a sister of *mine*," said John, striding impatiently across the room. "Why did you not anticipate him, Gertrude? and with right on your side, too."

" Had I been pecuniarily able to do so," replied Gertrude, " I had not the slightest *wish* to oppose a divorce, especially as I knew it could be obtained on no grounds that would compromise me. For months after Stahle left me, and, indeed, before, he and his spies had been on my track. Had there been a shadow of a charge they could have preferred against my good name, *then* would have been their hour of triumph! I have a copy of the divorce papers in my possession, and the only allegation there preferred is, that I did not accept Stahle's invitation to join him when he wrote me, in the manner I have related to you."

" But the world, Gertrude, the world," said the irritated John, " will not understand this."

" My dear John," said Gertrude, " they who *desire* to believe a lie, will do so in the face of the clearest evidence to the contrary. But I have found out that though a person (a woman especially) may suffer much from the bitter persecution of such persons, from the general undeserved suspicion of wrong, and from the pusillanimity of those who *should* be her defenders, yet even in such a position, a woman can never be injured *essentially*, save by her own acts, for God is just, and truth and innocence will triumph. I am righted before the world; my untiring industry and uprightness of life are the refutal of his calumnies. Leave him to his kennel obscurity, my dear John. I do not *now* need the blow that I am sure you would not have been slow to strike for me had you known how your sister was oppressed."

"I don't know but you are right, Gertrude, and yet—if he ever should cross my path, my opinion might undergo a sudden revulsion. Does he still keep up the show of piety?"

"So I have heard," said Gertrude. "The first thing he does, when he goes into a new place is to connect himself with some church. What a pity, John, such men should bring religion into disrepute."

"You think so, do you? And yet you refuse to expose it. It is just because of this that so many hypocrites go unmasked. Sift them out, I say—if there is not a communicant left in the church. I do not believe in throwing a wide mantle over such whited sepulchers."

"Do you suppose," said Gertrude, "that they whose houses are built on such a sandy foundation will quietly see them undermined? *Such* a hue and cry as they will raise (all for the honor of the cause, of course!) about your 'speaking lightly of religion and its professors!'"

"Very true," said John, "it is speaking lightly of its *professors* but not of its *possessors*. They might as well tell you to keep dumb about a gang of counterfeiters, lest it should do injury to the money-market; bah! Gertrude, I have no patience with such tampering; but to dismiss an unpleasant topic, you have plenty of employment, I see ;" and John glanced round the room at Gertrude's pictures. "I am proud of you, Gertrude ; I honor you for your self-reliance ; but what is your fancy, with your artistic reputation, for living such a nun's life ?"

"Well," said Gertrude, "in the first place, my time is too valuable to me to be thrown away on bores and idlers, and the Paul Pry family, in all its various ramifications. Autograph hunters I have found not without their use, as I never answer their communications, and they find me in letter stamps. But *entre nous*, John, I have no very exalted opinion of the sex to which you belong.

"Men are so gross and unspiritual, John, so wedded to making money and promiscuous love, so selfish and unchivalric; of course there are occasionally glorious exceptions, but who would be foolish enough to wade through leagues of brambles, and briars, to find perchance one flower ? Female friends, of course, are out of the question, always excepting Rose, whose title is no misnomer. And as to general society, it is so seldom one finds a congenial circle that, having resources of my own, I feel disinclined to encounter the risk."

"This isolation is unnatural ; Gertrude, you can not be happy."

"Who is ?" asked Gertrude. "Are you ? Is Rose ?

Where is the feast at which there is no skeleton? I make no complaint. I enjoyed more happiness in the five years of my first wedded life than falls to the lot of most mortals in a life-time. I know that such an experience can not be repeated, so I live on the past. You say I am not happy; I am negatively happy. If I gather no honey, I at least escape the sting."

"I wish for my sake, Gertrude, you would go into society. I can not but think you would form new ties that would brighten life. As a woman, you can not be insensible to your attractive power."

"I have no desire to exert it," replied Gertrude; "there are undoubtedly men in want of housekeepers, and plenty of widowers in want of nurses for their children. My desires do not point that way."

"You are incorrigible, Gertrude. Do you suppose there is no man who has sense enough to love you for yourself alone?"

"What if I do not want to be loved?" asked his sister.

"But you do," persisted John; "so long as there is any vitality in a women, she likes to be loved."

"Well, then, granting your proposition for the sake of the argument, please give me credit for a most martyr-like and persistent self-denial," said Gertrude, laughing.

"I will give you credit for nothing, till your heart gets thawed out a little ; and I think I know a friend of mine who can do it."

"Forewarned forearmed," said his sister.

CHAPTER XLIV.

"Rose, you are not looking well, this morning. Confess, now, that you did not sleep a wink last night. I heard the pattering of your little feet over my head long after midnight."

"Very likely, for I was unaccountably restless. I will tell you what troubled me. I was trying to think of some way to support myself; I wish I had a tithe of your energy, Gertrude."

"Well you have not, you are just made to be loved and petted. You are too delicate a bit of porcelain to be knocked and hustled round amid the delf of the world. Your gift is decidedly wife-wise, and the sooner you let my good brother John make you one, the better for all of us."

"What do you think of my turning authoress?" asked Rose, adroitly turning the subject.

"Oh, do it, by all means," mocked Gertrude, "it is the easiest thing in the world to write a book. It would be just the thing for a little sensitive-plant like you. I think I see it fairly launched. I think I see you sit down with the morning paper in your hand to read a criticism on it, from some coarse pen, dressed in a little brief authority, in the absence of some editor; a fellow who knows no difference between a sun-flower and a violet, and whose daily aspirations are bounded by an oyster supper, or a mint-julep. I think I see you thumped on the head with his butchering cleaver, every nerve quivering under the crucifixion of his coarse scalpel."

"But surely there are those who know a good book when they see it, and I mean to write a good book."

"You little simpleton, as if that would save you! Do you suppose you will be forgiven for writing a *good* book? No, my dear; the editor of 'The Daily Lorgnette,' takes it up, he devours a chapter or two, he begins to fidget in his chair, he sees there is genius in it, he gets up and strides across his office, he recollects certain books of his own, which nobody ever read but his publishers and himself, and every word he reads irritates that old sore. The next day, under the head of book notices you will see the following in the Daily Lorgnette :—

" 'Gore House, by Rose Ringdove.'

" 'We have perused this book; it is unnecessary to state in its title-page that it was written by a *female* hand. The plot is feeble and inartistic. In dialogue, the writer utterly fails; the heroine, Effie Waters, is a stiff, artificial creation, reminding us constantly of those females painted on the pannels of omnibuses, convuls-

ively grasping to their bosoms a posy, or a poodle.
There is an indescribable and heterogeneous jumbling
of characters in this volume. The authoress vainly
endeavors to straighten out this snarl in the last chapter, which has nothing to recommend it but that it *is*
the last. We advise the authoress of 'Gore House' to
choose some other escape-valve for her restless femininity; petticoat literature has become a drug in the
market.'

"How do you like that?" said Gertrude, laughing.

"Well, the editor of the 'Christian Warrior' sits
down to read 'Gore House,' he takes out his spectacles, and wipes them deliberately on his red-silk pocket-
handkerchief, he adjusts them on the bridge of his
sagacious nose; he reads on undisturbed until he comes
to the description of 'Deacon Pendergrast,' who is
very graphically sketched as a 'wolf in sheep's clothing.' Conscience holds up the mirror, and he beholds
himself, like unto a man who sees his natural face in a
glass. Straightway he sitteth down, and writeth the
following impartial critique of the book :

" 'We have read " Gore House." We do not hesitate to pronounce it a *bad* book, unfit to lie on the
table of any *religious* family. In it, *religion* is held up
to ridicule. It can not fail to have a most pernicious
influence on the minds of the young. We hope Christian editors all over the land will not hesitate, out of

courtesy to the authoress, to warn the reading public of this locomotive poison.'

"The editor of the 'Christian Warrior' then hands the notice to his foreman for an early insertion, puts on his hat, and goes to the anniversary of the Society for the Propagation of the Gospel, of which he is president.

"The editor of the 'John Bull' reads 'Gore House.' He is an Englishman, and pledged to his British blood, while he makes his living out of America, to abuse, underate, and villify, her government, institutions, and literature, therefore he says, curtly:

"'We have received "Gore House"—they of course who wish for *literature*, especially female literature, will look the other side of the Atlantic." He then takes one of the most glowing passages in 'Gore House,' and transposing the words slightly, passes it off for editorial in his own columns.

"The editor of 'The Timbrel' reads Gore House. He has a female relative, Miss Clementina Clemates, whose mission she thinks is to be an authoress. In furtherance of this design of hers, he thinks it policy to decry all other rival books. So he says:

"'We have read "Gore House." We ought to say we have *tried* to read it. The fact is, the only lady book recently published that we can heartily recommend to our readers is "Sketches of the Fireside, by Clementine Clemates."'

13

"The editor of the 'Dinsmore Republican' reads the book. He is of the Don Quixote order, goes off like an old pistol half primed, whenever the right chord is struck. Gore House takes him captive at once. He wishes there were a tournament, or some such arrangement, by which he could manifest his devotion to and admiration of the authoress. He throws down the book, unties his neckcloth, which seems to be strangling him, loosens his waistband button to give his breathing apparatus more play, throws up the window, runs his fingers through his hair, till each one seems as charged with electricity as a lightning-rod, and then seizing his goose-quill, piles on the commendatory adjectives till your modesty exclaims, in smothering agony, 'Save me from my friends, and I will take care of my enemies.'"

"But tell me," said Rose, "is there no bright side to this subject you can depict me?"

"Oh, yes," said Gertrude, "there are editors who can read a book and deal fairly and conscientiously by it and its author, who neither underrate nor overrate from fear or favor, who find fault, not as an escape-valve for their own petulance or indigestion, but gently, kindly, as a wise parent would rebuke his child—editors on whose faith you can rely, whose book reviews are, and can be, depended upon, who feel themselves accountable to other than a *human* tribunal for their discharge of so important a public trust."

"Well," said Rose, in despair, "if I might be Sappho

herself I could not run such a gauntlet of criticism as you have described."

"Far happier to be Cornelia with her jewels," said Gertrude, snatching up the beautiful Charley (I take it Cornelia had a glorious husband). "Fame is a great unrest to a true woman's heart. The fret, and tumult, and din of battle are not for her. The vulgar sneer for which there is no preventive, save the unrecognized one of *honor;* the impertinent tone of familiarity, supposed to be acceptable by those to whom a woman's heart is yet a sealed book; what are tears to oppose to such bludgeon weapons? No, the fret and din of battle are not for her; but if, at the call of trumpet-tongued necessity, she buckle on the armor, let her fight with what good courage her God may give her, valuing far above the laurel crown, when won, the loving hearts for which she toils—which beat glad welcome home."

CHAPTER XLV.

Miss Anne Cooper was a maiden lady of forty-two; a satellite who was well contented to revolve year after year round Madame Vincent, and reflect her *golden* rays. Madame Vincent had been a beauty in her day, and was still tenacious of her claims to that title. It was Miss Anne's constant study to foster this bump of self-conceit, and so cunningly did she play her part, so indignantly did she deny the advances of Old Time, that madame was flattered into the belief that he had really given her a quit claim.

Miss Anne's disinterested care of the silver, linen, and store-room was quite praiseworthy to those who did not know that she supplied a family of her relatives with all necessary articles from the Vincent resources. It was weary waiting for the expected codicil, and Miss Anne thought "a bird in the hand was worth two in the bush;" so if she occasionally abducted a pound or two of old Hyson or loaf-sugar, or a loaf of cake, or a pair of pies, she reasoned herself into the belief that they were, after all, only her lawful perquisites.

Yes, it was weary waiting for the codicil. Madame Vincent was an invalid, 'tis true; but so she had been these twenty years, having one of those india-rubber constitutions, which seem to set all medical precedents at defiance. She might last along for ten years to come—who knew?

Ten years! Miss Anne looked in the glass; the crow's-feet were planted round her own eyes, and it needed no microscope to see the silver threads in her once luxuriant black locks. Not that Miss Anne did not smile just as sweetly on her patroness as if she would not at any time have welcomed a call upon her from the undertaker. Miss Anne's voice, as she glided through the house with her bunch of keys, had that oily, hypocritical whine which is inseparable from your genuine toady, be it man or woman.

Miss Anne sat in the "blue chamber" of the Vincent mansion—a chamber that had once been occupied by young Master Vincent. Whether this gave it a charm in the lady's eyes or no, Miss Anne never had said. It was true that young Master Vincent, when he had nothing else to do, amused himself with irritating Miss Anne up to the snapping-point. They scarce met without a war of words, half jest, half earnest; but for all that, young Vincent's every wish was anticipated by Miss Anne. It was she who reinserted the enameled buttons in his vests, when they came from the laundress; it was she who righted his room, and kept all his little dandy apparatus (in the shape of perfumes, gold shirt-buttons, hair-oil, watch-guards, rings, etc.) in their appropriate places.

Your D'Orsay abroad, is generally a brute at home; selfish, sarcastic, ill-tempered, and exacting where he thinks it does not pay to be otherwise. All this Miss Anne turned aside with the skill and tact of a woman; occasionally quite quenching him with her witty replies, and forcing him to laugh even in his most diabolical moods. To be sure he would mutter some uncanonical words after it, and tell her to go to the torrid zone; and Miss Anne would smile as usual, drop a low courtesy, and glide from his presence; sometimes to go round making all sorts of housekeeping blunders; sometimes to sit down in her room, with her hands folded in her lap, and her great black eyes fixed immovably on the carpet, for all the world just as if Miss Anne were in love.

Old maids have their little thoughts; why not?

On the present occasion, as I have said, Miss Anne sat in "the blue chamber." She was paler than usual, and her Xantippe lips were closed more firmly together. The thread of her thoughts seemed no smoother than the thread between her fingers, beside breaking which she had broken six of Hemming's best drilled-eyed needles. At length, pushing the stool from beneath her feet, she threw down her work and strode impatiently up and down the apartment.

"To be balked after serving this Leah's apprentice-ship, by a baby! and by *that* baby! I could love it for its likeness to *him*, did it not stand in my way. It was such doll faces as that baby's mother's which could fascinate Vincent, hey?—soulless, passionless little automatons. Ye gods! and how *I* have loved him, let these sunken eyes and mottled tresses bear witness," and Miss Anne looked at herself in the glass. "That is all past now; thank heaven, that secret dies with me. Who would ever suspect *me* of falling in love?" and Miss Anne laughed hysterically. "And now that hope died out, that baby is to come between me and my expected fortune!

"Simple Chloe! She little thought, when she re-peated to me what she called 'her young mistress's crazy ravings,' that *I* could 'find a method in that madness.' Love is sharp-sighted; so is policy. That baby shall never come here. It should not, at any rate, for the mother's sake, pretty little fool!

"Madame will 'adopt' the baby, forsooth! She will fill the house with bibs and pinafores, and install me as head nurse, and to *that* child! All my fine castles to be knocked down by a baby's puny hand! We shall see.

"That old dotard, to adopt a baby at *her* time of life, when she ought to be thinking of her shroud."

"Ah, Anne, you there," said a voice at the door, "and busy as usual?"

" Yes, dear madame, work for you is only pastime."

" You were always a good creature, Anne," and madame tapped her affectionately on the shoulder.

" How very well you are looking to-day," said Anne. " Mourning is uncommonly becoming to you. Becky and I were saying this morning, as you passed through the hall, that no one would suppose you to be more than thirty."

" S-i-x-t-y, my dear, s-i-x-t-y," replied the old lady, cautiously closing the door; " but you should not flatter, Annie."

" It is not flattery to speak the truth," said Anne, with a mock-injured air.

" Well, well, don't take a joke so seriously, child; what every body says *must* be true, I suppose," and madame looked complacently in the glass.

" Anne, do you know I can not think of any thing but that beautiful child ? Don't you think his resemblance to our Vincent very remarkable ?"

" Very, dear madame, I am not at all surprised at your fancying him. He is quite a charming little fellow."

" Is n't he, though ?" exclaimed madame, with a pleased laugh; " do you know Anne I have about made up my mind to adopt him ? I shall call him Vincent L'Estrange Vincent."

" How charming !" said Anne, "how interesting you will look; you will be taken for his mother."

"Very likely," said madame. I recollect we were quite an object of attraction the day we rode out together; I think I *am* looking youthful Anne."

"No question of it, my dear madame—here—let me rearrange this bow in your cap; that's it; what execution you must have done in your day, madame."

"I had *some* lovers," replied the sexegenarian widow, with mock humility, as she twisted a gold circlet upon her finger.

"If report speaks true, their name was legion; I dare say there is some interesting story now, connected with that ring," suggested Anne.

"Poor Perry!" exclaimed madame—"I *did n't* treat him well; I wonder what ever came of him; *how* he used to sigh! What beautiful bouquets he brought me —how jealous he was of poor dear Vincent. I was a young, giddy thing then; and yet, I was good-hearted, Anne, for I remember how sorry I used to be that I could n't marry *all* my lovers. I told Perry so, one day when he was on his knees to me, but he did not seem as much pleased as I expected. I don't think he always knew how to take a compliment.

"Poor Perry!

"I could n't help liking him, he had such a dear pair of whiskers, quite à-la-corsair—but Vincent had the money, and I always needed such a quantity of dresses and things, Anne.

"Well—on my wedding-day, Perry walked by the

house, looking handsomer than ever. I believe the creature did it on purpose to plague me. He had on white pants, and yellow Marseilles vest, salmon-colored neck-tie, and *such* a pretty dark-blue body-coat, with brass buttons; *such* a fit! I burst out a crying; I never saw any thing so heart-breaking as that coat; there was not a wrinkle in it from collar to tail. I don't think I should ever have got over it, Anne, had not my maid Victorine just then brought me in a set of bridal pearls from Vincent; they were really sumptuous.

"Poor dear Perry!

"Well—I was engaged to him just one night; and I think the moon was to blame for that, for as soon as the sun rose next morning, I knew it would not do. He was poor, and it was necessary I should have a fine establishment, you know. But poor Perry! I never shall forget that blue body-coat, never—it was such a fit!"

"The old fool!" exclaimed Anne, dismissing the bland smile from her face as the last fold of madame's dress fluttered through the door; "after all, she might do worse than to adopt this child. I could easier get rid of that baby than her second husband. I must rein up a little, with my flattery, or she may start off on that track.

"Poor Perry, indeed!" soliloquized Anne, "what geese men are! how many of them, I wonder, have had reason to thank their stars, that they did not get what their hearts were once set on. Well—any will-o'-the-wisp who trips it lightly, can lead any Solomon by the nose; it is a humiliating fact;" and Miss Anne took a look at herself in the glass; " sense is at a discount; well, it is the greatest compliment the present generation of men could have paid me, never to have made me an offer."

CHAPTER XLVI.

"And you, then, are the mother of the beautiful child, I wish to adopt?" asked Madame Vincent, gazing admiringly at Rose.

Our heroine's long lashes drooped upon a cheek that crimsoned like the heart of a June rose, as she timidly answered:

"Yes, madame."

"You are extremely pretty, child, and very young to be a mother. Have you any other children?"

"None," replied Rose, "but Charley."

"And you would not give him up to me?" asked madame, coaxingly. "Do you think his father would object?"

"His father is dead, madame," said Rose, in a low voice.

"Pardon me, child, I did not know that you were a widow. *I* am a widow. It is very dull, being a widow; don't you think so, dear? Did your husband leave you property?"

"No," replied Rose, answering the inexcusable question, for she could not bear to seem disrespectful to Vincent's mother.

"That is a pity, dear; my husband left me plenty. I shall will it all to Charley, if you will only give him up to me. What was your husband's name, dear."

"Vincent L'Estrange Vincent;" answered Rose, startled at the strange sound of her own voice.

"Singular! Same name as my son's," said madame, "Very singular."

"He *was* your son;" said Rose, in the same strange, cold tone.

"My son never was married;" replied madame.

"God knows he told me we were so, and I believed him," answered Rose.

"He made believe marry you, then, did he?" asked the childish old lady. "He did that to a great many women, I believe. Gentlemen often do such things, so they tell me. Your child is of course illegitimate then."

Rose's lips moved, but no answer came.

"And what do you intend to do with him, child?"

"Bring him up to despise the sin of which his father was guilty," replied Rose, boldly.

"Oh yes, that's all very proper; but if you give him to me, there will be no occasion ever to mention it at all, or *you either*, child."

"Madame," said Rose, with a proud dignity. "Is it a mother who speaks to a mother such words as these? You love *your* son none the less that he made *my* name a reproach and a by-word, crimsoned my innocent cheek with shame, dimmed my eyes with unavailing tears. Shall I, think you, love *my* son the less that *your son* deserted him? Shall I love my son the less that through days and nights of tearful anguish his smile, his love, was all of heaven I ever dared to look for?"

" Oh, certainly not—oh, of course not," replied the old lady, nervously; "but you know he may not *always* love you as well as he does now, when he knows—"

" In God I put my trust;" said Rose, as tears streamed from her eyes.

" Well, don't cry, child—don't cry. I hate to see people cry. All I wanted to say was, that you would always be a drag on him, if he tried to rise in the world; but don't cry. It is right for you to trust in God, every body ought to be pious, it is so respectable. I have been confirmed myself; but don't cry, it will spoil your handsome eyes. You are young yet, perhaps somebody may marry you, if you keep quiet about this."

" I would never so deceive any man," answered Rose, with dignity.

" *Deceive!* oh, no, child, that would be *very* wrong. I only meant that you should say nothing about it; that is a different thing, you see. Now I loved a Mr. Perry much better than I did my husband, but it would have been quite foolish had I allowed it to be known, you know, because Vincent was very rich, and it was necessary I should have a handsome establishment. Oh, no! of course I do not approve of deception, that is very wrong, but there *are* cases where it is best for a woman to keep quiet. Well, how about Charley? have you quite decided not to part with him?"

"Quite," said Rose, "Charley must remain with me;" and, with a dignified air, she bowed madame to her carriage.

CHAPTER XLVII.

"A REGULAR little romance, I declare," said madame, laying off her black bonnet, and fanning herself languidly, "quite a little romance.

"*Vincent's* boy! no wonder he is so handsome; no wonder I was so attracted toward him. Vincent was a little wild, but very likely that young thing did *her* part of the courting. She is very handsome, and, with a little instruction under other circumstances—with a little instruction from me, I say, she would be quite presentable in society.

"It is very odd she would not give up Charley. I thought that style of people were always glad to get rid of their children; in fact, I think it her *duty* not to stand in the child's light. She is a Puritanical little puss, and quite queenly, too, for a Magdalen. I was quite dashed, as one may say, once or twice, by her manner, although I pride myself on my self-possession. She is really quite superior to her station; but Vincent, dear boy, always had indisputable taste; there never was a taint of grossness about him.

"He was very fastidious. I remember I put off his

father's funeral one whole day, in order that the tailor might alter the coat-collar of his new mourning-suit. Yes, and he was so sensitive, too, poor dear! he felt his father's death so much that he was obliged to go directly from the grave to the club-house, to dissipate his mournful thoughts.

"Ah! Anne, is that you? sit down; I have just returned. Do you know, the mother of that baby refused to give him up. She says it is one of our Vincent's children. She is a very pretty young woman, Anne—not a high-bred beauty, of course; that you never see, except in aristocratic circles, still, she is quite pretty."

"Very," replied Anne, quite nonchalently.

"Ha! you have seen her, then?" asked madame, with some surprise.

"My dear madame, I really would prefer saying nothing upon the subject. I answered your first question frankly, because I make it a point never to deceive you; but I really wish you would not question me, I dislike so much to speak ill of any one."

"But I insist upon knowing, Anne; in fact, I think it is quite unkind of you to have any secrets from me, so long as you have been in my confidence, too."

"Ah, well, dear madame, if you insist, I suppose I must yield, for I can refuse you nothing. The person you have been to see this morning is an arrant impostor. She is playing a deep game with you; her refusal is not sincere; she expects you will return and persist in asking for Charley, and intends then to make money out of the operation."

"Well, she is very much mistaken, then," said the old lady, indignant, as easily duped people are, who always fancy themselves a match for any double and twisted diplomatist, "very much mistaken, for I shall never go near her again. Then that story was all trumped up she told me about the baby being our Vincent's."

"Certainly," said Anne; "I tell you, my dear madame, she has played that game on several people beside you."

"Possible?" said the old lady, fanning herself violently; "the impudent little baggage! But how did you find it all out, Annie?"

"Ah! there, you must really excuse me, my dear madame. My informant is so afraid of being involved, that I was sworn to the strictest secresy on that point, but, I asure you, my authority is reliable."

"I have no doubt of it, my dear Anne, if *you* say so. But why did you not speak of it before?"

"Well, that was my first impulse, of course; but you see how it was. I was placed in very delicate circumstances, dear madame. Here I am a dependent on your bounty; you have been always like a kind mother to me; your heart was set on adopting this child; had I opposed it, you might have suspected my motives; that thought was too painful for me; and so, up to this

time, when you extorted it from me, I have been vacillating," and Anne looked lachrymose.

"You dear, good creature," exclaimed madame,
"you always had the best heart in the world. You
should not have tortured yourself so unnecessarily,
Anne. You know I never would imagine you guilty
of such mean motives. You may have my brown silk
dress, Anne, and the dark blue brocade. I had never
worn either when I was called into mourning. I declare, Anne, you have the best heart in the world.
You need not blush about it, child," said madame, as
Anne covered her face with her handkerchief to conceal a laugh. "You are too modest by half, Anne;
but it is always so with real merit."

"What an invaluable creature that Anne is," exclaimed madame, as she went out of the door in pursuit of the brown silk. "To think of the brazen-faced-
ness of that young woman! I declare I could not have
believed any body could tell a lie with such an innocent face. It is really almost past belief; what an invaluable creature Anne is. I never should be able to
get along without her. I must go to Mme. Descomb's
and select her a new dress hat. Just to think now
of the impudence of that Rose.

"I must furnish Anne with means to go on some
little excursion. I think I will buy her that pretty
music-box I saw yesterday.

"How wide awake Anne is to my interests! Had it not been for her I might have been taken in by that scheming young woman. I hope nobody saw me go to her house; I must warn Chloe against her, it will not do for her to go there again."

CHAPTER XLVIII.

Rose was sitting in her little parlor giving Charley his morning bath; the water was dripping from his polished limbs, and he was laughing and splashing about with the nude grace of a young sea-god; now catching his breath, as his head was immersed under water; now shaking back his dripping curls, and flashing upon you his dark bright eyes, as if life were all sunshine, and his infant sky were cloudless.

"I sall inform you zat you can leave my maison—my house—dis morning," said Rose's French landlady, entering the room without a preliminary rap. "You understand, mademoiselle—*dis morning*, I say—you are von bad woman, mademoiselle."

Twice Rose opened her lips to speak, but the color receded from her lips and cheeks, and she stood terror-struck and speechless.

"Zat is all ver' well," said madame, quite accustomed to see her country-women strike an attitude. "Zat is all ver' well; you did not expect I sall know any ting about it, but one personne tell me zat I know; you can go, for you are von bad woman."

"What is all this?" exclaimed Gertrude, opening the door and seeing Rose's pallid face and madame's angry gesticulations.

"Ah, ha! she has impose on you too!" exclaimed Madame Macqué. "She von ver' sly woman—ver' bad; she no' stay in my house long time."

"Woman!" said Gertrude, throwing her arm around Rose, "this is my sister; every word you speak against her you speak against me. She is as pure as that sweet child. If she leaves your house, I leave it."

"Ver' well—*trés bien*," said madame, shaking her overloaded French head-dress; "you can go, den—von day you see I tell you de truf when I say she von—"

"Don't repeat that again, in my hearing," said Gertrude, standing before her with sparkling eyes.

"Speak, Rose—dear Rose!" said Gertrude, kissing her cold face, as madame left the room. "Speak, Rose; do not let that miserable bundle of French trumpery crush so pure and noble a heart as yours. We will go away, Rose—you, and I, and dear little Charley. And, oh, Rose! when could I have a better time to plead for my brother's happiness, for yours, for my own? Put it beyond the power of any one to poison your peace, Rose; be *indeed* my sister."

Rose's only reply was a low shuddering sob, as she drew closer to Gertrude.

"Just as good as new," said Miss Anne, looking

complacently at herself in the brown silk. "Anne, you should be prime minister; you have a talent for diplomacy; femininity is too circumscribed a sphere for the exercise of your talents. You did that well, Anne—Madame Vincent thrown completely off the track, Rose crushed and out of your way forever; the baby ditto. Madame Macque is very careful of her reputation in *this* country, because she never had any in France. Ha—ha, Anne, you are a genius—and this brown silk is a proof of it. Now, look out for presents about this time, for your star is at its culminating point. Rose has beauty—has she? Vincent fancied her—did he? A rose's doom is to fade and wither—to be plucked, then trodden under foot;" and Miss Anne laughed one of her Satanic laughs.

CHAPTER XLIX.

Sally came into the kitchen just as the clock was striking seven. The Maltese cat heard the old clock, jumped up, and shook herself, just as if her dream of a ducking at the hands of the grocer-boy were true. Three stray cockroaches—cockroaches, like poor relatives, will intrude into the best-regulated families—scampered before Sally's footsteps to their hiding-places, and the little thieving brown mouse on the dresser took temporary refuge in the sugar-bowl.

Sally had been up stairs performing her afternoon toilet by the aid of a cracked looking-glass, which had a way of multiplying Sally's very suggestive to her crushed hopes. Sally, I am sorry to say, had been jilted. Milk-men do not always carry the milk of human kindness in their flinty bosoms. Time was when Jack Short never came into the kitchen with his can, without tossing Sally a bunch of caraway, or fennel, a nosegay of Bouncing Bettys, or a big apple or pear. Time was when his whip-lash always wanted mending, and it took two to find a string in the closet to do it, and two pair of hands to tie it on when found.

"Poor old thing!" the faithless John would now say to the rosy little plumptitude who had won his heart away from the angular Sally; "Poor old thing! I was only fooling a little, just to keep my hand in, and she thought I was in love."

Sally had as much spirit as the rest of her sex, and so to show John that she was quite indifferent about the new turn in their affairs, she set the milk-pan, into which he was to pour his morning's milk, out into the porch, and closed the kitchen-door in his false face, that he might have nothing upon which to hinge an idea that she wanted to see him. And more; she tied the yellow neck-ribbon he gave her on the last fourth of July round the pump-handle, and if John Short had not been blind as well as "short," he must have seen that "when a woman will—she will, you may depend on 't," and "when a woman won't—she won't, and there 's an end on 't."

Poor Sally, before she saw John, had lived along contentedly in her underground habitations, year after year, peeling potatoes, making puddings, washing, ironing, baking, and brewing; nobody had ever made love to her; she had not the remotest idea what a Champagne draught love was. She could have torn her hair out by the roots, when she did find out, to think she had so misspent her past time. It really *did* seem to her, although she was squint-eyed, that there was nothing else in this world of any ac-

14

.count at all. She had thought herself happy when her
bonnet was trimmed to suit her, or her gown a good
fit; but a love-fit! ah, that was a very different matter. Poor Sally! mischievous John!—the long and
short of it was, if Bouncing Bettys have any floral
significance, Sally should have been Mrs. Short.

Of course, she had no motive on the afternoon we
speak of, to look long in the cracked looking-glass; it
made no difference now whether she wore her brown
calico with the little white dots, or her plaid delaine
with the bishop sleeves; there was no use in braiding
her hair, or in putting on her three-shilling collar; she
had resigned herself to her fate. She even threw a
pitcher of hot water at the innocent organ-grinder,
because he played Love's young Dream.

Still you see, she goes on mechanically with her
work, putting the tea-kettle over the fire, setting the
six brass lamps in a regular row on the mantle, and
tucking the ends of some clean towels, out of sight,
in the half-open bureau-drawers. Sally is neat; but
John Short's little Patty is plump and rosy.

Ah! now she has some company—there is Miss
Harriet Place, who has the misfortune to have so stiff
a neck that when she turns it, her whole body must
follow. Miss Harriet has black eyes, affects the genteel, and speaks of "my poor neck" in a little mincing
way, as if its stiffness were only a pretty little affecta-
tion on her part. Her cronies wink at this weakness,

for Miss Harriet has a gift at trimming their bonnets, and putting finishing touches to all sorts of feminine knicknacks; then, here comes Alvah Kittridge, who is a rabid Free-will Baptist, and who lives at Mayor Treadwell's! where they have such fine dinners; at which the Mayor drinks a great deal, and "finds fault very bad," with every thing the next morning. Miss Alvah pays her way as she goes, both in stories, and maccaroons; the former her own, the latter Mayor Treadwell's.

Last, but by no means least, comes Mrs. Becky Saffron, all cap-border and eyes, the only other notice-able thing about her being her mouth, which displays, in her facetious moods, two enormous yellow tusks, one upper and one under, reminding the observer of a hungry catamount; this resemblance scarce diminishes on acquaintance, as Mrs. Becky, like all the skinny skeleton-ish tribe, is capable of most inordinate guzzling and gorging.

"Glad to see you, Miss Place," said Mrs. Becky (giving her cap-border a twitch), and getting on the right side of that stiff-necked individual, "I have not set eyes on you these six months."

"No," minced Miss Place; "I called at your board-ing-house, and they said you had gone somewhere, they could not tell where."

"Oh, I'm nobody; of course they would n't know; I'm nobody. I'm down in the world, as one may say.

I'm nobody but 'Becky.' I come and go; nobody cares, especially when I *go*," and Mrs. Becky gave her two yellow tusks an airing.

"I left my old place some time ago. I'm to *broth*-er's now." Mrs. Becky always pronounced the first syllable of this word like the liquid commonly designated by that syllable. "Yes, I'm to *broth*-ers now. His wife never wanted me in the house. She's dreadful pert and stuck-up, for all she was nobody; so I have always been boarded out, and been given to understand that my room was better than my company. But something queer has happened. I can't find out what, only that *broth*-er has got the whip-rein of his wife now, and has it all his own way; so he came and told me that it would cost less for him to keep me at St. John's Square than to board me out; so there I am.

"It is no use for *broth*-er's wife to teach me about silver forks and finger-bowls, about not doing this, or that, or t' other thing; can't teach an old dog new tricks. But I let her fret. I am not afraid of her now, for whenever she gets on her high horse, *broth*-er fetches her right off with the word "damages." I can't tell for the life of me what it means. I've seen her change right round when he whispered it, as quick as a weather-cock, and it would be all fair weather in one minute. It's curious. How do you like your new place, Alvah?"

"Places are all about alike," said Alvah, dejectedly. "See one, you see all. Damask and satin in the parlor; French bedsteads and mirrors in my lady's chamber, and broken panes of glass up in the attic; lumpy straw beds, coarse, narrow sheets, torn coverlets, and one broken table and chair, will do for the servants' room. Always fretting and fault-finding too, just as if we had heart to work, when we are treated so like dogs; worse than dogs, for young master's Bruno has a dog-house all to himself, and a nice soft bed in it; which is more than I can say. I declare it is discouraging," said Alvah. "It fetches out all the bad in me, and chokes off all the good. Mistress came down the other day and scolded because I washed myself at the kitchen sink. Well, where should I wash? There is neither bowl, pitcher, wash-stand, or towels furnished in my attic, and, after cooking over the fire all day, it is n't reason to ask any body not to wash wherever they can get a chance. It don't follow that I like dirt, because I have to do dirty work. I can't put clean clothes over a soiled skin. I feel better-natured when I am clean—better-tempered and more human like. When I first went out to live, I was conscientious like; but now, I know it is wicked, but I get ugly and discouraged, and then I don't care. I say if they treat me like a dog, I shall snatch a bone when I can get it. Mistress, now, wants breakfast at just such a time. She is too stingy to find me in proper kindling for my fire, so in course

it keeps going out as fast as I light it, and *henders* me;
and then she gets in a fury 'cause breakfast don't come
up.   Well, I stood it as long as I could; now I pour
lamp-oil on the wood to make it kindle; that does the
business.   I reckon it is n't no saving to her not to
buy kindling.   I know it is n't right; but I get aggravated to think they don't have no bowels for us poor
servants."

Mrs. Becky Saffern paid little attention to this narrative.   There was more attractive metal for her on the
tea-table, upon which Sally had just placed some
smoking hot cakes, and a fragrant pot of tea.   Mrs.
Becky's great yellow black eyes rolled salaciously
round in her head, and her two tusks commenced
whetting themselves against each other, preparatory to
a vigorous attack on the edibles.

"Green tea!" exclaimed Mrs. Becky, after the first
satisfactory gulp—"not a bit of black in it—that's
something like;" and untying her cap-strings, she
spread her white handkerchief over her lap, and gave
herself up to the gratification of her ruling passion,
next to gossip.   "How *did* you come by green tea in
the kitchen?" asked the delighted Mrs. Becky.

"Oh, I laid in with the housekeeper," answered
Sally; "she has dreadful low wages, and has hard
work enough to get even that.   I iron all her muslins,
and she finds me in green tea. 'Live, and let live,' you
know."

"That reminds me," minced Miss Place, who sometimes set up for a wit, "that's what I read on the side of a baker's cart the other day, 'Live, and let live;' but, unfortunately, right under it was written ' Pisin cakes !' "

About half an hour after this, Mrs. Becky choked over her sixth cup of tea; Miss Place's pun had just penetrated her obtuse intellect.

CHAPTER L.

"DEAR TOM,—

"The next best thing to seeing you, you witty dog, is reading one of your letters; but accept a little advice from one who has had experience, and don't throw away so many good things on one individual; economise your bon-mots, my dear fellow, spread them over your private correspondence as sparingly as they do butter on bread at boarding-schools. Ah! you will grow wiser by and by, when you find out how very rare is an original idea. Why—we literary people, if by chance we improvise one in conversation, always stop short after it, and turning to our friends say, 'Now remember, that's *mine*, don't you use it, for I intend putting it in my next book.'

"What am I doing, hey? Living by my wits, though not in the way of literature, which I find does not pay; for there has been such a surfeit of poor books that even a good one is now eyed with suspicion.

"At present, however, I am, thanks to Mrs. John Howe, in a comfortable state of wardrobe and purse. You should see this Venus! Who can set bounds to the vanity of woman? (This is in Proverbs, I believe; if it is not it ought to be.) At any rate, woman's vanity is the wire I am now pulling, to keep me in bread and butter.

"Mrs. John Howe is old, ugly, and shrewish; how she *would* rave, if she saw this! All her married life, she has led her husband by the nose. John is a good-natured, easy fellow, with no brains or education to speak of. Latterly, something has turned up between them, deuce knows what, I don't; but Richard is him-self again, smokes when and where he likes, and goes round like the rest of us.

"You will see that he is improving when I tell you that he has bought his wife off to mind her own busi-ness, and let him mind his, by an allowance of so much a year; and here's where the interest of my story comes in, my dear boy, for just so long as I can make Mrs. John believe that she is as young as she ever was, (and as beautiful, as by Jove! she *never* was), and that I can not exist one minute out of her presence, why so much the more hope there is for my tailor and landlady, confound them! *En passant:* I dare say *you* might wince a little at the idea of being supported by a woman; that only shows that you have not yet learned to recognize 'the sovereignty of the indi-

14*

vidual.' But the best thing is yet to come. Mrs.
John imagines herself a blue-stocking! though she
can not spell straight to save her life, and has not the
remotest idea whether Paris is in Prussia or Ireland.
You should hear her mangle Italian, which she has just
begun. It makes my very hair stand on end; I see
where it is all tending. She asked me the other day
about the divorce law; as if I would *marry* the old
vixen! Never mind, so long as the money holds out I
shall hoodwink her even in this.

"Write soon. I saw little Kate last week, fresh as
a Hebe, and beautiful as nobody else ever was, or can
be. Pity she is such a little Puritan! She would be
irresistible were it not for that humbug. I live in hope
that contact with the world, and intercourse with me,
will eradicate this, her only weakness. Bless her sweet
mouth, and witching eyes.

"Yours, as usual,

FINELS."

14*

CHAPTER LI.

"The dirge-like sound of those rapids," said Rose, as she tossed on her pillow at the public-house, at Niagara, vainly courting sleep; "it oppresses me, Gertrude, with an indescribable gloom."

"Your nerves are sadly out of tune, dear Rose; it will be quite another affair to-morrow, *i. e.*, if the sun shines out. Niagara's organ-peal will then be music to you, and the emerald sheen of its rushing waters—the rosy arch, spanning its snowy mist—beautiful beyond your wildest dream! And that lovely island, too. Dear Rose, life, after all, is very beautiful. But how cold your hands are, and how you tremble; let me try my sovereign panacea, music;" and drawing Rose's head to her breast, Gertrude sang—

"Tarry with me, oh, my Saviour!
For the day is passing by;
See! the shades of evening gather,
And the night is drawing nigh.
Tarry with me! tarry with me!
Pass me not unheeded by.

"Dimmed for me is earthly beauty,
Yet the spirit's eye would fain

Rest upon Thy lovely features—
  Shall I seek, dear Lord, in vain?
Tarry with me, oh, my Saviour!
  Let me see Thy smile again.

"Dull my ear to earth-born music;
  Speak Thou, Lord! in words of cheer;
Feeble, faltering, my footstep;
  Leaps my heart with sudden fear.
Cast *Thine* arms, dear Lord, about me,
  Let me feel Thy presence near!"

"Poor Rose," sighed Gertrude, as she kissed her closed lids, laid her head gently back upon the pillow, and released the little hand within her own. "If she could only bear up under this new trial; she is so pure and good that the thought of the sin the world wrongly imputes to her is wearing her life away. This journey, which I hoped would do so much for her, may fail after all. Poor wronged Rose! how can it be right the innocent should thus suffer?" but ere the murmur had found voice the answer came:

"For right is right, since God is God,
  And right the day must win:
To doubt, would be disloyalty—
  To falter, would be sin."

And laying her cheek by the side of Rose, Gertrude slept.

The next day was fine, and the faint smile on Rose's pale face was sweet as the much longed-for sunlight.

Our travelers descended to the ample drawing-room of the hotel to breakfast.

Rose glanced timidly about, scanning the forms which passed before her, as was her wont at a new place, and then the unsatisfied eye drooped beneath its snowy lid; and they who had been struck with the pensive beauty of her face, gazed upon it unnoticed by its object, whose thoughts were far away.

The tall Indian head-waiter was at his post, as purveyor of corn-cakes and coffee; and excellently well as he filled it, Gertrude protested, as an artist, against such a desecration of his fine athletic form and kingly air.

Human nature is, never more *en déshabille* than in traveling; and Gertrude's bump of mirthfulness found ample food in the length and breadth of the well-filled breakfast-table. The jaded pleasure-seekers, whose fashion-filmed eyes were blind to natural beauty, were talking of "doing the Falls in one hour." The little new-made bride sat there with love-swimming eyes, innocently expecting to escape detection in the disguise of a plain brown traveling-dress: pretty little simpleton! and casting such tell-tale glances at her new husband, too! The half-fledged "freshman" was there, with his incipient beard and his first long-tailed coat, making love and bad puns to a knot of his sister's mischief-loving female friends.

In came the pompous city aristocrat, all dignity and shirt-collar, following his abdomen and the waiter with measured steps and supercilious glance, to the court-end of the table. There, too, was the pale student, feasting his book-surfeited eyes on the pleasanter page of young beauty's April face. There, too, the unso-phisticated country girl, too anxious to please, exhaust-ing all her toilet's finery on the breakfast-table. There, too, the poor dyspeptic, surveying with longing eye the tabooed dainties, for which he must pay to Dame Nature if he ate, and to the landlord whether or no.

" Your spirits are at high-water mark this morning," said John to his sister, as Gertrude's quick eye took these notes of her neighbors. " I think you have made up your mind not to grow old. You look as handsome as a picture, this morning."

" As an artist, allow me to tell you that your com-pliment is a doubtful one," said Gertrude. " And as to old age, which is such a bugbear to most of my sex, I assure you it has no terrors for me. My first gray hair will excite in me no regretful emotions."

" Ah ! you can well afford to be philosophic now," retorted John, touching the shining curls around his sister's face.

" You don't believe me ? I assure you that the only terror old age has for me is its helplessness and imbecility. My natural independence revolts at being a burden even to those whom I love ;" and Gertrude's tone had a touch of sadness in it. " You remember old Aunt Hepsy, John ? how long her body outlived her mind; how at eighty years she would beg for tin carts, and soldiers, and rag dolls, and amuse herself by the hour with them, like a little child. This, I confess, is humiliating. In this view I can truly say I dread old age. But the mere thinning of the luxuriant locks, the filming of the bright eye, the shrinking of the rounded limbs, these things give me no heart-pangs in the anticipation. I can not understand the sensitiveness with which most men and women, past the season of youth, hear their age alluded to. It certainly can be no secret, for if Time deal gently with them the family register will not; and if the finger of vanity obliterate all traces of the latter, some toothless old crone yet hobbles, who, forgetful of every thing else, yet remembers the year, week, day, minute, and second in which (without your leave) you were introduced to life's cares and troubles.

"Beside, old age *need* not be repulsive or unlovely," said Gertrude; "look at that aged couple, yonder! How beautiful those silver hairs, how genuine and heart-warming the smile with which they regard each other! To my eye, there is beauty on those furrowed temples, beauty in those wrinkled hands, so kindly outstretched to meet each other's wants. Life's joys and sorrows have evidently knit *their* hearts but more firmly together. What is the mad love of youthful blood to the sun-set effulgence of their setting lives? God bless them!" said Gertrude, as, kindly leaning one on the other, they passed out the hall. "Old age *may* be beautiful!"

"Yes," replied John, "when the heart is kept fresh and green; that which neutralizes the counsels of old age is the ascetic severity with which it too often denounces innocent pleasure, forgetting that the blood which now flows so sluggishly in its veins had once the torrent's mad leap. But look, Gertrude, while I discuss this ham omelette, and see what is in the morning papers."

"Well—in the first place, ' dreadful casualty.' What *would* editors do, I wonder, without these dreadful casualties? I sometimes amuse myself, when I have nothing better to do, in comparing their relative tastes for the horrible, and their skill in dishing it up spicily to the appetites of their various readers. The ingenuity they manifest in this line is quite incredible.

"Observe now, the flippant heartlessness with which these city items, are got up, as if a poor degraded drunkard were the less an object of pity that he had parted with the priceless power of self-resistance! A man who could make a jest of a sight so sad, has sunk lower even than the poor wretch he burlesques.

"Well—let me see—then here are stupid letters from watering-places, got up as pay for the writer's board, at the fashionable hotel, from which they are written and which the transparent writer puffs at every few lines. Then here are some ingenious letters which the editor has written to himself, thanking himself for 'some judicious and sensible editorials which have lately appeared in his columns, and for the general tone of independence and honesty which pervades his admirable paper.' O, dear!" said Gertrude, laughing, "what a thing it is, to be sure, to get a peep behind the scenes!

"Then here is an advertisement headed, 'Women out of employment.' I wonder none of these women have ever thought of going out to do a family's mending by the day or week. I have often thought that a *skillful* hand would meet a hearty welcome, and a ready remuneration, from many an over-tasked mother of a family, who sighs over the ravages of the weekly wash, and whose annual baby comes ever between her and the bottom of the stereotyped 'stocking-basket.'

"But a truce to newspapers, with such a bright sun wooing us out of doors; now for Goat Island; but first let me prepare you for a depletion of your pocketbook in the shape of admiration-fees. You will be twitched by the elbow, plucked by the skirt, solicited with a courtesy or a bow; 'moccasins' to buy from sham squaws—'stuffed beasts' to see by the roadside—'views of Niagara,' done in water-colors, 'for sale,' at rude shanties. Then there will be boys popping from behind trees with 'ornaments made of Table Rock;' disinterested gentlemen desirous to 'take you under the sheet' in a costume that would frighten the mermaids; disinterested owners of spy-glasses 'anxious you should get the best view.' I tell you," said Gertrude, "for a damper the spray is nothing to it! You must be content to cork up your enthusiasm till these 'horse-leech' gentry are appeased.

"Do you know, John, that my '76 blood was quite up to boiling-point the first time I came here, when the toll-keeper on the Canada side demanded what was my business, and how long I intended to stay over there?"

"I can fancy it," said John, laughing; "did you answer him?"

"Not I," said Gertrude, "until I had ascertained that the same catechetical rule held good on the American side. Nevertheless, I would be willing to wager that I could smuggle any thing I pleased into Her Majesty's dominions under the toll-keeper's very nose, had I a mind to try it.

"I wonder," continued Gertrude, after a pause, "could one ever *get used* to Niagara? Could its roar be one's cradle lullaby and the spirit not plume itself for lofty flights? Could one look at it when laughing to scorn stern winter's fetters, as did Sampson the impotent green withes of the Philistines, dashing on in its might, though all Nature beside lay wrapped in old winter's winding-sheet? see it accepting, like some old despot, the tribute of silver moon-beams, golden sun-rays, and a rainbow arch of triumph for its hoary head to pass under;—ever absolute—unconquerable—omnipotent—eternal—as God himself! Could this be the first leaf turned over in Nature's book to the infant's eye, and *not* make it unshrinking as the eagle's?

"Hark! what is that?" exclaimed Gertrude, starting to her feet, and bounding forward with the fleetness of a deer.

Oh, that shriek!

High it rose above Niagara's wildest roar, as the foaming waters engulfed its victim! In the transit of a moment, they who for fourscore years and ten, through storm and sunshine, had walked side by side together, were parted, and forever! With the half-uttered word on his lip—with the love-beam in his eye —he "was not!"

"God comfort her," sobbed Gertrude, as the aged and widowed survivor was carried back insensible to the hotel. "How little we thought this morning, when looking at their happy and united old age, that Death would so unexpectedly step between; and still Niagara's relentless waters plunge down the abyss, shroud and se-pulcher to the loved and lifeless form beneath?"

Serene as the sky when the thunder-cloud has rolled away, calm as the ocean when the moon has lulled its crested waves to sleep, smiling as earth when from off its heaving bosom the waters of the flood were rolled, leaning on Him who is the "widow's God and Husband," the aged mourner whispered, "It is well."

"God has been so good to me," she said to Gertrude. "He has lifted the cloud even at the tomb's portal. Listen, my child, and learn to trust in Him who is the believer's Rock of Ages.

"The first years of my wedded life were all brightness. We were not rich, but Love sweetens labor, and so that we were only spared to each other (my husband and I), for us there could be no sorrow. Children blessed us, bright, active, and healthy, and, hugging my idols to my heart, I forgot to look beyond. I saw the dead borne past my door, but the sunshine still lay over my own threshhold. I saw the drunkard reel past, but *my* mountain stood strong! As I rocked my baby's cradle, my heart sang to its sweet smile—earth only seemed near, eternity a great way off. To-day I knew was bliss—the future, what was it? A riddle which puzzled the wisest; and I was not wise, only happy. Alas, the worm was creeping silently on toward the root of my gourd. It was 'the worm of the still.' One by one its leaves fell off. Silently but relentlessly he did his blighting work. Where plenty ruled, poverty came—clouds in place of sunshine—sobs for smiles—curses for kisses—tears for laughter.

"Bitter tears fell when they rolled by me in their carriages, whose wealth was coined from my heart's blood; but I did not chide *him ;* I toiled and sorrowed on, for still I loved. I know not where the strength came to labor, still I found my babes and him bread;

but, as week after week rolled by, and the reeling form still staggered past me, my heart grew faint and sick; for the hand which had never been raised save to bless us, now dealt the cruel blow; and the children who had been wont to wait for his coming, and to climb his knee, now cowered when they heard his unsteady footsteps. Each day I hoped against hope, for some change for the better, but it came not.

"One day a thought occurred to me by which I might perchance keep the demon at bay; I would watch the moment at which this craving thirst took possession of my husband. I would give him a substitute in the shape of strong hot chocolate, of which he was inordinately fond; I denied myself every comfort to procure it. I prepared it exactly to his taste—it was ready to the minute that the tempting fiend was wont to whisper in his ear. I was first upon the ground; I forestalled the demon. The sated appetite heeded not his Judas entreaties. My husband smiled on me again, he called me his saviour, his preserver; he again entered the shop of his employer; it was near the house, so it was easy for me to run over with the tempting beverage; I watched him night and day; I anticipated his every wish; my husband was again clothed, and in his right mind; we both learned our dependence on a stronger arm than each other's. Riches came with industry, our last days were our best days.

"And now, my dear child," and the old lady smiled

through her tears, " there is music to my ears, even in those rushing waters, for he who sleeps beneath them fills no *drunkard's* grave. What matters it by what longer or shorter road we travel, so that heaven be gained at last ?"

CHAPTER LII.

"DID I not tell you that old age was beautiful?" exclaimed Gertrude, to Rose, as they sought the privacy of their own apartments. "The world talks of 'great deeds' (ambition-nurtured though they be), yet who chronicles these beautiful unobtrusive acts of feminine heroism beneath hundreds of roof-trees in our land? too common to be noted, save by the recording angel! Now I understand the meaning of Solomon's words, 'Blessed is the man who hath a virtuous wife, for the number of his days shall be doubled.'

"Confess you are better, *ma petite*," and Gertrude kissed Rose's pale forehead; "nothing better helps us to bear our own troubles than to learn the struggles of other suffering hearts, and how many unwritten tragedies are locked up in memory's cabinet, pride only yielding up the keys to inexorable death!

"Sometimes, Rose, when I am mercilessly at war with human nature, I appease myself by jotting down the *good* deeds of every day's observation; and it has been a tonic to my fainting hopes to have seen the poor beggar divide his last crust with a still poorer one who had none; to see the sinewy arm of youth opportunely offered in the crowded streets to timorous, feeble, and *obscure* old age; to see the hurried man of business stop in the precious forenoon hours, to hunt up the whereabouts of some stray little weeping child; or to see the poor servant-girl bestow half her weekly earnings in charity. These things restore my faith in my kind, and keep the balance even, till some horribly selfish wretch comes along and again kicks the scales!

" And now Charley must needs be waking up there —see him! looking just as seraphic as if *he* never meant to be a little sinner! The tinting of a sea-shell could not be more delicate than that cheek; see the faultless outline of his profile against the pillow; look at his dimpled arms and fat little calves; and that little plump cushion of a foot. Was there ever any thing so seducing? I wish that child belonged to me.

" See here, Rose, look at those ladies pacing up and down the long hall, armed for conquest to the teeth. What an insatiable appetite for admiration they must needs have, to make such an elaborate toilet in the dog-days! Nothing astonishes me like the patient endurance of these fashionists at the watering-places; prisoning themselves within doors lest the damp air should uncurl a ringlet; wearing gloves with the thermometer at ninety in the shade; soliciting wasp-waists in the very face of consumption. They are what I call 'the working people;' for your mechanic has the liberty of cooling himself in his shirt-sleeves, and your sempstress, though Nature may have furnished her no hips, does not perspire in interminable piles of skirts. Rose, imagine the old age of such women—no resource but the looking-glass, and that at last casting melancholy *reflections* in their faces. Not that vanity is confined to the female sex—(Come in, John, you are just in time). I am about to give you an exemplification of the remark I have just hazarded, in the history of Theodore Vanilla.

"River House was full of summer boarders when I first saw him there; nursery-maids and children *ad infinitum;* ladies in profusion, whose husbands and brothers went and returned morning and evening to their business in the city.

"Of course the ladies were left to themselves in the middle of the day, and some of the most mischievous verified the truth of the old primer-adage; that 'Satan finds some mischief still for idle hands to do.' Theodore was their unconscious butt, and they made the most of him.

"Every evening they assembled on the piazza when the cars came in, and 'hoped,' with anxious faces, 'that Mr. Vanilla had not concluded to remain over night in the city.' The self-satisfied smile with which he would step up on the piazza rub his hands, and his

15

" ' Now really, ladies,'

" As he turned delightedly from one to the other, were a picture for Hogarth.

" Then after tea there was a preconcerted dispute among them, which should monopolize him 'for their evening walk;' and the innocence with which he would reply to all this fore-ordained wrangling,

" ' Now ladies *don't* quarrel, and I 'll engage to take turns with you,'

" Was too much for mortal risibles.   One lady would affect the sulks that 'he did not sit next her at table;' another, that 'he did not, like a true knight, wear her colors in the hue of his cravat.' Enveloped in his panoply of self-conceit, he was tossed back and forth on this female hornet's-nest, an agonized, but delighted victim.

" On one occasion a gentleman, jealous for his sex's honor, whispered to one of the lady ringleaders—

" ' You are too relentless; I really think this is wrong.'

" ' Do you!' answered the pretty tyrant, with an arch smile; 'I will engage one could throw just such a dust in the eyes of any gentleman you might select in this house (including yourself), even with this example before your and their eyes.' "

" Gertrude," said John, reprovingly, " do you remember what Solomon says—

"'A *wise* woman have I not found?'"

"John," mimicked Gertrude, "do you know the reason of Solomon's failure? It was because he met with a *pretty* woman, and forgot to look for a *wise* one!"

CHAPTER LIII.

"Good evening, Balch. Bless me! how gloomy you look here, after coming from the glare and music of the opera, its ladies and its jewels; you are as good as a nightmare, sitting there with your one bachelor candle, keeping that miserable fire company. One would think your veins were turned to ice, or that there was not a bright eye left in the world to make the blood leap through them. Turn up the gas, sing us a song, hand out a cigar; you are as solemn as a sexton."

"I dare say," replied Balch, in a melancholy key, as he languidly turned on the gas for his friend, and set a box of cigars before him. "I know I am not good company, so I shall not advise you to stay."

"A woman in the case, I dare be sworn," said Gerritt, lighting a cigar, "Lord bless 'em, they are always at the top and bottom of every thing!"

Balch gave the anthracite a poke, crossed his slippered feet, folded his arms, and looked at Gerritt.

"I knew it," said Gerritt. "I am acquainted with all the symptoms of that malady; let 's have it, Balch;

you can tell me nothing new in the way of woman's twistings and turnings. Bless 'em!"

"Bless 'em?" exclaimed Balch, unfolding his arms, placing both hands on his knees and staring in Gerritt's face. "Bless 'em?"

"Yes; bless 'em. I knew what I was saying, well enough. Bless 'em, I repeat, for if they do not give a man more than five rapturous moments in a life time, it is well worth being born for. Fact;" said Gerritt, as the speechless Balch continued gazing at him.

"Did you ever see Mrs. Markham?" asked Balch, finding voice.

The solemnity with which he asked the question, and his whole *tout ensemble* at that moment, was too much for Gerritt, who burst into an uproarious laugh.

"Ah, you may laugh," said Balch, "it is all very well; but I wish there was not a woman in the world."

"Horrible!" said Gerritt. "I shan't join you there; but who was this Mrs. Markham?"

Balch moved his chair nearer to Gerritt, and shutting his teeth very closely together, hissed through them,

"The very d—l."

"Is that all?" said the merry philosopher. "So is every woman, unless you get the right side of her. Women are like cats; you must 'poor' them, as the children say, the right way of the fur, unless you want them to scratch. I suppose you did not understand managing her."

"Were you ever on a committee of an Orphan Asylum?" asked Balch, solemnly.

"No—no;" laughed Gerritt. "Why, Balch, I beg pardon on my knees, for calling you and your den here, funereal; I have not laughed so hard for a twelvemonth."

"Because," said Balch, not heeding his friend's raillery; "*I have*, and Mrs. Markham was the matron."

"O—h—I see," said Gerritt. "You thought her an angel, and *she* thought that *you* thought the children under her care were well cared for, when they were not; is that it?"

"Ex-actly," said Balch, in admiration of his friend's penetration; "it was awful how that woman deceived every body. I don't mind myself, though I must say that I never want to see any thing that wears a petticoat again, till the day of my death; but those poor children, I can't get over it; and I one of the investigating committee, too! It was infamous that I did not look into things closer. But, Gerritt, you see, that Mrs. Markham—" and Balch looked foolish.

"I understand;" said Gerritt. "I see the whole game; well, what did you say about it? I suppose you did not content yourself with resigning?"

"No, indeed, and that comforts me a little. I had her turned out. I don't suppose (she was so plausible) that I should have believed Gabriel himself, had he told me any thing against her; but I saw her with my own eyes one day, when I called unexpectedly, abuse those children. She did not know I was within hearing, and tried afterward to gloss it over; it would n't do; and then, when the scales had fallen off my eyes, I looked back and saw a great many other things to which that scene gave me the clew. Then I went to Timmins and Watkins, two of her assistants, and after making me promise not to get them into any difficulty about it, they told me things that would make your very flesh creep; and I one of the investigating committee; but that Mrs. Markham was—"

"I have no doubt of it," said Gerritt; "but, my dear fellow, there is always a drop of consolation to be squeezed out of every thing. Suppose you had married her!"

Balch jammed the poker furiously into the anthracite, shaking his head mournfully the while, and the laughing Gerritt withdrew.

"Yes, yes," said Balch, "that *is* lucky; but poor little Tibbie! poor little Tibbie! that will not bring *her* back to life; and poor little Rose, too—and I one of the investigating committee! It is dreadful."

CHAPTER LIV.

The moon shone brightly on the trellised piazza of the —— House, at Niagara. The sleepy house-porter had curled himself up in the hall corner ; the sonorous breathings of weary travelers might be heard through the open windows, for the night was warm and sultry. Two persons still lingered on the piazza. Judging from their appearance, they were not tempted by the beauty of the night. Ensconced in the shadow of the further corner, they were earnestly engaged in conversation.

"I tell you she is in this house ; I saw her name on the books—'Gertrude Dean,' your ex-wife. What do you think of that—hey ?"

"The d—l!" exclaimed Stahle. "I can *swear*, now that I am out of school, you know, Smith."

"Of course," replied the latter, laughing ; "the only wonder is, how you manage to get along with so few vacations. To my mind, swearing lets off the steam wonderfully."

"How long has this admirable spouse of mine been here ?" asked Stahle.

"Don't know. Did n't like to ask questions, you know, until I had first spoken to you. She's flush of money, of course, or she could not stay here, where they charge so like the deuce. I should think it would gall you a little, Stahle, and you so out of pocket."

"It would," said the latter, with another oath, "had I not the way of helping myself to some of it."

"How's that? The law does not allow you to touch her earnings, now you are divorced."

"All women are fools about law matters. She don't know that," sneered Stahle. "She is probably traveling alone, and I will frighten her into it—that's half the battle. I owe her something for the cool way she walked round all the traps I sprung for her, without getting caught. I thought when I left her that she would just fold her hands, and let the first man who offered find her in clothes, on his own terms, for she never was brought up to work, and I knew she had no relations that would give her any thing but advice;" and Stahle gave a low, chuckling laugh.

"You see I always look all round before I leap, Smith. I can't understand it now, and I never have, why she did n't do as I expected, for she might have had lovers enough. She was good-looking, and it was what I reckoned on to sustain the rumors I took care to circulate about her before I left; but what does she do but shut herself up, work night and day, and give the lie to every one of them. I wrote to my brother,

Fred, to try every way to catch her tripping, to track her to every boarding-house she went to, and hint things to the landlord, carefully, of course. Fred knows how to do it; but you know if a woman does nothing but mind her own business, and never goes into company, a rumor against her will very soon die out. I kept spies constantly at work, but it was no use, confound her; but some of her money I will have. Here she is living in clover, going to the Springs, and all that; while I am a poor clerk in a grocery store. I feel as cheap when any Eastern man comes in, and recognizes me there, as if I had been stealing. I won't stand it; Mrs. Gertrude Dean, as she calls herself, has got to hand over the cash. If I can't ruin her reputation, I'll have some of her money."

" You advertised her in the papers, did n't you, when you left?—(after the usual fashion, ' harboring and trusting,' and all that)—were you afraid she would run you in debt?"

" Devil a bit; she's too proud for that; she would have starved first."

" Why did you do it, then?"

" To mortify her confounded pride," said Stahle, with a diabolical sneer, " and to injure her in public estimation. That stroke, at least, told for a time."

" A pretty set of friends she must have had," said Smith, " to have stood by and borne all that."

" Oh, I knew *them* all, root and branch. I knew I

could go to the full length of my rope without any of
their interference. In fact, their neglect of her helped
me more than any thing else. Every body said I must
have been an injured man, and that the stories I had
circulated *must* be true about her, or they would certainly have defended and sheltered her. I knew them
—I knew it would work just so; that was so much in
my favor, you see."

" They liked you, then ?"

Stahle applied his thumbs to the end of his nose,
and gave another diabolical sneer.

" Liked me! Humph! They all looked down on
me as a vulgar fellow. I was tolerated, and that was
all—hardly that."

" I don't understand it, then," said Smith.

" I do, though; if they *defended* her, they would
have no excuse for not helping her. It was the cash,
you see, the cash! so they preferred siding with me,
vulgar as they thought me. I knew them—I knew
how it would work before I began."

" Well, I suppose this is all very interesting to you,"
said Smith, yawning, " but as I am confounded tired
and sleepy, and as it is after midnight, I shall wish
you good-night."

" Good-night," said Stahle. " I shall smoke another
cigar while I arrange my plans. This is the last quiet
night's sleep 'Mrs. Gertrude Dean' will have for some
time, I fancy."

"Scoundrel!" exclaimed John, leaping suddenly upon the piazza through his low parlor window. "Scoundrel! I have you at last," and well aimed and vigorous were the blows which John dealt his sister's traducer.

Your woman slanderer is invariably a coward—the very nature of his offense proves it. There never was one yet who dared face a man in fair fight; and so on his knees Stahle pleaded like a whipped cur for mercy.

"Go, cowardly brute," said John, kicking him from the piazza. "If you are seen here after daylight, the worse for you."

"Very strange," muttered Smith the next morning, "very strange. Something unexpected must have turned up to send Stahle off in such a hurry. Well, he is a sneaking villain. I am bad enough, but what I do is open and above board. I don't say prayers or sing psalms to cover it up. I don't care whether I ever hear from him again or not."

15*

CHAPTER LV.

"How radiant you look this morning," exclaimed Gertrude, in astonishment, as she opened Rose's chamber door, and sat down by her bed-side; "your eyes have such a dazzling sparkle, and your cheeks such a glow. What is it, *ma petite?*" she asked, still gazing on the speechless Rose.

"Vincent is not dead," said Rose, slowly and oracularly, "Vincent is not false. The weight has gone from here, Gertrude," laying her hand on her heart. "I shall see him, though I can not tell you how nor where; but he will come back to me and Charley. I saw him last night in my dream—so noble—so good—but, oh! so wan, with the weary search for me. I hid my face—I could not look in his eyes—for I had doubted him—but he forgave me; oh! Gertrude, it was blessed, the clasp of those shadowy arms," and Rose smiled, and closed her eyes again, as if to shut out the sight of all that might dim her spiritual vision.

"Poor—poor Rose!" murmured Gertrude, terrified at the idea which forced itself upon her, "reason gone! Poor Rose!" and as she gazed, the warm tears fell upon the pillow.

Gertrude passed her soft hand magnetizingly over Rose's closed lids and temples; gradually the bright flush left her cheek, and she sank quietly to sleep.

"Was this to be the end of all Rose's sufferings? God forbid," murmured Gertrude. "Death itself were preferable to this," said she, her eyes still riveted on the beauty of that pale, childish face.

"Hush!" whispered Gertrude, with her finger on her lips, as her brother rapped on the door for her; she little thought that she had an unread page in her own eventful history to turn.

"I am so glad I did not see him," exclaimed she, when her brother finished his narration. "I should have felt as if a rattlesnake lay coiled in my path. He deserved his chastisement; and yet, John, I do not like this whipping system; it always seems to me as if a gentleman who stooped to it put himself on a level with the villain whom he punished."

"It is the only way, Gertrude," said the doctor; "especially where the law gives no redress. Besides, it is the only thing that appeals to that kind of fellow."

"But he is so vindictive;" said Gertrude, looking apprehensively at her brother, "he may lay coiled like a wounded snake, but he will yet make a spring."

"You forget that his Christian reputation stands in the way of any such little personal gratification," said John, sarcastically.

"He has been able, though, heretofore, to make a compromise with it," said Gertrude.

"Ah! he had only a woman to deal with," answered John, "and one whom he knew would suffer in silence, as many an injured high-minded woman has done before, rather than sacrifice the delicacy of her sex, by publicly brandishing the cudgel in her own defense, even in a righteous cause. *I* shall have no such scruples, and you will see that he understands it. A good sound flagellation is the only 'moral suasion' for such women tyrants; it is only against the defenseless such cowards dare wage war."

"Let us talk of something else," said Gertrude; and she related to John what had transpired between her and Rose.

John looked very grave, and sat absorbed in thought.

"I knew it would trouble you," said Gertrude; "it would be so dreadful should she lose her reason."

"I do not fear that," replied John; "I do not think her mind was wandering when she told you her dream. I think you will find that she will be perfectly sane when she wakes.

"Her dream,"—and John hesitated, "may prove true; stranger things have happened. Stronger chains of evidence than that which apparently overthrew her hopes have been snapped in twain, and, if—he should—be living—if—he—should prove worthy of her—dear as she is to me, I feel Gertrude, that my love is capable of self-sacrifice. I will use my best endeavors to bring them together.

"I shall never love again," said John; "I shall never see another woman who will so satisfy my soul, so pure, so childlike, so trusting, and yet so strong, so immovable in what she considers right—so vastly superior to all other women. I *had* woven bright dreams, in which she had a part," and John walked to the window to conceal his emotion.

Gertrude did not follow him; she knew from experience that there are moments when the presence even of the dearest friend is a restraint, when the overcharged spirit must find relief only in solitude and self-communing, and with a heart yearning with tenderness toward her brother, she stole softly from his presence.

CHAPTER LVI.

"Don't talk to me, Mrs. Howe," said her husband, slamming to the door, and dumping down in his arm-chair as if to try the strength of the seat. "If there is any thing I hate, Mrs. Howe, it is that tribe of popinjays, one of whom has just gone through that door; hate don't express it, Mrs. Howe, I detest, and abominate, and despise him."

"Well, now, Mr. Howe, I am athtonithed," lisped his wife, that lady not having yet accommodated her speech to the play of her new set of teeth. "I am thure he ith the moth elegant and refined and thivil thpoken young man I ever thaw; I never heard him thay an offenthive thing to any one in my life."

"Of course you haven't, Mrs. Howe; and that's just what I hate him for; a man who is so loaded and primed with civil speeches is always rotten at the core. I always steer clear of such a fellow," said John, forgetting the compliments to himself which he had heretofore swallowed.

"That man never sneezes without calculating the effect of it; he has the same smile and bow and ob-

sequious manner for every body; it is his aim to be
popular, and it may go down with women and soft-
headed men, but he don't take John Howe in. He is
an oily-tongued hypocrite. That's plain Saxon, Mrs.
Howe. I am astonished at you—no, I am not, either,"
said John, slamming himself down again into the
chair.

"Mrs. Howe!"

And John wheeled his chair close up to her, "did n't
you hear him the other day, when that tiresome, stupid
Mrs. Frink was here, inquire so touchingly after a bad
cough which he recollected she had when he met her
a year ago? Did you see the effect it had on the silly
old thing? I wonder she got out the door without
having it widened, she was so puffed up.

"Mrs. Howe!"

And John moved up still closer, "if that man should
meet our old cat in the entry after a month's absence,
he'd take off his hat, and inquire after that very pre-
cocious kitten of hers he had the pleasure of seeing
on the stairs when he was last here. Fact—I'm
astonished at you, Mrs. Howe," and John dumped
himself down again into the chair; "the man is a
jackass, a fool, a perfume-bottle on legs—faugh!

"Mrs. Howe!"

And John wheeled round again, "did n't he upset
that old squirrel-eyed Miss Price, by repeating a com-
mon-place remark of hers which she made him two

or three years ago, and which he had the brass to
say struck him so forcibly at the time that he never
forgot it? Did n't she go home in the full belief
that she had up to that time been terribly under-
rated by her folks at home? Certainly;—now do
you suppose he does all that for nothing, Mrs.
Howe? No—he gets his pay out of you all by an
invitation to a good dinner. He does the same here,
whenever it is more convenient to stop here than down
town, and then you and all the rest of these silly
women become his trumpeters.

"For his fine speeches to steamboat captains, he gets
a free pass in their boats; landlords of hotels, ditto;
that 's it, Mrs. Howe.

"I am astonished at you, Mrs. Howe.

"He gets presents of hats, presents of coats, presents
of canes, presents of pictures, presents of books and
stationery.

"As for the women, of course, as I said before, such
flummery takes them right down—just as it did you,
Mrs. Howe.

"May he be strangled in his pink and blue cravat
before he comes here to another dinner.

"That 's right, Jonathan, come in," said Mr. Howe,
as an unpolished, but good-hearted country cousin
strode over the carpet in his thick-soled boots; "that 's
right. You have come just in time to save me from
being sick at the stomach; sit down—any where, top

of the piano if you like ; put your feet on that Chinese
work-table, and hang your hat on that Venus. It will
do me good. And give me that bit of hay sticking on
your outside coat. Let us have something natural,
somehow."

Mrs. Howe retired in disgust, although she was too
much under the yoke to make any remonstrance, which
she felt sure would be thrown *in her teeth !*

In default of any more children, Mrs. Howe, like
many other ladies similarly situated, consoled herself
with her dog, Consuelo.

Seating herself in what she called her " boudoir," a
little room whose walls were covered with red satin
paper, which Mrs. Howe imagined particularly in harmony with her rubicund complexion, she took Consuelo
on her lap, and stroking his long silken ears, said :
" How like Mr. Howe, to prefer that clumsy country
cousin of his to the elegant Finels. There is just the
same difference between them that there is between
you, my lovely Consuelo, and that hideous yellow
terrier of the butcher's boy. I think I may say,
Consuelo, that both you and I are quite thrown away
in this house," and wrapping her pet in his embroidered blanket, she laid him down in her lap to sleep.

" Jealous ! ah, ha ! That 's it, Consuelo. That is
what sets Mr. Howe so against Finels ; as for his coming here for our good dinners, that is all sheer nonsense.
He sees plainly enough, with all his politeness to John,

that I am miserably sacrificed to him. I was not aware of it myself until after I became acquainted with Mr. Finels. Finels always pays so much attention when I speak. John, on the contrary, half the time, does not seem to hear me. It is not at all uncommon for him to leave the room or to fall asleep in the middle of one of my conversations. It is very irritating to a sensible woman. Finels always remembers some little remark I have made him. I think I must have been in the habit of throwing away a great many good things on John. John has grown very stupid since I married him.

"Finels says such pretty French words; I have not the slightest idea what they mean, but doubtless there is some delicate compliment conveyed in them, if I only understood the language. I think I will study French. Oh! that would be delightful, and then John can't understand a word dear Finels and I say;" and Mrs. Howe tied on her hat, and went in pursuit of a French grammar.

"What on earth is this?" exclaimed Mrs. Howe, as she entered the parlor two hours after, with her French bonnet and French grammar. "What on earth is this?" applying a tumbler which stood on the center-table to her nose, and tasting some remaining crumbs in a plate.

"What is it?" repeated John, puffing away, not at the chibouk, but at the old clay pipe. "What is it?

Why, it is the dregs of some molasses and water Jonathan has been drinking, and those crumbs are all that remain of a loaf of brown bread, for which I sent Mary to the grocer's. If he likes country fare he shall have it —why not, as well as your superfine Finels his olives, and sardines, and gimcracks? I pay the ' damages,' you know, Mrs. Howe;" and John's eye gave a triumphant twinkle.

"Of course, my dear—of course," replied that subjugated lady; " it is all right, my dear, and does great credit to your kindness of heart; but it is such a *very* odd, old-fashioned taste, you know ;" and applying her embroidered handkerchief to her nose, she motioned Mary to remove the remains of the homespun feast.

CHAPTER LVII.

OLD Mrs. Bond had taken her station on the sunny side of her piazza. Mrs. Bond was no sentimentalist, as I have said before. She had never read a line of poetry in her life; but she had read her Bible, and she loved to watch the glorious sun go down, and think of the golden streets of the New Jerusalem, with its gates of pearl, and walls of jasper. Many a blessed vision from that sunset-seat had she seen with her spiritual eyes; and many a sealed passage in the Holy Book which lay upon her lap, had then, and there, and thus, been solved; and many a prayer had gone from thence swift-winged to heaven.

The Bible contains great and mighty truths which none of us may safely reject; but apart from this, no mind, how uncultivated soever, can be familiar with its glowing beauty and sublimity, without being unconsciously refined.

Oh! how many times, even to the God-forgetting, has the beauty of its imagery come home with a force and aptness which no uninspired pen, how gifted soever, could rival!

How vital and immovably lodged, though buried for years under the dust of worldliness, its wise and indisputable precepts!

How like a sun-flash they sometimes illume what else were forever mystery-shrouded!

And now the last tint of gold and crimson had faded out, and one bright star sparkled like a gem on the brow of the gray old mountain, behind which the sun had sank—bright as the Star of Bethlehem to Judea's gazing shepherds, and like them, Mrs. Bond knelt and worshiped.

Broad as the world was her Bible-creed: it embraced all nations, all colors, all sects. Whosoever did the will of God the same was her father, sister, and mother; and like the face of Moses when he came down from the mount, hers shone that evening with the reflected glory of heaven.

The traveler could not have told, as he stopped before that little brown house, and stepped on its homely piazza, *why* he raised his hat with such an involuntary deference to the unpretending form before him; *why* his simple " Good evening, madam," should have been so reverently spoken; but so it was; and the kind old lady's welcome to a seat by her frugal board was just as unaccountably to himself accepted.

The traveler was a tall, dark-browed man, with a face and form which must have been once pre-eminently attractive; but now, his fine dark eyes were sunken, as if grief, or sickness, perhaps both, had weighed heavily there; and his tall form seemed bent with weakness. All this his kind hostess noted, and her nicest cup of tea was prepared, and the wholesome loaf set before him, and a blessing craved over it, from lips which knew no fear of man, with Heaven in sight. Perhaps this touched a chord to which the stranger's heart vibrated, for his eyes grew moist with unshed tears, and his voice was tremulous when he addressed his hostess.

"Can you tell me, madam, how far it is to the nearest inn?"

"A weary way, sir—a matter of fifteen miles, and you so feeble. You are quite welcome to stay here, sir, till morning; and your horse will be well content in yonder pasture."

"You are very kind, madam," said the stranger, hesitatingly; then adding with a smile, "travelers who have preceded me on this road must have borne a good name."

"There is nothing here to tempt a thieving hand," said Mrs. Bond. "I seldom think at night of barring yonder door. Where one's trust is in an Almighty arm, there is little room for fear.

"I can remember when yonder broad oak was but a sapling. I was born and married here, sir; through that door my husband and child passed to their long home. My time can not be long; but while

I stay, every stone and twig in this place is dear to me."

" With pleasant memories for company, one can not be lonesome," replied the stranger.

" No—and sad ones may be made pleasant, if one only knows how," and she laid her withered hand on the Bible.

As she did so a paper fluttered out from between its leaves. " Sometimes, though," said she, as she took it up, " one's faith is sorely tried.

" This now—this letter—it was from my child. I called her my child, and yet no blood of mine ever flowed in her veins; and she called me ' mother,' be-cause my heart warmed to her; God knows she had sore need of it, poor lamb.

" An old woman like myself may speak plain words, sir. He who was her child's father left her to weep over it alone. It was heart-breaking to see the poor young thing try to bear up, try to believe that he whom her innocent heart trusted, would turn out worthy of its love; but sometimes she would quite break down with the grief; and when she grew fretful with it, I did not chide her, because I knew her heart was chafed and sore.

" Her's was such a lovely babe; so bright, and handsome, and winsome. *She* was good and loving too. She had not sinned. She had been deceived and wronged. So she could not bear the taunting word, sir; and when it came, unexpectedly to us, she fled away like a hunted deer, through yonder door, till her poor strength gave out, and then we found her and the babe just like dead.

"I brought her home, and nursed her along, and thought to keep her, and make it all easy for her; but her young heart pined for *him*—she fancied, poor child, she could find him, and the world so wide—and that he would lift her pure brow in the taunting world's face, and call her ' wife ;' and so she fled away in the night, no one knew whither, and left me this letter, sir. My eyes are dim—but I have no need to read it, for the words come up to me by day and by night; read it yourself, sir—mayhap in your travels, you may hear of the poor young thing—I should so like to know of her, before I die.

"The light is but dim, sir," said the old lady, as the traveler took it in his hand, and held the letter between his face and Mrs. Bond's.

Yes—the light *was* dim, so were the traveler's eyes; he must have been sadly feeble too, for his hands trembled so that he could scarcely hold the letter.

"And you never heard from her, after this?" he asked, his eyes still riveted on the letter.

"Not a word, sir; it makes me so sad when I think of it; perhaps she may be dead."

"Perhaps so," answered the traveler, shuddering.

"May be you could make some inquiries, sir, if it

would not trouble you, as you go along; her name
was Rose, though she looked more like a lily when
she left us, poor thing! Rose—and her lover's name
was Vincent; perhaps you may have heard of *him*."

"The name sounds familiar," said the stranger;
"perhaps I shall be able to get some clew to it."

"Thank you," said Mrs. Bond, gratefully; "and
now, sir, as I get up early I go to rest early; so, if
you please, I will show you your room; it is very
plain—but it is all the spare one I have. It was poor
Rose's room;" and Mrs. Bond taking her candle, led
the way to it.

"There," said she, setting the light down upon the
table, "many a time when she stood at that little window, sir, she and the babe, people stopped here to ask
who they were, they were both so handsome, and so
different from our country folks.

"On that very little table she left her letter; it was
a long time before I could come here and feel that it
was all right she should suffer so, although I know
that God's ways are just; but I shall know all about
it when I get to heaven; perhaps it was only 'the
narrow way' to take *her* there—who knows? I would
rather be Rose than they who brought her here; and
yet," said the mild old lady, hesitatingly, "perhaps
they *thought* they did right, but riches make us take
strange views of things; it takes grace to be a *rich*
Christian. And when I feel displeased with Mrs.

Howe's heartlessness, I say, *money* might have turned *me* aside too—who knows? Good-night, sir; heaven send you sweet sleep;" and Mrs. Bond went down into her small kitchen.

And it was here—in this very room, that Rose had wept, and suffered, and wrestled with her great sorrow! On that very pillow her aching head vainly sought rest; at that window she had sat thinking— thinking—till brain and heart grew sick, and God himself seemed to have forsaken her; and down that road she had fled, like a hunted deer, with slander's cruel arrow rankling in her quivering heart!

Not on *that* pillow could sleep our weary traveler.

At the little window he sat and saw the night-shadows deepen, and only the shivering trees, as the night-wind crept through them, made answer to his low moan,

"Rose! Rose!"

CHAPTER LVIII.

"Dear Tom,—

"I am glad you are going abroad. You see I *can* be unselfish. How I wish *I* were going! Of course you mean to take notes on the way. For Heaven's sake, if you do, don't bore us with re-vamping the travelers' guide-book, like all your predecessors; don't prate stereotyped stupidities about Madonnas, and Venuses, and Gladiators, or go mad over a bit of Vesuvius lava, or wear Mont Blanc or the Rhine threadbare. Spare us also all egotistical descriptions of your dinners and breakfasts with foreign literary lions, and great lords and ladies. Strike out a new path, 'an thou lovest me, Hal, or I will write your book down with one dash of my puissant goose-quill.

"Mrs. John has gone to the dogs. Well, listen, and I will tell you. As John's allowance to her grew fitful, so did my attentions; a man can not live on air you know, or waste his time where it will not pay. Mrs. John pouted, and I whistled. Mrs. John coaxed, and I sulked. Mrs. John took to drinking, and I took

French leave, making love to little Kate, who, I hear, has lately had a fortune left her. Well, I had quite lost sight of old Mrs. John for some months; I only knew that her husband was a hanger-on at Gripp's gambling-house, and, like all steady fellows when they break loose, was out-heroding Herod in every sort of dissipation, leaving Mrs. John to take care of herself.

"Well, the other night Harry and I—you remember Harry? that clever dog who always beat us at billiards—Harry and I were coming home about midnight, when we came across a policeman dragging off a woman, who was swearing at him like a privateersman. That was nothing to us, you know, or would not have been, had I not heard my name mentioned. I turned my head; the light from the gas-lamp fell full upon her bloated face, and, by Jove! if it was not old Mrs. John! her clothes half torn off her in the drunken scuffle, looking like the very witch of Endor. Was n't it a joke? She died that night, at the station-house, of delirium tremens, shrieking for 'John,' and 'Rose,' and 'Finels,' and the deuce knows who. So we go. Have you seen the new danseuse, Felissitimi? If not, do so by all means when she comes to Baltimore. She will dance straight into your heart with her first *pas*. I'm off, like all the world, to see her.   "As ever, yours,

                                        "FINELS."

CHAPTER LIX.

"AND here we are in Boston!" said Gertrude. "Find me any thing lovelier than this Common," she exclaimed, as she seated herself under the trees one sweet summer morning.

"See! Beyond Charles River the hills stretch away in the distance, while the fragrant breath of their woods and hay-fields come wafted on every passing breeze.

"And the Common! one might look till the eye grows weary through those long shady vistas, on whose smoothly-trodden paths the shifting sunlight scarce finds place, through the leafy roofs, to play.

"Look, Rose, at those lovely children gamboling on the velvet grass, fresher and sweeter than the clover-blossoms they hide in their bosoms.

"See! Up springs the fountain! like the out-gushing of Nature's full heart at its own sweet loveliness; leaping upward, then falling to earth again, only to rise with fresher beauty. No aristocratic 'park' key keeps out the poor man's child, for Bunker Hill lifts its granite finger of warning there in the distance, and the little plebeian's soiled fingers are as welcome to pluck the butter-cups as his more dainty little neighbor's.

"God be thanked for that!" said Gertrude. "I well remember one balmy summer morning in New York, when my gipsy feet carried me out over the pavements in search of a stray blade of grass or a fresh blossom. My new dress was an 'open sesame' to one of the 'locked parks' under the charge of an old gardener. Lovely flowers were there, odorous shrubs, and graceful trees. The children of the privileged few, daintily clad, played in its nicely-graveled, shady walks.

"It was beautiful; but outside, the poor man's child, hollow-eyed and sad, crouched that balmy morning on the heated pavement, pressing his pale face close against the iron rails, looking and longing, as only the children of poverty *can* look and long, into that forbidden Eden!

"It made my heart ache. I could not walk there. That little pale, sad face haunted me at every step. The very flowers were less sweet, the drooping trees less graceful, and the lovely green hedge seemed some tyrant jailor, within whose precincts my very breath grew thick; and so," said Gertrude, "I thank God for this 'Common'—free to all—yes, *Common*. I like the homely, democratic word.

"Not that there is no aristocracy in Boston," said she, laughing; "on the contrary, the Beacon-street millionaire, whose father might have made his *début* three years ago as a tin peddler, looks down contemptuously

16*

on those who live outside this charmed locality. The
Boston Unitarian never dreams of sharing the same
heaven as the Boston Presbyterian, and this is the only
platform on which he and the Boston Presbyterian
meet! And 'High Church' and 'Low Church' are
fenced off and labeled, with a touch-me-not preci-
sion, for which the 'Great Shepherd of the sheep' furnished no precedent.

" Still, Boston is a nice little place. One does not,
as in New York, need to drive all the afternoon to get
out into the country. Start for an afternoon drive in
New York, you have your choice between the unmitigated gutter of its back streets, or a half hour's block-
ading of your wheels every fifteen minutes, in the more
crowded thoroughfares. Add to this your detention at
the ferry, blocked in by teams and carts, and forced to
listen to their wrangling drivers, and you can compute, if
you have an arithmetical turn, how much to subtract from
the present, or prospective, enjoyment of the afternoon ;
which, by the way, the first evening star announces to
be at an end, just as you arrive where a little light on
a fine prospect would be highly desirable. This, to one
whose preoccupied morning hours admit of no choice
as to the time for riding, may, perhaps, without wrest-
ing the king's English, be called—tantalizing ! But
what drives are *Boston* drives ! What green, winding
lanes, what silver lakes, what lovely country-seats,
what tasteful pleasure-grounds ! And the carriages,

so handsome, so comfortable; and the drivers so decent, respectable, and intelligent; so well-versed in the history of the city environs. Send for a chance carriage in New York, one hesitates to sit on its soiled cushions, dreads its dirty steps and wheels, and turns away disgusted from its loaferish driver, whiffing tobacco-smoke through the window in your face, and exchanging oaths with his comrade whom he is treating to a ride on the box. A handsome, cleanly public carriage, in New York, is as rare there, as a tastefully-dressed woman or a healthy-looking child.

"Then, Boston has its Sabbaths—its quiet, calm, blessed Sabbaths. No yelling milk-men or newsboys disturb its sacred stillness. Engines are not Sabbatically washed, and engine companies do not take that day to practice on tin horns; military companies do not play funereal Yankee Doodles; fruit-stalls do not offend your eye at street-corners, or open toy-shops in the back streets; but instead, long processions of families thread their way over the clean pavements to their respective churches, where the clergymen can preach three times a day without fainting away; where no poor servant-girl, whose morning hours are unavoidably occupied, finds, after a long walk there, her church closed in the afternoon, while her minister is at home taking his nap; where churches are *not* shut up in the summer months, while the minister luxuriates in the country at his ease."

"You are severe," said John; "ministers are but men; their health requires respites."

"I am not speaking of cases where a clergyman is really unable to labor," said Gertrude; "but that habit of closing churches whole months in the summer, strikes me most painfully. Death has all seasons for his own—sorrow casts her shadow regardless of summer's heat or winter's cold. I can not think it right that families should be left without *some* kind shepherd. Even then, with a substitute, every one knows there are sorrows, as well as joys, with which the most well-meaning stranger can not intermeddle.

"O, it is from the lips of one's *own* pastor the parting soul would fain hear the soul-cheering promise. *His* confiding ear that one would entreat for the tearful bed-side weepers! Verily those ministers have their reward, who, like their blessed Master, are 'not weary of well-doing.' It were worth some sacrifice of luxurious pleasure to ease one dying pang, to plume one broken wing for its eternal flight! It were sad to think the smallest and weakest lamb of the fold perished uncheered by the voice of its earthly shepherd. Ah! it was a life of self-denial that the 'Man of Sorrows' led."

"Quite a homily, Gertrude; you are evidently behind the progressive spirit of the times; when clergymen yacht and boat, and hunt and fish, and electioneer in the most layman-wise manner."

"I confess to conservatism on these points," said Gertrude; "I dislike a starched minister, as much as I dislike an undignified one. I dislike a stupid sermon, as much as I dislike a facetious or a ranting one; I dislike a pompous, solemn clergyman, as much as I dislike a jolly, story-telling, jovial one. A dignified, gentlemanly, courteous, consistent, genial clergyman, it were rare to find; though there are such, to whom, when I meet them, my very heart warms; to whom I would triumphantly point the carping unbeliever, who, because of the spots which defile too many a clerical cassock, sneers indiscriminately at the pulpit."

"Well—to change the subject, what have you to show Rose and me, here in Boston?" asked John.

"Use your eyes," said Gertrude; "do you not see that the gutters are inodorous; that the sidewalks are as clean as a parlor-floor; that the children are healthy, and sensibly dressed; that the gentlemen here do not smoke in public; that the intellectual, icicle women glide through the streets, all dressed after one pattern, with their mouths puckered up as if they were going to whistle; and that there is a general air of substantiality and well-to-do-ativeness pervading the place; a sort of touch-me-not, pharisaical atmosphere of ' stand-aside' propriety?

"Do you not see that slops are not thrown at your ankles from unexpected back doors, basements, or windows; that tenement-houses and palatial residences do

not stand cheek by jowl; that Boston men are handsome, but provincial, and do you not know that the
munificence of her rich men is proverbial.

"Yes, John, Boston is a nice little place; that its inhabitants go to church three times on Sunday, is a fixed
fact, and that many of them discuss fashions going,
and slander their neighbors coming back, is quite as
fixed a fact. If I should advise her, it would be after
this wise.

"Hop out of thy peck measure, oh Boston! and
take at least a *half* bushel view of things, so shalt thou
be weighed in the balance, and not be found wanting!

"And yet thou hast thy sweet Mount Auburn! and
for that I will love thee. What place of sepulture can
compare with it? Planted by Nature's own prodigal
and tasteful hand, with giant oaks and cedars nesting
myriad birds, now flitting through the sun-flecked
branches, now pluming their wings from some moss-
grown grave-stone, and soaring upward like the freed
spirit, over whose mortal dust their sweetest requiem
is sung.

"Beautiful Mount Auburn! beautiful when summer's
warm breath distills spicy odors from thousand
flowers, trembling with countless dewy diamonds;
beautiful when the hushed whisper passes through its
tall treetops, as weeping trains of mourners wind slowly with their dead beneath them.

"Beautiful at daybreak! when the sun gilds thy sacred temple; when the first wakeful bird trills out his matin song.

"Beautiful when evening's star creeps softly out, to light the homeless widow's footstep to the grave of him, whose strong arm lies stricken at her trembling feet.

"Beautiful when the radiant moon silvers lovingly some humble grave, monumentless but for the living statue—Grief!

"Beautiful, even when winter's pall softly descends over its sacred dust; when the tall pines, in their unchanging armor of green, stand firm, like some brave body-guard, while all around is fading, falling, dying; pointing silently upward, where there is no shadow of change.

"Beautiful Mount Auburn! beautiful even to the laughing eye which sorrow never dimmed; beautiful even to the bounding foot, which despair never paralyzed at the tomb's dark portal—but *sacred* to the rifled heart whose dearest treasures lay folded to thy fragrant bosom!"

CHAPTER LX.

"Is that you, John? because if it is, you can not come in," said Gertrude, opening the door just wide enough for her head to be seen.

"I am so miserable, Gertrude."

"Poor John! Well, just wait a bit, and I will open the door;" and darting back into the room, Gertrude shuffled away a picture on which she had been painting, and then threw open the door of her studio.

"Poor John, what is it?" and Gertrude seated herself on the lounge beside him, and laid her cheek against his, "what is it, John?"

"I am so dissatisfied and vexed with myself," said her brother, "I thought I was disinterested and unselfish, and I am not. I have caught myself hoping that Rose's dream might *not* prove true—that Vincent might never appear, so that I might win her—and she so bound up in him, too! I am a disgrace to my manhood, Gertrude, a poor, miserable, vacillating, unhappy wretch."

"No, you are not," said Gertrude, kissing his moist eyelids; "only a great soul would have made the generous confession which has just passed your lips; a more ignoble nature would have excused and palliated it, perhaps denied its existence; you *are* generous, and noble, and good, and I only wish you were not my brother, that I might marry you myself;" and she tried to force a smile upon John's face, by peeping archly into it.

"Do not jest with me, Gertrude; comfort me if you can. I too have had my dream; I am about to lose Rose. I can not tell you about it now, it is too painfully vivid. How can I live without love? without Rose's love? Tell me how you learned, Gertrude, to tame down that fiery heart of yours."

Gertrude only replied by her caresses; for, in truth, her heart was too full.

There is an *outward* life visible to all; there is an *inward* life known only to our own souls, and He who formed them.

Was Gertrude's heart "tamed?"

Ah, there were moments when she threw aside book, pallet, and pencil, when she could listen only to its troubled, mournful wailings, because there was nothing in all the wide earth, that could satisfy its cravings. Only in the Infinite can such a spirit find rest; and leaning her head upon John's shoulder, Gertrude sang:

> "Oh, ask thou, hope thou not too much
>   From sympathy below;
> Few are the hearts whence one same touch
>   Bids the sweet fountains flow:

Few, and by still conflicting powers,
   Forbidden here to meet,
Such ties would make this world of ours
   Too fair for aught so fleet;

"But for those bonds all perfect made,
   Wherein bright spirits blend;
Like sister flowers of one sweet shade,
   With the same breeze that bends.
For that full bliss of soul allied
   Never to mortals given;
Oh, lay thy lovely dreams aside,
   Or lift them up to Heaven!"

"You are a good girl, Gertrude," said her brother. "I am no Puritan, but your song has soothed me. There *must* be something more satisfying in another state of existence than there is in this, else were our very being a mockery."

"Poor John; he will arrive at the truth by and by," said Gertrude, as he left the room. "I think it is easier for woman to lean upon an Almighty arm; it is only through disappointment and suffering that man's proud spirit is bowed childlike before the cross. And how, when it gets there, the soul looks wondering back that it should ever have opposed its own poor pride of self to Calvary's meek sufferer!"

CHAPTER LXI.

How the wind roared! how the sails creaked and flapped! and the tall masts groaned! How the great vessel rolled from side to side, and tossed hither and thither, like a plaything for the winds and waves. The poor invalid groaned in his berth with pain and *ennui*. It mattered little to him whether the vessel ever made port or not. Sea-sickness is a great leveler, making the proud and haughty spirit quail before it, and disposing it to receive a sympathizing word from even the humblest.

"A rough sea, sir," said the captain, stripping off his shaggy deck-coat, and seating himself by the side of the invalid; "rough even for us old sea-dogs; but for a landsman, ah! I see it has taken you all aback," and the captain smiled as a man may smile who is quits with old Neptune in his fiercest moods.

"I can't say, though," continued the captain, "that you looked any too robust when you came on board. I suppose we must take that into the account. I hope you find yourself comfortable here—stewardess attentive, and so on. She is an uncouth creature, but seems

to understand her business. Ah! had you been aboard
my ship some years ago, you would have seen a stewardess! Such a noiseless step; such a gentle voice;
such a soft touch; it was quite worth while to be sick
to be so gently cared for."

The invalid made no reply, save to turn his head
languidly on the pillow; he was too weak, and sick,
and dispirited to take any interest in the old captain's
story.

"I wonder what ever became of her," continued the
captain, tapping on the lid of his snuff-box; "I made
all sorts of inquiries when I returned from my last
voyage. Such a boy as she had with her! You
should have seen that boy (bless me, I hope you'll
excuse my sneezing). Such a pair of eyes; black—
like what, I fancy, yours might have been when you
were young, and handsomer; he was a splendid child.
We thought one spell the little fellow was going to
slip his cable; but he managed to weather the storm,
and came out from his sickness brighter than ever.
Poor Rose! how she did love him!"

"Rose?" asked the invalid, for the first time betray-
ing any sign of interest.

"Yes; pretty name, wasn't it? and just sweet
enough for her too. But, poor girl, she was a blighted
Rose!" and the old captain set his teeth together, and
bringing his horny palm down on his knee, exclaimed,
"Great Cæsar! I should like to see the rascal who

broke that woman's heart run up to the yard-arm yonder. I don't care how fine a broad-cloth such a fellow wears; the better his station the greater his sin, and the more weight his damning example carries with it. If a man wants to do a mean action, let him not select a woman to victimize. Yes, sir, as I said before, I should like to have that fellow dangling from yonder yard-arm! I am an old man, and have seen a great deal of this sort of thing in my travels round the world. The laws need righting on this subject, and if men were not so much interested in letting them remain as they are, women would be better protected. Imprisonment for life is none too heavy a penalty for such an offense. It is odd," said the old captain, reflectively, "how a woman will forgive every thing to a man she loves. Now that poor little Rose—she clung to the belief that her lover had neither betrayed nor deserted her—is n't it odd now? and is n't it a cursed shame," said the old captain, striking his hand down again on his knee, "that the most angelic trait in woman's nature should be the very noose by which man drags her down to perdition? Hang it, I could almost foreswear my own sex when I think of it.

"But you don't agree with me, I suppose," said the captain, unbuttoning his vest, as if it impeded the play of his feelings. "You young fellows are not apt to look on it in this light. You *will*, sir, if you ever have daughters. Every such victim is somebody's daughter, somebody's sister. No man can indulge in illicit gratification—not even with a consenting party—and say he does no wrong. In the first place, as I look at it, he blunts his own moral sense; secondly, that of his companion; for it is well known that even the most depraved have moments when their better natures are in the ascendant; who can tell that *on him* does not rest the responsibility of balancing the scales at such a critical moment? Thirdly, the weight of his example on society; for none, not even the humblest, is without his influence; the smallest pebble thrown into a lake will widen out its circle; but I am talking too much to you," said the old captain; "I think of these things oftener since I saw poor Rose. You must forgive me if I said aught to displease you.

The invalid stretched out his hand, and said, with a languid smile, "I have not strength to talk to you about it now, captain; but God will surely bless you for befriending poor Rose, as you call her."

"Oh, that's a trifle!" said the captain; "it was a blessing to look on her sweet face and the boy's; you should see that boy, sir; any father might have been proud of *him*. Good-day; bear up, now. Nobody dies of sea-sickness. We shall make port before long. Let me know if you want any thing. Good-day, sir."

CHAPTER LXII.

"WEEPING! dear Gertrude," exclaimed John, as he entered his sister's studio, and seated himself by her side.

Gertrude laid her head upon his shoulder without replying.

"You do not often see me thus," she said, after a pause. "To-day is the anniversary of my husband's death, and as I sat at the window and saw the autumn wind showering down the bright leaves, I thought of that mournful October day, when, turning despairingly away from his dying moans, I walked to the window of his sick room, and saw the leaves eddying past as they do now. I could almost see again before me that pallid face, almost hear those fleeting, spasmodic breaths, and all the old agony woke up again within me. And yet," said Gertrude, smiling through her tears, "such blissful memories of his love came with it! Oh! surely, John, love like this perishes not with its object—dies not in this world?

"And my little Arthur, too, John—you have never seen my treasures. You have never looked upon the faces which made earth such a paradise for me;" and touching a spring in a rosewood box near her, Gertrude drew from it the pictures of her husband and child, and as John scanned their features in silence, she leaned upon his shoulder, and the bright teardrops fell like rain upon them.

"It is seldom that I allow myself to look at them," she said. "I were unfitted else for life's duties."

"It is a fine face," said John, gazing at that of Gertrude's husband. "It is a faithful index of the noble soul you worship. Your boy's face is yours in miniature, Gertrude."

"Yes; and I so deplored it after my husband's death; I used to watch so eagerly for one flitting expression of his father's."

John replaced the pictures in the box with a sigh, and sat a few moments thinking.

"Gertrude, do you know that your nature would never have fully developed itself in prosperity? The rain was as needful as the sunshine to ripen and perfect it."

"Yes, I feel that," said his sister. "And when I look around and see divided households; husbands and wives wedded to misery; parents, whose clutching love for gold swallows up every parental feeling; children, whose memories of home are hate, and discord, and all uncharitableness, I hug my brief day of unalloyed happiness to my bosom, and cheerfully accept my lot at His hand who hath disposed it."

CHAPTER LXIII.

"Dear Tom—

"Received your last letter by the Baltic. It was a gem, as usual. If your book is half as good, you will make your reputation and a fortune out of it. I knew you would like Paris; it is the only place in the world to live in. I hope yet to end my days there.

"And speaking of ending days, I have the most extraordinary thing to tell you:

"Jack—our glorious dare-devil Jack—has turned parson! Actual parson—black coat, white neck-tie, and long-tailed surtout—it is incredible! The little opera-dancer, Felissitimi, laughed till she was black in the face when I told her. It is no laughing matter to me, though, for he was always my shadow. I miss him at the club, the billiard-table, at King street, and every where else. It is confoundedly provoking. I feel like half a pair of scissors, and wander round in a most unriveted state.

"Such crowds as Jack draws to hear him! There is no church in town that will hold all his admiring listeners. I have not been, from principle, because I

17

think all that sort of thing is a deuced humbug, and I won't countenance it. But the other night, Menia did not perform, as was announced on the play-bills, and I looked about quite at a loss where to spend my evening. The first thing I knew, I found myself borne along with the current toward John's church. Then I said to myself, 'Now if that crowd choose to relieve me of the responsibility of countenancing John's nonsense, by *pushing* me into that church, well and good;' so I just resigned myself to the elbowing tide. And, by Jove! the first thing I knew, there I was, in a broad aisle-pew, sitting down as demure as if I were Aminidab Sleek.

"Well, pretty soon John came in. How well he had got himself up in that black suit! It was miraculous. I looked round on the women—*he* had them! With that musical voice of his, even that old hymn he read, sounded as well as any thing of Byron's. His prayer was miraculous!—I can't think how he did it; one would have supposed he felt every syllable; but you and I know Jack.

"Well, then came the sermon. 'Cast thy bread upon the waters, for thou shalt find it after many days.' He said it was in the Bible, and I suppose it was; I never heard of it before, but that may be for want of reading. By that time I was all eyes and ears. I knew he had impudence enough, so I was not afraid of his breaking down; and if he did, so much the better; there'd be something to laugh at him about.

"Now, Tom, you can't credit what I am going to tell you; that fellow began to relate his own experience; beginning with the prayers and hymns his mother taught him, and which he gradually lost the recollection of after she died, and as he grew older; then he described—and, by Jove, he did it well—his past downward steps, as he called them (I think that expression is open to discussion, Tom), the temptations of his youth, the gradual searing of conscience, and Satan's final triumph, when he cast off all restraint, and acknowledged no law but the domination of his own mad passions. Then he described his life at that point, *our* life—(I wonder if he saw *me* there?) he spoke of the occasional twinges of conscience, growing fainter, fainter, and at last dying out altogether.

"Then came his waking up from that long trance of sin, our meeting with that old lady in the street— (you remember, Tom), and the tearful look which she bent on him, when in reply to some remark of mine, he exclaimed,

"'Jesus Christ!'

"Then, how that look had haunted him, tortured him, by day and night; how it had wakened to new life all the buried memories of childhood—his mother's prayers and tears, and dying words; and how, after wrestling with it, through deeper depths of sin than any into which he had yet plunged, he had yielded to the holy spell, and that 'Jesus Christ' had now become to him, with penitential utterance, 'My Lord and my God.'

"Tom—there was not a dry eye in that church when Jack got through, no—not even mine, for I caught the infection (I might* as well own it) ; I felt as wicked as old King Herod ; and all day to-day—it is a rainy day, though, and I suppose, when the sun shines out, I shall feel better, I have not been able to get that sermon out of my mind. I don't believe in it, of course not ; hang me if I know what *does* ails me ; I am inclined to think it is a bad fit of indigestion. I must have a game at billiards. Write me.

"Yours,

"FINELS."

CHAPTER LXIV.

"How you grow, Charley," said John, tossing him up on his shoulder, and walking up to the looking-glass. "It seems but yesterday that you lay wrapped up in your blanket a-board Captain Lucas' ship with your thumb in your mouth (that unfailing sign of a good-natured baby), thinking of nothing at all; and now here you are six years' old to-day—think of that man? and I dare say you expect a birth-day present."

"Yes, if you please," said Charley.

"There, now; that is to the point. I like an honest boy. What will you have, Charley?"

"Something pretty for my mamma," said the loving little heart.

"Better still," said John; "but mamma won't take presents. I have tried her a great many times. There is one I want very much to make her, but she always says 'No.'" And John glanced at Gertrude.

"Mind what you say," whispered his sister. "He might chance to repeat it to his mother."

"So much the better, Gertrude. Then she will be sure to think of me at least one minute.

"But, Charley, tell me what *you* want. I would like to get you something for *yourself*."

"I want my papa," said Charley, resolutely. "Tommy Fritz keeps saying that I 'have n't got any papa.' *Have n't* I got a papa, cousin John?"

"You have a Father in heaven," said John, kissing Charley as he evaded the earnest question.

"When did he die? I want you to tell me all about him, cousin John, because Tommy Fritz sits next me at school and teases me so about not having any papa."

"Fritz?" repeated John, turning to Gertrude; "Fritz?—the name sounds familiar. Where could I have heard it? Fritz?" and John paced up and down the room, trying to remember.

"Yes, Tommy Fritz," repeated Charley; "and Tommy's big brother comes to school with him some days, and he saw me, and told Tommy that I had n't any papa."

"Did you say any thing to your mamma about it?" asked John.

"No," said Charley, with a very resolute shake of the head, "because it always makes mamma look so sad when I talk to her about papa; but I don't want Tommy to plague me any more. Is it bad not to have a papa, cousin John?"

"There are a great many little boys whose papas are dead," said John. "Yes, it is bad for them, because they feel lonesome without them, just as you do."

Charley looked very earnestly in John's face, as if he were not satisfied with his answer, and yet as if he did not know how better to make himself understood. Looking thoughtfully on the ground a few moments, he said—

"Was my papa good, cousin John?"

John drew Charley closer to his breast. "I did not know your papa, my dear, but your mamma loves him very much, and she is so good herself that I think she would not love him so were he not a good man."

"I'm *so* glad!" exclaimed Charley, with sparkling eyes. "May I tell Tommy Fritz that?" he asked, with the caution acquired by too early an acquaintance with sorrow.

"Certainly," said John, secretly resolving to inquire into this Fritz matter himself.

"Your mother is calling you, Charley," said Gertrude. "Poor little fellow," she added, as he ran nimbly out of the room. "Just think of a child with such a frank outspoken nature, burying such a corroding mystery in his own loving little heart, rather than pain his mother by asking for a solution. Poor Rose—the haunting specter which her prophet-eye discerned in her child's future, has assumed shape sooner than even she dreamed. Who can this 'big Fritz' be, John? and where could he have known Rose?"

"I have it," exclaimed John, stopping suddenly before his sister, with a deep red flush upon his face.

"This Fritz was a fellow-passenger of Rose's and mine on board Captain Lucas's vessel. The conceited puppy imagined that Rose would save him the trouble of gathering her by dropping at his feet—he found thorns instead of a rose, and his wounded vanity has taken this mean revenge. But he shall learn Rose has a protector," said John, folding his arms, and closing his lips firmly together.

"I shall do nothing rashly," said he, shaking off the clasp of Gertrude's hand. "Puppy"—he exclaimed— "contemptible coward, with all his pretensions to the title of a gentleman, to slander a woman!"

"Defining the word gentleman in that way," answered Gertrude, "the ranks would be pretty well thinned out. Some do it with a shrug—some with an uplifted eyebrow—some with a curl of the lip—some with a protracted whistle; and many a 'gentleman,' to make himself the paltry hero of the hour, has uttered boasting words of vanity, false as his own black heart; and many a virtuous woman has had occasion to repel insults growing out of this dastardly mention of her name before strangers, that else would never have been offered her. The crime is so common as to excite little or no reprehension, as to be little or no barrier in the intercourse between gentlemen. If every man who honors woman, and who finds himself in such unscrupulous society—testified his abhorrence by turning his back upon such a circle, the rebuke would soon tell. There *are* those whose standard of manly honor requires this in an associate.

"What! going, John?"

"Yes, I am too irritable to be good company; I must cool off my indignation by a walk in the open air. Go and sit with Rose, Gertrude; it may be that Charley may drop some word that will make known to her this new trouble."

"Never fear him," said Gertrude, "I don't know whether to call it instinct or tact, but he always seems to know what to say, and what to leave unsaid; he has the most lightning perceptions of any child I ever saw. No subtle shade of meaning in conversation seems to escape him, and he will often drop a remark which convinces you that he has grasped the subject at the very moment you are contriving some way to elucidate your meaning. Poor little Charley—it is always such natures whose heritage is sorrow."

17*

CHAPTER LXV.

THE old Bond mansion, though threatening to tumble down at every wind-gust, stood just where Rose had left it. The woodbine still festooned its piazza with green garlands in summer, and scarlet and purple berries and leaves in autumn. The tall butternut-trees still stood sentinel before it, the old moss-roofed barn leaned over on one side, like some old veteran whose work was almost done, and the iron-gray horse still took his afternoon-roll on the grass-plot before the door, kicking up his hoofs in the very face of old Time The brown chickens, once Charley's delight, had become respectable mothers of families, and clucked round after their lordly chanticleer, too happy to escape with half a dozen rebuffs a day from his majesty, and old Bruno, the house-dog, took longer naps on the sunny side of the house, and was less irascible at tin peddlers and stray cattle. The once nicely-kept little garden was overrun with pig-weed and nettles, and the tall, slender hollyhocks swung hither and thither with their flushed faces, like some awkward overgrown school-girl, looking for a place to hide.

It was five o'clock in the afternoon, and yet old Mrs. Bond had not thrown open the kitchen-door opposite the well-sweep, or filled the tea-kettle, or kindled up the kitchen-fire for tea. But look! a strange woman steps out upon the piazza; such a woman as every country village boasts; round, rubicund, check-aproned and spectacled, with very long cap-strings, turtle-shaped feet, thick ancles, and no waist. With her fat, red hands crossed over the place where her waist *once* was, she steps out on the piazza and looks over her spectacles, this way and that, up and down the road.

The little brook babbles on as usual, and the linden-trees and maples are nodding and whispering to each other across the road; but nothing else is stirring. So Mrs. Simms goes back into the house, and closes the door, and Bruno gives a low growl to signify that all is right, as far as he knows.

Then Mrs. Simms lays her hand on the latch of the sitting-room door, and softly glides in. It is very dark; just a ray of light is shining in through a chink in the shutter. She opens it a little further, and the pleasant afternoon sunlight streams in across the floor —across the pine table—across the coffin—across the placid face of good, dear, old Mrs. Bond.

She has gone to that city where "there is no need of the sun, nor of the moon, to shine in it, for the glory of God doth lighten it, and the Lamb is the light thereof."

And now the neighbors drop in gently, one by one. Not one there but can remember some simple act of kindness, which makes the warm tears drop upon the placid face, upon which they are looking for the last time. Mrs. Bond had no kin; and yet every trembling lip there, called her "mother."

Not for thee, "mother," whom the busy world honored not, whom the Lord of Glory crowned; not for *thee* the careless city sepulture, the jostled hearse, the laughing, noisy, busy crowd. Reverently the prayer is said; now the little, rosy child is lifted up, to see how sweet a smile even icy Death may wear; and now toil-hardened hands, though kindly, bear her gently on to the quiet corner in the leafy church-yard, to which she has so long looked forward. The mold has fallen on her breast, the grave is spaded over, and still they linger, loth to leave even to the fragrant night, the kindly heart which had beat so long responsive to their homely joys and sorrows.

Oh, many such an earth-dimmed diamond shall Jehovah set sparkling in his crown, in the day when he maketh up his jewels.

CHAPTER LXVI.

It is astonishing the miles one may pass over unconsciously when one's mind is absorbed in thought.
John strode rapidly down street, after his interview
with Gertrude, running against foot-passengers with an
audacity which his bland "beg pardon" scarcely
atoned for. Some scowled, some muttered "tipsy;"
an old apple-woman whose basket he upset, picked up
the half-dollar he threw her with a very equivocal look
of thanks, and a lady whose flounces he pinned to the
sidewalk, darted vengeance at him, from a pair of eyes
evidently made only for love-glances. Poor, distracted
John! pedestrians should have seen that his elbow had
a pugilistic crook in it, which might have notified any
one with half an eye, that he was in a state of mind.
But it is heart-rending how indifferent and stupid the
out-door world is to one's individual frames. The hard-
hearted teamster persists in halting his cart on the
only dry street-crossing, though bright eyes look down
imploringly at pretty gaiter boots; gentlemen who
have practiced before the looking-glass the most killing
way of carrying a cane, and finally settled down upon

the arm-pit style, mercilessly extinguish unwary eyes
with the protruding weapon. It matters not to the
smoker that he poisons the fresh air upon which one
has depended to cure a villainous headache. It matters not that the stain of the cigar-stump he tosses
upon your dress, is as indelible as the stamp of loafer-
ism upon the best-dressed man who smokes in the
street. It matters not to the grocer's boy, as he walks
with his head hind side before, that he draws a slimy
salt-fish across a silk mantle, or fetches up against a
brocade with a quart of molasses. It matters not that
you are unable to decide whether the world is not big
enough, or whether there are too many people in it;
the census keeps going on all the same.

As our hero was sufficiently unfashionable never to
have defiled his very handsome mouth with a cigar, he
had no escape-valve for his irritation but accelerated
motion; and that brought him, after a time, to the
door of a restaurant which stood invitingly open. Entering, partly from weariness, partly from extreme thirst,
consequent upon being in an excited state, he seated
himself in a curtained alcove, and tossing his hat on
the table, gave his order to the waiter, and listlessly
took up a newspaper. Ere his eyes were riveted upon
any particular paragraph, voices in the next alcove attracted his attention.

"Do you stay long in the city?"

"I think not; only a day or two."

"Well, there are plenty of things to look at, if you are fond of sight-seeing; and if your taste runs to women, we have plenty of fair faces. There is one in —— street—ripe, rosy lips—such a foot, and such a symmetrical little form; knows what she is about, too —demure as a nun and sly as a priest; took me completely in with her Methodist way. I thought she was what she pretended to be, and all the time she was carrying on a most desperate flirtation with a fellow by the name of Perry. She was a picture, that little Rose, and now it seems he has caged her at last."

"Rose? Married her?"

"Lord bless you, no—of course not. He schools the boy, and all that—pays the bills, etc.—you understand. The boy goes to school with my little brother; that 's the way I tracked her out. You see, it was on board ship I first saw her, and then I lost sight of her again until I got this clew. This whining Perry carried her off under my very nose—I—who have had such success; well, I don't wish to boast, but Perry's money was the thing—women are mercenary creatures. I suppose she passes here for respectable. They have a lady with them whom Perry pretends is his sister, to give it a more respectable air. No woman treats me with contempt without rueing it. By Jupiter, she was as imperious as a duchess because I honored her with a few compliments. I 'll turn their little comedy into a tragedy, as sure as my name is Fritz."

"I will save you that trouble," exclaimed John, darting into the alcove, and slapping him across the face with his glove. "There's my card. You know me, sir," and he stood facing him with folded arms.

It is half the battle to have right on one's side, and Fritz was taken at a liar's disadvantage. Conscious of this, he made no attempt at a retort, but pointing to "his friend," muttered something to John about "hearing from him."

John strode out into the open air, to the astonishment of the open-mouthed waiter, who stood, tray in hand.

"A word with you, sir," said the gentleman, whom he had just seen in Fritz's company, following him. "The lady who was the occasion of this quarrel— 'Rose'—I would speak of *her*."

"I am not accustomed to hearing her so familiarly designated by a stranger," answered Perry, haughtily.

"Pardon me!" exclaimed the gentleman, much agitated. "I—I—in fact, sir, I am a stranger to Mr. Fritz. We met casually in a railroad-car, and meeting me just now before De Marco's, he invited me in to take a glass of wine with him. I have declined having any thing to do as his second in this affair. His manner to you convinced me that he has no right to consider himself a gentleman. With regard to the lady, sir, it may seem to you an impertinence that I should speak of her again—the name attracted me—it is that of a dear lost friend—I fancied this might be she," and the speaker became more agitated. "Now—it is at your option, sir, whether to pursue the subject further."

John looked him in the face; there was goodness there, and must have been sorrow, too—for the eyes were sunken and the form emaciated, and his thin pale hands were as transparent as a woman's.

"Could this be *he?*" and John in his turn became agitated.

"If it were? should he lead him out of this laba-rynth of doubt? should he place in his hand the thread which should conduct him through its dim shadows out under the clear blue sky, 'mid soft breezes and blossoming flowers? or leave him there to grope, while he wooed the blessed sun-light for his own path?"

The temptation was but for a moment.

"You seem feeble," said John, kindly, though his voice still trembled with emotion; "do me the favor to accompany me home, and then we will talk of this more at length."

The two walked on, overshadowed each with the presence of a power, of which all of us have been at some eventful moment conscious, and over which the conventionalities of life have had no control. It did not seem strange therefore to either, that they who had exchanged words, so fraught with meaning to each, should walk on side by side in thoughtful silence.

CHAPTER LXVII.

ARRIVED at John's lodgings, he ushered the stranger into Gertrude's studio, of which she had given him the key when they parted, as she intended riding out with Rose. Motioning him to a seat, and adding that he would rejoin him presently, John left him there alone.

The stranger looked around; there were landscape, game, fruit, cattle, and flower pieces, and all so exquisitely painted that any other moment each would have been a study to him—now heart and brain were both pre-occupied. What was in store for him? He felt this to be a turning-point in his life.

A slight jar, and a picture, which stands with the back toward him, falls over. The stranger rises, and stoops to replace it !

Ah !—why that suppressed cry of joy ? Why those passionate kisses on the insensible canvas ? Why those fast-falling tears, and heart-beaming smiles ?

" It is not *your* mamma—it is *my* mamma," said Charley, stepping up between the picture and the stranger.

"His own eyes! his own brow! and Rose's sweet mouth! his own, and Rose's child!

"My God, I thank thee!" he murmured; but the thin arms that were outstretched to clasp his new found treasure, fell powerless at his side. To sorrow he had become inured; he could not bear the out-gushing fountain of joy.

John, who had been an unseen spectator, had not looked for this tragic termination of his test. On *his* kind heart his rival's head was pillowed, *his* hand bathed his cold temples, *his* voice assisted returning consciousness.

"Who is he?" whispered Charley, tiptoeing up to John.

"Ask him," whispered John, as the stranger slowly opened his eyes.

Charley advanced, then retreated a step—then, won by the beaming smile which irradiated the stranger's face, he asked,

"Did you come here to see my Aunt Gertrude's pictures?"

"No," replied the stranger, with the same bright smile.

"Did you come to see John?"

"No, my dear."

"Did you come to see me?"

"Yes."

"What did you come to see me, for?"

Drawing him closer to his heart, and wiping his brow, the stranger said, " See if you can not guess."

Charley looked at Cousin John, but the conflicting expressions which flitted over his face gave him no clew. He looked at the stranger—his dark eyes were brimming with tears, but the same smile still played upon his lips. Charley stood for a moment irresolute, then, with another timid look into his face, he said, "I don't know—*certainly*—who you are, but—"

" But what, my dear ?"

" Perhaps—you are my own papa come home."

No reply—but a deadly pallor overspread the stranger's face as he glanced in the direction of the door. John, who was standing with his back to it, turned around—and there—in the doorway, stood Rose with her small head bent forward—her lips apart—and her dilated eyes fixed upon the prostrate form before her. It was only for an instant—with a piercing cry, in which fear and joy both found utterance, she bounded to his side—kissed his brow, his lips, his eyes. Oh, was death to divide them then ? God forbid !

" Vincent—Vincent—my own Vincent !" and in that long, idolatrous kiss, her woman's heart absolved the past, whatever that past might be.

CHAPTER LXVIII.

"Sit down by me—tell me what you have learned from Rose," said John, the next day to his sister.

"His history is so singular," said Gertrude, "that in a novel it would be stigmatized as incredible, overdrawn, and absurd; in truth, a novelist who would not subject himself to such charges must not too closely follow Nature. If the gorgeous colors of our autumnal scenery were faithfully transferred to canvas, the artist would be considered a glaring, tasteless burlesquer. Both artist and novelist must learn to 'tone down' their pictures; but as my story is not for the critic's ear, but for yours, John, I shall tell it verbatim.

VINCENT'S HISTORY.

"Rose and Vincent were legally married by the Rev. Mr. Lehmann, a few miles from the boarding-school where Vincent first saw Rose. Vincent took her from thence immediately to the hotel, where his friend, the Rev. Mr. Lehmann, was staying for a few days previous to his departure for the Continent. The rector's brother, who was with him, was the witness to the ceremony.

" Rose and Vincent then left for a few days' sojourn in a neighboring city. There Vincent received intelligence of the dying condition of his aged father. As his father had been unapprised of his sudden marriage, he thought it not best to take Rose with him at such a time;—providing, therefore, every thing necessary for her comfort, and expecting to be gone at farthest but a few days, he took a reluctant leave of her—he little thought for how long a time.

" Part of the journey lay off from the regular public conveyances; and Vincent, being anxious to return to Rose as soon as possible, hesitated not, though the road was lonely, to perform it at night on horseback. On this night he was met by a gang of desperados, who, unknown to him, herded in the vicinity, and who attacked him and left him for dead, after possessing themselves of his watch, pocket-book, and papers. There he was found the next day, by a passing traveler, in an insensible state, and taken to the nearest farm-house. He was quite unable to give any account of himself; and not wishing to be burdened with the care of him, they put him into a cart and took him to the county poor-house. Here his sufferings, aggravated by neglect, assumed the form of brain fever, and from thence, after awhile, he was removed to the lunatic asylum, where he remained for a year without any symptoms of returning reason.

"His distress, when he finally became conscious of the length of time which had elapsed since he left Rose, was too much for his weak frame. A relapse ensued, and for months longer he vibrated between life and death.

"When consciousness again returned, though weakened in body and enfeebled in mind, he commenced his weary search for Rose. He could hear nothing except that part of her story which he gleaned from Mrs. Bond, and which only served to aggravate his distress. Since then he has traveled unceasingly in steamboats, railroad cars, and stages; haunted hotels, haunted villages, and loitered trembling in churchyards. There is no misery like suspense, and acting upon an already enfeebled frame, it sapped the very fountains of life, and reduced him so fearfully as to render him quite unable to bear the sudden shock of joy which so unexpectedly met him."

"Poor Vincent!" exclaimed John; "and I have grudged him his happiness."

"Dear John!"

"Where was Charley born, Gertrude?"

"In a Lying-in Hospital; in which poor Rose took refuge when the sorrowful hour drew near.

"Then," said Gertrude, resuming her story, "Rose's husband had a cousin of the same name as himself, extravagant, reckless, and dissipated, who, though only twenty-five, had run through a handsome property, inherited in his own right from his grandmother, besides making unreasonable demands upon the paternal purse-strings. The old gentleman at last remonstrated, and the young man's affairs being even worse than he had dared to represent, he became desperate and unscrupulous.

"The father of Rose's husband, who, spite of the profligacy of his nephew, cherished a warm attachment for him, had willed him his property, in case of his son's death. This the young spendthrift was aware of, and when he first heard of the old gentleman's illness, he planned with three desperados to murder his cousin, and remove the only obstacle to his immediate possession of the fortune."

"How was this discovered?" asked John.

"It was revealed by one of the gang on his death-bed, though not until after the instigator had met his own doom at the hands of a woman whom he had betrayed and deserted."

"Then," said John, after a pause, "Rose and her husband have no immediate means of support. It is happiness to know that I can be of service even now."

"But Vincent is not a man to incur such an obligation," said his sister, "enfeebled as he is."

"He must—he shall," said the generous John, "at least till he is stronger and better able to substantiate his claim to what is rightfully his own; he *may* get even more than his own," said John, "when the old lady in New Orleans finds out that he is the father of the beautiful child she fancied so much; the family likeness must have been well handed down in Charley's face."

"That is not strange," said Gertrude; "cases have occurred in which the family likeness having been apparently wholly obliterated, has re-appeared in the third or fourth generation."

"Well, Vincent's story passes belief," said John; "truth *is*, indeed, stranger than fiction."

18

CHAPTER LXIX.

HAD cousin John no war to wage with self? Could the long-hoarded hope of years be relinquished without a struggle? Could blissful days and nights, in which to breathe the same air with Rose, win even the faintest smile, were reward enough for any toil,—could such memories cease at once to thrill? Could he see that smile, in all its brightness, beaming upon another? —hear that voice ten fold more musically modulated whispering (not for him) words he would have died to hear—and not feel a pang bitter as death? Tell me, ye who have made earth-idols only to see them pass away?

No—cousin John felt all this; Rose lost all was lost —nothing to toil for—nothing to hope for—nothing to live for.

Was it indeed so? He dashed the unmanly tears away. Was he, indeed, such a poor, selfish driveler that the happiness of her whom he loved was less dear to him than his own? Was it no joy to see that sweet eye brighten with hope, though kindled by another? Was it nothing to see the shadow of shame pass from

that fair brow, and see it lifted in the world's scornful
face in loving pride to him who rightfully called her
"wife?" Was it nothing that Charley's little heaving
heart had found his own papa?

"Shame—shame—was *his* manly heart powerless to
bear what *she*, whom he so loved, had borne in all her
woman's feebleness?"

"I knew it would be so, John," said Gertrude, gazing into her brother's calm face, in which the traces
of suffering still lingered. "I knew you could con-
quer"—and tears of sympathy fell upon the hand she
pressed.

CHAPTER LXX.

"Sit down," said John, a few hours after, as Vincent rapped at his room-door. "I was just wishing for you, although it were cruel to monopolize you a moment, at such a time as this. Sit down—I want to confess to you," said John, with a heightened color. "It will make my heart easier—it will be better for both of us.

"Vincent—you have taken away from me all that has made life dear to me since I first saw your —— since I first saw Rose; and yet"—and John reached out his hand—"I can look on your happiness and hers, and thank God for it. It has cost me a struggle—but it is all over now. Peerless as Rose is—I feel that you are worthy of her."

"I can not find words to say what I would," said Vincent; "by my gain, my dear friend, I can measure your loss," and he grasped John's hand with unfeigned emotion. "Rose has spoken of you to me in a way this morning that, independent of this noble frankness on your part, would forever have insured you a brother's place in my heart. How can I thank you for it all?

How can I prove to you my gratitude for your kindness to me and mine?"

"By not leaving us," answered John; "by considering my ample means as yours, and Rose's, and Charley's; by making my otherwise solitary life glad, bright, and blessed by your presence; by placing a confidence in me which you will never have cause to regret," said John, with a flushed brow.

"I know it—I believe it—I know it—God bless you," said Vincent; "you can ask nothing that I could refuse. Had it not been for you, I might never have found my treasures. I will be your guest for a time, until I have established claims which I must not neglect, for those who are dear to me—and *then* our homes shall be one. God bless you, John, my brother."

Rose glided in! Oh how surprisingly lovely! with those love-brimming eyes and that sunny smile. Placing her little hand in John's, she said, "and my brother, too."

"Seal it with a kiss, Rose," said Vincent.

"That I will," exclaimed the happy little wife. "Kiss me, John."

"Me, too," said Charley. "Oh, John, is not *he* (pointing to Vincent) all of our papas? May n't I run and tell Tommy Fritz?"

CHAPTER LXXI.

It was a cold January night. The stars glowed and sparkled, and ever and anon shot rapidly across the clear blue sky, as if it was out of all reason to expect them to stay on duty such a bitter night, without a little occasional exercise.

The few pedestrians whom business had unfortunately driven out, hurried along with rapid strides, steaming breath, and hands thrust into their pockets; and, as their arms protruded, handle-fashion, they might have been mistaken for so many brown jugs in locomotion.

Through many a richly-curtained window, the bright lights gleamed cheerfully, while the merry song or laugh from within, might be heard by the shivering outsiders, quickening the steps of those who were so lucky as to have firesides of their own, and making the night, to those who had none, seem still more cold and drear.

Beneath one of these brilliantly-lighted windows, down upon the frosty pavement, crouched a bundle of rags, it scarce seemed more, so motionless had it lain there, for hours; for on such a bitter night no one felt inclined to stop and investigate it; and yet there was life within it, feeble and flickering though it was.

Now and then a pair of hollow eyes gleamed out, and gazed wildly about, and then the lids would close over them, and the head droop back again to its old posture.

Now and then a murmur issued from the parched lips, and one might have heard, had he been very near, the words—

"Mercy! mercy!"

And still from the window above, the bird-like voice caroled out its sweet song, and merry voices joined in the chorus.

Now a little child, with broad, expansive brow, and sweet, soul-lit eyes, parts the rich damask curtains, and pressing his little face closely against the window-pane, gazes out into the frosty night.

"How brightly the gleaming stars shine! I wonder how *long* have they shone? I wonder are they *really* all little worlds? and people in them? I wonder—" and here the child stopped, for the bundle of rags beneath the window gave a convulsive heave, and his quick ear had caught the words despair had uttered:

"Mercy! mercy!"

"Oh! papa—dear papa, Gertrude, John, oh, come!"

and with heart of pity and winged feet, little Charley darted through the dining-room door, out into the wide hall, and down the steps to the bundle of rags whence the sound issued.

The eyes had closed again, the head had drooped, and the poor thin, outstretched hands fallen hopelessly down upon the frosty pavement.

"Run in, Charley," said John; "the air is bitter cold. Move away, dear, and let me take this poor creature up."

It was a light burden, that bundle of rags, though the heart beneath it was so heavy.

Rose and Gertrude sprang forward and arranged pillows on the sofa for the dying woman, for such she seemed to be, and chafed her hands and temples, while John and Vincent dropped some wine between the pale lips.

Slowly she opened her eyes. Warmth! light! kind words! kind faces! Where was she?

Now Rose bends over her a face pitying as God's angels. The hollow eyes glare wildly upon it, a spasm passes over the pale face of the sufferer, and as she turns away to the pillow, she falters out,

"Oh! God forgive me! Mercy! mercy!"

"May He grant it!" said the shuddering Rose, hiding her face in her husband's bosom, as Markham's despairing, dying wail rang in her ears. "May God grant it, even at the eleventh hour."

When youth had passed, and, standing upon the threshhold of manhood, Charley looked out upon the tangled web of life, and saw (*seemingly*) the scales of eternal justice unevenly balanced, memory painted again, in freshened colors, *that* scene, and inscribed beneath it—

GOD IS JUST!

THE END.

JUST PUBLISHED.

LANMERE.

By Mrs. Julia C. R. Dorr,

Author of "Farmingdale."

1 Vol., 12mo. Price $1.25.

"Farmingdale" has won for its author a deserved popularity. In "Lanmere" she has not done herself injustice. It is a tale of great power and brilliancy.

LETTERS

OF MADAME DE SÉVIGNE.

Edited by Mrs. Sarah J. Hale.

1 Vol., 12mo. Price $1.25.

This book is the first volume of a series, which we are publishing under the general title of the library of

"STANDARD LETTER-WRITERS."

It is a work which should be read and studied by all. As a letter-writer, Madame de Sevigne's name ranks among the highest of those who have become famous for the beauty and conciseness of their epistolary correspondence. Her letters are models of excellence, and should be consulted, both as a text-book, and as a work of profound interest to the general reader. There is scarcely a subject worthy of notice but what her racy pen has dwelt upon, in a manner which at once instructs and entertains.

THE ELM-TREE TALES.

By F. Irene Burge Smith.

1 Vol. 12mo. Price $1.

Seated beneath a huge elm tree, a merry group listened to the beautiful stories which had been written for them. They were so well received by her little audience that the authoress concluded to present them to the great public, under the above title. The book contains three deeply interesting stories, entitled respectively, "JENNY GRIG, THE STREET SWEEPER;" "NANNIE BATES, THE HUCKSTER'S DAUGHTER;" and "ARCHIBALD MACKIE, THE LITTLE CRIPPLE." Boys and girls will be delighted with it; and children of an older growth will find it a volume of deep interest.

MR. HERBERT'S NEW WORK.

WAGER OF BATTLE,

A TALE OF SAXON SLAVERY IN SHERWOOD FOREST.

By Henry W. Herbert, Esq.,

Author of "Marmaduke Wyvil," "Henry VIII. and his Six Wives," etc., etc.

1 Vol., 12mo. Price $1.

"The story transports us back to the English forests, before the Norman and Saxon races had melted into one, and brings up a succession of domestic and rural pictures that are bright with the freshness of that primeval time. The present work is even richer in the elements of popular interest than Mr. Herbert's previous fictitious compositions, and will deservedly increase his reputation as a brilliant and vigorous novelist."—*New York Tribune.*

"'The Wager of Battle' is the best of Herbert's works."—*N. Y. Sunday Dispatch.*

"The story is one of intense interest."—*N. Y. Daily News.*

"The condition of the serf—the born thrall of that period, is accurately delineated, and the life, daily occupations, and language of the twelfth century placed vividly before the reader. There is no incident in the book that is tame and lifeless."—*N. Y. Picayune.*

"Herbert is the best living historical novelist."—*Cor. Boston Transcript.*

"It is a very beautiful tale—in its descriptive scenes, and in much of its coloring, reminding us more than once of Ivanhoe."—*Boston Traveler.*

"In this work, Mr. Herbert has bent his acknowledged genius to the agreeable task of creating a succession of highly attractive and interesting scenes, which completely transfer us, for the time, to the wild age to which they relate."—*Portland Eastern Argus.*

"This is an exceedingly able story, one which is sure to find favor with all classes of readers."—*Phila. Sunday Dispatch.*

"We like a good historical novel, and we know of no living writer better qualified to write one than Henry W. Herbert. In the present volume he gives a fresh, bold picture of Saxon serfdom in England before yet the two races of Norman and Saxon were mingled into one. The delineation of outward habits, and the customs of the time, are admirably done, and the story is one that can not fail to interest all who read it."—*Gospel Banner, Augusta.*

"A story of great interest. * * * Written in an attractive style. * * * Built upon a well-arranged plot. * * * The best of Herbert's works."—*Dayton (O.) Empire.*

"Herbert is a pleasing, busy, instructive, successful novelist historian."—*Boston Christian Times.*

"It displays much dramatic skill and felicity of description, and accurately depicts the manners, customs, and institutions of the Saxons and the Normans, at the time of their fusion into the great English race."—*N. Y. Chronicle.*

"Mr. Herbert's style is clear and fine, and the plot of his story well constructed."—*State of Maine.*

"One of the best stories of the author."—*Cor. Boston Traveler.*

THE RAG-PICKER;

OR,

BOUND AND FREE.

1 Vol., 12mo.   442 pp.   Price $1.25.

"This is a most stirring and pathetic story, illustrating the terrible power of human depravity on the one hand, and the importance of using the most efficient means to counteract it on the other. The author assures us that his statements are throughout nothing but sober verity ; and that many of the persons whose character and experience are here described are still living in various parts of the United States. If this be really so (and we have no right to dispute the author's word), we can only say that they form the most remarkable group of personages which have ever come within our knowledge. It is a most intensely exciting book ; but we do not perceive any thing that indicates ill-nature."—*Boston Puritan Recorder*.

"The tale is one of modern times and events ; the characters and personages alluded to are those who have lived in the present century, here and elsewhere, and the story is a most exciting one, well and powerfully written."—*Boston Transcript*.

"The most original in its conception, the widest in its scope, the most interesting in its narrative, and the best in its execution. The characters are drawn from nature ; we need no preface to tell us that, for they speak, think, and act to the life. * * * The ups and downs of honest old Davy, the hero of the book, the true-hearted Rag-Picker, read us a homily on the fickleness of fortune, and furnish an example which the proudest aristocrat might do well to follow. We lay aside the volume with a sigh that there is no more of it." —*N. Y. Saturday Evening Courier*.

"We have read this book, which claims to be a 'record of facts' by an eye and ear-witness, with thrilling interest at a single sitting."—*Boston Liberator*.

"The book is well and powerfully written, and the story is a most exciting one."—*Portland Transcript*.

"The narrative is rapid and spirited."—*N. York Evening Post*.

"It is replete with incidents, its characters are natural and distinctly shown, and the interest of the narrative is well sustained."—*Boston Atlas*.

"A good, a useful, and a meritorious book, and one peculiarly fitted for family reading." —*N. Y. Sunday Times*.

"It is highly dramatic, and keeps the reader intensely interested to the end."—*Portland Daily Argus*.

"It is written with spirit and power."—*American Courier*.

"The narrative warmly enlists the sympathies of the reader, and to the end sustains the interest without flagging."—*Chicago Christian Times*.

"It is beautifully written, and will be widely circulated, as it richly deserves."—*Christian Chronicle, Phila*.

"A well-planned and highly interesting story."—*Fred. Douglass's Paper*.

"The story is one of decided literary merit, and unexceptionable moral tone ; and is replete with life lessons drawn from life scenes."—*Boston Christian Freeman*.

"Well told, vivid and excellent in aim and tone."—*Cor. Boston Transcript*.

"It is written with distinguished ability."—*Boston Chronicle*.

"Is full of dramatic scenes of the most exciting kind."—*New York Life Illustrated*.

"A very readable volume."—*Dollar Newspaper*.

"It is full of vigor and dramatic power."—*New Bedford Mercury*.

"The author wields a vigorous pen."—*Glen Falls Republican*.

"No one will read it without a feeling of satisfaction."—*Oswego Palladium*.

"It may be deemed the protest of an energetic mind against the expression and lack of sympathy of one class toward another."—*Indianapolis Sentinel*.

"The story is, in truth, one of realities too sadly real, and, as such, impresses the reader with more profound sympathies for the unfortunate of our race."—*Dayton Gazette*.

"A most readable and interesting book."—*Pottsville Register*.

OLIE;

OR, THE OLD WEST ROOM.

The Weary at Work and the Weary at Rest.

By L. M. M.

1 Vol. 12mo., 456 pp. Price $1.25.

CONE CUT CORNERS:

The Experience of a Conservative Family in Fanatical Times;
Including some Account of a Connecticut Village, the
People who lived in it, and those who came
there from the city.

BY BENAULY.

1 Vol. 12mo., 456 pp. Price $1.25. Elegantly Illustrated.

LIFE OF HORACE GREELEY,

Editor of the New York Tribune.

BY J. PARTON.

Elegantly Illustrated. 1 Vol. 12mo., 442 pp. Price $1.25.

RUTH HALL:

A Domestic Tale of the Present Time.

BY FANNY FERN.

1 Vol. 12mo. pp. 400. Price $1.25.

" Every chapter has the touch of genius in it."—*Worcester Palladium.*

" It is a thrilling life sketch, with passages of great power and pathos."—*Maysville Eagle.*

" Flashes of gayest humor alternate with bursts of deep pathos ; so that the volume is relieved of all peril of monotony."—*N. Y. Tribune.*

" This is a remarkable book—a book to create a sensation."—*N. Y. Mirror.*

" Wherever the English language is read, Ruth Hall will be eagerly read."—*New York Picayune.*

" No one will fail to read the book through who reads the first chapter."—*N. Y. Sunday Courier.*

" Never did a tale abound in so many beautiful images."—*Philadelphia Mercury.*

" In point of interest it exceeds any work of fiction we have read for years."—*Eve. Journal.*

" Her words are red-hot, and her sentences seem to glow with the intensity of her feeling."—*Rutland Co. Herald.*

" The most lively and sparkling favorite writer of the present time."—*Burlington Gazette.*

" No one can fail to be interested in the narrative."—*Hallowell Gazette.*

" It is a powerful ; remarkable book."—*Springfield Republican.*

" It is a book that will make a sobbing among mothers and widows."—*Poughkeepsie Eagle.*

" Read it, you can not fail to be the better of it."—*Pittsburg Family Journal.*

" Whoever takes it up will read it to the close without sleeping."—*Plattsburg Republican.*

" The interest never flags."—*Knick. Mag.*

" In ' Ruth Hall' there is pathos, humor, and satire."—*N. Y. Life Illustrated.*

" We have read it through with unabated interest."—*Ithaca Chronicle.*

" A real *Heart Book*, a household book."—*Schoharie Democrat.*

" It sparkles with brilliants."—*Hartford Christian Secretary.*

" A fresh racy volume."—*Hartford Union.*

" Abounding with the keenest satire, and flashes of wit."—*N. Y. Christian Ambassador.*

" Will rival the choicest productions of English genius."—*Columbus (Geo.) Times.*

" Is the most intensely interesting book that we have ever read."—*Ellensville Journal.*

" Every page glitters with some gem of intellect, some bright truth."—*Tiffin (O.) Tribune.*

" No novel has created such a sensation."—*N. O. Bulletin.*

" Genius is manifested in every page."—*N. Y. Merchants' Ledger.*

" Thousands will read and re-read ' Ruth Hall' with deep and intense interest."—*Doylestown Democrat.*

" It is the most condensed and thrillingly interesting book ever written."—*Easton (Md.) Star.*

" It is instinct with the highest genius."—*Philadelphia Sun.*

" Presents a vivid picture of the trials of literary life."—*N. Y. True American.*

" Its scenes are drawn with power, pathos, and naturalness."—*Buff. Eve. Post.*

" The book shows *fact* to be stranger than *fiction*."—*Rome Excelsior.*

" A real sketch of human life, amid clouds, storm and sunshine."—*Lawrence Sentinel.*

" All the characters are portraits—every body has seen their prototypes."—*Waterville Journal.*

" Never have we read a book so true to nature."—*Keystone City.*

" A live book ; it is a tale of real life ; the story is powerfully told."—*Burlington Hawk Eye.*

" Abounds with gems."—*Nashville Banner.*

" It is an *evergreen*, fresh as are all the emanations of mind, ' not born to die.' "—*Lockport Democrat.*

" A book of extraordinary interest."—*Monongahela Republican.*

DR. LOWELL MASON'S
CHURCH MUSIC.

THE HALLELUJAH. A book for the Service of Song in the House of the Lord, containing tunes, chants, and anthems, both for the choir and congregation; to which is prefixed the Singing School, a manual for classes in vocal music, with exercises, rounds, and part songs, for choir practice; also, Musical Notation in a Nut-shell; a brief course for singing-schools, intended for skillful teachers and apt pupils. By LOWELL MASON. $1. Do. cloth extra, $1 25.

The publication of this, Dr. Mason's last work, was looked for with great interest by the musical public, as he had enjoyed peculiar advantages, and bestowed extraordinary labor in its preparation. It has not disappointed the expectations with regard to it. Thus far it has proved the most successful work of its class ever published, and it is believed that it will take its place by the side of "Carmina Sacra," by the same author, as a standard work in its department.

CANTICA LAUDIS; or, the American Book of Church Music; being chiefly a selection of chaste and elegant melodies from the most classic authors, ancient and modern, with harmony parts; together with anthems and other set pieces for choirs and singing-schools; to which are added tunes for congregational singing. By LOWELL MASON and GEORGE JAMES WEBB. $1.

THE CARMINA SACRA; or, Boston Collection of Church Music, comprising the most popular psalm and hymn tunes in general use, together with a great variety of new tunes, chants, sentences, motetts, and anthems, principally by distinguished European composers; the whole being one of the most complete collections of music for choirs, congregations, singing-schools, and societies extant. By LOWELL MASON. $1.

NEW CARMINA SACRA; or, Boston Collection of Church Music. This book is a careful and thorough revision of the favorite work heretofore published under the same title. The object has been to retain the most valuable and universally pleasing part of the former work as the basis of the new, omitting such portions as experience had proved to be the least serviceable and popular, and substituting choice tunes and pieces selected from the whole range of the author's previous works; appending, also, additional pages of entirely new and interesting music, from other sources. In its present form it undoubtedly comprises one of the best collections of sacred music ever published. $1.

*** More than 400,000 copies of the "Carmina Sacra" have been sold.

THE BOSTON ACADEMY'S COLLECTION OF CHURCH MUSIC. By LOWELL MASON. Published under direction of the Boston Academy of Music. $1.

THE PSALTERY. A new Collection of Church Music. By LOWELL MASON and GEORGE J. WEBB. Published under the direction and with the sanction of the Boston Academy of Music, and of the Boston Handel and Haydn Society. $1.

THE NATIONAL PSALMIST. A collection of the most popular and useful Psalm and Hymn tunes, together with a great variety of new tunes, anthems, sentences, and chants—forming a most complete manual of church music for choirs, congregations, singing-classes, and musical associations. By LOWELL MASON and G. J. WEBB. $1.

THE CONGREGATIONAL TUNE BOOK. A collection of popular and approved tunes, suitable for congregational use. By LOWELL MASON and G. J. WEBB. 30 cents.

BOOK OF CHANTS. Consisting of selections from the Scriptures, adapted to appropriate music, and arranged for chanting, designed for congregational use in public or social worship. By LOWELL MASON. 12mo, cloth. 75 cents.

THE BOSTON ANTHEM BOOK. Being a selection of Anthems and other pieces. By LOWELL MASON. $1 25.

THE BOSTON CHORUS BOOK. Enlarged; consisting of a new selection of popular choruses, from the works of Handel, Haydn, and other eminent composers, arranged in full Vocal score, with an accompaniment for the Organ or Piano Forte. Compiled by LOWELL MASON and G. J. WEBB. 75 cents.

CHURCH MUSIC.

THE SHAWM. A Library of Church Music, embracing about one thousand pieces, consisting of psalm and hymn tunes, adapted to every meter in use; anthems, chants, and set pieces; to which is added an original cantata, entitled "Daniel; or, the Captivity and Restoration;" including also the "Singing Class," an entirely new and practical arrangement of the elements of music, interspersed with social part songs for practice. By WM. B. BRADBURY and G. F. ROOT, assisted by THOMAS HASTINGS and T. B. MASON. $1.

THE NATIONAL LYRE. A collection of Psalm and Hymn tunes, with a selection of chants, anthems, etc. Designed for the use of all choirs, congregations, singing-schools, and societies throughout the United States. Compiled and arranged by S. P. TUCKERMAN, S. A BANCROFT, and H. K. OLIVER. 75 cents.

TEMPLE MELODIES. A collection of about two hundred popular tunes, adapted to nearly five hundred favorite hymns, selected with special reference to public, social, and private worship. By DARIUS E. JONES. 12mo. cloth, 62 1-2 cents. 12mo, roan, gilt, 75 cents. 12mo, cloth, full gilt sides and edges, $1. 8vo, cloth, 87 1-2 cents. 8vo, roan, gilt, $1. 8vo, Turkey morocco, extra gilt (pulpit copies), $3.

The different editions correspond exactly in all their contents, being *page for page the same*, varying only in the size of type and style of binding. This work has been extensively introduced into churches of various denominations, in different parts of the country, and has, we believe, given universal satisfaction in all cases. It is believed that it contains a very much larger number of really favorite and useful hymns and tunes than any other book.

PLAIN MUSIC FOR THE BOOK OF COMMON PRAYER. A complete collection of sacred music, for the worship of the Protestant Episcopal Church, designed especially for congregational use. Edited by Rev. G. T. RIDER, A.M. 50 cents.

This work has been carefully prepared to meet a long felt want, namely, of a book of chants and tunes for congregational use, that should contain, in convenient order and form, and attractive style, and at the same time at a reasonable price, all the music required for the use of the people.

THE LIBER MUSICUS; or, New York Anthem Book and Choir Miscellany, comprising anthems, choruses, quartetts, trios, duets, songs, etc. It includes pieces for the festivals of Christmas, Thanksgiving, and Easter, commencement and close of the year, dedications and installations, for funerals and fasts, etc., etc. Most of the pieces are new, and while their simple melody and ease of performance peculiarly adapt them to the wants of smaller choirs, they are also all the largest can require. $1.

THE CHOIR CHORUS BOOK. A collection of choruses from the works of the most distinguished composers. Compiled, adapted to English words, and arranged with particular reference to choir practice, and for the use of musical societies, by A. N. JOHNSON. In the large and varied collection which this book contains, five of the choruses are by Handel, thirteen by Haydn, seventeen by Mozart, six by Mendelssohn, and the remainder by Cherubini, Neukomm, Zingarelli, Romberg, Webbe, Naumann, Spohr, King, Steymann, etc. $1.

CHORUSES OF HANDEL'S MESSIAH. Complete vocal parts, forming No. 1 of the "Oratorio Chorus Book." This is the first of a series, the design of which is to furnish, in a compact and very cheap form, the choruses of the great oratorios, so that this standard music may be brought within reach of all. 50 cents.

THE PILGRIM FATHERS. A Cantata in two parts. Composed by GEORGE F. ROOT, assisted in the preparation of the words by Miss FRANCES J. CROSBY, the blind poetess. Paper, 25 cents.

This cantata was originally prepared for the pages of the "Hallelujah," and is now published as a supplement to that work.

GLEE BOOKS.

THE NEW YORK GLEE AND CHORUS BOOK. A collection of new and admired glees and choruses, for singing-schools, choir practice, Musical conventions, and the social circle. By Wm. B. BRADBURY and LOWELL MASON. (In press.) $1.

THE NEW ODEON. A collection of Secular Melodies, arranged and harmonized in four parts. By LOWELL MASON and G. J. WEBB. $1.

A revised edition of the most popular collection of secular music ever published in America, but which has for some time been out of the market. New Elements of Music have been prepared for it, and the places of such pieces as proved least attractive in former editions are occupied by arrangements of popular melodies, especially prepared for this new edition. It is the largest collection of secular music published.

THE GLEE HIVE. A collection of glees and part songs. By LOWELL MASON and G. J. WEBB. Revised and enlarged edition. 50 cents.

In the revised edition a few of the heavier and more difficult pieces have been laid aside, and their place, and a number of additional pages, are filled by lighter and more pleasing compositions.

THE VOCALIST. Consisting of short and easy glees, or songs, arranged for soprano, alto, tenor, and bass voices. By L. MASON and G. J. WEBB, Professors in the Boston Academy of Music. $1.

THE BOSTON GLEE BOOK. By LOWELL MASON and GEO. J. WEBB. Containing the choicest of the Standard English Glees. This work has been most admired of any similar publication, and has retained its popularity unabated. $1 25.

TWENTY-ONE MADRIGALS. Selected mostly from old and distinguished composers. By L. MASON and G. J. WEBB. 50 cents.

THE MELODIST. A collection of glees and part songs. By G. J. WEBB and WM. MASON. $1.

THE SOCIAL GLEE BOOK. A collection of classic glees, mostly from the German. By WM. MASON and SILAS A. BANCROFT. For skillful singers who are able to sing music of some difficulty with taste, this book is a treasure. It is filled with gems of the first water, which will not lose their luster by once wearing. The more these gems are sung, the better they will be liked. New edition. Price reduced to $1.

FIRESIDE HARMONY. A collection of glees and part songs. By WM. MASON. $1.

FOR MEN'S VOICES.

THE YOUNG MEN'S SINGING BOOK. A collection of music for male voices, intended for use in Colleges, Theological Seminaries, and the social circle, consists of, Part I.—The Singing School. II.—Glees and part Songs. III.—Choir Tunes. IV.—Congregational Tunes. V.—Anthems, Chants, etc. By GEORGE F. ROOT, assisted by L. MASON. $1.

THE GENTLEMEN'S GLEE BOOK. A selection of glees for men's voices, from the most admired German composers. By L. MASON. This is the only work of the kind published in this country. It contains a very choice selection of the very best of the German glees for men's voices. $1.

JUVENILE MUSIC.

BRADBURY'S YOUNG SHAWM. A collection of School Music. By W. B. BRADBURY. The features of this new book are, 1st, a brief elementary course, in which tunes and songs in the body of the work are referred to, instead of mere "exercises," printed in the elementary department: 2d, Musical Notation in a Nutshell; or, Things to be taught; furnishing to the teacher a synopsis of such subjects as he will need to introduce from lesson to lesson; 3d, a great variety of new juvenile music. 38 cents.

THE SONG BOOK OF THE SCHOOL ROOM. Consisting of a great variety of songs, hymns, and Scriptural selections, with appropriate music. Containing, also, the Elementary Principles of Vocal Music according to the Inductive Method. Designed to be a complete Music Manual for Common or Grammar Schools. By LOWELL MASON and G. J. WEBB. 38 cents.

THE PRIMARY SCHOOL SONG BOOK. In two parts; the first part consisting of songs suitable for Primary Juvenile Singing Schools, and the second part consisting of an Explanation of the Inductive or Pestalozzian Method of teaching Music to such schools. By LOWELL MASON and GEORGE JAMES WEBB. 18 cents.

THE BOSTON SCHOOL SONG BOOK. Sanctioned by the Boston Academy of Music. Original and Selected. By LOWELL MASON. 20 cents.

LITTLE SONGS FOR LITTLE SINGERS. For the youngest classes, the nursery, etc. By LOWELL MASON. 18 cents.

WILDER'S MUSICAL ELEMENTARY. An improved text-book in the first principles of Singing by Note, with a variety of recreative school music. A new and revised edition of this popular work, to which are added many new pieces. By LEVI WILDER, Teacher of Music in Brooklyn Public Schools, etc., etc. 28 cents.

WILDER'S SCHOOL MUSIC. A collection of pleasing pieces for schools and juvenile classes. By L. WILDER, Teacher of Music in Brooklyn Public Schools. 18 cents.

HASTINGS'S SABBATH SCHOOL SONGS. A collection of many original tunes and hymns for Sabbath schools. By THOMAS HASTINGS. 18 cents.

JUVENILE ORATORIOS; the Festival of the Rose, Indian Summer, and the Children of Jerusalem; designed for Floral and other Concerts, Singing and Common Schools, etc. By J. C. JOHNSON, originator of the Floral Concerts in Boston. The Oratorios are arranged to be sung entire or in parts, to suit the taste and occasion. 30 cents.

THE TEMPLE OF INDUSTRY. A juvenile Oratorio. By J. C. JOHNSON, author of Juvenile Oratorios. 20 cents.

MUSICAL WORKS FOR ACADEMIES AND SEMINARIES.

THE MUSICAL ALBUM. A Vocal Class Book for Female Seminaries, Academies, and High Schools. By GEO. F. ROOT. The demand for new music in female seminaries, academies, etc., and especially from those who have used the "Academy Vocalist," has led to the preparation and publication of this work. The elementary instruction, exercises, solfeggios, and rounds, together with the anthems, etc., are taken by permission from Mr. Mason's popular work, "The Hallelujah." 63 cents.

THE ACADEMY VOCALIST. A collection of Vocal Music, arranged for the use of Seminaries, High Schools, Singing Classes, etc. By GEO. F. ROOT, Professor of Music in Abbott's Collegiate Institution, Spingler Institute, Rutger's Institute, etc. Including a complete course of elementary instruction, vocal exercises, and solfeggios. By L. MASON. "The Academy Vocalist" is the standard text-book of a large portion of the most esteemed academies, seminaries, high schools, etc., in the land, and has already passed through ten editions, which proves it a most acceptable work. 63 cents.

THE FLOWER QUEEN; or, the Coronation of the Rose. A cantata in two parts. Words by Miss F. J. CROSBY, a graduate of the New York Institution for the Blind. Music by G. F. ROOT, editor of "Academy Vocalist," "The Shawm," etc. 50 cts.

331145